Pure Hearts

Jeannine Allison

Pure Hearts
Copyright © 2017 Jeannine Allison

ISBN-13: 978-1548011949
ISBN-10: 1548011940

Edited By: Stephanie Parent
Cover Design by Hang Le Designs
Formatting by Champagne Formats

All rights reserved. No part of this publication may be reproduced, distributed, or transmitted in any form or by any means, including photocopying, recording, or other electronic or mechanical methods, without the prior written permission of the publisher, except in the case of brief quotations for a book review.

This novel is a work of fiction. Names, characters, places, and events are products of the author's imagination. Any resemblance to actual persons, living or dead, or actual events is purely coincidental.

Dedication

To my dad, and all the other pure hearts in this world.
Thank you for making life a little brighter.

Prologue

Catherine

Twenty years ago...

I STOOD IN THE DOORWAY OF OUR CLOSET—SCRATCH THAT, *my* closet—and took in the state of it. The only things my soon to be ex-husband, Tyson, left behind were his "World's Greatest Dad" T-shirt and a ceramic mug Nicky made him a couple years ago. The mug was lopsided and painted an unfortunate color combination of brown and green (brown for his dad's favorite color and green for his). Nicky had been so proud of it, even more so when Tyson told him it was the best gift he'd ever received.

A tear slipped out of the corner of my eye and ran down my cheek. I didn't wipe it away, nor did I try to stop the ones that followed. It was pointless given the circumstances.

My husband no longer loved me. But becoming a twenty-five-year-old divorcée wasn't what caused the ache in my chest.

It wasn't even the fact that I'd be raising our son alone.

No. Any and all grief I felt was for my little boy in bed across the hall. Because what Tyson failed to mention before he left was that I wasn't the only one he didn't love anymore.

He was a coward. When he left he told Nicky he still loved him, that he'd only fallen out of love with me. Tyson made promises he knew he wouldn't be keeping right before he walked out our front door, leaving me to break our son's heart.

I could understand him leaving me. We weren't in love and didn't have any business being married. Tyson and I had married for Nicky's sake when I was only seventeen. As we grew up, we realized we wanted different things out of life. We struggled for money and always had to watch our spending. I didn't mind. I didn't need much. I was okay with a small life and big love. Tyson seemed to want the exact opposite.

Nicholas was my big love, and because of that he never felt like a responsibility. It felt like a privilege to be his mother. But Tyson grew dissatisfied with our quiet life. He wanted more money, a flashier job, less responsibilities…

Our son was, apparently, the biggest one of all.

How would I explain that to an eight-year-old? How would this fit into Nicky's perception of himself, and the world?

I'd get over it. My worth wasn't tied to Tyson's presence in my life. Like with any change, I'd miss him, but I definitely wouldn't mourn him.

With a sigh and a quick swipe to rid my face of any tears, I turned off the closet light and walked out of my bedroom toward Nicky's room. He was lying in bed, his spacesuit pajamas on and hands relaxing behind his head.

"Hey buddy." I walked in and sat down on the edge of the bed before pushing some of the hair out of his eyes.

"Hey," he whispered, giving me a sad smile.

I stayed quiet for almost a minute. "I want to talk about your dad."

"He's not coming back, is he?"

I jerked, taken aback by his response. I needed to tread carefully. This discussion felt like a minefield. "Why do you think that?"

Nicky shrugged, his eyes meeting the ceiling. "Paul said when his dad left he never came back either."

"I see… and did Paul say anything else?"

My son paused, his jaw tensing. "He said it's because Dad doesn't want me anymore. Is that true?" Nicky murmured, shattering my heart into more pieces than I thought imaginable.

"It's complicated," I said slowly, the lie feeling like ash in my mouth.

Nicky looked at me, and his little eyebrows worked, trying to understand. "How? He either loves me or he doesn't, right?"

I didn't know what to say. For all their naivety, children got one thing right. Love. My sweet boy was right—love wasn't complicated. Everything else was, and unfortunately everything else bled into love, giving the illusion of complexity. But no matter what other troubles my ex was going through, if he truly loved Nicky, he'd be here right now.

I must have stayed quiet too long because he nodded and refocused on the glow in the dark stars affixed above him. I had nothing to correct him with anyway.

How could a child possibly understand abandonment? How did a son reconcile the fact that his hero no longer wanted to be his father?

I didn't get angry often, but right now I was furious. I wouldn't lie to my son, and sadly telling him his father loved him felt like a lie. So I offered the only truth I could.

"It's not your fault, Nicky."

Another shrug.

"How could it be? I'm still here," I said, putting my hand over my heart. "If it was your fault, wouldn't I leave too?" His gaze collided with mine, and before he could speculate, I added, "And that will *never* happen, Nicholas. The only way I'm leaving you is if God decides it's my time, and even then I'll go kicking and screaming."

I felt victorious when he gave me a smile, complete with the wide gap between his two front teeth.

"I guess it's okay. He wasn't here much anyway." Another flash of fury moved through me. I looked down and saw his tiny fist relaxing as he spread out his fingers. "You make better pancakes than Dad anyway."

Grinning, I grabbed his hand. "How 'bout I make some special ones tomorrow morning? Chocolate chip?"

Instead of smiling wider like I expected, his lips dipped down and his attention moved to something behind me.

"Baseball tryouts are tomorrow," he whispered. "Dad was gonna take me."

"I'll drive you. Pancakes first and then—"

He shook his head, dropped my hand, and climbed out of bed. "That's okay." My shattered heart broke even further when he grabbed his sports bag—too heavy for him to carry—and dragged it across the room toward his closet. "Maybe I'll try out next year."

Nicky closed the door but didn't turn around. I waited for a sniffle or the shake of his shoulders—anything to indicate he was crying and needed me. It never came.

A few minutes later he turned around, his expression blank as he got back into bed.

"Chocolate pancakes sound real good," he said before giving me a hug. I held on tight, waiting until he was ready to let go. Nicky giggled when I held on even after his arms had dropped to the side.

Falling back against his bed, he smiled up at me. Tyson was a fool if he thought he'd find something better.

"Night, Ma."

I grabbed the covers and pulled them to his chin before bending down and kissing his forehead. "Night, dear. I love you."

"Love you, too," he mumbled. His eyes were closed by the time I made it to the threshold. I turned off the lights and closed the door until only a sliver of space remained.

I quickly walked into my room, my back hitting the door as soon as I shut it, before I collapsed, tears flooding my eyes.

I didn't want him to hate his father. I didn't want to turn him against Tyson, just in case Tyson ever did want to be back in his son's life. But my primary job was to protect Nicky, and how could I do that if I wasn't honest about the kind of man his father was?

Sleep never came. I sat there all night, thinking of what I was going to say the next time we talked about Tyson.

Turns out, it didn't matter.

Nicky never asked about his father again.

He never talked about trying out for baseball again.

And he never fully trusted another person again.

One

Nick

IT WAS TRUE.

Your life flashed before your eyes when you died. And what a shitty life it had been, filled with broken promises and betrayals.

My whole childhood, my ma and I struggled to get by...

Four years ago, I came home to my girlfriend setting the dining room table, boasting a wonderful surprise...

Twenty years ago, I watched my father walk out the door, promising his love and time...

That memory was particularly brutal, even if I didn't always acknowledge it. It was the first time I truly understood disappointment. I was only eight, but my father taught me an invaluable lesson. He showed me that a person's first and foremost loyalty was to himself. Not even blood mattered.

The memories were fewer and further between as I slowly regained consciousness.

My head was pounding, and my stomach felt like it was being ripped out of me. There was a light shining my way. I lifted my head toward it, immediately regretting the decision when the brightness caused another throbbing sensation to shoot through my brain.

Next came the screams.

Then pain. *Everywhere.*

"Hello? Sir? Are you okay?" The voice was high-pitched and frantic, but definitely a man's. "Sir?"

What's going on?

More screams.

More pain.

I wanted to open my mouth. I wanted to let him know… I wasn't even close to okay. When I tried, I was cut off by another bloodcurdling scream.

God, her screams. The pain sounded excruciating as I struggled to remember what happened.

"Lily, I don't…" The man sounded torn. The ache in my head was intensifying.

"We're gonna… oh God, we're gonna lose her—" she started before letting out a horrifying scream.

"I don't…" The man trailed off and I heard his pounding footsteps fading as he ran away from me. A moment later the sound returned, and this time his voice carried toward me like a death sentence. "I'm sorry! I have to go… I can't…" he shouted, his voice sure and filled with purpose.

And then he was running away again, providing me with another memory of a person doing something unforgivable.

I heard the car drive away, leaving me here alone.

To die…

Iris

It's a girl!

Grinning like a fool, I walked down the hospital corridor toward the maternity ward, remembering the words my mom had screamed in my ear when I answered the phone this morning. My smile faltered slightly when I thought of my sister's troubles, but I shook it off. I needed to focus on the positives. My beautiful nineteen-inch, six-pound-and-nine-ounce niece, Mirielle, was doing better. I heard the relief in my mother's voice when she relayed how my sister was beside herself with joy when she held her daughter for the first time.

I looked down at the four balloons wrapped around my wrist—three pink and one yellow—before squeezing the giant teddy bear in my other arm closer to my chest. I couldn't think of anyone who deserved to be a parent more than my big sister.

Calla was five years older than me, but she never treated me like the annoying little sister. Not when Mom made her pick me up at a friend's house. Not when she had to miss parties to babysit me. Not even when I raided the makeup on her vanity and broke her favorite bottle of perfume.

I never felt unwanted around her. She was like a mother to me, not because ours was lacking—our mother was wonderful. Calla just had that way about her. She was *born* to be somebody's mother. Mirielle was one lucky baby.

My smile widened with each person I passed, and I couldn't help but pick up my pace. I had just turned a corner when I came to an abrupt stop. A man and woman stood in the middle of the hallway about fifteen feet away. He was clearly a doctor—dressed in maroon scrubs and a black cap, with a mouth mask pulled down around his neck—and she must have been a patient's family member based on how exhausted she looked, apparent even from here.

He only stood about half a foot above her and was filled out like he took care of himself, which made sense since he was a doctor. I'd be in excellent shape too if I knew all that could go wrong. I quickly glanced down at my slight pooch, something my solo Taco Tuesday parties were most certainly responsible for.

Shaking my head, I lifted my gaze back to them. The woman looked like she took care of her body too, but somehow she seemed especially frail and tiny in comparison to the doctor. Her black pants and gray sweatshirt appeared slept in and the brown knot of hair on her head had definitely been pulled at a few times.

"He's my baby boy!" she wailed, clutching her chest as it heaved with sorrow. My lips immediately dipped down into a frown and my eyes quickly filled with sympathetic tears. The doctor tried to keep his face impassive and professional, but I could see a crack in his demeanor, a break in his heart. There was no way to watch this grieving mother without feeling *something*.

"I'm sorry, ma'am. Your son has experienced extensive renal trauma, and our only option right now is dialysis. He'll eventually need a new kidney, without one—"

"He'll die? My *son* will die?"

The doctor placed a hand on her shoulder; all pretenses of impartiality were gone as he lowered his face toward hers. And even though I knew it was wrong, I inched forward.

"Ma'am, there is plenty of time, and there are a few different options. Some patients live on dialysis for years. The important thing to focus on right now is that he's stable and all his other injuries will heal. He should be waking up shortly."

He offered her a soft smile.

I looked on with blurry vision at this mother so desperate to save her son. Glancing down at the stuff in my hands, I felt my expression morph into a glare, like somehow the cheerful presents were responsible for this woman's suffering.

I lifted my head in time to see her eyes widen, her stare moving past the doctor. "Oh God... I'm—I'm not going to be a mother anymore."

The doctor didn't offer her any more words. He simply wrapped his arms around her and let her cry on his shoulder, her face aimed my way.

My heart broke into a thousand pieces.

I recognized the look in her eyes. Fear. Complete and soul-consuming fear.

The doctor may have told her that her son had time, but that wasn't what she heard. When you were going through a trauma, when you were so distraught you could barely stand— like how she was leaning on the doc—you only heard fragments of what someone was telling you. You only listened to the bits that reconfirmed your fears, justifying your reactions. Everything else was lost.

Fear, and a deep love like that, could lead to desperation. I'd seen it. I'd *lived* it.

"*Paging Dr. Moore,*" a voice announced over the PA system. The doctor seemed torn as he gazed down at the broken woman in his arms before glaring at the speaker in the corner. After his name was called once more, he regretfully pulled away and told her he had to leave.

"Okay," she whispered. He gave her shoulders one more squeeze before walking away. A waft of air hit me as he passed by and I stared after him. Dr. Moore hesitated at the end of the hall, only a couple of feet away from me, unable to stop looking at the woman. When his eyes caught mine, he gave me a brisk nod and hurried away.

My gaze moved back to her. She was stumbling away, blindly slapping the wall as she walked in the opposite direction. I wasn't sure what compelled me forward, but I followed her.

Thankfully I was wearing my Keds instead of something impractical and noisy, although I was pretty sure a bomb could explode and she wouldn't hear it. Grief did that—it dulled all the other horrible things. Her own personal bomb had detonated and nothing could compare.

She paused in front of a door, her hand on the knob and her head bent, like she was gathering strength to go inside. I skirted back around the corner. It felt wrong to spy on this woman, but I wanted to make sure she was okay.

Iris, you idiot, she'll never be okay again…

This I knew from experience. Because even if you survived a tragedy, it would always be a part of your narrative. The only way to handle a hardship was to make it a part of who you were, with purpose and pride. Taking initiative made sure *you* were the one weaving it into your story. Not the tragedy. Not the faceless noise coming from all the people trying to help. *You.* It gave you a power you would've otherwise lost.

The only thing we could really control in life was our reactions; everything else was up for grabs.

As for me, I didn't "let go" of my tragedies, I held on as tight as I could. I forced them into my psyche the way *I* wanted. And I didn't "move on," leaving it all behind. I brought it with me everywhere.

I wondered if this woman would be able to do that…

I stuck my head out and watched her pull the door open before disappearing inside. Snapping out of my daze, I came out of hiding and looked up. It was a chapel.

My family wasn't overly religious, but we did believe in God and I liked to think we all tried to live in a way that would make a higher deity proud.

I hovered outside for a moment before removing the balloons from my wrist and tying them around one of the bear's arms. Then I set him down just outside the door and stepped inside. My eyes immediately found her in the empty room. She was sitting in the front row as she crossed herself and began softly praying.

My bravado from seconds earlier faded, and I suddenly felt like I was betraying a deeply private moment. I quickly turned to leave when I ran into a pew, clipping my shin and biting back a wince. Glancing behind me, I cringed. The woman was staring right at me.

Now that I could see more than her profile, I couldn't help but notice how pretty she was. Despite her disheveled appearance, the bluish marks under her eyes, and the devastating way her lips turned down, I could tell she was beautiful. The dark circles didn't detract from the slight hope shining in her eyes. Nor did her frown take away the prominent laugh lines around her mouth. She was most likely going through the worst moment of her life, but I could tell she would bounce back, that she was one of the good ones who lived life for the happy moments and didn't dwell on the sad ones.

My brother often told me I overreached, went too far past what was "normal" and made people uncomfortable. I never agreed. But right now, I thought, he might have a point.

"I'm so sorry," I rushed out before turning to fully face her. I refrained from grabbing my sore leg as I stood tall and walked forward a couple steps.

"It's all right, dear." She cleared her throat. "Who are you here for?"

"Pardon?" I choked out.

"What's the name of the person you're here for? I'll include him or her in my prayers." She tried to smile. And despite her lips never making it up her cheeks, I could see the warmth in her eyes and how genuine she was being.

I knew she was a good one.

"Oh. Umm… n-no one." My throat suddenly felt dry, guilty for… well, I wasn't sure. "My sister just had a baby." This time her smile inched a little higher.

"Congratulations. Children are"—she covered a sob with her hand. When she removed it, she was shaking her head—"a precious gift from God."

"I'm sorry," I whispered. Her brows puckered in confusion before rising in question. "I heard you talking to the doctor," I explained, hitching a finger to the door behind me.

She lowered her head. "I'm sorry for the scene I caused."

"No, no." I rushed forward, wincing at the ache in my knee, only to stop a pew behind her. "I didn't mean… I just… actually, I'm not sure what I meant."

Her lips pulled even higher as she scooted down and patted the spot next to her. I gingerly sat down to her left and she immediately took my hand with her right one. "Will you pray with me?"

"Of course."

"Thank you." She squeezed my hand. "What's your name?"

"Iris."

"I'm Catherine." She wrapped her left arm around me. "And what's your sister and the baby's name?"

"Calla is my sister, and her daughter is Mirielle."

"Beautiful names," she whispered. I smiled and we bowed our heads.

Catherine cleared her throat. "Dear Heavenly Father, Iris and I humbly come to you today, and ask that you watch over our loved ones. Please bless Calla with a speedy and complication-free recovery. May her child, little Mirielle, be graced with health and joy. And..." When she paused I squeezed her hand harder, trying to ground her here and not let the pain take her mind to a dark place. My encouragement seemed to work as she took a deep breath and continued.

"Gracious Father, please send a kidney for my Nicholas. He... he's all I have, and even if the hospital can keep his body alive, I'm afraid his spirit will be crushed. I do not know your plans; maybe someone else needs one more, maybe Nick needs to experience this, but if he doesn't, I ask for your mercy. And lastly, bless sweet Iris for checking on a complete stranger. In the name of the Father, and of the Son, and of the Holy Spirit. Amen."

"Amen," I echoed, feeling more at peace than I was expecting. She disentangled herself from me and crossed herself again. I looked at her and some of the heaviness in her eyes was gone, and her breaths seemed to be coming to her more naturally. Like the act of praying made her life a little bit easier to live in that moment.

"Thank you. That was beautiful." Tears brimmed in my eyes; she had no idea the effect her words had on me. I'd been trying to stay strong and positive, but truthfully I was a bit shaken.

Calla had been struggling to get pregnant for nearly three years, and when she was diagnosed with preeclampsia a few weeks ago, the entire family had rallied around her. Especially her husband of eight years, Kent.

The doctors were concerned, but she wasn't far enough along at that point to induce labor. Her husband took her home and made sure she was on strict bedrest, and even though no one doubted she was doing everything in her power to keep herself and the baby safe—her pride wasn't a factor—we all still worried.

Then last night she started experiencing abdominal pain and blurry vision. Given her condition and the possible complications, it was important that Kent got her to hospital as fast as he did.

They were forced to perform an emergency C-section after Mirielle's breathing had become too weak. Thankfully they got her out quick enough. The doctors said if Kent had gotten her here even a few minutes later, it might have been too late for Mirielle.

My sister and niece were both stable right now, so I wasn't immediately concerned, but it would be premature to think we were out of the woods. And this prayer helped more than I thought it would.

"You're welcome, dear."

I gazed into two of the most sincere eyes I'd ever seen, still struggling with her own grief while trying to celebrate my joy, and I knew there was only one thing I could do.

"Excuse me," I said softly to the nurse behind the counter. Catherine was still in the chapel and my sister's bear and balloons were still sitting outside it.

"Yes?"

"I need to speak to Dr. Moore." I was incredibly grateful I'd had the sense to remember his name.

She nodded and began shuffling pages. "For who?"

"I'm sorry?"

"What patient of his are you concerned with?"

"Oh, I actually don't know. I met this woman, Catherine, and her son needs a kidney. She's not a match, and well... it's a long shot..."

"You want to see if *you're* a match? That's highly irregular and I'm not sure it's appropriate—"

"I want to see if I can save someone's life, what's inappropriate about that?" I asked. She paused and gave me a suspicious look. I sighed. "Could you please tell me where to find Dr. Moore?"

"What can I help you with, miss?" I whipped my head around to the new, deeper voice. It was Dr. Moore. I stepped away from the nurse and noted how his eyes flared in recognition.

"Dr. Moore," the nurse started. "This isn't—"

"I'll handle it from here, Jessica. Thank you." He tilted his head down the hall and I trailed behind him.

"I'm Dr. Moore." He held his hand out. "I'm a trauma surgeon in the ER."

Nodding, I shook his hand. "Iris."

"How can I help you, Iris?"

"I have an odd request..." I hesitated, even as his eyebrows rose in interest.

Was this too crazy? Was this taking my desire to help people one step too far?

I immediately dismissed those thoughts. Surely there was no limit to kindness. I berated myself for even questioning it.

My mother always said the second you let other people's perceptions dictate how you lived your life, you lost. And I had no interest in losing who I was. I wanted to be nice and kind. I wanted to go out of my way to help an elderly lady with her groceries, or a middle-aged man who, while rounding up his kids in his minivan, had dropped a soccer ball and groaned in frustration when it rolled away from him.

And I wanted to give Catherine's son one of my kidneys.

It didn't have to make sense to anyone else. Well… maybe the doctor, I at least had to convince him.

"I overheard your conversation with Catherine." I pointed toward the end of the hallway where he had consoled her earlier.

"Yes?" He looked wary now, and I couldn't say I blamed him.

"I have two kidneys, and you know, you can live with just one." I slammed my mouth shut; God, I was an idiot when I was nervous.

The doctor's lips quirked. "Yes, we did go over that once or twice in my training."

"Right." I swallowed before closing my eyes, psyching myself up. My eyes flew open as I said, "I want to help him. I want to…"

My lips snapped together as his expression flattened. Even though I hadn't said the words, he knew what I was going to say. But he gave me absolutely no sign of what he was thinking.

Did he think I was crazy? Was he devising a plan to get me to the psych ward without a scene? Or maybe he thought I was pulling a cruel prank? Maybe he thought I was idealistic and acting on a whim. He could have even been impressed. But I didn't know; he was frozen and mute. It felt like an eternity before his body relaxed and he spoke again.

"You want to give Mr. Blake one of your kidneys? Is that what you're saying, Ms.…?"

"Chamberlain," I filled in. "And yes, that's exactly what I'm saying."

Two

Nick

I'D PASSED OUT LISTENING TO THE HORRIFYING SCREAMS of a scared woman. I woke up to the soft whimpering of a scared woman.

I forced my eyes open and they immediately met the top of my mother's head. She was bent over my hand; I could feel the rosary beads pressing into my skin, a glorious reminder that whatever prayers she sent upward had been answered.

My fingers twitched under hers and with that action her head snapped up. Her warm brown eyes were rimmed red and she looked haunted.

"Ma," I croaked out.

"Oh, Nicky." She quickly glanced heavenward and crossed herself, murmuring her thanks, before bringing her full attention back to me. One of her hands came up and cupped my cheek.

I tried to smile, but my dry lips cracked, protesting the

movement. "It must be bad if you're not going to give me grief for not shaving."

My ma chuckled. "Hush. I was getting to it." She clucked her tongue, but didn't say anything else.

Flipping my hand over, I wrapped my fingers around her wrist. "What happened? It's pretty foggy."

"You were in a car accident."

"Bad?"

Ma nodded. "Almost." She smiled as she brought her rosary beads up to her mouth and kissed the cross. "The Lord saved you. He sent us an angel."

I gave her a genuine smile, not daring to mock her like I normally might. We were both devout Catholics, but her faith ran deeper than mine. She felt it in every single atom of her being. It ran through her, like the blood pumping in her veins, involuntary and necessary to her survival. Her belief and trust in our God was unwavering; she believed he sent miracles and that everything happened for a reason.

My faith was a little shakier. Where hers was analogous to blood, mine was more like skin. It provided me with a tremendous amount of protection, but there were layers to it, and it was constantly changing and regenerating. And in some places, there were scars. Permanent, damaged, ugly reminders that while God *was* great and protective, he couldn't solve everything.

I believed in God as much as my ma, but I also believed in humans, and the horrible lengths they could go to destroy the heavenly things God gave them. Ma said I needed to trust God's grace above everything else, but it was always a struggle for me. I tried to keep my cynicism at bay in front of her. It never worked; she was a smart woman and not much got by her.

"An angel, huh?" I asked. "Was it some killer surgeon who saved me?"

She shook her head. "No, dear." She was practically vibrating in her seat as she relayed everything.

No-contact car accident.

Other driver fled the scene.

Left to die.

Critical condition.

Damaged both kidneys.

Dialysis.

Ma crying in a chapel.

A miracle.

A savior.

"Wait, wait," I rushed out as I tried to sit up, seemingly more aware of the pain in my midsection now that I knew everything. "You can't let some random woman give me her kidney..."

"What choice do we have? You *need* a kidney, Nick." Her bottom lip trembled before she looked down at her lap where she had folded her fidgeting hands. I immediately knew my ma wouldn't be able to donate since we had different blood types. No tests were needed. But to ask a stranger? To *trust* a stranger?

I looked away from her tears, feeling like an asshole. "I know, Ma. But like the doctor said, we have time. It's not life or death right now. If I take this woman's kidney she's gonna be linked to us *forever*. What if she expects something? What if she—"

"She won't," my mother said resolutely. The tight grip she had on her cross was probably making an indent on her palm. "You haven't met her. She's a good one. A kind soul, Nicholas."

My mother thought that about everyone. That was the

flaw in thinking God touched everything; she thought everyone had a bit of good in them.

She grabbed my hand with both of hers and pressed a kiss to my knuckles.

Closing my eyes, I tilted my head back against the pillow and thought about what she was asking of me: to trust a complete stranger. The idea was so terrifying it brought forth a question about a person I'd never wanted to think about again.

"Have you thought about asking Dad?" The words tasted bitter on my tongue. I hated that I called him *Dad*—I hadn't in years. Ma and I had only talked about him a handful of times, but he was always Tyson. Never Dad.

Regardless, there was something about lying in a hospital bed, discussing my need for one of his vital organs, that made calling him anything else impossible. He was forever linked to me whether I wanted him to be or not.

My ma hesitated; the grip she had on my hand loosened as she slowly started rubbing my fingers. "I have," she finally whispered. "It's been a few years, but I think I still have his number. I just don't know..."

She didn't have to say it. The fact that I let it slip past my lips and give tangible proof to his absence when I spent so long pretending he never even existed was painful enough. I didn't need her to confirm what I knew before I asked: he wouldn't give me one of his kidneys.

It was ridiculous to think a man who couldn't spare an afternoon for one of my cooking competitions would part with a kidney. I hadn't seen or spoken to him since he left twenty years ago. Ma kept in contact so he could pay child support, but other than that he wasn't a part of our lives.

Lifting my head, I opened my eyes and met hers. "Never

mind. It was a stupid thought." I shook my head to highlight my foolishness.

I hadn't actively brought up my father in years and I knew my mother always struggled with how to broach the subject. She wanted to protect me from him, but she also wished for me to know him if he was ever interested. How could you let someone spread their wings and soar, and protect them at the same time?

You couldn't. Living meant hurting.

"Maybe he's changed," she said, a bit of hope in her eyes. "He's older, he could have—"

"No, Ma. Your initial reaction was right. He probably wouldn't donate one, and even if he was interested, I wouldn't want it. It'd probably be out of guilt."

I came to peace with his absence a long time ago. At least as much as I could.

My mother shook her head, a sad smile on her lips. "You can't let your pain—or your pride—rule your life."

"It's not." But even as I said it, I felt a weight on my chest from all the painful memories and how I let them change who I once was. With a sigh, I leaned back again. "I'm kinda tired, Ma. Can we talk about this later?"

"Of course," was her immediate response. "Please think about this. The doctors still need to test her compatibility. She's having the tests done this week, but if she is a match..." She shook her head, tears welling again. "Our lives have already changed, and dialysis is an uncertain future. It's like a hold, a pause, while we wait and hope for a kidney. If you take this one being offered to you, you'll be able to start living again now. You can get used to your new life, make plans and start getting better. Please, Nicky. Do this for me," she begged.

When I was a kid I got called a mama's boy, and it was

always said with disdain. I didn't get it then or now.

Was it because I respected her?

Loved her?

Wanted to talk to her every day?

Maybe. But I never felt any shame in it. My ma did more than give birth to me. She was the only family I had. She was a mother *and* a father, and she made sure I never felt like I was missing out on anything.

I'd do anything for her.

So with a reluctant smile, I said, "Okay."

Her eyes closed and she let out a breath of relief. "Thank you, dear." She leaned forward, kissed both cheeks, and pulled me into a hug.

Maybe if those kids who made fun of me took half a second to think about all the amazing things their mothers did for them, they'd have done the same.

Despite my love and respect for her, I couldn't rid myself of my suspicions. Randomly donating a kidney, to a stranger no less, was *not* normal. There was zero chance this woman was doing this out of the goodness of her heart. I understood my mother's desperation, but my guard would definitely stay up.

The fact that we knew my own father wouldn't even consider giving me a kidney made trusting a stranger's decision to do it ten times harder.

I smiled and found genuine ease in her happiness, assuaging her worries and giving her peace of mind, but I secretly vowed to figure out what this woman could want, and to make sure she didn't get it.

Iris

Like ripping off a Band-Aid. That was how I had to treat this.

I had been toying with the idea of becoming a living kidney donor for over six months. When I first told my family they were relatively supportive, but somewhere in the back of their minds, I was sure they'd thought they could talk me out of it. Maybe given enough time and persuasion they could have, but not after I met Catherine Blake in that chapel.

I was a believer in signs. And that was most definitely a sign. A large, flashing, neon sign that I was meant to do this.

As I got out of my car, I straightened my dress and tucked my long, chestnut brown hair behind my ears before making my way up the driveway. I cut across the perfectly manicured lawn and knocked once on the large wooden door, stepping through without waiting for an answer.

"Mom? Dad?" I called out, shrugging off my light jacket and hanging it on the coatrack. It was mid-May in Boston but some of the bitter cold was still hanging on.

After I left Dr. Moore a week and a half ago, I grabbed my sister's things and hightailed it to her room, almost an hour after I was supposed to arrive. No one noticed; everyone was too wrapped up in Calla and Mirielle. I didn't bring it up, letting Calla and Kent have their moment.

The doctor called the next morning so we could begin setting up appointments, and within a week the tests were done. When Dr. Moore called yesterday morning and told me I was a match, I knew I had to come clean to my family.

My sister had been discharged a couple of days after delivering. Thankfully Kent worked for an awesome company that granted new fathers two weeks paternity leave. I knew my parents were dying to go over and hover, but Kent made it clear they wanted some time to themselves. Besides, we all knew Calla would call if something was really wrong. There was no way she'd risk her child for anything.

I walked into the kitchen and found my brother, Aster, sitting at the counter, shoveling cereal into his mouth. He may be a couple months short of thirty, but he had no trouble reverting into a teenager. Aster lived in New York City and had come up once Calla went into labor. He had been saving to take two weeks off, and was staying with our parents until he left in a couple days.

"What's up?" he mumbled.

"Nothing. Just needed to talk to Mom and Dad about something."

He sat up straight, a suspicious glint in his eyes. "Oh no."

"What?"

"I know that look," he said, pointing his spoon my way. "Nothing good ever comes from it."

"I don't know what you're talking about."

"Uh-huh." He didn't sound convinced.

"So where are they?" I asked.

"Don't know about Dad, but one guess where Mom is." Aster tilted his head toward the backyard. Chuckling, I smacked a kiss on his cheek before heading outside.

My mom *lived* for her garden. She loved growing fruits, vegetables, herbs, and pretty much anything she could. But nothing surpassed her love for flowers. It was no coincidence that me and my siblings were named after flowers. Well, actually, mine *was* a coincidence.

My parents had been content with Calla and Aster; they'd always longed for one boy and one girl. But for some reason, one day, my mother decided she wanted to have a third child, and she wanted to adopt him or her. I was nine years old when they found me.

Dad said it was love at first sight for him. Mom didn't deny the feeling either. She said when she found out my name was Iris, it felt like a sign. I suppose I got my love of signs from her. I was hoping that meant she would understand why I had to do this.

I believed in miracles and destiny; I believed the Chamberlains were always meant to be my parents. My birth parents never really felt like mine. They belonged to each other more than me. I wasn't bitter about it. Maybe God knew their time here would be short and I was simply proof of their love; I was the reminder that a great love could be had in a short and sometimes difficult life. I didn't really know, to be honest, but I'd always felt like I belonged with the Chamberlains.

The two of them took me in when they didn't have to. They gave me my life back, and I'd always wanted to be able to change someone's life in some meaningful way too. To give them another chance when they thought they weren't getting one. That was the reason I'd already looked into becoming a living donor, and even though Nick's situation wasn't dire, meeting Catherine made me feel like I was meant to help *him*. Like my interest was always meant to lead me here.

Aster would no doubt roll his eyes, but I knew my parents wouldn't. They always supported their children.

My mom's bright yellow sun hat stood out like a beacon the second I shut the door. "Hey," I called out as I walked toward her.

"Iris, honey, what brings you by?" She smiled for a second before it quickly dropped. "Is it your sister? Have you heard something?"

"No, Mom. Relax." She let out a breath. "You and Dad need

to stop worrying so much."

"Impossible. It's a parent's job to worry. Besides, with the complications and Mirielle almost not making it…" she trailed off and shook her head, like she couldn't even entertain the idea.

"I understand. But they're okay now, and shouldn't it be a comfort that trained medical professionals felt they were both well enough to be discharged?" I asked softly. My mom stood up, brushing dirt off her jean capris, giving me a dubious look. I held up my hands in surrender. "Fine. Worry."

She smiled and linked her arm through mine, steering me back up to the house.

"So what brings you by then?" she asked again once we were inside, patting Aster on the back before heading to the sink to wash her hands.

Some people had the amazing ability to articulate exactly what they were feeling. To lay everything out in a poignant way and speak with power and conviction.

I was not one of those people. It all sounded great in my head, but once I opened my mouth, especially if I was nervous or excited, word vomit was all I was capable of.

My mom and brother stared at me as I told them everything. They were used to making sense of my disjointed monologues, so they kept up. I could tell by my mother's worried—what a shock—expression, as well as my brother's disapproving one, that this might be a harder sell than I originally thought.

"Iris," my mother began, her voice soft and hesitant. "I love how much you care about other people, I do. But—"

"There's no buts, Mom. This man will *die* if he doesn't get a kidney."

Aster rolled his eyes. "Stop being so dramatic. He has months, if not years. You don't need to fork over a kidney for a stranger. If you're in need of feeling good about yourself just go volunteer at a homeless shelter or something."

A glare to the back of his head was all the response I gave my brother. I focused my attention solely on Mom.

"They've already run my tests, and Dr. Moore is sitting down with Catherine and Nick today to tell them I'm a match. I'm going back in a few days to discuss setting up the surgery and to meet Nick. It—"

"You're crazy," my brother muttered. I'd tried to ignore my brother's mumblings, but after that comment I couldn't.

"You don't understand, fine. But that doesn't make me crazy—" His scoff interrupted me and my mom shot him a withering glare. She was the sweetest, but you did *not* want to be caught in her crosshairs.

"Actually the fact that you're crazy makes you crazy," Aster said, clearly not caring about upsetting our mom. He lifted his hands when he noticed our narrowed eyes.

"Won't this affect your health? I'd hate to come back and say I told you so."

No, you wouldn't.

"It's not like I'm giving him my heart, Aster. I'm going to live a normal life."

"There's always risk—"

"You're right. Just like there's always a risk when I get in a car, so should I stop driving?" He rolled his eyes again, his patent move. "You're being ridiculous," I added for good measure.

Aster dropped his attitude. "I want to make sure you're gonna be okay. You're still my baby sister."

I let down my defenses too. "I know. But I… I have to do this. I'm going to help him." My mom was now smiling as she leaned over and brushed a stray wisp of my hair behind my ear.

"Of course you are, sweetheart. That's what you do. I just

want you to be sure. This is a big deal."

I nodded. "I know. But you weren't there… seeing her, speaking to her… I felt…"

"Like you were in the right place at the right time?" she guessed.

"Yes! Exactly."

My mom smiled. "Okay, well of course we'll support you. Whatever decision you make."

I knew that despite his reassuring words, my brother still thought this was over the top and insane. And even though I loved him, I didn't care what Aster thought. If the worst thing about me was that I was too nice, too giving, too caring… I'd wear those labels proudly.

Three

Nick

I was about to meet the woman who was going to give me my kidney... her kidney... a kidney...

Shaking my head, I looked out the window. I was still having trouble getting used to the idea. When my ma told me that this woman—Iris, I learned—was a match, I felt conflicted. Despite my bah humbug attitude, I was grateful for this opportunity. My ma had been right. This was a huge life change. Between the medical bills and the dialysis that chipped away hours of a day, I would most certainly become depressed if this was my life for years.

But part of me also felt guilty. Now that I'd had time to digest my situation and research the statistics online, I realized how fortunate I was. I was twenty-eight years young and had only been on dialysis for a couple weeks. There were many people out there who were far older and who had been waiting on a kidney for years. People who had felt these strains much longer than me.

Why did I deserve this chance?

Was it selfish of me to take it?

Why has Iris picked me? I kept asking myself.

It heightened my suspicions, bringing about even more guilt. I shouldn't have agreed to this. It wasn't going to end well. We didn't know this woman. We didn't know—

"Knock, knock," my ma chirped. I glanced over just in time to see the slightly ajar door swing open, lightly bouncing off the wall. Her smile was wide when she walked into the room. She seemed so weightless and joyful compared to the woman hunched over my hand two weeks ago.

Despite how vivacious she was, my gaze was pulled to someone else. To the woman walking in behind her. I couldn't fully see her yet—her head was turned, looking back and laughing at something in the hallway.

I stared at the back of the woman's head. Her light brown hair was pulled into a high ponytail, the ends touching the top of her back, just below where a string of pearls sat on her neck. I couldn't tell whether they were real or fake. It didn't matter either way. That simple necklace still spoke volumes about the type of woman she was. She wanted the appearance of wealth, to seem "elegant." I'd known women like her my whole life. Two-faced. Women who—

All thoughts of other women were obliterated when she turned toward me. Large, chocolate brown eyes, framed by thick lashes, met mine. They were warm and sincere as an even bigger grin spread across her light pink lips. She looked… effervescent. That word wasn't a regular part of my vocabulary, but it was the first one to come to mind.

I was gaining a kidney.

My ma was getting her son back.

This woman... Iris... *she* was losing something, and somehow she seemed happier than Ma and me combined.

She appeared a couple inches shorter than me, with B-cups and a slight curve to her waist. Her light green sundress was modest, ending just below her knees, and her shoulders were covered with a white sweater.

Damn, she's pretty.

That probably meant she was even more used to getting her way. Well, whatever she wanted, we weren't giving it to her. Not that we had much anyway. Distrust crawled up my spine and settled in my brain, reminding me there was no way this woman was going to give me her *kidney* without stipulations.

I straightened my back along with my resolve and met her chipper expression with my stony one. She was completely unaffected. Her smile stayed wide and her eyes remained bright.

"Nicky, this is Iris. Iris, my son, Nicholas."

"Hi." She gave a tiny wave. Ma grabbed her arm and brought her next to my bed. Iris immediately held out her hand. "It's great to meet you."

"Yeah. You too." The skepticism in my voice was heavy, and if my ma's scalding gaze—a look that still caused me to shrink back like a five-year-old—was any indication, neither woman missed it. When I glanced back at Iris, she still appeared sincere despite by my gruff behavior. Regardless, my mother hated disrespect in any form, and I knew she wouldn't let my attitude fly just because I was laid up in the hospital after almost dying.

"Nicky," she scolded.

"Sorry, ma'am." After giving her a sheepish, please-forgive-me grin, which she accepted with a nod, I looked to Iris. "Seriously, uh, thanks."

Internally, I cringed. I didn't *want* to be an asshole. But not knowing her motives was seriously affecting my ability to be a gentleman. And I couldn't exactly cross-examine her with my mother in the room.

"Don't mind him, dear. I could blame his apish tendencies on the accident, but honestly, my Nicky has never had a way with words. And his social skills, or lack thereof, have always been appalling, no matter how hard I tried to correct him." I flinched as she pinched my cheek.

"No worries. I'm a teacher—dealing with difficult personalities is half the job."

"Oh, you are?" She smiled at my "angel." "What grade?"

"Second." Iris beamed back, clearly in love with her profession.

"That's wonderful. But don't make excuses for Nicky. Your students are seven-year-olds, not grown adults." Ma shot me another pointed look.

A phone rang and we both watched my ma dig around in her purse until she pulled it out, waving it in the air like she'd scored a massive victory. Her bag wasn't large and she didn't keep much in it, but she repelled technology. To the point where merely finding her phone made her feel triumphant.

"Be right back." I watched her affectionately squeeze Iris's shoulder before stepping out.

The door shut and our eyes instinctively found each other. I was sizing her up. She just continued to smile.

It wasn't natural.

"Why are you giving me your kidney?"

She shrugged like she wasn't even a little bit put off by my distrustful tone or very apparent scowl. "I'd been thinking about it for a while. I'd already done some research and when I met your mother, it seemed like fate." Iris reached behind her and dragged the chair next to my bed before taking a seat.

"Convincing my family wasn't easy—"

My eyebrows rose. "You're an adult. Shouldn't you be making your own decisions?"

"I do. But their opinions matter to me." She arched her eyebrow and somehow her expression was smug and sincere all at once. "Are you trying to tell me you don't care about your mother's opinion?"

Damn.

She had me. "It's different."

"Of course it is." Iris was grinning as she reached into her purse and pulled out a magazine. Silence settled around us, and she started flipping through her issue of *People*. She was completely calm, while I was crawling out of my skin. How wasn't she unsettled by the quiet?

"What do you want?" I asked.

She didn't hesitate. "Currently I'm craving a lemon bar."

I rolled my eyes, even as my lips involuntarily tipped up. I quickly forced them back into a frown. "I mean, what do you want from *us*? Why are you doing this?"

"I'm doing this because I want to. I am curious, though—what do you think I could want from you?" she asked, eyes still on her magazine.

"Money is the most obvious."

Her lips quirked into a smile. "That would be illegal. Besides I don't need money."

"You're a teacher," I said, like it should be obvious.

When I didn't immediately continue, she raised her eyebrows and asked, "So?"

"And?"

"And what?"

"You're telling me you're a teacher, with no other job, and you don't need money?" I tried to look down at her left hand but her fingers were hidden. "Your husband must have a pretty cushy job."

Iris took a deep breath before closing her magazine and folding her hands over it, left hand on top, as she wiggled her ring finger. "I'm not married."

She rolled her eyes when I continued to stare her down. "Fine. Not that it's *any* of your business, but I have a trust fund."

I started laughing; I couldn't help it. How often had I seen rich kids go out of their way to do something nice to make themselves feel better? Too often to count. It wasn't always malicious, and I figured it wasn't that way with Iris either. It didn't matter though, the results were always the same. They typically backed out, especially if it was something big. And this was freaking *huge*.

I shook my head. "Look, it's a nice offer," I began, trying to keep the conversation civil like my mother would want. "But you'll change your mind. And that will just hurt my mother more. So please tell her the truth now."

Her brows furrowed. "Why would I change my mind?"

"This isn't a pencil you're letting me borrow in algebra class or a five-dollar bill you're loaning me so I can get a fucking sandwich. It's a freaking *organ*. It's a big decision, and not one that should be made on a whim. You saw my mother crying in a hospital chapel, I get it, you felt bad. You made a rash decision. The sooner you tell her, the better." Civility hadn't lasted long and my entire speech reeked of condescension.

I closed my eyes and rested my head against my pillow, listening for the sounds of her departure. When I heard none, I cracked open one eye. She was frowning, her fingers lightly tapping the cover, and I couldn't for the life of me figure out what she was thinking.

"She can't handle any more heartbreak or disappointment,"

I tried again, softening my voice.

"I think it's you." Her eyes were now sharp on mine.

I froze. "What?"

"Don't worry," she said casually before focusing her stare back down and opening her magazine once more. "I'm not going to change my mind."

Iris

He was staring at me like he didn't know what to make of me. I could practically feel his eyes boring holes into my skull.

I saw him lift his head out of the corner of my eye. "So why me?"

"Don't flatter yourself," I said, my gaze on the same page it'd been on for the past five minutes. "I didn't even know who you were. But if I had, I'm sure your winning personality would have sold me."

"It was for my mother," he guessed.

"Give the kid a prize." I smiled to soften the joke.

Nick grunted as Catherine came fluttering back in. I closed the magazine and turned in my seat. Her smile was so big she seemed to be making up for her son's lack of one. My lips automatically lifted. How this bitter man came from this caring, warm woman was beyond me.

She'd just opened her mouth to speak when my phone started ringing. I caught a glimpse of the name and smiled. "Looks like it's my turn," I said with a laugh. I stood and excused myself. Nick seemed relieved, while Catherine urged me to hurry back.

I ducked into the hall, almost crashing into a nurse and

causing her to drop the files she was holding. I apologized and bent down to help her, but she waved me away with an impatient hand.

"Watch where you're going," she muttered as she picked up the last folder before straightening and walking down the corridor, all without a backward glance at me.

"Hi, Calla," I greeted as soon as I answered the phone.

"Hey." I didn't know how a single word could exude so much exhaustion. It had only been two weeks, but my sister was clearly feeling the effects of being a new mother.

"Is everything okay?"

"Yeah. I just miss my baby sister." I could hear the smile in her voice and it lessened some of my concern.

Exhaling, I said, "Me too. I'm sorry I haven't stopped by. I've been at the hospital a lot this week and—"

"The hospital?" Her voice spiked with alarm. "Are you okay? Why—?"

"Yeah, yeah." I rushed to assure her before I stopped, suddenly remembering she had no clue what was going on.

"Oh, okay. Good. What are you doing there?"

"I'm… I'm meeting with a mom and her son." She stayed silent. "When you were admitted a few weeks ago, I met this woman, Catherine, in the hospital chapel. She was upset over her son. He was in an accident."

Calla was still quiet, but somehow it seemed more pronounced now. I tried to figure out the best way to word this. After a few pointless seconds, I realized there was no gentle way to tell her. "I'm giving him one of my kidneys."

I held my breath. Truthfully, I had no clue how Calla would react. She wasn't like Aster.

He could easily turn a blind eye to a homeless man on the street. I'd even seen him throw some looks of disdain their way. That wasn't to say he was a bad person, but he would only help those he felt were worthy. He had no sympathy for those who made poor choices or whose actions caused disastrous consequences.

I never understood how he looked at everyone and saw only the bad; why not choose to see the good? Maybe it made me naive or foolish, but I didn't want to live my life seeing the worst in people. How was it my place to judge the worst thing a person's ever done?

But Calla wasn't like me either. She thought I trusted too easily too.

"You w-what?" she stuttered over the phone, sounding slightly panicked.

I exhaled. "I'm donating my kidney."

More silence.

"Iris—"

"No," I cut her off, hoping I could stop her before she said the same things Mom, Dad, and Aster had. "I know your concerns are going to come from a good place, and I respect your opinions, but I need to do this."

"How will it work with school? You already missed a few days for Mirielle's birth."

"It's not like I'm in a hospital bed being rolled into surgery right now." I gave a small laugh, trying to cut the tension. "The procedure won't be for a couple months. It'll be in the middle of summer and will give me plenty of time to rest."

Calla was quiet. She wouldn't be as vocal as Aster, but I really needed one person completely on my side right now. And since that was usually my sister, I didn't think I could handle her not standing by me.

My eyes moved to the room across the hall. I watched the nurse from earlier, the one who gave me the stink-eye, help a patient from her bed to a wheelchair. The little girl couldn't have been any older than eight or nine, and she looked terrified. Her wide eyes were bouncing between her parents who were arguing in the corner of her room. From what I could gather, they were divorced and the father had their daughter when she got into some kind of accident.

"This is your fault!" the mother screamed before poking him in the chest. "You're a terrible father."

Looking back at the girl, I saw her upper lip tremble and her tiny hands shake as she gripped onto her hospital gown. The nurse knelt down in front of her and grabbed her hands. I was too far away to hear what she said since she wasn't yelling, but the girl giggled and nodded, forgetting all about her parents and the unforgivable shouts they were hurling at each other. Shouts which were hurting their daughter more than they would ever hurt each other.

The nurse stood and walked over to her patient's parents. They appeared shocked and a little chagrined at whatever she said, and both nodded before the nurse wheeled the little girl, still smiling, away and down the hall.

My lips lifted. *This* was what I always tried to explain to Aster.

Why would I choose to remember her snide comment to me, when I could remember the wonderful way she made that girl's day a little brighter? It seemed like a no-brainer.

"Okay," my sister whispered into the phone. "Just be careful."

As we said our goodbyes, I tried to figure out what was causing the more-than-average apprehension in her voice.

I was still lost in my thoughts, staring at the ground, when someone tapped me on the arm. Looking up, I saw the nurse from earlier standing in front of me, her hands tucked into the pockets of her scrubs.

"Hey," she began slowly, clearly embarrassed. "I wanted to apologize about before." She waved her hand toward the area where her papers had fallen. "I wasn't paying attention either. I'd…" The nurse gave me a wobbly smile as her eyes started shimmering with tears. "I had just delivered some bad news to a patient."

My lips curved down and I put a hand on her arm. "I'm sorry to hear that. Don't worry about earlier." When I smiled she seemed relieved.

"Thank you." A code went out and she gave me a quick nod before dashing down the hall along with a few other medical professionals. My grin inched up even higher as I turned back toward Nick's room.

Catherine and Nick were exchanging heated whispers when I walked back in.

"Sorry, should I head back out?" I pointed to the hallway.

"Nonsense." Catherine stood. "We were just finishing up."

I smiled at Nick, hoping his mother had managed to make him less ornery. The glare he was sending me indicted she had not. Catherine started talking about the weekly dinners she and Nick always had, completely oblivious to her son's distrust and growing displeasure with my presence.

"You know what would be wonderful?" she asked as she sat on the edge of her son's bed, her body facing me. "If you came over and joined us for dinner on Sunday."

I saw Nick shoot up a little from the corner of my eye, clutching his midsection when he moved too fast.

"Oh, Nicky." His mother stood up and laid a hand on his shoulder. "Take it easy." She walked around his bed, where there were fewer cords and machines, and begin fussing with his pillows. Catherine smiled over at me. "But really, you must come over, dear."

"I—"

"Ma," he said, cutting me off. "Don't put her on the spot." Looking at me, he said, "Sorry about her. We're sure you're very busy and have no time." Nick nodded and grabbed his phone, effectively ending the conversation before it had really begun. He refused to look at his mom, who was glaring at him.

"I'd love to come."

Nick's head whipped in my direction, and when his mother's expression brightened and she skipped back around to hug me, his mouth dropped open. I met his eyes. He seemed shocked, like he couldn't possibly believe I'd be defiant. Just because I wanted to make people happy didn't mean I let them walk all over me to do it.

He was about to learn there was a lot more to me than met the eye.

Four

Iris

Two months later...

THE PROCEDURE WENT SMOOTHLY AND I WAS RESTING in my hospital room. My head was tipped back and my eyes were closed, a content smile on my face as I thought about the last two months.

Much to Nick's dismay, I came over every Sunday for dinner like Catherine wanted. They usually alternated but since Catherine was staying at his place until the surgery, the dinners were at his apartment.

I couldn't be sure, but I didn't think his surly attitude was about my presence alone. He seemed itching for her to go back home so he could be alone.

Catherine hardly let him do anything. The first few weeks I could understand—he'd still looked pretty banged up. But he seemed a lot better toward the end. It hadn't mattered. I was pretty sure the only time she let him do something for himself was when he went to the bathroom. Otherwise, she took care of it. I could tell it bothered Nick, but while he may have been a jerk to me, he was near saintly with his mother. He never said a thing.

Aster would have yelled at our mom on day one.

Perception was funny that way. At first glance one might look at Aster and see an upstanding son, someone who was compassionate and well-mannered, and he was, but only in the public eye. To his family and close friends he was something entirely different. Not bad, just not as thoughtful as he initially appeared. While Nick, who appeared cold and grumpy, had the softest spot in the world for his mother, and no doubt his friends too.

Unfortunately he never saw me that way. The dinners had been an odd combination of pleasant and awkward since the Blakes clearly didn't have the same feelings toward me. Eight meals with Catherine's bright smile and kind words, while Nick glowered at me every time she turned her back. Anytime I tried to ask him a question he shut the conversation down with one-word answers.

There was clearly a story there. No one arbitrarily decided to be a distrusting jerk. A few times I'd lain awake at night and thought about what his story could be. He had a wonderful mother, and she mentioned two very close friends that Nick had known since childhood. Maybe it had something to do with his father?

I didn't know much, but one night, after Nick had excused himself to his room and Catherine offered me some coffee, she told me a bit about her life. Including the fact that Nick's father left them when Nick was eight years old.

My mind constantly worked, trying to figure out what

could have happened to make him so rigid. At first glance he seemed like any other guy. Light brown hair that was slightly longer on top than the sides. Warm, chocolate brown eyes that he had the ironic ability to make cold as ice. His upper lip and jawline were covered in a thin layer of dark brown hair, hints of his skin peeking through. It looked well-maintained, while also giving off a messy, I-don't-care-what-I-look-like vibe. Nick was a couple inches taller than me, maybe around six foot, and even though he didn't look ripped, it was obvious he took care of himself.

Then there was his smile… so elusive, yet undoubtedly beautiful.

Every girl had a kryptonite when it came to a guy's physical appearance. Some were normal: abs, eyes, tattoos. And some were weird. Like my college roommate, Anita, who was strangely attracted to toes. I still shuddered whenever I thought about it. But to each their own.

My kryptonite? Dimples.

I couldn't resist a man with dimples. It was a tantalizing combination of sexy and cute that had rendered me speechless on a few occasions in high school.

And, of course, Nick had dimples. He made it hard for me to tell since he was constantly scowling at me. And when he did smile—always at his mother—he would duck his head, like he couldn't even let me see someone else make him happy. But I'd caught a glimpse of them; now if only I could figure out a way to have them aimed at me.

I mean, I gave the man my kidney, the least he could do was flash me a dimple…

Loud knocks on my bedside table jolted me from my loopy thoughts—I could blame the pain medication, right?

"Iris?"

I jerked at the sound of Aster's voice. He'd come up for the procedure and had been here for about an hour visiting me. Things had been a little tense between us since I announced my decision two months ago.

"Sorry, what were you saying?" I asked.

Sighing, he leaned forward in his chair. "I was telling you about my date with Becky."

"Oh, right. How was it?"

He shook his head. "It was okay. I don't know if we're going to go on another."

"Why not?" I asked with a frown.

"I wasn't feeling it." He shrugged and started playing with the clasp on his watch.

"This isn't some preteen movie where there's butterflies and sparks. It takes time."

"Maybe…" Aster sighed and leaned forward, his complete attention on me. "Look, Iris, I wanted to talk to you about what I said a couple months ago, when you told us about all this…"

Sitting up straighter, all signs of being loopy gone, I reached for my brother. "Aster—"

I cut myself off as our heads swiveled toward a voice outside the door. I exhaled, recognizing Catherine's exuberance, just before she entered.

"Iris, dear, I thought—" She stopped in the doorway when she saw Aster sitting next me. "Oh. I'm terribly sorry. I didn't mean to interrupt."

"No, no. Don't be silly." I smiled and waved her forward. She had yet to meet any of my family.

She looked oddly sad as her gaze shifted between the two of us.

"Is everything okay? Is it Nick?" I asked, my smile

dropping and panic taking over. She seemed fine when she first walked in, but I couldn't imagine what else would put a frown on her face right now.

"He's fine. I'm sorry, I didn't mean to worry you. Nicky's doing excellent. The doctor is hopeful that he'll make a full recovery."

I relaxed against the bed. "Thank God."

Aster shifted around awkwardly, and I knew it was because of his original reluctance to support my decision. I could see the guilt creeping into his expression. Despite the weirdness from Aster, Catherine rounded the bed and held her hand out to him.

"Hi. I'm Catherine. Nicholas's mother."

"Oh." He discreetly wiped his palm on his pants before placing his hand in hers. "I'm Aster."

Her smile was warm and genuine, back to the bubbly woman I knew. "Well, it's lovely to meet you." She stepped away and dropped his hand.

"I'll just… uh…" He hitched a finger toward the door before hurrying out.

"Was it something I said?" Catherine joked.

"No. He just isn't all that comfortable with this." I waved my hand in the direction of the beeping machines and the wires that hooked me up to them. Her lips dipped down as she sat on the bed and took my hand. It always looked strange on her. Almost as if she frowned so infrequently her lips were having a hard time remembering what to do.

"You didn't feel pressured, did you?"

"What? I—"

Before I could continue Catherine started talking again, staring down at her hand, the one not holding mine and gripping a crucifix instead. She never was without it in the hospital. "Nick said you might've felt that way." She blew out a frustrated breath. "And with you saying how Aster was uncomfortable… I'm sorry if I made this hard on you. If I—"

"Stop." Her head snapped up. "All you asked me for was a hand to hold while you prayed. Nothing else. You had no way of knowing what I was going to do. I had *two months* to think on this. And I'd been thinking about becoming a living donor before I met you. You didn't pressure me into a single thing. Except maybe trying that falafel last month, which I must say, was delicious and one of the best decisions I've ever made."

Catherine's unnatural frown quickly gave way to a smile. "It was good falafel, wasn't it?"

"The best," I seconded.

"Your only." She grinned.

"Still the best." I squeezed her hand.

"I didn't mean to run your boyfriend off," Catherine said. My gaze instinctively moved toward the still open door before settling back on her. I'd never explicitly stated that I didn't have a boyfriend over the past two months, but I had assumed my lack of reference was an answer in and of itself.

Also, ewww…

"Aster isn't my boyfriend. He's my older brother." I pretended not to notice how her face lit up with those words. Shaking my head, I squeezed her hand. "I'm glad you stopped by. My parents were here yesterday, but they haven't been by today yet."

"Of course, dear. So has your actual boyfriend come to visit yet?"

I grinned. "Catherine… are you fishing?"

"Me? Whatever do you mean?"

I busted out laughing. "You know you're supposed to be subtle when fishing, right?"

"Subtlety isn't my style." She didn't repeat her question, just raised her eyebrows expectantly.

"No. My boyfriend hasn't stopped by, because he doesn't exist."

Catherine tsked. "That makes no sense. How is a girl like you single?"

"How is a woman like you single?" I countered.

She blushed before waving the conversation away. "All right, all right. Let's get to business."

"Business?"

"Yes." She pointed to a wheelchair outside the door. "I thought you might want to see Nick."

I smiled as she went to grab the wheelchair, not waiting for an answer. Truthfully, I *did* want to see him, which didn't make any sense considering he never wanted to see me. You would think I'd have grown tired of him, or annoyed. But I hadn't. Maybe because he was never outright rude, and I saw plenty of things that made me believe in his inner goodness.

How he pulled the chair out for his mother when she sat down at the table. The way he always corrected her when she said something negative about herself. His use of "please" and "thank you." And not just to his mother.

And although he didn't trust me, he was still considerate of *me*. Like how he got up to fill my ice water when he noticed it was empty.

They said actions spoke louder than words, and Nick's actions were *screaming* at me. He was a good person. He thought of others and did nice things, but for some reason, he was trying his hardest to hide it.

Nick

"What do you think?"

"I give it a week," he answered.

"A week, really? That's insane…"

"Nope, that's Nick. He'll be itching to get back in the kitchen within a week."

She tsked. "I think you're wrong. He's smarter than that."

"We rarely make wise decisions when our passions are involved."

"Is that so?" Her voice came out lower and with a hint of seduction. I heard him take a step closer to her.

"Yeah. Remember that time we thought it'd be a good idea to have sex on a—"

"Guys," I interrupted, my eyes still closed. "I can hear you." I cracked open one eye to see my two best friends standing next to my bed, mere inches separating them. They both gazed down at me. Lindsay had a shit-eating grin on her face and Kevin looked like I'd just cock blocked him.

I arched an eyebrow. "Really? You thought you'd get lucky in my *hospital room*?"

He shrugged as a lazy grin crawled up his face. "You never know."

"You weren't about to get lucky. I knew he was awake. But you, my dear Nicky, probably could have used the story. How long has it been since you've had sex? And it was a *really* good story…"

"Surprisingly, hearing about my two best friends having sex is *not* a turn-on. And you knew? Why the hell—"

"Why were you pretending to be asleep?" she tossed back before I could finish.

"Because I was hoping you would leave."

Neither was affronted by my reply.

"Exactly. That was your punishment."

"But it was also supposed to be a reward since he hasn't gotten laid in months?" Kevin asked.

Her dark eyebrows furrowed. "Shut up. You're supposed to be on my side."

"I am." Kevin kissed the corner of her mouth. "Always, baby."

I rolled my eyes. One of these days they would get stuck in the back of my head thanks to these two, which would be unfortunate since I was now on my way to a full recovery.

The last of my injuries had pretty much healed up, and after spending almost twenty-four hours in the ICU following the transplant, I would only be in this room for a few more days before being discharged. To say I was ready to get back to my life would be an understatement. Ma was hovering, fretting over every little thing, and she wouldn't stop talking about Iris.

Did you know Iris volunteers at the public library, teaching adults how to read?

Did you know Iris double majored?

Did you know Iris walks her neighbor's dog every other day, since she's old and can't walk well?

Did you know Iris is currently solving the poverty crisis, curing cancer, and establishing world peace?

Okay, I made that last one up. But with the way my ma was talking, you'd think Iris was the greatest thing to ever happen to the planet.

I was still unsure of her. Yes, she had been great the past few months, but we still didn't know her motives. And I was sure they'd come to light after the surgery, which made Ma's fangirl moments all the more difficult to listen to. My mother was the type to cling to any girlfriend I had. She'd always wanted a daughter and I was concerned about the attachment she was forming to Iris. As Iris had pointed out months ago, it seemed unrealistic to expect anything from her. She had her own money and we were no one important. Realistically, what could I think she wanted? I didn't have a clue. *That* was what terrified me.

But I also recognized how lucky I was. Most of the people I met at the dialysis center these past two months had been waiting for years, with no clue as to when they'd be getting a kidney. I went through the hours of treatment, feeling drained and dejected afterward, but I had the satisfaction of knowing I'd be receiving a transplant soon. They didn't have that. My troubles, while exhausting, were small compared to theirs.

"Where's your mom?" Lindsay asked, breaking me from my thoughts. I sat up and glanced toward the empty chair she'd been occupying when I drifted off.

"Huh. I don't know. She must be still in the hospital somewhere. She wouldn't leave without saying good—"

"Lindsay! Kevin!" The three of us looked to the doorway where my ma stood. My eyes immediately dropped to the person in front of her. Iris was sitting in a wheelchair, staring between my friends and me with a smile on her face.

"Hey." Lindsay broke away and practically fell on Iris. Based on her wince, and my own pain, I knew it had to hurt, but she said nothing. I'd opened my mouth to say something, when Iris caught my eye and shook her head.

"We're so grateful you did this for Nicky."

"Of course."

Lindsay pulled away, but before my ma could wheel her all the way in, Kevin was striding forward and holding out his hand. "Yeah. It's an amazing thing, what you did."

Iris shook his hand and waved his words away. "Just trying to help out."

A slightly awkward silence descended, and we all just stared between each other. I didn't know Ma was bringing Iris in here, and truthfully, I wished she hadn't. My friends knew about her, but I'd never had any intention of them meeting. That would complicate an already troublesome situation.

Soft laughter floated through the room as Iris responded to something Lindsay said. My eyes lingered on Iris. She still looked exuberant. Even with my annoyance and distrust, she pulled me in. She was magnetic. There were dark circles under her eyes and general exhaustion pulled at her features, but she still glowed.

My gaze moved to her head, and I noted her flat hair from lying in a hospital bed for the better part of two days. She wasn't constantly fidgeting or trying to fix it, she just let it be. The ends curled near her breasts, and I couldn't help but wonder if her hair was as soft as it appeared. It'd been almost a year since I ran my fingers through a woman's hair, and up until this moment I hadn't realized how much I missed it.

I forced myself to look away. I regretted it as soon as I met Kevin's cocky stare and Ma's hopeful smile.

"Any news on the guy who ran me off the road?" I asked. Nothing ruined a party more than that question, especially considering how fired up it got me. I knew how unrealistic it was to expect results considering no-contact car accidents left little to no evidence, but I still had to hope there was a way to bring the bastard to justice.

"No." I felt like a jerk when my ma's smile slipped, but the distraction worked. I didn't need her getting any more ideas about Iris. She was a romantic who was hell-bent on finding me a girlfriend. She moved around Iris, who was still busy talking to Lindsay, as she shook her head. "Insurance is covering most of it. You're working with them now—"

"No," I bit out again. "I shouldn't have to pay a dime. I'm willing to do anything to find this guy. He *knew*, he fucking knew what he'd done and he left." My hands involuntarily formed fists, and the room got eerily quiet. I looked up, and sure enough Iris and Lindsay were both staring at me. I tried to soften my voice; it wasn't my mother's fault, after all.

"You remember what the doctor said, right? If that other car hadn't come along a minute or two later like it did, I'd be dead."

"But he did, Nicky—"

"The guy didn't know that, Ma. He committed a crime and I don't care how difficult a no-collision car accident is to solve, I want him found."

Ma sat down on the bed and wrapped her hand around mine, relaxing the fist I'd formed. "We understand, Nick. And they're not giving up."

I looked at Kevin and Lindsay, who were nodding in agreement. But Iris seemed confused. I didn't know why since I knew my mother had told her this at one of our weekly dinners.

"Being the angel you are, I suppose you think I should forgive him?" I asked her.

"Nicky," Ma admonished. For once I didn't care. I kept staring Iris down, brow raised.

"It's fine, Catherine," Iris said as she looked at her with a smile. And for some reason her reasonable, adult-like response pissed me off even more. When she turned back to me, there wasn't anything other than polite indifference on her face. "I guess I don't understand the point of holding a grudge against someone, especially if you don't know the circumstances." She waved her hand my way. "What is being angry getting you?

And maybe he had a good reason... maybe there was an emergency or—"

"*I* was having a fucking emergency." Fuck, was she serious right now?

"There was another car. He thought—"

"Exactly. Thought. Not *knew*. *Thought*. He was gambling with my life." Iris was silent for a moment, and I could practically feel the collective breath being held by my friends and mother.

"I'm not trying to defend him for his sake. I'm doing it for yours. Holding on to your anger won't help you. He'll just be taking more from you. I'm not saying what he did was right. But maybe there was no right decision. Maybe he did the best he could."

"Or maybe he's an asshole," I refuted. But even as I said it, I knew it wasn't the truth. I remembered the woman's screams. Was she injured in the accident? If so, why didn't the cops put it together? I had too many questions and absolutely no answers. And while Iris may be able to assume the best and move on, I couldn't.

"Maybe I should go back to my room," Iris said softly. I ignored my mother's apology on my behalf and Kevin and Lindsay's mumbled goodbyes. My gaze stayed out the window, not looking at anyone until my ma and Iris shuffled out.

"That was kinda harsh, Nick."

I didn't say anything. Part of me agreed, but another part knew that despite my gruff delivery, I was right. If I had died on that road, if that other car had kept driving, this would be an entirely different situation. Just because it happened to have a happy ending didn't change the fact that the driver leaving me was wrong.

Right was right. Wrong was wrong. And all that "the world

has shades of gray" bullshit was just that… bullshit. Seeing the world through that lens was dangerous. It gave people a convenient excuse to justify their mistakes.

Maybe it was easy for Iris to see the world that way because she'd never been on the receiving end of someone's shitty choices. She was never left with the consequences of a shattered world.

There was a right and wrong choice to be made that night. The other driver made the wrong one. And maybe next time he did, the results wouldn't be so happy. Wrong decisions had to be punished, even if everything turned out okay.

Black and white made clear lines. The world had no room for gray.

Five

Nick

I stared at the plate of food in front of me. It was hard to be in the restaurant and not run back to the kitchen and start cooking. If Kevin didn't show up soon, I might just do it. I still had a couple of weeks before the doctor wanted me returning to work, but I was itching to get back to it. Cooking for myself at home wasn't quite the same.

Kevin had been right at the hospital. People rarely made good decisions when passion was involved. Passion was like a drug. And I was a junkie who needed his fix.

People might have looked at me and called me a workaholic, and in the technical definition, I suppose that was true. But it was different for me. This wasn't just work, it was my *passion*. When they said if you did what you loved you'd never have to work a day in your life, they were right.

I was still lost in my thoughts when my phone vibrated across the bar, my ma's name flashing and her smiling face staring up at me. Guilt lodged in my throat as I debated not answering. Things had been tense between the two of us the past couple of weeks. The fight I'd had with Iris hadn't been addressed when my ma came back in the room. I knew she was disappointed; she didn't have to say a word. And she knew it, so she let me stew in my discomfort.

"Hey," I answered.

"Hi, dear."

I immediately became suspicious—her voice held way too much enthusiasm for someone who was still semi-pissed at me.

"What's up?" I asked.

"Nothing. I was calling to see if you'd come over for dinner tomorrow night." Some of the tension left me.

"Yeah, sounds good."

She paused. "Okay, around seven?" And before I could say anything else she added, "Oh, and Iris is coming over too."

So nonchalant, like she was a normal part of our lives. Technically for the past few months she had been, but I thought that would stop once the surgery was finished.

Exhaling roughly, I dragged a hand through my hair and gripped the ends. "Ma—"

"No," she bit out, a sudden fierceness to her voice that I wasn't familiar with or prepared for. "I know what you're going to say. But just because *you* don't understand her generosity and you'd rather prepare for the worst instead of hoping for the best doesn't mean Iris has ulterior motives."

"Ma—" I tried again.

"I get it," she whispered, all the venom gone as quickly as it came. "It's what you have to do to survive. You have to think that way. But can't you understand that the way I see the world is what *I* need? That Iris sees the world the way *she* needs to? I know you're a good person, Nicky, and that you're struggling, but *please* do this for me. Come to dinner and actually *try*."

Taking a deep breath, I willed myself to calm down. She was right. I was being a jackass. Though neither of these two things were news to me.

"Okay, and I'm sorry. I don't want you to become too invested. How about this… I'll try and be a little nicer, as long as you try and keep your distance? Just a little bit?"

She didn't say anything for a few minutes. "Sure, dear. If it means that much to you, I'll be a little more careful."

"Thank you." And just like that, we were good. I exhaled in relief as a large hand came down on my shoulder. I turned to find Kevin grinning down at me while Lindsay moved back behind the bar.

"Hey, Ma? I gotta go. Kevin and Lindsay just got here. I'll see you tomorrow?"

"Sounds good. Love you."

"I love you, too."

I hung up and swiveled on my stool.

"How ya doing, man?" Kevin asked with a slap to the back.

"Not bad. Ready to get back to work."

"You can't rush these things," Lindsay chimed in, nodding her hello while she tied her apron around her waist. I knew she was thinking about her stepfather, whom she was very close to, and the complications he had from his surgery. He went back to work too early and ended up back in the hospital for a week. And even though his surgery—septal myectomy—and job—construction foreman—made the likelihood of problems far greater than mine, I kept my mouth shut. That time had been hard for Lindsay, and despite the differences, I knew she was only looking out for me.

Besides, my friends had been surprisingly understanding about my behavior at the hospital, and I didn't need to be alienating anyone else.

"You're right." I smiled and knocked on the bar to get her attention. "I'm taking it easy, I promise." She gave a smile of gratitude and understanding.

"Why don't we order some food?" Kevin asked, grinning between us. "It won't be as good as Nick's, but it'll fill us up."

Lindsay looked up at Kevin with hearts in her eyes. Leaning against the bar, she shifted her gaze between us. "What'll you guys have?"

"Damn, I could really go for your wings," Kevin murmured to me, his eyes glazing over. "Surely making only *one* thing wouldn't do any harm—"

"Kevin Macy," Lindsay said sternly, using his middle name, which he hated. I chuckled, just like I did every time he got reprimanded and she used his middle name to do it.

"Fine," he grumbled. He didn't look too annoyed—I doubt he ever could. He and Lindsay had been together since the first day of high school, and now they were getting married in a couple months.

Lindsay had been Kevin's crush when she first moved here in eighth grade, and once he got the balls to ask her out the summer before high school, she became his high school sweetheart. They were *that* couple. Kevin was a wide receiver on the football team and Lindsay was the captain of the volleyball team. They were unanimously voted prom king and queen. Still, they waited. They dated for nearly ten years before he popped the question. While they both loved each other fiercely, they knew college could change them into different people. They wanted their marriage to last. I never doubted it would.

Even in rough times, when normal people would have taken a break or simply walked away, they didn't. They *fought* for it. I came to realize that was the path to a successful relationship.

Not love or trust—although those were definitely important—but the willingness to fight for it. Because no matter the couple, there would always be a fight that looked like it would be the last. The couples that were meant to be together fought against their struggles, not against one another. They wanted to make it right, even if that meant admitting they were at fault too. Even "the one" took work.

That was how I knew Colleen and I were never supposed to last. When the shit hit the fan, I had no interest in fighting for the relationship, or her. Not in a malicious way, or to be cruel. I just didn't want it, or her, enough to overlook what she'd done.

I looked at Kevin and Lindsay and knew we'd never had anything close to what they had. And despite what Colleen did to me, I wasn't so cynical that I couldn't be happy for Kevin and Lindsay. Hell, I helped him pick out her ring, and I was currently helping Lindsay set up a secret man-cave for Kevin as a wedding present.

Regardless of what my mother thought, I knew there were still decent people in the world. I just wasn't sure I'd ever be able to trust someone enough to open myself up that way.

My heart stopped. Because for some reason, Iris popped in my head.

***

Ma was bustling around her tiny kitchen, accidentally hip checking the counter every couple minutes in her excitement. Her brown hair was pulled back into a tight bun, not a hair out of place. She was dressed in a dark blue skirt that fell just past her knees and a white shirt. I had to stop myself from rolling my eyes. She looked like she was having tea with a queen.

"You took out the good wine, right?"

I held in my sigh of annoyance. "Yes, Ma."

"And you laid out the nice plates? The ones with the angels on them?"

"Ma," I said, walking over and putting my hands on her shoulders, forcing her to stop and face at me. "Everything is perfect. You did a great job." Her smile lit up the room. "But why are you going all out?"

"This woman gave you something, something she didn't have to. Something that will affect her for the rest of her life. The least I could do was serve decent wine and make sure her plate doesn't have a chip in it." She withdrew herself from my hold. "Sometimes the things we do aren't about the people we're doing them for. Sometimes they're just about us, about how we treat people, regardless of who they are or what they did. In this case, it's a little of both. I really like Iris, and I won't have your Grinch attitude ruin that."

"Okay, okay." I held up my hands. "I'm sorry. I just hate to see you running around frantic."

"I won't apologize for caring about making a good impression. And this is her first time over at my apartment. It's important to me."

"Noted." I tried to give her my best *forgive-me* smile. It worked, and I relented even more. "Would you like me to get the tall candles out?"

I was always amazed at how wide my ma's smile could get. "Yes, dear. That's an excellent idea. Thank you."

She bought both of us a set about a year ago. Mine were collecting dust in my closet. I told her pigs would fly before I casually used long-stem candles.

Passing her, I placed my hand on her shoulder and

squeezed. "No thanks necessary. I'm sorry I gave you a hard time." This time I didn't add an excuse; they invalidated an apology anyway.

"You're forgiven. Now scoot." She laughed as she whipped the towel at my back.

After placing the candles on the table, I sat at the counter, my gaze nervously shifting to the clock. In the blink of an eye, a knock sounded through her apartment.

"Oh, she's here. Will you grab it? And be nice," she added sternly before grabbing a mitt, opening the stove, and carefully taking the food out.

Getting up, I slowly made my way to the door. I looked through the peephole. She was smiling, a dish in her hands and her purse dangling from her shoulder. From what I could tell she was wearing a bright purple dress under her coat. I shook my head and unlocked the door before swinging it open.

"Hi." Her greeting was immediate and genuine. How could a girl whom I've done nothing but rebuff be so happy to see me?

"Hey. Uh… c'mon in." I stepped back and my gaze involuntarily dropped to her ass as she passed. I shut the door and leaned against it for an extra minute or two.

"Iris, dear?" my ma called out.

"Hi, Catherine. I brought some of that dessert we talked about last time." I looked over to see Iris setting the store-bought container on the counter before enveloping my mother in a hug.

A few minutes later we were all seated around a table full of food. I may love cooking, but I always appreciated my ma's home-cooked meals.

"As always, this smells delicious, Catherine. Thank you again for having me."

"You're always welcome, dear. I can't wait till you try some of Nicky's food." Iris glanced toward me, brows raised. "Nick is a chef," my mom boasted proudly.

"Really?" Iris asked, eyes bright and smile broad. "How didn't this get brought up earlier?"

"It was kinda difficult with my ma constantly fretting and doing everything for me," I joked. My ma smiled over at me and I raised my brows, saying, *See? I can be nice…*

"You know," Iris began. "There's a Cultural Fair during the first few weeks of school. Each class is assigned a country and the students have to present on it. Five students talk about geography. Five talk about history, etc… and the teacher is responsible for the food, and well, I'm horrible at cooking…"

Uh-oh. I knew where this was headed, and judging by the excitement in my mother's eyes, so did she.

"I know it's only the beginning of September, so it's about a month away, but maybe you could help me?" she finished with a hopeful grin. They were both waiting for an answer. I wanted to say no. This woman was trying to worm her way into our lives, and we still had no idea what she wanted.

Then I made the mistake of really looking at my ma, the woman who gave up so much for me. She looked hopeful and resigned all at once. She knew I wanted to say no, she was expecting it, but as always there was a tiny glimmer of hope. And I really loved that look on her, so I shrugged and said, "Sure."

The way her expression completely blew apart made it all worth it. She actually squealed. "Oh, this is great news," she exclaimed before clapping her hands and wrapping one arm around Iris.

And something about the way she held on to Iris just a little bit longer than normal made me think how decisively *un*great this was.

I had a feeling we weren't getting rid of her anytime soon.

Iris

I slumped back in my seat, so full I thought I might explode.

"Wow, I'm stuffed. Really, thank you for having me over. Everything was wonderful." I turned from Catherine to her son. "I can't wait to see your cooking in action."

He grumbled something unintelligible. Frowning, I leaned forward. I could understand his behavior when he was in the hospital. After all, I'd be pretty ticked if someone ran me off the road and left me for dead. But now? And aimed at *me*? Someone who'd tried to help him? I didn't have any excuse for his behavior. I wasn't angry—he didn't know me enough to actually hold any ill will toward me. But why? That was what always got to me about the angry, cruel people in the world… *why*?

With my elbows on the table and my arms crossed, I finally asked him the question I'd been dying to know. "Why are you so prickly?"

He laughed, a real, deep laugh, like no one had ever accused him of that before. And I almost saw the dimples! "Prickly? Most—"

His mother cut him off and placed a hand on my arm. "My dear, that is very generous of you. Bastard is the most common insult."

My eyes were wide as Nick scowled, but Catherine was unaffected by the entire thing.

"Nicholas, you should say thank you."

His scowl deepened. "I'm not thanking her for insulting me."

I hadn't meant to offend him. Frowning, I said, "Prickly isn't necessarily an insult… more like… a quirk."

Nick didn't seem to take it that way. Grabbing his plate, he stood up and walked to the sink.

"Don't worry about him, dear. He woke up on the wrong side of life." Nick's mom chuckled as she picked up both our plates.

"Oh, let me—"

"Nonsense," Catherine interrupted. "You're my guest."

She joined Nick at the sink. He was trying to hold his glare, but I saw the glimmer of affection in his gaze. Nick may have tried to act firm, stone cold, and uncaring; but he could never make it reach his eyes. His jaw was sharp, his lips in a flat line, but his eyes always held love.

There was something about him that made me not want to give up. He made me want to take a chance. I was willing to prick myself on a thorn, just to get close to the beauty of a rose. Because I knew it was there. He tried to hide it, but I could still see it.

"Do you go to church, Iris?" Catherine asked above the water Nick had turned on.

"Not with any regularity."

"Well I do hope you'll come with us sometime—I'd love for the churchgoers to meet a real-life angel." Catherine was beaming, but behind her I saw Nick roll his eyes as he placed a dish on the drying rack. And despite the fact that he clearly disagreed, there was a warmth to his expression as he looked at his mother. He may not understand or agree with her, but he clearly loved and respected her. When he caught me staring his features chilled.

"I would be honored," I answered.

"Excuse me for a minute. I'll go grab a program." His

mother smiled at me before walking to what I presumed was her bedroom.

"Thank you again." I turned back toward Nick. "I really appreciate you having me over."

"Why?" I shook my head; I thought we'd cleared this up when his mom was out here. He leaned forward, keeping his voice down. "Look, I'm not trying to be a dick. But my ma has the tendency to see only the good in people."

"And that's a problem?" I asked with a quirked brow.

"It can be. I don't know what you want—"

Okay, now I was getting exasperated. "I don't want anything," I hissed, unable to keep the annoyance out of my voice. "I don't know what happened to make you so distrustful. But I had nothing to gain from giving you my kidney. I did it because you needed it. I came to dinner because your mother asked me to, and I agreed to go to church because I *like* your mother. My decisions were never based on *you*. I simply saw Catherine, suffering and in pain at the hospital, and I empathized. I know what that feels like—"

Nick laughed, but it was cold and mean. And I knew the words that followed would be the same. "You wouldn't know pain and suffering if it bit you on the ass. You talk about growing up in your perfect, cookie-cutter mansion, with more money than you know what to do with—"

"Money doesn't buy happiness," I interrupted.

"Oh, so you grew up unhappy?"

Gritting my teeth, I answered, "No, I didn't. But that doesn't mean—"

"That's what I thought. We didn't have much growing up; I had to work and earn my way into adulthood. And I'm sorry you're bored out of your mind, playing around with all of Mommy and Daddy's money, trying to make up for the extravagant lifestyle you led by wandering around looking for do-gooder tasks to make you feel better about your vain life. You don't know *anything* about the hell my mother has been through."

I rarely got angry, especially over people like Nick who weren't worth it. If I were to get angry, it was usually at Aster. But Nick had no right to talk to me this way.

I looked toward Catherine's room before leaning forward. My voice was even and calm.

"Let's get something straight. Just because I smile and want to see the best in people and believe thinking positively is the way to go, just because I wear bright purple dresses and I like makeup and getting my nails done, doesn't mean I live a vain life or didn't work for what I have."

He opened his mouth to respond, but I cut him off. "I talk to babies in a high-pitched voice, but that doesn't mean I'm not smart, and I try to save random crickets and spiders that get in my house, but that doesn't mean I'm weak.

"I went to college. I studied hard, and when I graduated I got my job on my own. I stayed late, worked weekends. I worked hard for what I have, all of which *I* paid for."

"I—"

"No. You don't have the right to come into my life and judge me for doing well for myself. I won't apologize for working hard and doing what I enjoy as a result of it. Did I have help? Sure. My parents paid for my schooling, but they've also set up scholarship funds for others. I won't apologize for having a good life. Or for trying to help others."

I pushed my chair back and grabbed my purse.

"And for the record, there's a lot about me you don't know. Things that sucked. Things that were heartbreaking. But I *chose* not to let those be the things that defined me. I'm a strong and capable person, and that was my choice. None of it happened by chance. And your flawed perception of me won't change me either."

And with that, I walked out.

Six

Iris

"Can you believe it?" she whispered; her tone was an odd blend of disgusted and gratified.

"Are you sure?" Terry asked softly.

"Uh-huh. Barrett got twelve months in prison for—"

Shaking my head, I left the teachers' break room, leaving my two coworkers and their gossip about another teacher's husband to themselves.

I had no interest in it. Although I was sure I'd end up hearing about it eventually—work gossip spread quicker than germs through a daycare, and no one was immune.

Something I had learned working with children… adults weren't a real thing. Most just pretended really well.

It was the first week of school, and already teachers were gossiping about what other teachers had done over the summer. I shook off the thought. I didn't want to participate, even passively by thinking about it.

Sipping my coffee, I walked into my classroom and sat at my desk before looking over my lesson plan.

The first unit of the year was a general overview of world cultures, where we went over all the wonderful aspects of diversity and how important every person was to society. Then at the end of the three-week lesson the school held a Cultural Fair and each class was assigned a different country to research and present. My students had Italy.

I loved it. Truthfully, there wasn't much about my job I didn't love, but this was one of the few lessons the kids really enjoyed. It almost seemed like play to them rather than actual work.

The only thing I didn't love was the cooking, and now I was saddled with that alone.

My plan to befriend Nick flew out the window when I walked out Catherine's door a week ago. I wouldn't try if it meant I was being insulted the whole time. Even though I could let his attitude roll off my shoulders, that was a lot of shrugging, and I wasn't convinced Nick was worth it at this point.

The warning bell rang and I finished my coffee before I started organizing my desk and writing on the board. I listened to the eager pitter-patters of kids shuffling in. Kids who hadn't figured out they were supposed to hate school and rebel against everything. I loved teaching, but I was doubtful I could teach anyone over the age of eight or nine. I couldn't see myself enjoying it as much. I had such a passion for learning, and I wanted to instill that in as many kids as possible.

Everyone was still jittery coming off summer break, yet somehow they managed to stay focused, for the most part, on the lessons. Math, language arts, and science all went well. But when we came in from recess they struggled with the social studies and foreign language sections. And before I knew it, the day was ending and it was time to go.

"Okay, guys. We made it through our first week of school. Don't forget to start working on your Class Culture assignments. Three weeks will be here quick." I finished with a smile as everyone packed up and the bell rang. Their excited chatter rose in a flurry. I heard the door open and kids shuffling out. Once I was seated behind my desk, I took out my planner and began planning out my weekend.

I was babysitting Mirielle for the first time alone tomorrow. Calla was hesitant, but after nearly four months, I insisted she and Kent go out and spend the day together.

"Oh, excuse me, dear." My head snapped up.

"Catherine." I rose as she held the door open for the last of my students.

"It'll be wicked fun!" Matthew shouted at Abby.

With a shake of her head and a chuckle, she glanced at me. "No matter how long I live here, I don't think I'll ever get used to that."

My brows crinkled. "Used to what?"

"The word 'wicked.'"

"Where are you from?" I asked, realizing we'd never really touched on Catherine's background. She'd mainly kept the focus on me or Nick during our dinners.

"Oh, a bit of everywhere. I was an Army brat." She smiled. Then grew a little awkward and shifted around uncomfortably.

"Is everything okay?" I asked, walking forward to draw the blinds so we could have some privacy.

"Yeah, I…" She blew out a breath before walking to one of the front desks and taking a seat. I walked around and took the seat next to hers. "I wanted to apologize for what Nicholas said last week. I came out and you were gone. He wouldn't tell me the particulars, but I can only imagine—"

"Catherine." I reached out and grabbed her hand. "Please don't apologize. I'm sorry I walked out. It was rude, and you've been nothing but kind and courteous to me. I shouldn't have done that to you."

"Oh, I don't want you apologizing either, dear."

I chuckled. Weren't we a scene? Two women asking for forgiveness when it should have been someone else doling out apologies.

"You don't need to say sorry for Nick either. I'm not mad or offended. But I also respect myself enough not to be spoken to that way. I hold no ill feelings toward either of you. Someday, when Nick gets his head out of his butt, it'd be nice to see you guys regularly."

Catherine turned in her chair and grabbed one of my hands, wrapping it in both of hers. "Oh, I'd love that. And he will. He just… this has messed with him."

I nodded. I understood that, but like Catherine had said weeks ago, he wasn't a child. Eventually he had to accept his situation and rise above it.

"Well, as soon as he figures out I don't want anything from you guys maybe we'll have that chance."

"I've told you his father left when he was a kid, and his ex…" She frowned at the mention before shaking it off. "He'll see you're not like Colleen."

"Colleen?" I asked.

She waved her hand, almost like she hadn't meant to say it. "It's not my story to tell."

"And you're sure Nick will want to tell me?"

"Someday he will." She stood up and shouldered her purse. "I know it may not seem like it, but he needs someone like you. I know you both thought I was pushing you together for romantic reasons, but that wasn't it—well, that wasn't *only* it," she added with a smirk.

"I could see you balancing each other well. He needs some light and color in his life. And as much as I hate to admit it, people like you and me need cynics like him. Nick may be wrong about you, but he has been right about a few other people I tried to bring into our lives." She paused, looking sad and a little lost. "He doesn't *want* to see the bad. He's just seen it too many times to ignore it."

"I understand."

Catherine nodded and walked toward the door. "Please remember that. I know my son. He'll apologize. It might take a little time and it might be hard for him…"

"I promise I'll be civil."

She chuckled. "Oh, I know you will, dear. I don't think you're capable of anything else. I'm just hoping for something a little bit more than civil."

I was speechless as she winked and walked out the door.

Nick

"*Dammit!*" I shouted, throwing the charred meat and the pan into the sink. The waitress who had been clearing her tray jumped, causing the glass tumbler she had yet to remove to fall to the floor and shatter. She started while I was still healing, so this was the first shift I'd worked with her.

I had never been a social butterfly. I mostly kept to myself at work, nothing beyond the occasional laugh if I overheard something funny. But I was never outwardly angry either.

"Hey, Amanda," Kevin said as he walked up to us. "Why don't you go help Lindsay set up the bar?"

She quickly nodded, bolting before I could apologize. Even though it was a Friday, lunch had been slow. The other chefs were lingering, hoping to hear the boss reprimand me. Because Kevin would. He may have been my best friend, but that didn't mean I got away with stuff. It was the same way for Lindsay.

Luckily Kevin was a fair boss, only offering constructive criticism and never belittling you. Today was a bit different. He turned around and snapped at them. "Back to work."

"There're no orders," Aaron said, waving his hand toward the ticket holder—my lonely ticket was the only one on there. Aaron was in his mid-fifties, and ironically he wasn't one of the ones trying to catch some gossip. He was a good guy, and like me, he kept to himself. He came in, did his job, and then went home to his husband and kids.

"When was the last time the refrigerators had a good, *deep* clean? Was it—?"

Kevin didn't get the second question out before the guys were scrambling. Suddenly they all found things to do, except Aaron. He didn't mind hard work, even if there were ulterior motives to Kevin's question. Aaron did what was asked of him, no questions, no complaining.

"Aaron, do you mind finishing up that order while I talk to Nick?" My boss slapped me on the back.

"Sure, not a problem." Aaron immediately started working, fixing my mistake.

I was half a second from flinging Kevin's hand off me when he hissed, "Move," and gave me a little shove toward the back door. I expected him to tear into me the second the door shut, but he surprised me. Kevin calmly walked to the end of the alley before turning to face me. His lips were set in a firm line and his brows furrowed as his gaze roamed over my face. After a minute or two of me impassively staring back, he sighed.

"What's up?"

"What do you mean?"

Kevin raised his eyebrows. "Don't do that shit. That was the third dish you screwed up today."

I cringed. It was actually the fourth. Standing up straighter, I said, "I'll pay for—"

He literally growled this time. "Cut the shit, Nick. I don't care about the money. I care about *you*." He frowned. "Is it the surgery? Do you need more time—?"

"No." I exhaled loudly and ran a hand through my hair. "No, it's nothing like that. I don't know…"

But that was a lie. I knew *exactly* what was wrong.

I couldn't stop thinking about Iris and how I spoke to her. She hadn't deserved it. She wasn't the reason I was in a funk. Truthfully, I'd been a dick to her from the beginning out of fear. Not fear that she was the same, but fear that she was different. That she might be someone who was true to her word.

Most people said fear came from the unknown, and I suppose some did. But fear also came from knowing. And I knew she would be the one who would call me out on my shit and make me reevaluate my life.

That was why she was constantly on my mind. It wasn't her momentary anger that had me down, it was the look in her eyes. The steel. The strength.

How did she do it?

I shook my head. It didn't really matter how. She deserved an apology regardless.

"I gotta go," I said, turning and walking away from Kevin, who shouted at my back. "I'll call you later." I absentmindedly waved at him before jogging to my car.

After climbing in, I sat there for a second, trying to think of another solution. But apart from calling the hospital and asking the staff to violate HIPAA policy, there was only one way to get what I needed.

Biting the bullet, I picked up my cell phone and dialed her number. My ma answered immediately.

"Hello?" She sounded a bit out of breath.

"Hey."

"Nicky! Hi, dear. This is a pleasant surprise." Her voice was high-pitched and a bit nervous. Before I could question her odd behavior, she plowed ahead. "Is everything okay? How was your first day back at work?"

I rubbed the back of my neck. I didn't think I was going to be able to get the words out. "Eh, it could have been better. I messed up a few dishes."

"That's not like you. Are you feeling okay? Is it—?" I cut her off the second her voice started to reach a panicked shrill.

"I'm fine. It's nothing to do with the surgery or accident. Nothing like that. It's kinda… well it's just in my head, really."

She paused. "What's wrong?"

Scrubbing my hand down my face, I decided to get it over with it. "I think I need to talk to Iris. Clear the air. You wouldn't happen to have her address, would you?" I held my breath.

"Of course. Give me a minute." I could hear the blinding smile in her voice, even as she tried to tamp down her excitement.

I chuckled. "I'm not fooled by your tone. You've been playing matchmaker from day one."

"I don't know what you're talking about," she practically sang. The words were smug, like she was talking to a little kid. "I'll go grab it."

With a sigh, I leaned my head back against the seat as I heard her put the phone down. My eyes were closed when I heard her say, "He's calling about Iris."

At that, they shot open. Who was she talking to? My ma didn't date and she hardly had any friends. I always felt guilty, but she'd said she preferred it that way. And when I grew up and moved out, and she stayed the same, I figured that had been the truth.

She giggled at something the other person said.

I pulled the phone back; maybe I'd fallen asleep and was imagining things. Nope, I was still on the phone with my mother... who *giggled*.

"Nick? I have it—"

"Who's there?" I interrupted before I could think better of it.

"What?"

"I heard you talking to someone... who was it? Is a guy over?"

Great, I sounded like her dad lecturing her about boys...

Her voice lowered. "Yes, I have a guest over. And yes, he happens to be male. Is that so inconceivable?"

I winced at the embarrassment in her voice. "No, Ma. Of course not. I didn't mean it that way."

She easily dropped her defenses. "I know. Touchy subject, I suppose."

"I really didn't mean anything by it. I was just surprised. You never had many friends, even after I left..." I cringed again. My jaw was awfully sore from all the time my foot spent in my mouth.

"I know," she whispered. "It wasn't because I didn't want any. I guess I was so comfortable in my loneliness that I didn't even realize I was lonely." She paused, and I could imagine her shaking her head. "I don't know if that makes any sense."

"It does," I assured her. It was easy to get into a routine, to think you were happy, when you were really just content. My mind drifted to Iris... Iris who always seemed happy, who had a smile for everyone. I wondered if part of Ma breaking out of her shell was because of Iris.

Just another thing you owe her... my cynical mind added. But I was starting to think maybe she really didn't have an ulterior motive. It'd been nearly two months since the surgery, four since we met, and not a single thing seemed suspicious.

"I really like him."

I took a deep breath, reminding myself that however hard it was for me, my ma deserved this. I just had to make sure whoever this guy was deserved her. But one crisis at a time.

"Then I'm happy for you."

She let out a breath of relief. I didn't think she'd stop seeing him if I had a problem, just like I didn't stop seeing Colleen when my ma wasn't convinced she was for me, but we always liked to have each other's backs. We always wanted to support one another.

We finished the phone call after she gave me the address and I told her I wanted to meet this guy soon. I was in slightly better spirits as I drove to Iris's house.

I just hope she'll accept my apology.

I arrived twenty minutes later, about half an hour past six. She lived in exactly the kind of place I would imagine. In the suburbs, with her house situated at the top of a cul-de-sac, looking immaculate.

Pulling to a stop, my gaze ran across her wraparound porch. She had a cushioned bench beside her door and flower beds running along the walk to her front door.

Before I could psych myself out, I unfolded myself from the car. Then I opened the door to the backseat and grabbed the flowers I'd picked up on the way over. My long legs carried me up to her door in no time. I glanced down at my slightly sweaty palms, feeling ridiculous.

What was I nervous about? It wasn't like she was going to slam the door in my face or something.

But then I realized that almost made it worse. When someone was exceedingly nice to you after you'd been nothing but a dick, it made you feel even shittier.

I took a deep breath, and before I could obsess about it any more, I raised my fist and knocked.

Iris opened the door with a bright smile. I watched it falter when our gazes clashed. Honestly, I expected it to drop completely, but I kept forgetting we weren't the same. She would still try.

"Nick," she said, surprise lacing her tone. "What are you doing here?" Her tone was the epitome of polite, like she hadn't told me, essentially, to go fuck myself the last time we spoke.

"I wanted to apologize," I blurted out as her eyes traveled to the orange chrysanthemums in my hands.

Iris's eyes flared slightly and her smile slipped a degree or two. They were subtle changes that I wouldn't have caught if I hadn't been staring at her so intently. She almost seemed stunned silent.

"Can I come in?" I asked.

She glanced over her shoulder. Panicking, and thinking I was losing my chance, I quickly reached out and grabbed her hand. Iris startled and looked back at me, her eyes wider than ever. She shook off the expression before smiling again. Then she opened the door all the way and welcomed me in.

Letting go of her hand was harder than I'd expected. Once I did, I followed her into the main part of the house.

"Are those for me?" Iris asked, pointing to my hand.

"Oh, yeah. The florist said tulips were great apology flowers. But I don't know..." I shrugged. "I liked these."

She gave me a huge grin as she took them to the kitchen and began filling a vase with water. "Chrysanthemums are my favorite," she admitted.

I laughed. "No shit?"

"Ask anyone." Iris placed the flowers on the counter by the window before turning back toward me. "Would you like something to drink?"

"No, I'm good."

"Okay."

My gaze wandered around her house as I took a seat at her table. It was nice. The windows were large and the curtains drawn back, letting in the natural light. Her furniture was all white, but there were splashes of color everywhere. The blood red pillows, the baby blue vases spread through the family room, the yellow and green cutlery I could see on her drying rack near the sink. Her house was just like her; simple and unassuming, yet bright and impossible to ignore.

I turned back toward Iris. Grabbing the back of my neck, I stared at the floor, trying to figure out what to say. Apologizing wasn't my strong suit. And even with my guilt, I wasn't sure I'd been completely wrong. I didn't think I had to apologize for not immediately trusting a stranger.

She grabbed a mug on the counter before coming and sitting across from me.

"Do I get my apology now?"

"What?"

"You came over to apologize?"

"Yeah, but…" I waved my hand at the vase. "I brought flowers."

See? I sucked at apologizing. Colleen only really needed roses or jewelry when I pissed her off.

Iris smiled, and I imagined it was the exact smile she gave her second-graders, bemused and patient. She nodded toward the vase. "The chrysanthemums are lovely, but I also like words. I don't believe in holding grudges. I believe in forgiveness. But that doesn't mean I hand it out for free. So, the floor's yours…" She lifted her drink to her mouth and finished it.

I laughed. Genuinely laughed.

I didn't always understand her.

But somehow I'd come to like her.

And I'd hurt her.

My smile fell with that thought.

I leaned forward, outstretching my arms and asking for her hands. She was surprised, but she willingly placed them in mine. Looking at our joined hands, I ran my thumbs over her knuckles and thought about what to say.

"This is a fairly little thing, especially since we don't know each other all that well… you probably only need a few words," she joked, sensing how uneasy I was.

I smiled to myself. She was teaching me how to apologize. How ridiculous was that? And what did it say about her that *she* was trying to make *me* more comfortable? I'd never met someone who tilted my world upside down as much as she did. I didn't know right from left, up from down, and suddenly everything I'd thought was true was being questioned. I wasn't sure I knew how to live in this world Iris was creating.

It should've terrified me. I guess part of it did, which was why I'd resisted for so long. But now I couldn't help but want more. More of her, more understanding, just… more.

With a deep breath, I looked up and locked eyes with her. "I made judgments based on things from my past that had absolutely nothing to do with you. I know it doesn't erase what I said or the fact that it hurt you. But it had nothing to do with who you are, which I know you know. You're kind and sweet and nice, and maybe that was what made it so hard to believe. I've never met someone so... good. I'm not used to it." I cleared my throat and broke our stare, the connection becoming too much. "But I want to be. I want to get used to it. Used to you." I stared down at our hands before cursing myself for my cowardice and gazing back up into her eyes.

"I'm truly sorry, Iris. Will you forgive me?"

She scrunched up her face in deliberation. Then she started moving her head from side to side, and I cracked a smile right before she said, "Hmmm, apology accepted... I guess."

Just like that. Somehow she made me work for it while also making it feel effortless. I wondered if I'd ever figure this girl out. We were smiling at each other when I realized I'd done what I came to do, and my continued presence was most likely awkward for her.

"I should probably get going," I said as I broke our connection and stood up. She grabbed her mug and headed to the sink while I walked toward the door.

"Oh! And—" I spun around, expecting her to still be in the kitchen, surprised to find her right behind me, as she ran into me from my abrupt turn. "My bad." Steadying her with my hands on her shoulders, I chuckled. "Man, you move fast... and quietly."

She laughed with me. "What were you going to say?"

I let go of her and stepped back, rubbing my hand over the back of my neck. "I was gonna say I'll still help you. With your school thing. The food."

Jesus, I sound like a caveman.

She managed to keep herself from grinning, even though her eyes were lit with humor. "As long as you're sure you don't mind…"

"I don't," I immediately answered.

Nodding, she crossed her arms, seeming a bit anxious. "Would you be able to meet me somewhere tomorrow?"

"Yeah." I pulled out my phone and asked for her number. After she gave it to me, I sent her a quick text. "There. Just let me know when you decide where."

This time, Iris smiled, with her lips, her eyes, her entire being…

Before I did something stupid, I turned around, opened the door, and left.

But for some reason I felt like I was leaving a part of myself with her.

Seven

Nick

Iris: Boston Common. The George Washington statue. Two o'clock. xx

I STARED DOWN AT THE TEXT MESSAGE IRIS SENT ME LAST night before glancing at the clock above the bar. Kevin didn't have me scheduled to work today, but I knew I had to come in and give him an explanation for yesterday.

It was five past noon now.

"Nick?"

Looking up, I saw Kevin walking out from the back hallway. "Hey." I nodded, watching him settle behind the bar.

"What's up? And if you're here to ask me to sneak you on the schedule today, I can't. Lindsay would kill me."

I smiled and began twirling the coaster in front of me. "No, it's not that. I thought you deserved an explanation for yesterday."

"As your boss or your friend?"

"Both."

He was grinning as he pulled out a bottle of beer, popped the lid, and slid it to me. "Good answer. I gotta say I was pretty pissed when you took off. You'd been moaning and groaning for months about getting back to work, and yesterday you were suddenly fine with fucking things up? I call bullshit."

I briefly smiled before taking a sip. "It—"

"And don't even think of lying," he interrupted, pointing a finger at me. "Or I'll sic Lindsay on you."

"It was about Iris. We had a fight." Kevin straightened and his eyebrows rose.

"So you were a dick?" he asked. I narrowed my eyes. "What? Tell me I'm wrong."

I gritted my teeth in frustration. Not because of what he was saying, but because he was right. I hadn't been purposefully trying to hurt her; despite my douchebag tendencies and knack for saying the wrong thing, I never wanted to intentionally hurt someone. Especially her.

Because, somehow, and without really meaning to, I was starting to care for Iris. And being in an argument with someone you cared about put a gray cloud over everything, which was why I'd avoided relationships in the last few years.

Woahhh.

A relationship?

"Hey," Kevin said, thankfully breaking me out of the rabbit hole my thoughts were about to take me down. He squinted, intrigued and unsure. "You being a dick isn't a new occurrence. You feeling bad, on the other hand… holy shit." His eyes grew wide, and I didn't like the thoughts I could see brewing behind them.

"She's nice, okay? I'll give everyone that. So yeah, I felt

bad. But doesn't anyone else think she's unnaturally friendly? I mean, who's *that* happy all the time? She could have a bird shit on her head and her first thought would probably be, *well at least he isn't constipated.*"

Kevin chuckled and leaned back. "You like her."

So much for escaping the rabbit hole…

It wasn't intentional, but I remained quiet, a fact Kevin eagerly pounced on. "You do. Oh my God, Lindsay totally called this. How the hell does she do it?" he whispered to himself, his voice filled with awe and affection for his fiancée.

"I don't *dis*like her," I mumbled, looking at my beer.

"I'll take it," Kevin said, and I could hear the smile in his voice. I rolled my eyes. "And don't worry. Lindsay is pissed at me like three times a day. So I'm sure Iris will forgive you soon. She doesn't really seem like the kind of girl to hold a grudge."

My gaze collided with his when I lifted my head. "Well she certainly wasn't happy. But yeah, she's already forgiven me." Kevin didn't say anything; he just leaned back, a smug expression on his face, and crossed his arms.

"Hey guys," Lindsay said. We both turned to see her walking toward us.

"Hey, babe," Kevin greeted. He immediately tugged her forward and gave her a light kiss on the cheek. Her lips lifted as he pulled away.

"What were you guys talking about?"

"Nick's new—"

"Hey," I cut Kevin off with a frown. Lindsay turned in his arms and faced me.

"C'mon. You're finally healed and back at work, what could be so bad?" When I stayed silent, she made her way over to me. "Nope. I'm not letting you mope when things are finally looking up. What's my motto?" Lindsay asked in an annoyingly perky voice.

Rolling my eyes, I said, "To live life like you're a dog with its head out the window."

"Exactly." She beamed, while Kevin and I started laughing, like we always did when her life motto came up. Lindsay's lips tipped down and she glanced back at Kevin. She opened her mouth to say something, but he beat her to it.

"God, I love you."

Lindsay blushed and looked down at her feet. I shook my head and stood up. Before I could walk away, her head snapped up and she leaned across the bar, grabbing my arm. "Hey. It's a great motto to live by. I mean, have you ever seen an unhappy dog with his head out the window?" Her face was completely serious now.

"I know, Linds. You tell me that every time."

"Well maybe someday it'll make it through your bonehead brain," she said with a slap to my head. Kevin grinned as he reached forward, wrapped his arm around her waist, and with one strong tug, pulled her into him.

"So what were you guys talking about? And why was he so cranky?" she asked Kevin, and I knew he was gonna spill.

"Nothing."

"Nick's future girlfriend," he said at the same time.

"I'm leaving," I muttered as I dropped some money on the bar.

"Aww… don't be like that. It's cute. She'll be the Beauty to your Beast," Kevin called out to my back. They both chuckled when I held up my middle finger in response.

Kevin was right… I *did* like her. I didn't necessarily want to like her, but I did.

While I didn't understand it, I couldn't help but be pulled in by her. My ma was right. Iris was like a miracle. And even though I may not have believed in them, I couldn't help but take notice when one appeared to be taking place right in front of me.

Trying not to glance at my watch for the fifth time, I anxiously waited by the statue. Iris would be here any minute, and I was more nervous than I'd ever been. My apology last night felt like wiping the slate clean.

I wasn't sure what she saw in me, but I was determined to do better this time around. Second chances were a gift most threw away, so sure that a person willing to give them one other chance meant they could squeeze two or three more out. I knew different. I was hardly one to grant second chances let alone third or fourth ones, and I had a feeling that while Iris was kind enough to give me another chance, she wouldn't give me any more. Somehow she was strong and vulnerable all at once.

My gaze was on the ground as I kicked at a rock, when I saw a stroller stop a couple feet away from me. I lifted my head, preparing to offer a stranger directions, and my eyes collided with a pair of unmistakable warm brown ones. I didn't need to look at her mouth to know she was smiling.

"Hi."

"Hey. I'm glad you could make it," she said as she stepped closer. I glanced down, and I was a bit amazed that just the sight of Iris had temporarily made me forget about the stroller.

Wide blue eyes stared up at me as the little girl—based on her pink flowered headband—sucked on a yellow pacifier. Her chubby arms waved toward me, almost like she was saying hi.

"I think she likes you," Iris said. Then she reached down and tickled the baby's belly, causing a loud giggle to pierce the air when the pacifier fell out of her mouth.

"Is… is she… yours?" I asked. I hadn't meant to ask that first, or be so blunt and awkward, but the truth was, I didn't know much about Iris's life. I only really knew the small things. I knew she wasn't married, but that didn't mean she was single. Hell, she could have had a house full of children and a boyfriend, and maybe they just weren't home last night. Though I didn't remember seeing any pictures.

Iris straightened. "You think I had time to give birth to a child in the last few months while I was busy donating a kidney?"

I rubbed the back of my neck and looked down. "Ah, yeah, I guess I didn't think about that."

She was smiling when my eyes found her again. "She's my niece. Actually… she's the reason you have a kidney." My brow furrowed as she explained, "I was in the hospital that night because my sister just gave birth."

"Really?"

"Yeah."

I glanced at the little girl again. "What's her name?"

"Mirelle. It means miracle in French."

It was pretty, if not unusual. I wondered for a moment if it was a trendy way to keep their daughter unique. Rich people always did weird shit like that.

"How'd they come up with it?" I asked, because despite my attempts to turn over a new—less bitter—leaf, I couldn't help but assume the worst. Habits were hard to change.

"My sister had been trying for nearly three years to get pregnant. About two years before Mirelle was conceived they started fertility treatments. After four months one took…" She trailed off and looked toward her niece. "They lost him five months in," she whispered. When she turned back, there were tears in her eyes.

"It broke my sister's heart."

You would think I'd be used to being wrong about this girl and her family, but I was still stunned silent. There was no way she was lying—her grief was too genuine. It was the first time I'd seen anything less than a smile on Iris's face. It was a horrible sight, and something I never wanted to see again.

"Hey, it looks like everything worked out," I said, pointing down at Mirielle. I was rewarded when that bright signature smile took up residence on Iris's face. All felt right in the world again.

"Yes it did. They didn't try again for another eight months, and seven months later she was conceived. They were hesitant to get their hopes up again. But with each passing month, their excitement grew. When the seven-month mark came, they started picking names. A French colleague of Kent's suggested it and my sister fell in love. Mirielle has been responsible for so many miracles." Her smile transformed into something more meaningful as she looked at me.

My mouth felt dry when she continued to stare at me. I admired that about her—she never shied away from her feelings or seemed embarrassed. She may have thought the same about me, but she'd be wrong. Distrust and anger masked everything else. It was hard to be embarrassed when your heart was so heavily guarded. And now that it wasn't, it felt like I was putting it on a chopping block.

I cleared my throat and pointed down the sidewalk. "Should we start walking?"

Nodding, she turned the stroller around and began pushing. It was a beautiful day out, the temperature hovering in the high sixties, and people were everywhere. Boston Common was spacious enough that it didn't feel crowded, but there was a myriad of things going on: teenagers playing Frisbee, people jogging, having picnics, or walking dogs. I couldn't remember the last time I enjoyed a day like this. It was nice.

"Did you have a good morning?" she asked.

"Yeah, not bad." I shoved my hands in the pockets of my jacket. "Yours?"

"It was great. I'm spending the whole day with this little one." She leaned forward and brushed Mirielle's leg. "How are you adjusting to everything?"

I blew out a breath. "Pretty good, I think. I have to set alarms on my phone to remember my meds and all the appointments, but I think it's just a learning curve. I'll get used to it in no time."

"That's good," she said with a smile. We were quiet for a few minutes as we kept walking. It wasn't awkward; it was the kind of quiet that came when you were comfortable with another person.

"Can I ask you a question?" I asked.

"Of course."

"Last week you said things in your life weren't always easy, that there were times of heartbreak. What did you mean?"

She frowned. "Why are you asking me this?"

"My ma trusts you completely. But I'd be lying if I said I wasn't still struggling a bit," I admitted with a cringe. I didn't want to piss all over my second chance, but I wanted to be honest with her.

Iris faced forward again, the brief silence filled with tension this time. "And you think if I tell you about my past it will justify something?" Off my silence, she sighed. "I didn't expect your trust, Nick. That's earned. I understand that. All I ever wanted was your respect. You don't have to trust a person to treat them with respect."

I rubbed my hand down my face. "You know what's pathetic? This is me trying."

We walked a little farther before she said, "The Chamberlains adopted me when I was nine years old."

She paused, and my mind flooded with the horror stories I'd heard about foster care. Abuse. Neglect. And things far too horrifying to even think about…

"Nothing like that happened," she quickly added, recognizing the expression on my face. "I actually don't remember much about my time with other foster parents. I know they were decent homes. Nothing terrible happened, nothing ruined me." I stayed silent. I'd asked for her story, the least I could do was let her tell it without interruptions.

"I'm not happy because my life has been perfect, Nick. I'm happy because I decided to be. I know you probably think it was easy for me. But it took work."

Iris pulled the canopy over Mirielle, blocking her from the sun so she could drift to sleep. "My birth parents died when I was seven years old. I had no siblings and no extended family. I was alone and scared, forced into an imperfect system with no guarantee of ever leaving."

She took a deep breath before continuing, "Most of the information I have is secondhand. My birth father never had an easy life. He didn't finish high school, too busy running around with drug dealers and thieves. I guess the only option he saw was a life of crime. Then he met my birth mother, and his whole life changed." She smiled and her eyes were bright with the happy memory. "He fell in love with her immediately, and he tried to turn his life around. He proposed after only two months, and within a year they were married and had me. In one of his letters he wrote that it was everything he never knew he wanted, and he couldn't have imagined a better life. He never thought he'd get a happily ever after."

Her eyes filled with tears and the small smile she'd had slipped. "Then she got cancer. It was fast spreading and required a lot. A lot of drugs. A lot of treatments. And a lot of money. What could my parents do? She was a diner waitress and he worked in a garage." She shrugged.

"So he went back to what he knew. Selling drugs, stealing..." Shaking her head, she said, "He wasn't a bad person. He just wanted to save the love of his life. I don't condone what he did. I know it wasn't right. But I think it's a mistake to condemn people for the worst thing they've ever done. You probably think he deserved what he had coming—"

"Hey." I had to stop her now. In an effort to protect myself these past few months, I'd put on a mask. A mask of a monster considering how she thought of me. I didn't want her to see me that way anymore. I stopped in the middle of the sidewalk and lightly gripped her elbow. When she paused beside me, I slowly dragged my fingers down her arm until I was holding her hand in mine. We were both quiet for a moment, our eyes on our connected hands.

"I'm not judging, I promise," I said. She nodded in response.

"He got caught. And with his priors, his sentence was a lot longer than it might have otherwise been. Not that it mattered—she died a month after he was sentenced."

Tears fell from her eyes, but she reached up and quickly wiped them away. "I think he blamed himself," she whispered. "But I was there. And despite my young age, I know there wasn't anything else he could have done for her."

My hand squeezed hers. God, I couldn't even imagine. Watching your wife, the mother of your child, and the love of your life wither away before your eyes, powerless to stop it.

"I was put in foster care because of her death and his imprisonment. I remember being told I'd be released to my father once he got out." Her eyes dipped, and my heart broke. "He never did. He died three months after she did." Iris laughed, the sound unhappy and getting stuck in her throat. "You'd think it was prison that killed him. It's not exactly a safe place. But that wasn't it… he just… died. His heart stopped and they couldn't find a reason. They ruled it natural causes." Our entwined fingers became blurry as I stared down at them.

"Iris…" I murmured.

"I think…" She looked up at me, her face wracked with despair. "I think he died from a broken heart. I think he couldn't handle living in this world without her. And I think he knew, because his last letter felt like goodbye."

"He wrote you?"

She nodded. "My mom had started writing me letters when she got sick, first just general ones. Then she made some for important milestones. Sixteenth birthday, eighteenth, graduation, wedding, etc…

"Once he was arrested, he did too. Like I said, I think he knew he wouldn't be able to live without her. I remember some of his letters, how I could *feel* his love for her just from his words."

"Did he write letters for all the milestones too?"

She shook her head. "He said he wouldn't know what to say, that his life wasn't one to mirror. He said that was what Mom was for. Mainly he apologized a lot. But honestly the letter was so him, and I wouldn't have wanted it any other way."

When she looked at me her eyes held strength, not sadness like I was expecting. "My life could have turned out a lot differently if it weren't for the Chamberlains. And even though I was never a bitter person, I promised myself I would appreciate everything. I wouldn't dwell on what I couldn't change. I would live life to the fullest and help as many people as I could."

"You had all these thoughts at age nine?" I smiled, my hand involuntarily squeezing hers. A nonverbal *I'm here. You have me.*

"Yes. I was very smart." I was relieved when her lips followed mine. Then she shrugged, almost embarrassed but not quite, and pulled her hand away. She started pushing the stroller again as I stepped beside her.

The next few minutes of our walk were filled with nothing but the sounds of our surroundings, both of us lost in our thoughts.

Mine were scattered. I couldn't quite wrap my head around the fact that Iris had experienced so much loss and found a way to smile in spite of it.

Strength wasn't about being the loudest or the most aggressive, like I had been the last few months.

Strength was about standing behind your convictions. About speaking when you should, not just because you could. About being happy with who you were even if no one else was.

Others might not know it by looking at her, but Iris was one of the strongest people there was.

Eight

Iris

It was Sunday morning, almost three weeks since Nick and I walked around Boston Common. We had started texting, and we'd seen each other at the last three Sunday dinners at Catherine's. But other than that, this would be the first time we'd be hanging out, face-to-face, just the two of us.

The Cultural Fair was tomorrow, and we were going to spend today shopping and cooking the dishes. I'd just blown out one of my favorite candles, Lemon Zest, when someone started knocking.

Quickly moving from the kitchen to the door, I smoothed down my dress and adjusted my necklace. I paused in the entryway and grabbed my purse before opening the door with a wide grin.

"Hi."

Nick chuckled as he backed up so I could exit. "Excited?"

"Yes, this is my favorite unit. I love how the kids get into it." He was nodding when I turned to lock the door. We walked toward his car in silence, and when we reached the passenger side, Nick placed a hand on my elbow. I turned around to find him reaching for the handle. I had to suppress my smile as I put my left foot inside and sat down. He softly shut the door once I was in and walked around the front of the car.

"Do you mind if we stop for coffee?"

"No, coffee sounds perfect," I answered while both of us buckled up. Nick flicked on the radio and we made the ten-minute drive with just the sound of soft rock in the background, only turning it down when he pulled up to the drive-thru.

"Welcome to Dunkin Donuts, what can I get for you today?"

Nick placed both our orders before pulling forward and waiting behind the car ahead of us.

"How have you been?" he asked, his gaze straight ahead.

"Not bad. You?"

"Okay."

Even though he started the conversation, he seemed at a loss for how to continue it. "How are things at the restaurant?"

"Better." He exhaled, and only then did I realize how tightly he was gripping the steering wheel. "No mess ups or broken glasses." Nick looked a little embarrassed. "Although I'm pretty sure Amanda is still afraid of me."

"She'll come around," I said matter-of-factly before grinning. "You're like a Sour Patch Kid—first you're sour, then you're sweet." Nick chuckled and shook his head as the car in front of us left. When he rolled up to the window, I pulled my wallet out.

Nick's hand landed on top of mine. "I got it."

"That's not necessary. If anything, I should be buying yours since you're helping me out."

My breath hitched when his fingers squeezed around mine. "I've got it, Iris." I nodded, watching him pull away from me and grab some money out of his wallet.

My gaze was drawn to the car behind us. A mom and a girl I assumed was her daughter, who looked around ten or eleven, were laughing. Then the girl twisted and grabbed a shopping bag out of the backseat, it reminded me of the mom and daughter dates me and my mom used to have. Getting breakfast, going to the mall, grabbing coffee…

I smiled at the sight. I could almost hear the girl's giggles as she held a dress up against her chest. The mom's eyes radiated love. It was such a wonderful sight.

My eyes came back just as Nick handed off the cash. I leaned across the console, ignoring the sharp inhale he took when I brushed his chest. "Excuse me," I said to the barista.

"Yes?" She briefly glanced at Nick when she handed him his change before giving me her full attention.

I held out my credit card and nodded to the car behind us. "Could you go ahead and put their order on my card?"

She stuck her head out the window, her brow furrowed, and looked back at the car. When her gaze came back to mine, she told me they both got large specialty drinks, a dozen donuts, and two breakfast sandwiches. I said nothing, simply held out my card with a smile.

"Their bill is almost twenty-five dollars," she sputtered.

"Maybe they're celebrating something." I held my smile, practically pushing my card into her hand and almost crawling onto Nick's lap to do it.

"Oh—okay." She took the card, looking slightly embarrassed, and quickly swiped it. "Did you want a receipt?" she mumbled.

"No, thank you." I tried to give her another genuine smile, but she was avoiding my eyes as she handed the card back.

"Your coffees will be right up." The barista quickly shut the window and moved farther into the shop. With a sigh, I slumped back into my seat. My eyes were forward, but I could feel Nick's gaze on me.

"What?" I asked, exhausted by the thought of having to justify this to someone else.

"Nothing. I just… what if you're wrong?"

"About what?"

"About them celebrating."

I shrugged and chanced a glance at him. He didn't look annoyed, just curious. Maybe he really was trying to see things differently.

"It reminds me of stuff my mom and I did on the weekends."

"But you don't know. What if they do this all the time?"

My shoulders lifted again. "So what if they do? It's still a nice gesture, and maybe they'll appreciate it so much that they'll pass it on, and maybe that keeps happening, and one day it finds a person who *is* celebrating or who had a bad day and needed some comfort." I turned to face him. "It's not my job to decide who's worthy. Who am I to decide something like that? I'm just a person. No more. No less. I saw a chance to do something nice, and I took it. Maybe the narrative I formed is a lie, maybe it's not. It really doesn't matter to me. I'd rather do too much than not enough. And I believe you have to put out what you expect to get back."

Looking over his shoulder, I saw the barista about to return with our order. "You want the world to be softer? To be a little kinder? A little gentler?"

He slowly nodded. "Yeah… I'm skeptical, but it's a nice thought."

The barista opened the window and handed him our drinks. "Here ya go." After we thanked her and got back on the road, Nick seemed tense.

"Someone has to start it," I whispered. "Probably more than one person. And how is everyone supposed to do that if they're holding grudges or only doing things based on their perception of what a person deserves?"

I looked out the window, lost in a memory. "Once, when I was around twelve, my mom and I were at the grocery store. We were standing in line and there was this mother and her daughter in front of us. The little girl was crying because she wanted a stuffed bear—to replace the one she'd lost—but her mother couldn't afford it. So my mom stepped forward and handed her the money for the bear like it was nothing. The mother was amazed. She kept thanking us, telling my mom that the bear her daughter lost helped her sleep at night because she was afraid of the dark.

"At first glance it looked like the little girl was throwing a tantrum. But really, she just wanted to feel safe again." Turning to face Nick, I cleared my throat. "My mom did that. She gave a little girl her comfort back, and she got to experience another mother's overwhelming gratitude. All for the price of a small stuffed animal. Six dollars can buy you a lot in this world. But it can't buy you that, nothing can."

"So, how'd you become a chef?" I asked, switching topics after things became a little too heavy for a casual Sunday afternoon drive.

"We didn't have a lot growing up. Experimenting with food

became an easy way to pass the time. Granted, we didn't have a lot of food either, so the first few concoctions were unusual. But when I was older, I got a job in a restaurant and the rest is history. I didn't want to go to college. It was too expensive, and this was an easy way to make a decent career. Connections can get you a lot of places in this industry."

I was frowning, and when he noticed, he asked, "What?"

"A *decent* career? *Connections*? It doesn't sound like you love your job."

His expression smoothed. "I do. Sorry, I tend to lead more with the practical than the emotional. Drives my mom nuts. But practicality is important."

"So is passion." His eyes briefly moved to mine, flaring a bit at the word before frosting over and returning to the traffic ahead of us.

"Fortunately, I am passionate about cooking. But I'll be the first to admit, if I hadn't thought something lucrative would come out of it, I might not have pursued it."

I clucked my tongue. "That's a tragedy."

"Well lucky for us, that didn't happen," Nick said as he pulled into the lot and parked the car. "So, what's the country we're cooking for?"

"Italy."

"You're kidding," he whispered, almost to himself. "Italian food is some of my favorite." His smile was wide, and I could see that passion he felt for food simmering under the surface.

We were silent as we exited the car and walked inside. Nick grabbed a cart, looking completely submerged in his thoughts, and I could only assume he was thinking about ingredients.

"Okay, so," he began, and I could tell he was trying to tamper his excitement, but it wasn't working. Passion could not be dampened. "I make a delicious mushroom risotto, or a bolognese-stuffed bell pepper—"

"Nick," I said gently, placing my hand on his arm.

He briefly looked down. "Yeah?"

"The kids are eight."

"Yeah?" he repeated.

"I don't know many eight-year-olds who would want to eat a bolognese-stuffed bell pepper," I said softly.

He frowned. "So you're saying you want cheese pizzas? Because surely you could have done that." There was no anger in his voice, just disappointment.

"You'd be surprised at what I could screw up," I said with a smile. I didn't add that part of the reason I'd asked for his help all those weeks ago was because I was trying to befriend him. "And no, I don't want that. But we need to think about the fact that the kids might not be so adventurous."

"Hmm… okay. Well, we could start with bruschetta. Maybe do a lineup and have them make it themselves, pick their toppings?"

My hand involuntarily squeezed his bicep. "Yes! That's perfect, Nick."

He stared at my hand, swallowed roughly, and nodded before turning back toward the cart. My arm fell away with the movement. "Good. What else?"

We spent a little under two hours in the store. When I ended up saying that pizza should probably be one of the recipes, he scowled and insisted on getting the ingredients for a mushroom risotto, too. I conceded; at the very least he and Catherine could have a nice meal.

Nick and I were loading up the trunk of his car as a random idea hit me.

"Hey, you know what you should do?" He turned toward me, his brows lifting. "You should keep a journal. Like a gratitude journal or…" I trailed off when I noticed his frown.

"That sounds like something for a kid, Iris."

I tilted my head. "Why is being grateful only reserved for kids?"

"I didn't mean it like that. I'm grateful for stuff. Ma and I list those things every time we pray. But why do I need to write them down?"

"You're the one constantly talking about trying to see people in a better light; I thought maybe this would help. Writing things out is cathartic and I think if you had a tangible list of the things you're grateful for, you'd be more appreciative and optimistic. You'd see the world a little better. Besides, it couldn't hurt, could it?"

Nick shook his head as he loaded the last bag and shut the trunk.

"Okay, I guess I'll try it, even though I'm sure I'll feel ridiculous."

"I promise not to tell a soul." I mimed locking my lips with a key and tossing it over my shoulder.

We rounded the car, but not before I saw a smile inch its way up his face, dimples and all.

Nick

We were laughing as we started putting the food in Tupperware, waiting for the risotto and pizza to cool. I'd forgotten how good it could feel to laugh like this. Sure, I had my ma, Kevin, and Lindsay, but it'd been years since I'd experienced the company of someone new. I'd forgotten how nice it was to share stories, and laugh at old memories that no else knew yet. To discover someone else's favorite things.

When the risotto looked cool enough to eat, I eagerly dipped my fork into it. Tasting the food I'd created—especially if I did it from scratch—was my favorite aspect of cooking. It felt like magic, how I could take something from its barest form and transform it into something that bursted with flavor.

After I nodded my approval, Iris grabbed a fork and shoved it in the center. I laughed at the amount of food she piled on—I couldn't even see the fork apart from its handle. She'd thought I bought it for another time. But I knew after cooking all this food that we would be starving, too.

As I watched her lift the piece of silverware to her mouth and slowly chew my food, I realized I was wrong. Watching other people taste my food was what I loved most about cooking.

Then she moaned, proving me wrong once again. I had a feeling having *her* taste my food would be my new favorite part of cooking.

"Nick," she mumbled. She brought her hand up to cover her mouth so I wouldn't see the bits of food she was still chewing. "This is phenomenal."

I smiled brightly. I loved knowing that she enjoyed my cooking so much she couldn't even wait to finish chewing.

"Yeah?" I feigned humility, a puppy dog look on my face like I wasn't sure. I was. There was no shame in admitting that what I studied, what I trained for, what I was passionate about, was something I excelled in.

Her eyes widened. "Seriously? Yes. This is the best thing I've ever put in my mouth."

My eyebrows shot up and a grin played on my lips. I hadn't thought it possible, but her eyes widened further as she realized what she'd said. I stood, enraptured, as I witnessed Iris Chamberlain blush for the very first time. A rosy pink color traveled across her cheeks, settling into a deep crimson, as her mouth opened and closed like a fish.

"I gotta say, I like a challenge. I bet I could find something even better to fill that pretty mouth with," I murmured before dragging my tongue across my bottom lip.

I followed her blush, down her neck, and wondered how far south it went.

Again, I'd forgotten how nice it felt to flirt with a woman. But I also knew that wasn't quite right. It wasn't just some woman; it was *Iris*. There was no one else like her, and I knew I wouldn't have this feeling with someone else.

"T-that didn't come out right," she sputtered.

"No?" I teased.

She grunted, grabbing a nearby dishtowel and chucking it at my face. "You're a jerk."

"Nah, I'm just prickly."

We both dissolved into laughter until Iris's tapered off. I frowned. "What is it?"

"You're…" She shook her head and shifted a little closer. "You're not who I thought you were," she whispered, looking up at me through her lashes. Her gaze burned into me, *through* me. I'd never met a woman who made me feel as unsettled as she did.

"You aren't either. I don't…" I sighed, frustrated with how something as simple as *goodness* could confuse me. "I didn't understand how you could be so good. And I didn't understand why that was something that bothered me." I shook my head. "It should be the simplest thing in the world, to accept kindness. Hopefully this journal will help me do that."

Part of me still thought it was silly. Part of me thought about how much Kevin would make fun of me if he ever found out. But Iris was right—it couldn't hurt. And I knew the knowledge was safe with her. She wouldn't make fun of me.

"I hope so too," she said with a smile. "I think you have a lot of love in your heart, Nick. I'd hate to see it wasted. And I think the journal will work. Because do you know what happens when you look for something?"

I smiled. "You find it."

"Exactly. And if you never looked for goodness, how were you supposed to find it? Now that you're looking for positive things, for love and all you're grateful for, you'll find it. Just like before when you were searching for bad in the world and you found it. Your pessimism isn't rooted in who you are. You can change what you look for. You can decide to find something worth living for, rather than just the crappy things."

I thought about how much I wanted that, and yet how difficult it still seemed. "What if I've already found the bad? How do I forget it?"

"You don't." She shrugged, like it was easy. Maybe it was. "It'll always be a part of you. You'll remember the lesson it taught you, and you can be wary in the future. I'm not saying to trust everyone and everything. I'm just saying maybe think of those experiences as the exceptions, not the rules. Don't use your tragedies as a lens to see by; use them more like a rearview mirror. Just a reminder of what's behind you." Iris looked out the window absentmindedly.

"My brother used to think I should be mad at the world. He thought I should walk around like the world owed me something because of the unfortunate circumstances of my childhood."

I wanted to reach out and grab her hand, to offer her comfort, but I curled my hand into a fist and restrained myself. She turned and stared at me closely, and I imagined she was trying to see the wound—or wounds—from my past. "You're mad about something, right?" Iris spoke after a beat or two of silence.

I nodded. She gave me her kidney; I could at least give her the truth. Or parts of it anyway.

"What about Catherine?"

"What about her?" I asked.

"She's wonderful. And not many people have someone like your mother. I've seen tons of kids who don't have anything close to Catherine. Why not be grateful for her? Why not focus on that?" I didn't know what to say, but she continued, like she knew I wouldn't have a response.

"This works however you want it to, Nick. You decide how much weight you give to these things. *You*, no one else. I decided a long time ago that instead of being sad about what almost broke me, I'd be grateful for what saved me. I look at the Chamberlains and all they do, and they're my reason. Not necessarily them as people, but what they stand for. How they helped me when they didn't have to, cared for me when others were scared to. I could have taken my pain and let that shape my narrative. I could have let bitter anger be the thing that fueled me. But I didn't. I made helping people the thing my heart beats for." She shrugged, almost embarrassed. And I realized she probably was. She probably encountered assholes like me all the time. People who gave her shit simply for caring. It broke my heart that she seemed to be bracing herself for a negative reaction.

Why had I looked at this woman and her kindness as the weird thing in this world? Why was malevolence expected and generosity abnormal? What kind of world did we live in where *those* were the standards?

She picked up the fork and took another bite, pink touching her cheeks as she most likely recalled our flirty conversation from minutes ago. When she noticed me staring, she swallowed and grinned, trying to shake off the tense atmosphere.

"So, what are you gonna find? What is the thing you're gonna live for? What little slice of this world are you gonna steal and call your own? What is your heart going to beat for?" Iris asked, most likely expecting a goofy answer.

But I just stared at her, stunned into silence. My eyes traveled around her house as I tried to catch up with my thoughts and feelings.

Sensing she'd put me on the spot, she said, "It's just something to think about."

Yeah, that and about a million other things...

And when the word finally came to me, I couldn't say it. At least not to her. Because I was beginning to think that the thing I was going to live for, the thing my heart would beat for, and the thing worth finding... I'd already found.

She was standing right in front of me.

Nine

Iris

THIS ISN'T SOME PRETEEN MOVIE WHERE THERE'S *butterflies and sparks.*

I'd been wrong when I said that to Aster a couple months ago. Because I was feeling them now. They didn't happen right away, considering Nick had been so stubborn in showing me who he really was. But now that I saw it, there was no way to tamp down the butterflies.

It was true what they said. People became more attractive once you got to know them. And since I'd always found Nick to be good-looking, I was especially enamored now that he'd warmed up to me. I was sure the dimples didn't hurt. Before he had kept them in a steel vault, but now it seemed he was throwing them my way every chance he got, like he knew they were my weakness.

As Nick was leaving last night, he asked if he could come to the fair today. I told him he didn't have to but he insisted.

More than that, he actually seemed like he wanted to be there. Part of me thought it was a bad idea. I was afraid I'd lose focus with him there. But realistically it didn't matter—Nick was all I had been thinking about, whether he was present or not.

I was digging around in the trunk while Nick finished talking to his mom, whom he'd been on the phone with when I pulled up a few minutes ago.

"Okay, well have fun, Ma," Nick said as he met me at the back where I had most of the stuff already taken out. He hung up and looked down at his phone for a couple seconds. I placed my hand on his arm to get his attention, but even when I had his eyes on me I left it there, enjoying the warmth of his skin.

"Is everything all right?"

He frowned, looking extremely confused and honestly, adorable. "My mother has a date tonight."

"Really?" Nick arched an eyebrow at my squeal, but I didn't care. I wrapped my hand more firmly around his forearm and asked him again, "Really?"

"Yeah."

He didn't sound happy about it. He'd mentioned his mom was talking to someone, but he didn't know who and at the time they were just friends.

"What's wrong? Is the guy a jerk?" I honestly couldn't imagine Catherine going out with anyone who wasn't a complete saint.

"No, it's… Dr. Moore."

"The ER doctor?" Nick nodded and shifted his gaze back to his phone. "That's wonderful! Isn't it?"

"I guess… it's just… she's never dated before. I can't even remember a time she went on a single date."

I grabbed the last few things out of the trunk while he continued deliberating. "Maybe she thought it'd be weird for you.

You're not a kid anymore so she can afford to think about herself a little more."

He slowly lifted his head. "Yeah, I guess. She sounded a bit nervous, but I'm happy for her. I am."

I smiled. "Are you sure? It sounds like you're trying to convince yourself more than me." The last word was more of a grunt as I slammed the trunk shut and moved to lift the large cooler.

"Woah, woah. I'll get that." Nick rushed forward and took it from my hands. I watched him for a minute as he trekked across the lawn, my eyes invariably drawn to his butt. He wore jeans well and I literally had to shake my head to clear it. I reached down and grabbed two of the bags before trailing after him.

Don't look at his butt. I don't care if it's perfect. You're at your job right now… with children.

Luckily I pulled my eyes up in time. My stare met the back of his head right before he stopped and turned around by the entrance. With the cooler still in his hands, he nodded his head for me to lead the way.

The fair was taking place in the cafeteria, located in the center of the school. Not a long trek, but I was suddenly grateful Nick was here to help me lug all this stuff in. It had been hard enough when I was putting it in my car this morning.

Once we found the table, he told me to start setting it up while he brought everything else in. I laid a tablecloth with the Italian flag on it over the long table before grabbing the paper plates and plastic silverware.

Twenty minutes later, after everything was set up, I turned toward Nick and smiled. "Thanks again for all your help, I really appreciate it."

"No problem. So what's the game plan?"

"You're sure you want to stay?" I double-checked.

Nick shifted around. "I do. Is that weird?"

"No, not at all. I just wanted to make sure. I'd love for you to stay."

"You won't get in trouble?"

I waved off his concern. "Nah. A few of the other teachers have their husbands with them so…" I trailed off, blushing, when I realized the implication. "Not that—" I cut myself off before there was a repeat performance of our implied blow job conversation from last night. He grinned, obviously thinking the same thing. When he opened his mouth, I held up my hand.

"Remember, we're in a school." I laughed as he quickly shut his mouth and gazed around, looking guilty for whatever he had been thinking.

"I feel that way too," I assured him.

"What way?"

My thoughts drifted to his jeans and how he looked in them. "Like I can't think about anything other than education. Students tend to think we have no lives outside of school. They probably think we sleep here. And the older kids definitely think we're asexual. After a while it kind of feels wrong to think about anything else."

Nick grinned and leaned forward. "And what wrong thoughts have you been having, Ms. Chamberlain?"

I tried. I really did. But I couldn't help the way my eyes dropped to the front of his jeans. My face felt like it literally caught on fire. I quickly averted my gaze. Unfortunately I made the mistake of looking into his eyes. Eyes that were heated and hungry. Nick's mouth dropped open, almost like he was as surprised as I was. *Doubtful.*

Clearing my throat and fiddling with the silverware, I

attempted to redirect… everything, by answering his original question.

"No, it won't be a problem. The principal loves me, I'm sure she wouldn't mind making an exception." He was silent but I didn't dare look at him. Instead I busied myself by fixing things that were completely fine and going over the game plan.

"So the kids will arrive in about thirty minutes. I'll go back to my classroom to meet them and after a few words all six second-grade classrooms will congregate in here. The children will sit in front of that stage." I paused, pointing to the other end of the cafeteria where several rows of chairs were set up. "Three classes will present in the morning, then we break for lunch. They'll come back here and visit all the tables, grabbing some food and learning more about the other countries. Then after lunch the last three classes will present." I took a deep breath before finally looking up at him. "Does that sound good?" I asked, my gaze tangling with his.

He nodded and I was relieved when the atmosphere returned to normal.

My thoughts, however, stayed as immoral as ever.

Nick

Don't.

That was the one-word mantra I had to keep repeating to myself as Iris moved around the room. Every sway of her hips drew my eyes to her ass and every burst of laughter had me grinning like an idiot.

Iris walked up to me as her class finished presenting, the last of the day. "So, what'd you think?"

"I think you're amazing," I said, not thinking, just going

with the first thing that came to mind. It was true, but it probably wasn't what she meant.

Her wide smile slipped into something softer, more intimate. "Thanks," she said softly. "For everything. Even though I couldn't hang out with you as much as I would have liked, I really enjoyed having you here." I wondered if she knew those words made me feel ten feet tall.

Taking a deep breath, I worked up the courage to do what I'd been thinking about all day.

"Do you wanna come over to my place tonight? I thought I could cook us dinner?" My hands were now shoved in my pockets so she couldn't see how my fists had clenched waiting for her response. This girl was seriously tying me up in knots.

She'd just opened her mouth to respond when a woman I hadn't seen yet came up to us. "Oh, Iris. Everything was wonderful. I had Mr. Andrews sneak me some of the food, and yours was sensational… absolutely delicious."

"Thank you." Iris turned to me and placed her hand on my arm. "Nick actually cooked the food. He's a chef."

I was floored by the amount of pride in her voice.

"Ohh… well, it was wonderful." The woman looked me up and down, a sly grin on her face. "I'm Judy Ward. I teach fifth grade. I volunteered to help out the second-grade teachers with the cleanup."

I nodded. Iris and I got here early with two other second-grade teachers for the setup, and there were a few teachers from other grades who volunteered to help. She told me the remaining half were responsible for the cleanup along with other volunteers. That way the second-grade teachers didn't have to do everything.

"Yes, it was very nice of you." Iris smiled, but I saw a slight crack in it. Between that and the flex of her fingers, I knew it took a lot for her to stay cordial to this woman.

"Unfortunately I just got a call and I don't think I can stay." Judy pouted, and I had to force myself not to roll my eyes. "You wouldn't mind covering for me, would you?" She didn't wait for an answer before typing out a response on her phone with a laugh. When she looked up, she didn't even spare Iris a glance; instead her eyes locked on mine.

"So, Nick… would you like to get dinner sometime?" Judy asked.

Iris's hand jerked against my arm before she pulled it away. I frowned down at the place where it had been. Without thinking, I turned toward Iris, following the warmth she brought and was now taking away.

"Nick." My head jerked back to Judy.

Oops. I guess I forgot about her.

And judging by the annoyed, pinched look on her face, she knew it.

"Sorry, Judy. I'm unavailable." I made sure to shift my gaze to Iris. Her smile exploded, and damn, that smile did things to me. Distractedly, I glanced back to Judy. "And Iris actually can't cover for you tonight. We have plans."

I wrapped my arm around Iris's shoulders and steered her toward the exit. Raising a hand, I called back, "And thanks for volunteering to help so Iris could bug out early." A soft chuckle drew my gaze down. "Too much?" I asked once we were outside, my arm still in place.

"No. Just right. She's a bitc—" Iris cut herself off, but I caught it. Stumbling back, eyes wide and lips tipped up into a shocked grin, I stared down at her.

"Iris…"

"Rose," she supplied her middle name with a smile.

"Iris Rose—wait, *Rose*, really? That seems more than

coincidental…" She told me about her mother's obsession with flowers, but what were the chances of finding a kid with a first and middle name to match how she named her other children?

"I didn't have a middle name. Mom gave it to me when I was adopted."

I squeezed her shoulder. "Okay, I'll buy it."

"Oh, thank God." She brought her hand up to her forehead. "Now I'll be able to sleep tonight."

We both chuckled, neither of us saying anything as we continued walking, my arm still around her shoulders. And at some point our footsteps slowed, prolonging our time together.

Shaking my head, I said, "I still can't believe you swore."

"Almost swore," she corrected with a finger in the air.

"I feel like there's a bigger story there."

On an exhale, she responded, "She used to date Aster, my brother."

"Bad breakup?"

Iris scoffed. "That's an understatement. I can't believe she'd hit on my—" She abruptly stopped, her eyes flying to mine. I waited, brows raised. "My friend."

I let her off the hook and we walked in companionable silence to our cars. When we got to hers, I paused with my hand on the driver door. I pulled back, the door still shut. "Can I ask you something?"

Iris blinked back her surprise. "Sure."

"If I hadn't been there, would you have stayed for her?"

She looked down, shuffling on her feet a bit. When her gaze met mine she seemed ashamed. "Maybe." She winced as she said it.

"I know you're not a pushover, so why would you let her walk all over you?" I asked. "Especially if you don't like her."

With an exhale, she slumped against the door. "I don't

know. Sometimes I don't even realize I'm doing it. I just think about how it will be helping and I say yes." She shrugged. "I know sometimes I may be helping someone who doesn't deserve it. But I guess I'd rather be like that than *not* helping someone because I thought they were lying and I turned out to be wrong. Does that make sense?"

"Yeah, it does." I stood in awe for what felt like the hundredth time.

"And yes," she said.

"Huh?"

"I'd love to have dinner." Her eyes lit up with an idea. "I'll meet you at your place. I'm going to bring a surprise."

This wasn't an official date. I knew that when I asked her over. I knew that as I set my kitchen table with the two long candlesticks I'd swore I'd never use. And I knew that as I quickly ran back to my room and changed my shirt. But somewhere in my mind I must have decided it was a date. Or a pre-date? Maybe a rehearsal date?

Because when Iris showed up five minutes ago telling me that my ma and Dr. Moore were on their way over, I felt unreasonably annoyed.

"Why would you invite my mother and her *date* over?"

"Well you said she was feeling nervous—I thought some friendly faces might help." She shrugged, looking a bit chagrined. "Do you really dislike him that much?"

"Who?" My brows bunched. Her confused expression matched mine.

"Dr. Moore?"

"Oh." I cleared my throat and tugged on the collar of my shirt before walking back into the kitchen. "No, it's not that—"

I was cut off by three soft knocks. Now I was thanking God for my mother's arrival. I had zero way of explaining that blunder away.

Iris turned to answer the door, while I returned to the stove to finish the meal.

"Hello, dear," I heard my ma chirp as Iris ushered them inside.

"Dr. Moore, good to see you again." I could hear the grin in her voice.

"Please, call me Trevor," he responded just as my mother came to stand beside me.

"Hey, Ma."

She wrapped an arm around me and leaned her head on my shoulder. "Thank you for inviting us over," she whispered. "Iris told me that you knew how anxious I was about my date and wanted to make sure I was comfortable." Ma squeezed me. "I really appreciate it, Nicky."

I felt like shit. Not only had Iris tried to help my ma— which I initially resented—but she gave me the credit for it.

Clearing my throat, I turned toward her, her arm falling away in the process. "Actually, it was all Iris's idea. I didn't even know you two were coming over until she showed up and told me."

I cringed, waiting for the look of disappointment to enter my mother's eyes. It never came. Instead her lips lifted into the most brilliant grin.

"What?" I asked with a curious smile. She shook her head, her eyes flitting over to Iris and Dr. Moore.

"I think it's curious that you both tried to make the other look good. I can't recall you doing that for your other friends," she finished, putting extra emphasis on the word *friends*, before she left my side and joined her date.

Ten minutes later we were seated around the table. Ma had already prayed and we were passing around the dishes.

"I love the candles, Nicky. Are they new?" I looked up and found her smirking, with a hint of mischief in her eyes.

"Yes," I said with a fake grin as I plopped a pile of potatoes on my plate. "I thought I'd start classing the place up." Ma couldn't hold back her chuckle. Trevor smiled and softly brushed his thumb along her jaw. I watched her cheeks turn pink under his attention. She cleared her throat and threw him a small smile.

"So, how was the fair?" my mother asked Iris as she passed me the rolls.

"It went great! Nick was kind enough to stay and help." I felt tingles explode up my arm when Iris placed her hand on my arm. "And everyone loved his food."

"I'm not surprised," Dr. Moore added, his eyes on me. "I've only had a few bites, but it's delicious."

I gave him a tight-lipped smile and thanked him. For once, I wasn't trying to be a hard-ass for the sake of it. I just felt it was my duty, as her son, to make sure he was worthy of her. He gave me a subtle nod like he understood and wasn't offended.

Iris obviously didn't see it because she dug her nails into my arm. I looked over and she mouthed "be nice." She didn't seem mad, though—it was almost playful. I smiled, a full one that no doubt showed off my dimples, and maybe I was imagining it, but I thought her grin widened too.

I couldn't stop the flood of overwhelming joy that filled my chest. This all felt so right. I felt comfortable around her in a way I'd never experienced before. If we were dating this would be the moment I grabbed her by the neck and kissed her… just for the hell of it. Just for being her.

Our eyes disconnected and her hand fell away when Dr. Moore started asking her more questions about her job. I caught my ma's smirk as she pretended to be increasingly interested in her string beans.

The rest of dinner continued in much the same fashion. Iris did something cute, I'd try to hide my grin, and my ma would swoon like a fangirl.

I had to—begrudgingly—admit that Dr. Moore was a gentleman. He pulled the chair out for my mother when she sat. He didn't pull out his phone (you'd be surprised how often I'd pass through the restaurant and see couples on their phones during a date). And he regularly glanced at my mother (usually when she wasn't looking) like he couldn't believe she was real.

"I'll clean the dishes," he volunteered. "Nick, you've already done so much, and you ladies deserve to relax."

I watched as he stood and started collecting plates. When he gave my ma's shoulder a quick squeeze, I snapped out of it.

"I'll help."

"Really, I don't mind—"

My mother placed her hand over his on her shoulder. "Nicky is very particular with his cookware."

"You wash and I'll dry?" I compromised when it looked like he still wanted to argue.

"Sure."

We got settled into an easy routine, while my mother and Iris sat on the couch and caught up. I glanced at Dr. Moore out of the corner of my eye.

"So, Dr. Moore—"

"Trevor," he interrupted.

"Dr. Moore, how long have you been seeing my mother?"

He shook his head, trying to hide his grin. "I've been

talking to her for a few months now."

"I see." I turned to look him over. "You're successful and relatively good-looking, so why are you single? What's wrong with you?"

Dr. Moore started laughing so hard the girls looked over. Both narrowed their eyes at me.

"What? I'm funny." My mother playfully shook her head, while Iris gave me a soft smile.

"I've always been very dedicated to my job, Nick. That's what's wrong with me," he said good-heartedly.

"But my mother has changed that?"

"Most definitely." I carefully dried my paring knife before focusing on him. He was completely unruffled.

"And you're not annoyed that Iris and I crashed your date?"

He smiled, patient and kind. "Not at all. Your mother relaxed considerably once we got here. The happier she is, the happier I am."

Either I was surrounded by paragons of good, or I was seriously losing my touch for being an asshole. No one seemed affected by my gruff behavior anymore.

"Something tells me you know what that's like."

"What what's like?"

"Meeting a woman who changes you, who causes you to put your whole life into perspective."

My gaze shifted to Iris. She was listening intently to whatever Ma was saying. Because that was what she did. She gave you her full attention, she made you feel special and important. Whether that was the teacher in her, or just who she was, I couldn't be sure. But I knew one thing for certain: she treated everyone like they mattered. It was an admirable trait. Unfortunately, it made reading her extremely difficult.

My mother's comment about friends floated through my

brain. She was right—of course—I was different with Iris. But how was I supposed to tell if the girl who was kind to everyone felt anything deeper for me?

Then Iris looked over at me, her eyes colliding with mine. And in that moment, I knew. It was the way her body was always slightly turned toward me, or how her smile remained just a couple of inches higher when she looked away from me. They were subtle gestures; some might even say I was reading too much into them. But I knew that wasn't the case.

Because I knew *her*.

I knew she used at least two paper towels to dab the grease off her pizza. She did her best to step over the cracks in the sidewalk. She wasn't a fan of surprises. She had an unhealthy—in my opinion—love for lemon bars and lemon-scented things.

I also knew that when she got married she wanted any gifts to be donations to her favorite charity, St. Jude's, in lieu of actual presents. I think that was the first time I stared at her in awe. Iris had tried to brush it off, saying she just wanted to pick out her own things, but I knew better.

The main, motivating factor was her kindness.

Her pure heart.

I glanced back at Trevor. "Yeah, I know exactly what that's like."

Ten

Iris

I HADN'T SEEN NICK SINCE MONDAY. THE DAY HAD BEEN perfect, even with Judy randomly showing up and making things a little awkward. As I left his house that night and hugged his mom goodbye, she seemed exceedingly happy as she told me she wanted to double date again. When I told her Nick and I hadn't been on a date, she grinned and patted me on the cheek like a child.

As the week went on I couldn't get that interaction out of my head. Every time I talked to him, the thought was there.

Are we more?

Part of me thought we might be. And that tiny part was able to convince me that I needed to ask him.

I was looking at our texts from earlier today, when we had joked about him doing little things in an effort to see the world better.

Nick: I tried to help a pregnant woman with her groceries

last night.
  Me: *That was nice :) I'm sure she appreciated it.*
  Nick: *Yeah, not so much…*
  Me: *:(Why not?*
  Nick: *She wasn't actually pregnant :/*
  Me: *Oh.*

After I explained to him that you NEVER assumed a woman was pregnant, unless you actually saw her delivering the baby, I asked him to come over tonight. He had to work, but he was adamant he could cut out early and stop by for a bit. It was Friday night and I had no reason to be up early, so it worked out perfectly.

I tried to convince myself I wasn't nervous as I sat at my kitchen table with a glass of liquid courage in front of me, staring at the clock on the microwave. It was forty minutes past eight, and if he got out early like he thought, he should've been here twenty minutes ago.

I was so jittery I practically flew out of my seat when I heard a knock on the door. I reached the server by the front door and paused. Facing the mirror, I took a deep breath and tried to calm down. It'd been a long time since a guy had affected me this way.

My cheeks were flushed and my hair was straight with a slight curl to the ends. I was also wearing a little more makeup than usual: tinted moisturizer, mascara, and some red lipstick. All of this was paired with hip-hugging jeans and a white blouse that hung loose around my frame. You wouldn't know by looking at me that I'd spent all evening lounging in my pajamas as soon as I got off work today.

I took one last deep breath before pivoting toward the door, checking the peephole to confirm it was him, and opening it.

That deep breath proved worthless. Nick was wearing light-wash jeans that conformed to every inch of him, and a long-sleeved, dark blue Henley with the top two buttons undone. I gulped, and when my eyes skimmed his jaw I noticed his beard was neatly trimmed—something his mom told me was pretty rare. I followed his hand as he brought it up and pushed back his still-wet hair.

And then he killed me.

With his head still lowered, he peeked up at me from under his lashes and smiled, those dimples slaying me on the spot. On anyone else, the pose might have seemed ridiculous, but Nick was one hundred percent sincere, and despite his gruff exterior, he was actually kind of sweet and shy.

"Hey," he said, rocking back on his heels. "Sorry I'm late. I wanted to run home and shower first. I tried to be quick, hence the wet hair." Nick motioned to the damp locks and shrugged.

I gripped the door frame. I was pretty sure I'd never wanted to kiss anyone more. Between insisting he could come over at nine o'clock after a double at work, wanting to look nice, and rushing over, I'd never felt so wanted. I still wasn't sure what this meant to Nick, but I was hoping it meant the same to him as it did to me. Otherwise it'd be really awkward when I asked him out tonight…

"Iris?"

I shook my head and lifted my gaze.

Crap. Had I been staring at his lips?

"Yeah?"

He chuckled and motioned behind me. "Can I come in?"

"Oh, yeah, yeah. Of course," I babbled like an idiot, almost tripping on my welcome rug in my hurry to back up. Once he passed, I slowly shut the door and leaned my head against it for a second, trying to compose myself.

I turned around and found him staring at me. "Are you okay?" he asked, his concerned gaze roaming over my face.

"Yeah. Sorry." I hiccupped as I brushed past him. We walked into the kitchen and I pointed to the almost empty wineglass. "This is why I usually don't have wine."

"Ah. Rough day?"

"No. I just felt like a glass. What about you? Do you want anything to drink?"

"Beer?"

"Coming right up." I was thankful to have something to do. After grabbing it and popping the lid, I handed the bottle over. He eagerly accepted, draining nearly half of it in one gulp.

"I talked to Amanda today."

"Amanda?" I asked. I couldn't remember where I'd heard the name before. Truthfully, I was having trouble concentrating in general.

"The waitress I practically chucked a pan at."

"Ah, right. And?"

He walked over to the couch and sat down with a sigh. "It went fine. She doesn't seem as nervous around me anymore, but…" Nick shook his head and started picking at the label on his bottle.

"I wasn't always this way." He immediately snapped his mouth shut. I didn't say anything. It seemed like he was working through something. "I don't mean to keep beating a dead horse. I know we've talked about this already. It just really hit me today, how people see me."

I walked toward the couch, leaving my wineglass on the table, and sat down on the opposite end. "But now you have a chance to change that perception," I said softly.

"Because of you," he whispered back. The air froze in my lungs, and when he turned to look at me, I lost it completely.

"I'm serious. You've done more than you know. More than I can ever thank you for."

My hands twitched, begging me to grab one of his, but I managed to refrain. "I'm glad."

He shook his head, looking more put off by the idea. "I like you, Iris. I like being your friend." I tried to keep a neutral face as he dropped the "friend" bomb. "I don't always understand you, how you can be so good, so pure… but I want to."

"I don't understand the problem."

"The problem is, what am I giving you?"

I frowned. This was definitely not how I imagined tonight going. And it was such a flip from when we first met. Then he accused me of wanting something from him; now he was practically despondent because he thought he had nothing to give.

"I worry that while you're helping me, I'll eventually hurt you." His gaze shifted to the fresh chrysanthemums I bought in the middle of the week. "You're like this blooming flower, gorgeous and new and untouched. I'm afraid I'm the boot that will step on you, that will kill you."

I stayed quiet for a few minutes. I knew what I wanted to say, just not how to say it. When it finally came to me, I slid down the couch and took his hand.

"No, Nick, you're not. You're like the weather. Your anger is a passing rain cloud. And I'm strong enough to withstand it and wait for the sun. And the rain, like your pain, is temporary. You'll find your way again. No one's course is permanent. Destiny, fate, whatever you want to call it… is a constantly evolving creature that we get to shape. Don't take the coward's way out by locking yourself in some perceived box of loneliness and despair, saying it was meant to be this way. It's meant to be whatever way you want it."

I was smiling, but his face remained stoic until my lips

slowly dropped. My slightly alcohol-clouded mind went through what I'd said. It made sense and wasn't insulting. Maybe Nick needed more encouragement. Maybe this was a bigger project than I'd realized—

Startled, I jumped back when he put his beer on the table and suddenly stood. One hand was resting against my wildly beating heart as he grabbed my other arm, yanking me up.

I swayed slightly, but only for a second before he was pulling me into his chest and wrapping his arms around me.

"Thank you," he whispered directly into my ear. I shivered as my brain finally caught up and I weaved my arms around his waist.

Melting into him, I turned my head and rested it against his chest, listening to his heartbeat.

"You're welcome," I finally responded.

I started to feel guilty. This was obviously a big deal for Nick, a personal and emotional moment. And all I could think about was how good he felt pressed up against me.

He made *hugs* feel erotic. I couldn't even begin to imagine what everything else would feel like.

Nick

We pulled apart. But I didn't have a chance to feel embarrassed.

"Jeez, Nick. We need to have some fun."

"Yeah." I rubbed the back of my neck. "Sorry about that." Truthfully, I hadn't meant to go there. After she asked me to hang out, I jumped at the chance and immediately started thinking of ways to ask her out. Even when I got off work, I tried to put the conversation with Amanda out of my mind, but as soon as that awkward silence descended, I realized Iris was the only person I wanted to talk to about it.

"Do you ever let loose?" she asked, not waiting for an answer before she grabbed my hand. "C'mon."

"Where are we going?"

"Nowhere. But what we *are* doing is having an impromptu dance party."

I immediately pulled my hand from her grip. "No we're not."

She didn't respond, just bounced over to her iPod dock in front of her kitchen window. I watched her pull out her iPhone and hook it up. Her ass stuck out as she leaned against the counter and scrolled through her music.

I wondered if she had any idea what she did to me when she did shit like that. Probably not a fucking clue.

"Perfect!" she exclaimed, her ass already moving even though the song had yet to start.

Jesus.

This was not going to end well for me. I forced my gaze away, but was immediately drawn back when the song started. It sounded like techno, and for some reason that was the last thing I expected Iris to listen to.

She turned around, a wide, heart-stopping smile on her face as she danced toward me. I laughed at the exaggerated way she moved her hips. When she reached out for my hands, I shook my head and stepped back.

"Uh-uh, no way." I raised my hands to further demonstrate my point. She didn't care. Instead she jumped up and grabbed them before interlocking our fingers in a gesture that felt far more intimate than this silly dance party we were apparently having.

Then she started shaking… everything. Her ass swayed back and forth and her chest shimmied closer to me, all while

I stood there.

I couldn't think of a single other girl who would do this around me. Lindsay might, but only because we'd been friends for years. But Colleen never acted this way. She never looked this free.

"You're seriously just going to stand there?" Iris hollered over the music.

Very reluctantly, and with a roll of my eyes, I started lightly bouncing. Really, it couldn't even be called dancing, but you wouldn't know that with how Iris lit up. She jumped a little higher and brought us closer as she moved her head back and forth.

"What is this?"

"'Shake It' by Metro Station. Ever heard of them?"

"I can't say I have."

"Oh. Well, it's a great song to dance to."

"Clearly."

Iris finally called me out. "This isn't dancing," she said as she spread my arms and looked down at me. She faked a shiver and put on a look of disgust, but all the while her lips tipped up.

"It's as much dancing as you're going to get."

She pouted, her breathing becoming more labored as she continued to dance enough for the both of us. When I figured we had less than a minute left to the song, I tried a little harder. Shaking my own ass with enthusiasm and bobbing my head to the beat.

Iris shrieked, squeezing my hands as she closed her eyes and lost herself in the music. My movements slowed again—unintentionally this time—as I took her in. It was beautiful to watch her be completely comfortable with who she was. And Iris had no idea.

I'd thought she was beautiful when I first met her. Anyone

with eyes could have seen how gorgeous she was. But this hot-burning attraction that seemed to sizzle in the air whenever she was around was one hundred percent her personality, which made all the things I'd already adored even more stunning.

I knew some women thought being silly was a turn-off, and maybe to some men it was. But never to me. That was what I wanted from a woman: sexy and silly.

The song switched and a light melody floated through the living room. Iris immediately stopped and moved toward the dock. I stopped her by grabbing her hand. She couldn't hide her surprise as her eyes lifted to mine. Honestly it was a bit of a surprise to me too. I'd hated dancing with Colleen.

Iris's expression transformed to one of delight. She placed her other hand on my shoulder and we slowly began to sway back and forth. Now that she was pressed against me, without thoughts of Amanda and my abysmal personality clouding my mind, I could appreciate it a bit more. And I couldn't imagine a scenario in which Iris in my arms could possibly be anything less than wonderful.

Her heart thudded against my chest, pounding like it was trying to get out, like it was too great to stay in her body. I could barely detect a difference in mine—my heart was beating only slightly faster than usual. And to me those differences seemed to speak volumes about how different we were.

Iris was living to the fullest. She was doing everything she wanted. She was living life to her extreme and feeling so much joy her heart wanted to beat out of her chest with the excitement of it all. And me? Mine was only pumping slightly harder. I existed, and then there were those rare moments when I dared for something more. But I never lived to my fullest.

I'd been working at Kevin's place for nearly three years, and while I loved it, something I'd never told anyone—not my two best friends, not even my mother—was that I wanted more. Somewhere in the back of my mind I'd dreamed of starting my own restaurant. But I never did anything with it.

I didn't want to be a passerby in my life anymore. Just letting things happen to me. I wanted to *make* things happen. Iris's soft voice interrupted my thoughts.

"Nick?"

"Hmmm?" I looked down to see her frowning. "What's wrong?"

"I was going to ask you that." She nodded between us. "You stopped."

I stared down at my feet, like I didn't know what they were doing and had no control over them. "Oh. Sorry. I didn't mean to. I was just thinking."

"'Bout what?"

We stayed close together, my arms wrapped around her waist and hers looped around my neck, the tips of her fingers ghosting along my hairline.

"Can I tell you something kind of silly?"

"Yeah."

"I think I want to open my own restaurant one day."

Her eyes widened and she straightened. "That's not silly at all." She slapped my chest. "I didn't know you were thinking about doing that. Catherine never mentioned it…"

We both smiled. Yes, my mother had a habit of telling everyone every accomplishment I'd ever made. I wouldn't be surprised if, when I was younger, she told the grocery clerk right when I wiped my ass for the first time.

"She doesn't know," I confided.

Iris's eyes softened. "She doesn't?" I shook my head. "What about Kevin? Have you gotten his advice?"

She was asking one question, but I knew it was meant to answer several others.

Am I the only one you've told?

Are we becoming more than we've been?

"He doesn't know either." I roughly swallowed, my hands tightening their grip on her hips and pulling her forward.

One of Iris's hands came up to brush some of the hair out of my face. "I think it's a wonderful idea, Nick."

"Yeah?" I asked. I feared people would think I was just some foolish kid with a dream, and that nothing would possibly come from it.

"At the risk of sounding like an after-school special, you can do anything you set your mind to."

"You really believe that, don't you?" I asked, more to myself than her.

"Of course. If you want to start your own restaurant, I believe you can. I'll even help you if you want."

I didn't doubt that for a second. She really, truly believed in me. And I could tell she would stop at nothing until I had my dream. Iris was that kind of friend. She stood by you and broke down barriers with you, all while giving you the credit. She was adaptable and optimistic.

Iris did more than just make lemonade out of lemons. She made the lemonade, planted the seeds to grow a damn tree, and probably used the peel for some kind of crazy skin scrub (that was a thing, right?).

She was smiling up at me, waiting for an answer.

I didn't know how, but she was always smiling. If I walked around with a perma-grin like hers, I'd look like the Joker on crack. She made it look effortless, like smiles were made for her face. And I suddenly found myself wondering what her smile would taste like, if I were to slowly press my lips against hers and steal that smile for myself. I imagined her tasting like lemon, sweet and fresh, and before I was tempted to find out, I stepped back.

"I'd like your help."

"Done," she answered easily. My eyes moved to the clock on the wall; it was thirty minutes past nine. I needed a distraction that wasn't her lips.

"Wanna watch a movie?"

Iris nodded and walked me over to her DVD case. "Pick whatever you want."

"It's your house."

"And you're my guest," she countered.

Rolling my eyes, I blindly picked something. I didn't think I'd be able to focus on it anyway. Iris put in the DVD while I walked back to the couch, picking up my beer and draining it.

"Mind if I grab another?"

"Not at all," she said, back still to me.

"Do you want more wine?"

She turned around then, face still flushed, probably from the wine and dancing. "Better not. I'll probably grab some iced tea in a bit."

I saw the pitcher when I went to grab my beer. Pulling it out, I started looking for a glass. I finished up and moved back to the couch where Iris was already sitting. She beamed when I handed her the tea.

"Thank you."

"No problem."

My eyes were forward, but I could feel her watching me. When I glanced at her, she was assessing me for… something.

"You okay?" I asked.

Iris took a deep breath before putting the tea down and

swiveling to face me. "I'm going to ask you something. And it might be a bad idea to ask it right now since we'll be stuck here for two hours, or it might just be a bad idea altogether… either way, I'm going to ask."

"Shoot." Putting my bottle down, I turned her way and gave her the same amount of attention. I tried not to worry about what she was going to say, but knowing I was going to end this night asking her out had me fearing every word out of her mouth.

Her eyes stayed unwaveringly on mine as she asked, "Do you want to go on a date with me?"

I froze. Was she really asking me out? It seemed impossible considering I was still fifty percent certain she was going to turn me down.

I must have stayed quiet too long because she frowned and turned back toward the TV. "I made it weird, huh? I didn't mean to make you uncomfortable, just forget it." She smiled before reaching forward and grabbing the remote.

Forget it?

Like hell.

I was still partially frozen, watching as she continued on like everything was normal. The tips of her ears were red, but that was the only indication she was embarrassed. She wasn't going to make me feel bad, and I doubt she would think less of herself. It was so refreshing, *she* was so refreshing, how could she think I'd say no?

Maybe because you didn't say yes, idiot…

Oh, that.

"Iris." I moved down the couch until I was right next to her, and placed my hand on her arm.

"Yeah?" She met my eyes.

"Yes." She raised her eyebrows. "I only hesitated because I

was surprised."

"That a woman did the asking?"

Shaking my head, I chuckled. "Maybe a little bit of that. I mean, I've seen it happen a few times, but nothing this sincere. That wasn't really what surprised me though."

"What was?"

"That I was planning on asking you out before I left tonight."

Her eyes flickered with an emotion I couldn't pinpoint, as her lips tipped up. "Really?"

"Really," I confirmed with a nod.

The opening credits played while we stared at each other with goofy grins.

"Next Friday?" she asked.

I frowned—that was a week away. "We can still see each other between then, right?"

Iris giggled. "Of course. I have a family thing tomorrow, otherwise I'd make it then."

"It's not a problem." And it wasn't. I was just anxious to finally take her out.

We were both still smiling as Iris used another remote to dim the lights and we settled back against the couch. I didn't go back to my end, and she didn't seem to mind. At some point we moved until our sides were touching and my arm was resting on her shoulders.

Somehow we managed not to take it any further. But I was pretty sure it was going to be torture this next week, waiting for Friday.

Iris and I hugged once more before I left, and I drove home in a blur, everything else clouded by my excitement. The first thing I did when I got to my apartment was something I should have done a week ago, as soon as I first started using it.

I went to my nightstand, pulled out my "grateful" journal, and added one more thing to the list.

Iris.

Eleven

Nick

I WAS NERVOUS.

Which was really fucking ridiculous. How a twenty-eight-year-old man was scared to go on a date was beyond me, but there was no denying it. My palms were sweaty and my mouth felt uncomfortably dry. It was a little after noon on the following Saturday. Once I figured out what I wanted to do for her, I asked Iris if we could change the date from Friday to Saturday.

I was dressed in jeans and a plain black T-shirt. When I told her to be ready this early and to wear something she'd be comfortable in, she spent all week trying to figure out what we'd be doing. Every morning I woke up with a text from her trying to guess. She never got close.

Slamming the door, I walked around my car and toward her house. I swallowed, hoping to alleviate my dry throat, and quickly banged on her door three times. She was equally fast in answering, almost like she was waiting nearby. The idea that I wasn't alone in my excitement and nerves made me feel better, but it didn't calm my racing heart.

Iris was wearing jeans, a lightweight navy blue sweater, and boots that went to her ankles. Her makeup was minimal, maybe just some blush and whatever that black stuff was girls put on their eyelashes. It didn't really matter. I'd seen her with no makeup, with a completely made up face, and various things in between, and she always looked beautiful.

The idealistic part of me thought that maybe it was all her goodness shining through. Then I remembered what I saw when she walked into my hospital room all those months ago, and I knew she was one of those rare few whose inner beauty matched her outer beauty.

I'd never considered myself homely, but every time I looked at her I couldn't help but feel out of my league. Not because I was insecure with myself, but because I was so in awe of *her*.

I'd been standing there for several minutes, jaw hanging open and eyes devouring her, before I realized I was one or two mannerisms away from looking like a cartoon character in love. It wasn't until I met her eyes that I realized she had been doing the exact same thing.

God, she was gorgeous. How was I supposed to make it through an entire date—especially the lengthy one I had planned—not knowing what her lips tasted like? They looked pillow-soft, and I licked my own in response.

"I just… I need to do this before we go," I whispered, lifting my gaze to meet hers. Iris's eyes widened and her breathing stalled. Making my intentions known, I moved closer, slowly lifting my hands and cupping her cheeks. "I won't be able to concentrate if I don't, which will lead to another car accident, and then you'd have to give me another organ…" I cracked a smile as she chuckled, some of her nerves floating away. "It'd be a mess."

"We wouldn't want that..." Iris trailed off, breathless, with a sweetness to her voice that I didn't think I'd ever get used to.

"No, definitely not," I whispered. I nervously swallowed before my hands tunneled into her hair, gently cradling the back of her head. She froze for a moment, almost like she couldn't believe this was happening. Her body quickly relaxed. Then her eyelids lowered and the small smile that had been on her face disappeared with the slight parting of her lips.

Eyes closed and head tipped back, she was waiting for me.

I took my time, slowly shuffling forward until I had her back against the door. Her hands came up and gripped my biceps, her chin jutting out just a little bit. No words passed her lips, but she was speaking all the same.

Kiss me. Hurry.

My lips involuntarily tipped up as I teased her a little bit longer, trailing my hands down her cheeks to the sides of her neck, my thumbs meeting in the center to slowly caress the skin between her collarbones. To anyone looking in it would probably look like I was strangling her, stealing her breath and life. They'd be wrong. She was stealing *mine*.

She stole it every time I looked at her.

And she ripped apart my life—in the best way possible—and changed everything I thought I knew. Every time she spoke or did something remarkably kind, I was rethinking everything.

I was staring at my thumbs when Iris softly moaned, dragging my attention to her face. Her eyes were still closed, but the skin between her eyebrows was pinched. Leaning forward, I kissed her there, feeling it stretch and smooth. My lips moved down the bridge of her nose, not applying any extra pressure, just a slow drag, until I reached the tip. I placed the softest kiss there before slowly withdrawing and moving down. Our faces were no more than an inch apart, our mouths so close I could feel the heat off hers. It pulled me in until my mouth rested against hers.

Finally.

And that soft, almost innocent, touch was all we needed. It was like the shotgun at the start of a race, and once we heard that sound—or felt that first touch—all bets were off… *we* were off.

Our mouths opened at the same time, trading moans and immediately seeking out the other's tongue. My skin instantly heated and everywhere she touched felt like a spark of electricity.

Her hands drifted up my arms, gripping my shoulders and trying to pull me closer. I skimmed my hands down the front of her until I reached the top of her jeans. Winding my arms around her waist, I tugged her flush against me, allowing her arms to wrap around my neck. Iris's fingers sought refuge in my hair, and I groaned loud and long at the contact. She responded by pulling my lower lip between her teeth, lightly nipping, before soothing it with her tongue.

It felt like we'd been kissing for hours when we finally broke apart, panting. I immediately dove back in, only to discover the Beatles were wrong—love was definitely *not* all we needed. We also needed oxygen, which was pretty damn inconvenient right now.

This time we were laughing as we pulled away from one another.

"I haven't…" She trailed off and shook her head.

"What?" I whispered, unable to stop myself from placing a soft kiss on the corner of her lips. She brought one hand up to her mouth. Leaning back, I watched her trace her lips, and I swear to God, I could *see* the stars in her eyes.

"It's never... I don't..."

She was flustered and speechless, but I knew exactly what she was trying to say. Because I'd never felt anything like that before either.

In theory, it should have been like any other mind-numbing kiss. But it was nowhere close; there was no comparison. I wasn't sure what made it so different. Were her lips softer? Her hands greedier? Her moans raspier? Her bites a little sharper?

None of those seemed exactly right... it was all just *more*.

Iris's kiss was what I imagined taking the first hit of a new drug would be like. It was exhilarating, and unlike anything I'd ever experienced. There was a delicious buzz going through my head even as my entire body felt relaxed, practically melting against her.

People always said that nothing was like the first time. Nothing compared to the first taste. That was what drove addicts—they were constantly chasing their first high. Only to discover they could never quite reach it again.

My lips found hers once more, and just like that, I became an addict.

Iris

I had been standing in front of my full-length mirror, my head twisted so I could see how my backside looked, when a firm knock echoed off the walls of the hallway and reached my bedroom. I was never the kind of person to get nervous before a date, but for some reason, this felt like more than a date. And I practically sprinted to the door.

Now, as I was experiencing something that definitely didn't feel like a first kiss, I knew I had been right. This was *more*.

I retreated, tipping my head back against the door. Nick's lips met the column of my throat, gentle and assured, while he whispered words of praise into my skin.

"So soft."

"Gorgeous."

"How'd I stay away so long?"

"We're going to be late," I murmured.

Nick chuckled and stepped back from me. The only place we were touching now was his hands on my hips.

"You don't even know where we're going or what we're doing."

"True, but I still don't want to be late for it."

He smiled, his thumbs applying extra pressure where they lay underneath my shirt, against my skin. "Let's go then."

Grabbing my hand, he pulled me off the porch and down the driveway. I was in a daze as he opened my door and helped me in. He softly shut it before jogging around to his side of the car.

When he slid into his seat and started the car, he glanced over at me and gave me a nervous smile. "Okay, so this date is… unconventional."

"We're not going to a graveyard, are we?" I asked as he pulled into traffic.

"What?" His startled eyes quickly flew to mine then went back to the road. "Did a guy actually take you there?"

"Not me; a friend in college." *That's what happens when you pick your date based on his toes…*

I crossed my legs and shifted my body so I was angled toward Nick. "No, my worst one was a third date. He took me to a wedding."

He shrugged. "That's awkward and kinda fast, but not too bad."

"Ah-ah." I held up my finger. "I wasn't done. The wedding was for his ex-girlfriend."

"Hmm… well that's definitely weird, but not necessarily—"

"He wasn't invited."

Nick chuckled. "Okay, that's really bad."

I laughed, watching him throw me a flirty grin. "Yeah. It was a big wedding, so at first no one noticed us. But he seemed determined to make a scene." I shook my head.

"And second place goes to the guy who took me to a strip club. It was our third or fourth date and he thought it was time I met his regular dancer. He was even so generous as to offer her up to give me a lap dance."

"So the bar is set pretty low for me?"

Grinning, I said, "My point was that this is a giant display of trust I'm exhibiting right now. I haven't let a guy take me on a blind date in years."

"I'm honored." Nick stopped at a light before bringing his hand over to cup my face. "I promise it's nothing like any of that. But it's not dinner and a movie, or a picnic in the park."

We were smiling at each other, his thumb lightly brushing over my cheekbone, when a horn blared behind us. Nick jumped, pulling his hand away and immediately slamming on the gas. With a shriek, I gripped the armrest and held on to my seat belt.

"Sorry." He gave me a sheepish look.

"No worries." Calla was a nervous driver so I was used to abrupt driving.

I started paying better attention to our surroundings and… "Are we going to your apartment?"

"Yup."

I looked at him out of the corner of my eye. I didn't think his "unconventional" date would be a nooner at his place, but I was at a loss for what we might be doing.

We spent the rest of the car ride in silence. When we arrived at his place, I unbuckled and reached for the door handle before he stopped me with his hand on my wrist.

"Let me." With a smile, he got out and jogged around the front of the car. Nick held the door open and offered his hand. He kept my hand in his as he shut and locked the doors. We walked up the path until we stood in front of his door.

"Close your eyes," he instructed while he put his key in the lock. Once they were shut, I heard the door squeak open before feeling Nick against my back, holding on to each hand and leading me over the threshold.

His apartment smelled good, like coffee and pine. Definitely the work of a candle. Nick chuckled into my hair when I inhaled deeply.

"You like?" he whispered.

"Yeah. I didn't picture you for a candle person."

Another laugh tickled my ear. "There's a lot you don't know about me, Iris." He paused and when he spoke again there was a serious and wistful quality to his voice. "That's my fault, but now I want you to know everything."

"Me too," I whispered, aware of the lump in my throat.

He shuffled us forward a bit more before moving to stand directly beside me.

"Okay," he said, and without the advantage of sight I could hear the nervous pitch to his voice. "You can look."

I opened my eyes and let my gaze float over the two rooms I was standing between, unsure of what I was seeing. To the left of us, where his couch was in front of his main window, there was a variety of things laid out on the coffee table. Small packs of tissues, deodorants, toothbrushes, toothpastes, tiny bottles of mouthwash and shampoo, and bars of soap.

On the bar that separated the kitchen and the family room, there were stacks of blank copy paper, envelopes, and a roll of stamps.

And on the far counter sat a bunch of ingredients, but I couldn't make them all out from here.

"What is all this?" I asked with a sweep of my hand.

"Well… I thought we could do some volunteer work?" Nick awkwardly chuckled when the statement came out as a question.

My breathing stalled. This couldn't be…

"None of this is terribly original. I just googled it and these seemed the easiest." He walked over to the coffee table. "So over here we have a couple bathroom items." He pointed to the backpacks on the ground that I hadn't seen earlier. "I thought maybe we could make hygiene kits for homeless people. There's also a blanket in the bottom of the backpack already. If you can think of anything I forgot we can always stop at the store before we hand them out." Nick's speech was hurried and he wouldn't look at me.

"And over here I thought we could write some letters to the troops…"

I stopped listening. I didn't mean to. I wanted to hang on every word he said. My gaze drifted over everything, and I couldn't help it when tears pricked at my eyes. Who did something like this? This was perfect…

I'd dated a few guys over the years, and most treated my need to volunteer or go out of my way to help people like Aster did. Sometimes they would treat me like a child, as if I didn't understand, as if I was naive and didn't know all the horrible things that could happen or what people could do.

They were condescending.

And the thing was, I didn't need them to come with me or to want to help. But I hated the feeling that they were rolling their eyes behind my back. I knew they didn't mean to be rude about it, but that almost made it worse. They genuinely thought I was a joke. I never truly admitted to myself or anyone else how much that hurt. Maybe I just hadn't realized it until I was standing here in front of a man who may not understand this part of me but still treated it with respect.

"Iris?" My head snapped up and I met his worried gaze. "Are you all right?"

I wondered how long I'd zoned out for. "What? Yes, yes. Sorry. I'm great." *More than great.*

Nick's lips pulled down. "Are you sure? I mean, if you'd rather do dinner and a movie, we can do that." He ran his hand over his head and tugged at his hair. "Like I said, I know it's nothing terribly original in terms of giving back…" He shrugged, like he was a little embarrassed. Like this wasn't the nicest, most thoughtful thing anyone had ever done for me. "I thought… ah… never mind." The tense smile he gave me broke my heart and immediately had me snapping out of the haze I was still floating around in.

He had just turned toward the door when I grabbed his arm and pulled him back around. "No, I don't want that. This is perfect, Nick." I looked around the room once more. "Definitely the best date I've ever been on."

His features relaxed as his lips kicked up into a goofy grin. Nick's fingers skated down my arm until he was holding my hand, giving it a light squeeze before he started talking. "The date hasn't even started yet."

I stepped closer, removing my other hand from his bicep to touch my lips. "Really? My lips seem to a recall a rather spectacular kiss." I frowned and looked down at his chest. "Maybe that was with another guy? It—"

Nick's mouth crashed down on mine without letting me finish, his lips stealing my air and thoughts all at once. This kiss was hungrier than before, like he was branding his lips on mine so I'd never be able to forget him. His tongue quickly demanded entrance, which I eagerly gave. My moan spurred him on and before I knew it, my hands were in his hair, his hands were cupping my ass and I was being lifted. My legs instantly wrapped around his waist as my back hit the wall.

Nick's body pinned mine, allowing his hands to roam. He slipped his palms under my shirt and softly caressed my hips. When I moaned, he broke away and started dropping kisses down my neck before coming back up and resting his lips against the shell of my ear.

"Iris." I shivered at the deep, dark way he said my name. It almost sounded like a threat, but I didn't understand why, nor did I understand why it turned me on the way it did.

"Who's kissing you?" he whispered, his fingers ghosting over the skin along my stomach and causing me to tremble.

"Whaaat…?"

Nick chuckled as his fingers inched up toward my bra.

"I said, who"—kiss—"is"—kiss—"kissing"—kiss—"you?"

"Y-you?"

"That's right." One hand moved a couple inches further and skimmed the side of my breast. I shuddered and my breathing hitched. "And the only way you won't know it's me is if you're so out of your mind with pleasure that you don't even know your own name." His hand left my breast and moved around to my back before he drew a soft line down my spine. "Understood?"

I nodded, only exhaling when he pulled his hands out of my shirt and gently set me on the ground. He stepped back and my gaze involuntarily dropped to the front of his pants.

Clearing my throat, I stepped away from the wall. "Okay, so, uh, where do you want to start?"

When I met his eyes, they were lingering on my body, clearly saying we'd already started. He wasn't wrong.

Oh boy… this was going to be a long day.

Twelve

Iris

"WHERE SHOULD WE START?" I REPEATED, quickly adding, "And I want the non-pervy answer."

He grinned and pointed over his shoulder. "Maybe the cookies, since those will need to bake and cool."

"Cookies?"

"Yeah." Nick smirked. "Weren't you paying attention?" Unabashed, I shook my head.

Chuckling, he grabbed my hand and pulled me into the kitchen. "We're making cookies to take to some firehouses."

"Gotcha," I replied, looking over the ingredients.

We spent the afternoon laughing and having fun. Nick had me do the baking, but he oversaw the whole thing so I didn't "kill the firemen," as he so nicely—and accurately—put it. He didn't stand next to me or sit on a stool. Nick spent almost the entire time pressed against my back with his arms wrapped around me. And despite the close proximity, and him whispering in my ear half the time, it never felt sexual. It was just comfortable.

After that, we sat at the counter and each wrote ten letters to troops overseas. At first I thought it might be awkward, that I would run out of things to say and repeat myself. But the words flowed easier than I expected. I'd just finished number ten when Nick announced he had to go to the bathroom and would be right back. He kissed me on the cheek, brushing his nose against mine before walking down the hall.

Sucking in a breath, I tried to focus on anything other than the heat pulsing through me. My eyes landed on his letter; he'd flipped it over and shoved half of it underneath the others he'd already sealed shut. I knew I shouldn't do it, but I reached forward anyway, slipping the paper free and turning it over. After looking over my shoulder to make sure he wasn't coming, I froze. This wasn't me, and if I was ashamed at being caught, that meant I shouldn't be doing this. I turned around, ready to put it back, when I saw my name in the middle of the page.

I started at the beginning of the paragraph, because even though it was wrong, I couldn't tear my eyes away. My curiosity was too strong.

You're probably wondering why I'm writing you. I guess people write for all kinds of reasons. Mine's probably the weirdest.

There's this girl. Isn't there always? Her name is Iris and she's... honestly, I don't know that there's a word for her. She's completely unprecedented. You wouldn't believe she was real. Sometimes I still don't.

Even how we met is completely insane... she gave me her kidney. A complete stranger. Even when I was a complete dick to her in the beginning, she didn't care. She smiled. She never faltered in her decision.

She's incredible.

And that's why I'm writing you. We're on our first date right now, and we're doing different volunteer-type things. I was actually worried she would think it was lame or something. I don't know why. She seems to be loving it.

Iris may have brought me here, but I meant what I said at the beginning of this letter. I appreciate your sacrifice. I never thought of myself as a bad person—I've discretely bought breakfast for vets before, and a few other things that kept me behind the action. But she made me see the profound effect a personal touch can have, just knowing someone cares. Not just doing the bare minimum to make yourself feel better.

So that's what I'm saying... I want you to personally know how much I appreciate what you're doing and the sacrifices you've made. If you'd like to keep talking, I'd love for our letters to continue. I'd love to read about the woman who's changed your life, like Iris has changed mine.

"It's kinda nice knowing you're not perfect," Nick whispered behind me. I yelped and grabbed my chest. Once my heart calmed, I turned around, guilt written all over my face as I blindly placed the letter down behind me.

"I'm so sorry. I just—"

He leaned forward and cut me off with a quick kiss. "Relax. I don't mind."

I stayed silent as I watched him finish the letter and tuck it away in the last envelope. Once he was done, we moved over to the couch and, with the soothing sounds of Adele in the background, packed up the care kits. The silence between us wasn't awkward. It felt... right. Natural. Like this was our place and we did this every Saturday. I couldn't stop the grin that crept up my face with that thought. I knew it was dangerous and presumptuous, but I couldn't help how I felt.

After we finished the letters, we arranged the cookies on several platters before we started loading up his car. It took us five trips. We had ten trays of cookies, twenty letters, and thirty backpacks. I shut the trunk after putting in the last load of bags while Nick locked his front door. We met at the passenger door. With a smile, he gently tipped my chin up and his lips met mine. It was another sweet, soft kiss that had my mind spinning and my heart pounding.

I pulled back and leaned against the car, biting my bottom lip. His eyes flared as his gaze focused there.

"Thank you, Nick. This was… amazing."

"Hey," he murmured, putting his hands on my hips and drawing us together again. "It's not over yet."

"What's next?" I asked softly.

"Well, I was going to suggest blood donation, but unfortunately I can't because of my rejection meds. Besides, if you get weak in the knees I want to know I was the reason, not massive blood loss." We both chuckled as he pushed a piece of hair behind my ear. My breath caught at the intimate gesture. I'd always been one of those girls who swooned more at the little things.

"There'd be no doubt," I whispered, my eyes trained on his lips, while I swayed into him for effect.

"After we drop all this off I thought we could go to dinner. Unless you're sick of me?" Nick asked with a grin.

"*So* sick, actually."

I was still gazing up at him adoringly, so I wasn't prepared when Nick reached around and pinched my butt—hard—causing me to yelp and reflexively slap his chest.

He chuckled, and I couldn't even stay mad. "I was right,"

I said.

"About what?"

"This date. Sore butt aside—and yes, I know how that sounded. No dirty comments necessary," I quickly added, slapping my hand over his grin before he could say anything. Nick kissed my palm. I smiled and pulled my hand away, revealing those dimples once more.

"I knew this date would be perfect," I finished. The date wasn't the best I'd been on because he took me to a fancy restaurant and ordered the most expensive bottle of wine, or brought me to the hottest club, or gave me lavish flowers and candy.

What made it perfect and romantic was how personal it was. How much thought he put into this. It seemed everything Nick did, he did with me in mind.

And it wasn't even halfway over.

My palms were sweating as I sat in the passenger seat and watched him walk around the front of the car. We'd just gotten back from dinner and I was trying to figure out how to prolong the date. In reality it had been about seven hours, but it seemed to fly by. The butterflies in my stomach went crazy as Nick opened my door and held out his hand. I climbed out and he softly shut it behind me.

"Hey." He gave me a mischievous smile, grabbing my hips—those seemed to be becoming a favorite—and walking me backward until my back met the car door.

"Hi," I whispered back. He was still grinning down at me, when a cold blast of air blew by and I shivered.

"Here." Nick stepped back and pulled the wool black scarf

he'd grabbed before we left from around his neck. I watched him lift it over my head and fit it around my neck. My heart practically melted as he gently lifted my hair so it wasn't caught underneath. He didn't see any of this. Nick missed all the feelings I was sure were blatant on my face, because he was too busy watching his hands. Like making sure I wasn't cold and my hair wasn't caught were the most important things to him.

Once he was satisfied, he brought his gaze to mine. Our eyes stayed locked as he wrapped each of his hands around one end of the scarf, folding the material over and over again, our bodies coming closer with each turn of his wrist until we were only inches apart. And with one final twist, Nick pulled me into him without even touching me.

His warm, sweet breath fanned across my lips seconds before he made contact. The kiss was unhurried and quite possibly the sweetest kiss I'd ever had.

Unlike earlier, when the first kiss was all about the newness, and the second was raw and hungry, this was different. It wasn't…

I'm kissing you because I've been dying to for weeks and I can't go another second without it.

Or…

I'm kissing you because I'm powerless against it, practically starved for your lips.

It was simpler than that. It was *I'm kissing you because I want to, and I don't care who's watching or what else is out there. Kissing you is all I want to do in this moment.*

When he finally pulled back, my lips felt worshipped and wrecked in the most delicious way.

"Wow," I murmured. And like that was a secret password, Nick gave me the widest, brightest smile I'd ever seen, his dimples like proud exclamation points on how happy he was.

"So I did good?" he asked. There was no nervousness in his question, no quiver to his voice. He had to know this date was incredible by all my reactions.

"The best date I've ever been on," I whispered intently. His smile melted into something softer, his dimples receding, but he stilled looked radiant. Maybe because his eyes were bright with excitement.

"C'mon." He uncurled his hands, leaving his scarf around my neck, before turning and offering me his arm. I eagerly took it and leaned my head against his upper arm as we walked up to my house. His footsteps slowed, like he was trying to prolong the date too.

We disentangled from each other on the porch. I felt his gaze on me as I reached into my purse and pulled out my keys. Only when I unlocked the door and threw my keys back in my bag did I look at him. His eyes were soft on me and the corner of his lips were tipped up in a barely there smile.

"I had a really great time today," I said softly, cringing as I realized we'd essentially just had this conversation.

"Me too," he whispered back with a grin. I watched with bated breath as he stepped into my space, both of his hands framing my face before he turned us. My back gently hit the door at the same moment his lips met mine. It was another soft kiss, my personal favorite. I was never a fan of clothes being ripped off or up-against-the-wall sex. I didn't need rough and fast to feel how much Nick wanted me.

His tongue sneaked out to part my lips, and I eagerly let him in, our tongues immediately tangling. With a slant of his head he took the kiss deeper. I was immobile, his hands still holding me hostage, not that there was anywhere else I wanted to be.

A few minutes later I broke away. Panting, I turned my

head, desperate for air. Nick's hands fell away, ghosting down my body until they landed on my hips. His kisses moved from my cheek and down my neck until he reached my collarbone. I moaned as he brought his kisses back up, kissing under my jaw, stopping right by my ear. It was my weak spot. And based on the grin I felt there, Nick had figured it out.

My hand reached out to grab the doorknob behind me.

The moment was ruined when he slipped his hand under my shirt and the tips of his fingers began making soft designs on my stomach. Because I giggled. Freaking *giggled*, like a fourteen-year-old.

Nick stilled his hand and pulled back, looking amused.

"Ticklish?" he murmured.

"Just a bit." We stayed that way, staring at each other, until our grins eventually fell away.

"Do you… do you want to come in?" I finally asked, gripping the doorknob painfully tight as I waited for his answer.

He smiled, leaning in and placing a sweet kiss on my forehead. Then he pulled back and asked, "You won't think I'm easy if I give it up on the first date?"

I laughed as we swayed closer together before I nipped his lower lip. "No, and I won't tell. Your virtue will be safe with me."

Our laughter tapered off and we met in the middle for another kiss. It started slow, the warmth from his lips spreading through me and settling in my chest. I breathed him in, and as my mouth opened wider, Nick took advantage. His tongue sliding inside and wrapping around mine.

My back hit the door once more and Nick's hard body pressed into mine. His hands framed my face, while mine clung to his sides, begging him closer. When his palms descended and settled on my chest, I shivered, my knees almost buckling.

"Iris," he whispered. He was barely a breath away, so close

that my name became a kiss.

"Come in." It was no longer a question as I reached behind and opened the door. Without taking my eyes off Nick, I walked backward across the threshold, his fingers skimming until I was too far away and they fell.

When he made no move to follow, I faltered, shifting on my feet and tightly gripping the door. For as confident as I tried to be, sex always made me shy. I didn't hate my body and I wasn't inexperienced. But it was never casual to me. It always meant something, and I always felt like I was giving a piece of myself away when I slept with someone for the first time.

And I'd never slept with someone on the first date. I'd had a single one-night stand, and even though I didn't feel ashamed, I definitely didn't enjoy it like I thought I would.

"You getting shy on me, Iris?" Nick asked, finally stepping closer.

"I don't, uhhh… I don't normally"—I waved a hand toward the bulge in his pants—"on the first date." Except this didn't really feel like the first date. And truthfully, it wasn't. We had meals together. We'd gone to a movie once, and babysat for my sister a few times, falling asleep on the couch when it got too late.

"I don't know why I keep comparing this to everything else," I murmured.

It's incomparable.

I'd never really been friends with someone before dating them. All of my past relationships began in a similar manner: we'd meet, go out, kiss on the second date, sleep together on the seventh, and from there things progressed differently based on the guy and what my life was like at the time.

This thing with Nick was entirely different. First date or not, I felt closer to him than I ever had to anyone else. My nerves were still there, but only because I realized how important he was to me, how much I wanted this to work out.

"It's okay if you've changed your mind. We don't have to do this if you're uncomfortable." It sounded like it physically pained him to say it, yet he didn't try to convince me. Not one single word.

I believed there were key moments to falling in love with someone. Moments from *I could fall in love with this person* to *I am falling in love with this man* to *I'm undeniably in love with him.*

This was one of those moments. I could so easily see myself falling in love with Nicholas Blake.

He leaned forward and placed a soft, gentle kiss on my mouth, shifting his body away so I couldn't feel his hardness against my stomach. My eyes stayed open, wide with awe. When he pulled away and smiled, it was genuine, like being here with me really was enough.

I took a deep breath, ready to set my fears aside when he closed the door and leaned against it, a serious expression on his face.

Nick looked down and I swore I saw a slight blush race over his cheeks. His eyes met mine again, this time with resolve. "Would you feel better if we got to know each other better?"

"What?" I asked, stunned. I tracked him as he walked past me, toward my living room. "Nick, I was just—"

"I'll sit at one end, and you'll sit at the other." He pointed to the opposite side of the couch as he took a seat. "And we'll get to know each other better. But whatever question you ask, you also have to answer." Nodding, I slowly moved forward.

"That seems fair." I joined him on the couch, practically sitting on the armrest to keep from jumping in. He smirked when he noticed and I shuffled down so I didn't look quite so weird. I didn't want to be nervous, I trusted Nick, but I couldn't ignore the slightly uneasy feeling that I was doing something wrong.

"Iris?" I glanced up and met his solemn expression. "You could know everything about me, but if you don't feel comfortable sleeping with me, you don't need a reason. I'll respect your decision, you know that, right? This"—he paused to wave a hand between us—"isn't about sleeping with you. I want to know more about you too."

Jesus. How could I not feel safe around this man?

Despite my momentary freak-out, this admission right here made me feel more ready than I ever had. But I was almost positive Nick wouldn't let it go. He'd want to be sure.

So now—because I was crazy—I was going to have to sit here and "get to know him," when the only thing I *really* wanted to get to know was his—

"You okay?" Nick suddenly asked.

"Yeah," I croaked out. I cleared my throat while he started thinking of his first question.

Crap.

This was going to be a long night...

Thirteen

Iris

This might be the dumbest thing I'd ever done.

"So I think I heard this on a show once... but isn't there a rule that you shouldn't sleep with a guy unless you know his middle name? Or was it his mother's maiden name? That probably makes more sense..." He trailed off, deliberating between the two.

How was he so unaffected? I was two seconds away from sitting on my hands to stop myself from reaching out and grabbing him, and he seemed calm as could be.

"Hmm... either way, you already know the maiden name: Blake. But my middle name is Jonah."

I clenched my fists. "That wasn't really a question." I nodded my head at him.

"I suppose not. What's your favorite color?"

I chuckled. "Really? That's the thought-provoking question you want to ask?"

"We gotta start easy, babe." We both froze as the term of endearment so easily rolled off his tongue.

I cleared my throat and grabbed a pillow to keep my hands preoccupied. "Right. It's yellow."

"Green."

"What was your first job?" I asked.

"Busboy."

"Tutor."

"It sounds like you always knew what you wanted to be," he said thoughtfully as he rested his arm along the back of the couch.

I relaxed some. Talking about students was definitely a mood killer. "I have. Growing up I noticed that not every kid had parents as great as mine. And I saw the difference a teacher could make. I wanted to give kids the chance to have at least one adult in their life who cared about them. But even before I actually thought about the reasons why, for job interviews and admissions and stuff, I always just knew it was what I wanted to do. It was like someone asking me my hair color or where I was born; it was a fact. I was going to be a teacher."

Nick shuffled infinitesimally closer. "It was the same way for me. With Tyson gone and my ma working, I had to learn to cook for myself a lot of the time. She always felt bad, but I loved it. And when I was old enough for people to start asking what I wanted to do with my life, my first thought was cooking. It was the perfect balance for me. There were general guidelines to follow, but there was also a freedom to do whatever I wanted."

"It's nice when your job overlays with your passion. Not many people have that."

"Yeah." His hand twitched like he was trying to stop himself from reaching out and grabbing me.

"I think it's your turn again," I said softly.

"Oh, yeah."

As I was sitting there trying to think of my own next question—anything to keep my mind from straying—I realized it wasn't as easy as it seemed. Not when you wanted to know *everything* about the other person.

"I guess it's a little harder than we thought, huh?" I asked with a laugh.

Nick pointedly looked down at his lap. "No, it's as hard as I thought it'd be." My eyes widened, following his stare.

Jesus. That certainly wasn't helping.

When my gaze flew back to his face, he was smirking. With a shrug, he said, "Between talking about cooking and you looking good enough to eat, I'm surprised it's not harder."

Clearing my throat, I reached for my phone on the table. "How about we look up some questions?"

I heard Nick chuckle, my eyes still avoiding his as I scrolled through my phone. Most of them were fairly normal…

What's your biggest dream?
What's your biggest fear?
What would you change about yourself?
Do you want children?

My brows furrowed. Others were less normal. "What the heck kind of icebreakers are these?" I murmured.

"What's the question?"

"If you were a vegetable, which one would you be and why?"

"Tomato," he answered easily. Laughing, I glanced up at him.

"Why?"

Nick reached his hand over and rubbed the inside of my

wrist. "That's your favorite," he whispered. "You always piled extra tomatoes on when my ma made burgers. I've even seen you eat a raw one a time or two. And if I'm going to be a stupid vegetable, I'm damn sure going to be your favorite."

I swallowed and looked down at his thumb still drawing soothing patterns over my veins.

"I've noticed everything about you. Even when I was being a jerk, I was collecting information. Like how sometimes you absentmindedly smell your hair."

I shrugged, suddenly feeling self-conscious. "I like the smell of my conditioner."

"Me too." He grinned, but got serious just as fast. "You get cold easily and always have a spare sweater in your purse or car. You talk to every animal you see. You catch the eye of any baby you pass and wave. And every time after you crack your knuckles, you cringe, but then your face eases into contentment. Like even though it might be bad for your joints, it relaxes you. You—"

I cut him off, gently placing my fingers against his lips. "You really noticed all that?"

"And more. Iris," he whispered. Looking up into his eyes, I sucked in a breath. There was no heat there, no playfulness, just sincerity. Nick scooted closer, until our legs were touching. "We don't have to do anything you don't want to. I won't be mad if you ask me to leave, and I won't think less of you if you want to have sex on the first date. Hell, that'd be pretty hypocritical and stupid since that's what I've been dying to do all night. We can do whatever you want. Stop thinking about what it'll mean or what I want, just do the first thing you think of, just—"

I leaned forward and sealed my lips over his. It was a quick and soft kiss. I pulled away, only an inch or two, as his eyes fluttered open. "I hope that was a precursor to picking plan B, otherwise that was plain cruel," he teased.

Biting back a smile, I crawled into his lap. We were *definitely* doing this.

I was completely gone. I attacked him.

My hand wound around his neck and I pulled him to me. My kisses were relentless, my hands greedy, and my body was practically vibrating with need. Nick kissed me back, his tongue swooping in like it had found its place in our kiss. One of his hands landed on my hip to steady my body, while the other cupped my neck, his thumb brushing over my jawline. He broke away, kissing his way across my cheek and toward my ear.

"Iris," he whispered. "I can wait. For you, I'd always wait."

Tears came to my eyes as he pulled away and I stared down at him. "I know. That's why you don't have to." My voice was scratchy, raw and emotional and very transparent. It was the sound of a woman swooning.

"You're a good man." He blushed and tried to look away. I gripped his chin, forcing his eyes on mine. "I mean it. And if you feel uncomfortable taking all the credit, I'm fairly certain your mother is responsible for most of that goodness."

He chuckled, any remaining tension fled with my words. "Well if you didn't want to have sex tonight, talking about my mother was a surefire way to do it. My blue balls are officially cured."

I laughed, too; relieved we were getting back on track.

"Hmm," I whispered. "Let me see what I can do about reversing that…"

Nick

Our shirts were off and we stood staring at each other, our breaths coming out in labored pants. Iris was—much to my dismay—still wearing her bra. I had been shocked by the intense lust that shot through me when she removed her shirt. Her bra was simple: a plain white material, with two small sections of lace running along the sides, complete with a tiny pink bow in the center. It screamed innocence, and yet I'd never found anything quite so sexy. It didn't plunge and it wasn't strategically cut so her nipples were showing or some weird shit like that.

Fists clenched, I forced myself to take in the rest of her even though all I wanted to do was pounce… again. She was leaning against the wall right next to her bedroom door, where I pinned her when we first walked in. But now I wanted to take my time.

My eyes fell to her lower abdomen, where the small incision from her surgery was. My scar was a lot larger. And again, just like with our heartbeats, I thought about the irony of it. Because it took so little of Iris to give, while it took so much for me to accept and receive. For me to trust and let someone care for me.

But somehow we were here.

Together.

Sometimes I didn't have a clue why she cared for me. Why I was falling for her was completely obvious. But I still wasn't sure I had much to offer in return.

I shuffled forward and brushed my fingers over her scar, my eyes following the movement.

"You didn't hesitate, did you?"

Iris reached her hand over and traced my incision. "Maybe

for like, half a second." She grinned and my lips followed. "But that worry was background noise based on other people. In my heart…" She paused, lifting my hand to her chest. "In *here*, there was never any doubt or hesitation. And it was the best decision I've ever made."

Falling to my knees in front of her, I dropped kisses along the puckered, pink skin. Her breath hitched and her fingers weaved into my hair. At first there was nothing sexual about it, it was just an acknowledgement of how our story started. Then my kisses changed direction, bringing the atmosphere with them.

I worked my way toward the top of her jeans.

"You're so beautiful," I murmured into her skin, grinning when I felt her shiver.

Her hands loosened and began slowly running through my hair. I rested my chin on her stomach and stared up at her soft smile.

"Today was perfect," she whispered. "I've never had a better time."

My fingers flexed against her hips. "Me neither. And that was my goal… to make it perfect." I moved my hands down and around, gripping the back of her thighs. Her breath hitched as my fingers inched higher before sliding under her jeans and brushing the top of her panties.

My eyes were still fixed on hers as I removed my hands and slowly started working her jeans down and off. I tossed them somewhere behind me, my gaze now settled on her white panties. They were just like her bra—simple, a soft material that covered her completely except for two strips of lace around her hips. And there in the center was a small pink bow. It was soft, beautiful, and understated, while being the sexiest thing I'd ever seen, just like Iris.

Unable to stop myself, I leaned forward and placed a soft kiss on the bow. I looked up to find her eyes were no longer on me; they were squeezed shut and her head was tipped back. But when I gripped the sides of her panties and slowly began peeling the material down her legs, her eyes shot open and landed on mine.

My eyes didn't leave her as I removed her underwear, gently grabbing behind each knee to help her step out of them. She whimpered when she saw me pocket them.

"I hope those weren't your favorite," I said with a grin. Iris swallowed hard before quickly shaking her head. Slowly standing, I dragged my hands along the inside of her thighs, gently brushing my fingers through her wetness when I reached the apex.

Stepping back, I removed my jeans, standing before her in only my boxers. Iris gulped and bit her bottom lip, looking tortured.

I returned my hands to her. She moaned as I took my time, smoothing my hands across her stomach, past her still-covered breasts until I reached her shoulders. I gently kissed her lips before turning her to face the wall. Her hands were bunched at her sides. I reached down and pried her fingers loose. Iris's breath hitched as I ran her fingers between her legs, slowly swirling one around her clit.

"N-Nick... please..."

"Do you feel how much you love this?" I asked before pressing my nose against the back of her head, inhaling the sweet scent of strawberry wafting from her hair. Iris moaned in response and wiggled her naked ass against me. My other hand ghosted up her back until I reached the clasp of her bra.

"I'd rather feel how much you love this," she whispered, her cheek pressed against the wall and her head turned. Removing our hands from her legs, I gently brought hers back and placed it over my boxer-clad cock.

She whimpered and I groaned when she wrapped her hand around me and squeezed. My head fell to her shoulder as she continued to rub, trying to torture me like I was torturing her. I shook my head and refocused.

Take care of her first.

I lifted my head and removed her right hand from my dick before quickly undoing her bra, shoving it over her shoulders and down her arms before dropping it on the ground beside us. Then I grabbed both her hands, and placed her palms above her head. My hands skimmed down her arms and neck, quickly changing course to her frontside, each grabbing a breast.

"Nick." Her voice caught when I pinched her nipples. "I need..."

"Yes?" I whispered in her ear. "If you want something, all you gotta do is ask."

Before she could answer, I dragged one hand down her waist and settled between her legs.

"I want... yes... t-that," she murmured as I sank two fingers inside her. Iris timidly rocked her hips into my hand. I increased the pace until she was teetering at the edge, about to fall over and drop. Then I slowed and removed my fingers completely.

"What the....?" she started, sounding like she was in genuine pain, before I spun her around and slammed my mouth against hers, stealing her thoughts, breath, anything I could...

The kiss was rough and filled with need, and when we parted, her hands were balled into fists once more. I stepped back, my gaze roaming over her, naked and wanting. Her lips and nipples were red from my attention, her pussy so wet I could see it from several feet away, and her heart was beating so fast I could see her pulse hammering in her neck.

With a growl, I took her hand and led her to the bed. She was about to get what she wanted because I couldn't hold back much longer.

She sat on the edge and quickly crawled back, her eyes never leaving mine. I swallowed roughly, grabbing her ankle before she got too far. As much as my dick wanted in, I had to taste her first.

I dropped to my knees again.

"You're on your knees an awful lot," Iris quipped.

"All the better to pleasure you, my dear…" I replied with a grin. Then I leaned forward and ran my tongue through her folds. Iris let out a delicious groan and fell back on the bed. This time I was relentless. It didn't require much, she was still worked up, and when I sealed my mouth over her clit and sucked, she exploded. Her moans echoed off the walls as her hands pulled at my hair. When it became too much she started shoving me away. I slowed but kept my mouth where it was.

"Nick, I can't… please."

I sat back on my heels and licked my lips, watching Iris lift her head and study me. Her movements were sluggish and her eyes were hooded. Standing up, I slid my boxers down. Iris leaned up on her elbows and appraised me from head to toe, suddenly a lot more alert. She shuffled backward when I put my knee on the bed and crawled toward her.

I was lying beside her, my elbow propping me up as my lips found hers. She shuddered when I dragged my finger up her inner thigh and between her legs. I continued to kiss her as I made a path up her stomach and across her breasts. Reluctantly I pulled my mouth away.

"Do you have a condom?" I asked. I had a couple in my wallet in my jeans, but that seemed too far. Thankfully she nodded. Then she turned away from me and reached into her nightstand. I barely held in my groan at the sight of her ass. Palming her hip, I leaned forward and lightly nipped one of her cheeks. Iris yelped before spinning around, slamming her back on the bed with a string of at least six condoms in her hand.

I plucked them from her grasp. "It's a lofty goal," I said, climbing over her and spreading her legs. "But I'm up for the challenge."

"You bit my butt," she whisper-hissed, trying to sound angry, but her stuttered breathing gave away her intense arousal. I chuckled, leaning back as I rolled on a condom. My hands ran up her thighs and around until I was grabbing her ass.

"It's an ass worth biting." I dragged her forward until I was settled against her entrance. When I looked up her eyes were riveted on my dick.

I'd love nothing more than to watch myself disappear inside her, but I'd have plenty of time for that. Right now all I wanted to do was watch her face. I wanted to see the pleasure race across her as I filled her for the first time.

Pushing in slowly, I watched Iris bite her lip as her eyebrows furrowed. When I was fully seated, I couldn't even describe the sheer bliss I felt or what I saw in her expression. Her head dropped back and her eyes met mine. As I began moving, she set her lip free, her mouth falling open to allow the sweetest sounds out. Moans. Whimpers. Pleas.

I nearly lost my mind.

Reaching for her hands, I intertwined our fingers before pinning them by her head. Our bodies were practically glued together. Her tits rubbed against my chest. Her legs wrapped around my waist. Her heels pressed into my ass, urging me on. But she didn't need to—nothing could stop me right now.

I rested my forehead against hers, our eyes opened and

locked as I gradually moved faster. Her breath hitched and I saw beads of sweat form across the tops of her breasts.

"I feel..." she started.

"I know," I whispered. It felt amazing. Incredible. Life-changing. And a bunch of other fantastical words that wouldn't really measure up to what was happening between us.

Iris leaned up and kissed me. We only lasted a few seconds until our movements forced us away. I lifted my head.

"Look," I murmured, making sure her eyes were where I wanted them before shifting my gaze lower. I groaned as I finally watched myself disappear inside her. Iris eagerly took me with each raise of her hips.

She whimpered, her heels digging in harder and her fingers trembling around mine. "Faster," she begged. "Please..."

I looked up; her head was tipped back and her eyes were shut. I dropped kisses across her jaw until I reached her ear.

"Is this what you want?" I asked as I picked up the pace.

"Yes... God yes," she moaned.

"I could spend hours between your legs... fucking you, tasting you, teasing you." She clenched around my dick and I smiled into her neck. "You like that, huh? You like hearing what I'll do next?"

I slowed my pace when she didn't respond. "Hmm... Iris?" I looked down into her eyes and saw desperation.

"Y-yes, I like it," she said. She let out a breath of relief as I moved faster than before. "Yesssss..."

"You like my cock?" I teased. Her head thrashed against the pillow as she whimpered another yes. "You like my tongue flicking against your clit and my fingers pinching your tits?"

We were both so close, and I could feel how much my words were affecting her. "You know what I'd like?" I licked a path up her neck, feeling her quake beneath me as my lips met her ear again. "I can't wait for you to ride me, Iris. To dig my fingers into your ass until I leave marks, to watch your tits bounce in front of my face until I have no choice but to lean forward and draw one into my mouth, to watch you grind your clit against me, so desperate to make yourself come…"

"Nick!" she shouted, coming so forcefully she jerked beneath me. "Oh God… don't stop…"

I didn't; I slammed into her over and over until she insisted she couldn't take anymore. Only then did I come, with my dick buried deep inside her, sparks of pleasure radiating down my spine.

"Iris," I groaned into her neck. "Fuck, you feel so good."

Our breaths were loud as we struggled to come down from our high. I knew it was pointless, though. Because just like our first kiss, I knew I'd never recover from this.

Fourteen

Nick

We'd laid in bed until almost eleven o'clock before I—regretfully—had to leave. After stopping by the pharmacy to pick up some more of my medication, I went home and started cooking. Kevin and Lindsay were coming over to my apartment to watch football, and I'd agreed to make my special wings for Kevin, as well as Lindsay's favorite dip.

It seemed insane, but even after spending all day with Iris yesterday, I couldn't wait to see her again. Not that I would have to wait long, because even though she knew nothing about football, she eagerly accepted my invitation to watch the games with us.

I hadn't been this happy in a long time. Not because I'd been sad or angry. Truthfully, I hadn't been much of anything. My mother and I had been in the same place up until recently, so content in our lives that we didn't even notice things were missing.

It was strange, because one would think that nearly dying was what would have turned it all around for me. That might have been the case for my mother. I knew many had profound epiphanies after a near-death experience, they saw the light and realized how precious life was and how we had to make the most of every day… yada yada yada. But that wasn't me. I was fairly certain I would have been an insufferable prick until the day I died, near-death accident or not.

It wasn't the possibility of death that woke me up. It was her.

Her presence, her radiance and positivity, it existed outside of life and death, happy and sad; she was remarkable. And she didn't even know it.

Now, Iris was sitting next to me on my couch, my arm around her shoulders, while Kevin and Lindsay sat on the recliner by the door—Lindsay on his lap. The halftime performance was on, but none of us were paying attention. As the wedding got closer it seemed all we did was talk about it. Even with almost everything picked out and done, somehow there was something to obsess over or some magazine she had to read. And now that Iris was here, someone who knew none of the details, Lindsay was more than happy to share.

I was zoning out, the conversation about color scheme not holding a bit of my attention, when Lindsay asked Iris a question.

"You're coming to the wedding, right?" She was practically bouncing on Kevin's lap with excitement.

My eyes jumped to Iris's as a slight panic moved through me. "I didn't—" I started, only to be interrupted by Lindsay.

"You didn't invite her?" she asked, her wide eyes going back and forth between us.

"Not because I didn't want to," I rushed to say, my gaze on Lindsay. "I just… you sent invitations out months ago and I didn't want to ask. I didn't want to mess with the bride, you know?"

I looked down, hoping Iris could see the truth in my words. This wasn't me having cold feet about our relationship—no, my feet were nice and toasty. I may have been uneasy about her in the beginning, but now that we were together, I was one hundred percent in.

Iris smiled before leaning over and placing a kiss on my cheek. "It's okay," she whispered, with nothing but sincerity in her eyes.

"Oh please," Lindsay began. "I'm as chill as they come, you know that. I appreciate the thought, but you can ask me things about the wedding. I'm not running around like a chicken with my head cut off."

"Yeah, but you're always talking about it and—"

"Because I'm excited." She smiled down at Kevin, cupping his face in her hands. "I'm beyond ready to marry the love of my life."

They kissed. It was brief and full of nothing but love. When Lindsay pulled away and faced us, she said, "Do I want things to be perfect? Of course. Everyone does. But will I have a meltdown if things go a little differently? No, because the most important thing is staying the same."

"She's not lying. I haven't seen her cry over a wedding detail once," Kevin said, his eyes stuck on his soon-to-be wife. "Lindsay's the perfect woman." He placed a kiss on the corner of her mouth.

Lindsay beamed and sat up straighter. "That's right, I am. So yes, of course she can come."

"Really?" My arm tightened around Iris's shoulders. I

didn't even wait for Lindsay's response before twisting toward my girlfriend and grabbing one of her hands.

"Iris, will you go to their wedding with me?"

She laughed. "Of course."

I quickly leaned forward and captured her lips with mine, my tongue effortlessly sliding in and tangling with hers. It was the kind of kiss that made you forget other people were in the room. Hell, it made me forget other people were on the planet.

It wasn't until her fingers were pulling at my hair and my hand had fallen to her ass, ready to lift her into my lap, that I registered the very loud coughing in the background. Iris ripped her mouth away, and her cheeks turned pink when she heard how loud our breathing was.

"Dude," Kevin said, his eyes on me. "I know I said I was bummed about Linds not letting me get any triple-X channels, but you didn't need to give me a show."

Lindsay chuckled as she backhanded him in the chest. He easily caught her hand and brought it up to his lips for a kiss.

It was funny; when I was single, their inability to go a minute without touching or kissing something on the other drove me insane. But now it wasn't as annoying.

"Ohmygod," Iris muttered as she tried to sink into the couch.

"Hey, you know what would be awesome?" Lindsay asked, clearly trying to draw attention off my girlfriend's raging red cheeks. I must admit, I liked a blushing Iris quite a bit.

"What?" I asked.

"If Iris was a bridesmaid! That way you can walk down the aisle together."

"Oh." Iris scooted up on the couch. "That's really sweet, but you don't have to—"

Lindsay started waving her hands, cutting Iris off. "I don't do anything I don't want to."

"So you're okay with it being uneven?"

"Uneven?" She tilted her head, confused, before recognition hit her. "Oh no no. You wouldn't be an add on, just walking by yourself. You'd take someone's place. The girl walking with Nick. You guys look about the same size. Don't you think, Nick?"

Iris's eyes widened, and I knew she was thinking about how she couldn't take someone else's spot. Lindsay must have understood the look too, because she quickly assuaged her worries.

"The girl Nick's walking with is my cousin, Anne. She loathes any kind of attention and has been dreading this. But since Kevin had three groomsmen, and apparently I only have two friends, I needed an extra person. So really, this is perfect. I felt awful about asking Anne, but I really didn't have anyone else."

"You swear?" Iris looked to Kevin and me for confirmation.

"Really." I looked down at her and squeezed her hand. "Anne is going to be over the moon when she finds out. And I'm not just saying that because I want you on my arm."

"Well okay, if you're really sure—"

"She is." They all chuckled as I cut her off before quickly kissing her on the lips. I wasn't giving her any reason to doubt how much I wanted her there. My kisses traveled across her cheek until I reached her ear. "I'm insanely happy right now."

When I pulled back she was grinning. "I am too," she whispered. "More than seems possible."

Iris

The game was in the last five minutes of the fourth quarter, and the Patriots were killing the opposing team. I was told that wasn't surprising.

I knew nothing about football, so when Nick and Kevin started talking about corner routes and pass protection, I was officially bored.

Lindsay caught my eye and grinned. Apparently I wasn't covering my boredom well. She stood up and, with an affectionate pat on Kevin's shoulder, moved past him.

"Wanna help me make some drinks?" Lindsay asked while the guys continued talking.

"Yes," I said a little desperately, practically jumping up. Lindsay had already turned toward the kitchen and Kevin's gaze was on the television, watching the announcer draw blue lines all over the place, when Nick wrapped his hand around the back of my thigh. I looked down to find him smiling up at me. He didn't say a word, just squeezed my leg once and turned toward the TV.

The gesture sent my heart aflutter, like he was saying, *I'll miss you*. Which was ridiculous because I was only moving a few feet, but when a person is that immersed in something, it's nice to know that they're still thinking of you, tracking where you are.

Dopey grin still in place, I finally followed Lindsay into the kitchen.

"I'm really glad you were able to make it," she said with a smile before she reached into a cabinet and took out a couple glasses. Lindsay already had club soda, white rum, sugar, mint leaves, limes, and strawberries out.

"What are we making?"

Lindsay raised her eyebrows. "You've never had a strawberry mojito?"

Shaking my head, I took a seat at the counter. "Nope. I'm not much of a drinker to be honest. And when I do it's usually a glass of wine or a beer."

"Would you prefer a beer? I don't think the guys drank them all yet," she said, already halfway turned toward the fridge.

"No, that's okay. I'd love to try one."

"They're the best. Oh! I almost forgot." Her voice dropped to a whisper as she quickly looked over my shoulder into the living room. I turned and found the guys in the exact same position, leaning forward and pointing at the screen while they discussed the game as if someone was going to come ask their advice on it.

When I swiveled back around Lindsay had preheated the oven and taken a bag of pizza rolls out of the freezer. After grabbing a thin pan, she quickly—and rather quietly—started arranging them on it, her eyes going to the guys every couple seconds.

My brows were bunched, but my lips kicked up into a smile. After one of Lindsay's not-so-discrete checks of the living room, she took in my expression.

With a small snort, she immediately started laughing. "I must look crazy right now."

"Just a little bit," I said with a smile as she put the last row of rolls on the pan. The oven dinged and she easily slid the food in and set a timer, letting out a breath of relief when she was done.

"Sorry. Nick's really picky about food, and he hates when I eat those. But they're too damn good to give up. I had to sneak these in." She paused as she started making the drinks again. "Have you ever been on the receiving end of one of his food rants?"

"I can't say I have."

"Oh. He must be saving that particular brand of crazy for when you've fallen too far to back out."

I looked over my shoulder at Nick. A warm feeling raced through me as I watched his smile eat up his face, those dimples I loved so much coming out to play.

Nick caught me staring and grinned wider. I stared back, unashamed, while my lips slowly pulled up. He winked before looking away and talking with Kevin again.

I turned back around, blushing, to find that Lindsay had finished making the drinks and mine was waiting in front of me. Without looking up at her, I wrapped my hands around it, peering down with a smile. "I've fallen pretty far," I admitted in a whisper.

Out of the corner of my eye, I saw her lean against the counter, the drink she was so excited for was now forgotten.

"I think he has too."

My gaze moved up. "Really?" I wasn't insecure in my relationship, but there was something about hearing from family and friends—who'd known him for years and watched him grow, who'd seen his other relationships—that provided a whole different kind of relief.

"You're the first," she said softly.

"The first what?"

Her eyes darted to the other room before coming back to me. It was the first time I'd seen Lindsay so serious. "The first relationship he's had since…"

"Colleen?" I guessed, remembering the words his mother had said to me in passing a couple months ago. But Nick and I hadn't discussed her yet. And I didn't feel comfortable hearing about it from someone other than him, when he was ready to tell me.

"He hasn't told me anything," I added when I saw the disbelief in her eyes. "His mom accidentally mentioned her once."

Lindsay nodded, leaning back and grabbing her drink. "I'm not trying to gossip. He should be the one to tell you, when he's ready. I just want you to know this is big for him. It's not a whim. He's a relationship guy, and he's been wary of starting one for years. For him to want to try again must mean you're pretty special, and I want to make sure you're not taking it for granted."

She looked at me like I imagined a mama bear would look at someone trying to get near her cub for the first time.

"I'm not," I swore, my voice a tad too loud and impassioned for a casual conversation. But when I looked in the other room the guys were still lost in the world of football. Turning around, I finished, "I promise. I may not know the details, but I know how hard it was for him to open up to me. I won't do anything to jeopardize that."

I sat still, holding my breath, like I was waiting for a verdict to be read.

"I believe you." Lindsay smiled, and I couldn't help but think about what a beautiful and radiant bride she would be.

I didn't want to bring the mood back down, but I did have one other question that I wasn't sure Nick would be able to answer as impartially.

"Did he love her?" I asked quietly. Sure enough, her grin dropped.

Lindsay took a moment before answering, swirling the straw in her drink. "He loved her like you love your first set of makeup. It's new and shiny, and you're excited to finally have it.

But when it breaks or gets old, you start testing out some other stuff and you discover what crap the first set was." She slapped her palm over her face. "God. That was a terrible analogy because all makeup gets old. But did it make any sense?"

I chuckled as she peeked through her fingers. "Yeah. I think it did."

Lindsay removed her whole hand and said, "I liked Colleen, don't get me wrong. We were friends even. But she and Nick were never right for each other. If it hadn't been what happened, it would have been something else. It's who she was. She was nice, but she could also be very selfish."

I nodded and looked down at my drink.

"One last thing and then we can talk about fun stuff again," Lindsay said, bringing my head back up. "What happened damaged him a little bit, and it definitely changed him. But if he mourns anything, it's the person he was. He's not mourning her or their relationship. Sometimes guys are stupid at explaining stuff like that, so I just wanted you to know."

With a grateful smile, I thanked her and finally took a sip of her mojito.

Holy sh—

"This is delicious." I immediately took another sip while Lindsay grinned.

"Right? They're my favorite. I can't—"

"Lindsay!" Nick shouted as he came into the kitchen. "What's that smell?"

Only then did I realize the aroma of pizza was swirling in the air.

"Iris wanted them," she blurted out. I shot her a wide-eyed look before glancing back at Nick, who was frowning down at me.

"Was there something wrong with what I made?" he asked

as he crossed his arms. I carefully set my drink down.

"No. I—"

All of a sudden, Nick grabbed my hand and yanked me up. I saw Lindsay's grinning face right before he threw me over his shoulder.

"I'm sorry," Lindsay said on a laugh—not sounding sorry at all. "I thought he'd go easier on you."

Between the blood rushing to my head and Nick's palm on my butt, I couldn't think of a response. I just laughed along with everyone else as he carried me out of the room.

I'm not falling.
I've already hit the ground.
And I've never felt better...

♥♥

After Kevin and Lindsay left that night, I hung around for as long as I could. But since I had to be up early for work, we just relaxed on his bed and watched a movie. Okay, we watched half a movie and spent the other time making out.

The movie clicked off about ten minutes ago and I was trying to convince myself to leave. But it was rather difficult with him softly running his hand through my hair, occasionally stopping to massage my scalp. The longer we lay in silence, the more my thoughts circled, and they kept coming back to one: Colleen.

I finally took the plunge. "Hey, Nick?" I whispered.

"Hmm?"

"Can I ask you something?"

"'Course," he mumbled, sounding near sleep.

"Who's Colleen?" I felt him solidify under me, and I

immediately backpedaled. "Your mom mentioned her once. You don't have to tell me—"

Nick's hand found mine and he squeezed. "It's not that. I want you to know. It's just hard."

I stayed silent, my arm still firmly wrapped around his waist as I waited. "The simple answer is she's my ex-girlfriend."

"And the complicated answer?" I softly asked.

"She's one of the main reasons why I'm so distrustful and bitter. I don't pretend not to know why I'm this way, but I also know it's far more complicated than just her. I am also aware that, like you've mentioned, I have a choice. I can decide to overcome it all, and I'm trying right now. It's hard but it's definitely worth it." I felt him smile as he pressed a kiss to the side of my head.

"Did she cheat on you?" I couldn't really imagine anything else. That was a huge reason why people became distrustful and had a hard time in future relationships. But I thought about all the sweet and wonderful things Nick did, and I couldn't understand how a girl would cheat on someone this attentive and caring. What more could another man have to offer?

"No. She…" He blew out a breath and I almost told him to stop, because I could tell how difficult this was for him. "She was pregnant," he finished on a pained whisper.

I froze. I definitely wasn't expecting *that*. Was he trying to tell me he had a kid? No, that wouldn't be possible. Catherine would be doting on and on about that child for days. And there was zero chance Nick wouldn't be a part of his kid's life. Whoever ended up with Nick as a father and Catherine as a grandmother was a lucky kid.

Woah. A little soon to be thinking about kids, huh, Iris?

Okay, well if not that, then what?

Oh. Crap. Had his child died? It wouldn't explain the

betrayal, but that would certainly make me—

Nick chuckled, sounding a little relieved to find something to smile about, and I looked up at him.

"What?"

"Quit trying to guess. I'm gonna tell you." Nick paused, some of the darkness coming back as he swallowed roughly. "Colleen had an abortion."

"But…" I trailed off. That didn't make sense. Nick might not have been as devout a Catholic as his mother, but there was no way he'd agree to—

I froze and pushed away from him. Sitting up, my wide eyes looked into his. "No," I whispered. "She…?"

I couldn't even finish the thought, let alone the sentence.

"Yeah," he said miserably. His gaze left mine as he stared down at his hand bunched into a fist. "I didn't find out about the baby until it was too late."

"How?"

"A voice mail on her home phone." He laughed, but there was no joy in it. It sounded sad and pained. "Colleen was so weird about still having a landline, and in the end that was the thing to bite her in the ass. We had keys to each other's places and I had stopped by to crash on my lunch break because her house was only five minutes from the restaurant where I was working at the time. I walked in just as the phone rang one last time before switching to the voice mail. I remember smiling when I heard Colleen's voice asking them to leave a message." When he paused, I brought my hand up and started rubbing slow circles on his chest. He exhaled, like he was letting out all the bad and preparing to take in the good… me. And when he kissed the side of my head, I knew I'd been right—I was giving him exactly what he needed.

"I was already heading up the stairs when the message

started. Honestly I was so beat I'm surprised I even paid attention. But I heard the words clinic, and appointment, and checkup, and I jogged back down to listen. She was my girlfriend, I was worried." I shuffled closer and hugged him tighter.

"Then I heard the rest. I must have stood there in shock for at least ten minutes before I replayed it. Not just once, but five times. I even looked up the doctor and called to be sure. I knew they wouldn't have been able to tell me about a patient, but I wanted to confirm what they did. The lady must have thought I was insane with how many times I made her repeat that it was an abortion clinic and that abortions were the primary procedure they performed."

"I'm so sorry, Nick. I can't even imagine…" The words sounded weak and pathetic… nowhere near the magnitude I really felt.

He shook his head and when he began speaking again he sounded distant, methodical, like he was reading a book about someone else's life. "I didn't go back to work, and I didn't answer any of her phone calls. I just sat down on her couch and waited for her. She was so relieved when she came home and saw me sitting there. That relief quickly turned to fear when she saw the look on my face. I asked her, I laid out everything I heard, and point blank asked her if it was true. If she killed our unborn baby.

"I don't know what I was expecting. I guess some part of me thought she'd have an explanation. But of course she didn't. She was straightforward when she told me. I didn't yell, and I didn't cuss her out or start punching a wall. I just stood there and stared, trying to figure out how this person I'd spent years of my life with, could do what she did."

My fingers continued drawing circles on his chest. "Did you guys want kids?"

"I thought so… we had stopped being diligent about protection. We weren't *trying* to get pregnant, but I guess we figured it wouldn't be the worst thing in the world. At the time, we were all the other saw."

I tried to ignore the sharp ache those words brought.

"The reality of it proved more difficult for her to accept. Colleen started crying, blubbering about how she was sorry and she loved me, but she had to do it. I asked her one more question. But she didn't need to answer, I saw the look in her eyes… she never would have told me. She had zero intention of telling me we created a child, or that she killed it."

"Do you know why she did it?" I asked.

He laughed, this time it was dark and filled with anger. "Because of her fucking job. She was a model and she didn't want it ruining her body." Nick sighed before looking down at me. "And that was when I started seeing people's decisions through the frame of, *what are they getting out of it?*"

I watched him shake his head, like he wanted to rid himself of his pain. Then he gently cupped my face with his hands.

"Iris," he whispered. "I don't want to be like this. I don't want to see the world this way. I want to see it the way you do. I want to look at a field of flowers and not just see the weeds. I want to get lost and not get angry, but think of it as an adventure somewhere new. I want to see the best in someone, not the worst.

"But I genuinely don't know how. Colleen made that decision without a single thought as to what it meant to anyone but her. My father left my mother and me and he never looked back at the damage he caused. I want to give that guy who ran me off the road the benefit of the doubt. Maybe he had no choice, but I just can't…" He trailed off, helpless.

I didn't say anything, instead I just wrapped him in a hug.

One he quickly returned, holding on tight.

Everything about Nick made sense. His surly and distrustful nature, his reluctance to believe I gave him my kidney for "no reason."

And I couldn't entirely blame him. I'd always thought we had a choice in how we viewed the world, but maybe sometimes the past had a greater hold on us than we were capable of breaking.

Nick had been forced to view the world this way. It was as if he'd been standing in a room and suddenly the lights went out. His eyes would have no choice but to adapt to the darkness.

Maybe his heart adjusted to the dark the same way.

Fifteen

Iris

Two weeks had passed since our first date, and we'd managed to see each other every day. Things between us felt different now that I knew about Colleen. I felt more connected to him, and I was so grateful I hadn't given up on him. Because despite his past, he could come out on top of this.

Even under all the destruction of his life and his thoughts, the real Nick was still there. Like the foundation of a home, all the rubble in the world wouldn't change what it was built on—you just had to be willing to dig past it all. To bring him into the light. I was confident I could. I'd already started to see changes in him.

I found it funny that the people who needed the most compassion, who needed the greatest show of affection, rarely got it. People smiled at others who were already smiling, but they so rarely smiled at those who were frowning.

It made no sense. But people seldom did.

Like Calla.

I was about to introduce Nick to my family for the first time, minus Aster who was in New York and wouldn't be coming back until Thanksgiving. We were all having dinner at my parents' house. And when I called to ask if she, Kent, and Mirielle would come to meet my new boyfriend, I expected her to be thrilled. Instead she seemed standoffish, stuttering and saying she didn't know if they could make it. Mom was able to convince them, but it still left a weird feeling in my stomach.

I was staring at the flowers Nick brought me a couple days ago, all these thoughts still swirling, when I heard his knock. Shoving my sister and her weirdness to the back of my mind, I scurried toward the door.

After I yanked it open, I immediately drank him in. He was wearing black jeans and a fitted, dark-green, long-sleeved shirt. He'd even trimmed his beard.

I felt like a teenager again. Butterflies in my stomach. My heart trying to pound its way out of my chest. My lips powerless against lifting into a smile.

"I'm almost ready." I held the door open wider and started backing away. "I just need to grab a few things and put on my shoes."

Turning away from him, I walked over to the server that was a few feet away. My pearl earrings sat next to my purse, cell phone, and keys, and my heels were on the floor waiting to be broken in. I heard the door close and his feet shuffle closer.

I grabbed one stud, securing it in my left ear, and then picked up the other. My head was tilted to the side, exposing my neck to him, when Nick's hands found my hips and he pulled me back into him. I sucked in a breath.

"Hi," he whispered.

"H-h-hey," I stuttered back, like an idiot. He chuckled as his left hand skimmed up my side and around my back. When he made it to my neck, he brushed all my hair so it fell on my left side. I shivered as his hand traveled underneath the hair and around my throat. Then he moved his hand up until his fingers were cupping my jaw.

I was frozen. His assault was a wonderful mixture of tender and possessive. My second stud fell to the floor as he began dropping kisses on the back of my neck. I forced my eyes up and into the mirror that hung on the wall.

Nick's head was bent, but I could see that his eyes were closed. The kisses moved down and across my upper back, his nose trailing over the top of my shoulder.

Lifting his face back up, he rested his chin on my shoulder and murmured, "You look incredible."

He applied more pressure to my neck and I moaned in response. Nick quickly pulled away and turned me around. My breaths were coming out in pants as he narrowed his eyes. Something flashed behind his eyes and a wolfish grin took over his face. Grabbing my hand, he moved me a couple inches left, just past the server, and backed me up into the wall. His hand moved to my chest, his palm flat against my cleavage and his fingers spread wide and touching the bottom of my throat.

"You liked that, didn't you?" His voice was husky and deep, and I shivered at the promise in it. I couldn't speak, my eyes fluttering closed as he wrapped his hand around my neck and squeezed just like before.

"I could always find out myself," he whispered. My eyes shot open as his other hand dropped to my leg, right at the hem of my dress. He flattened his palm against my inner thigh, slowly dragging it closer to my aching center, bringing my dress up with it. Nick paused at the apex of my legs, his finger making a slow sweeping pass at the hem of my panties before he cupped me, putting delicious pressure on my throbbing clit.

"Yessss..." I moaned. But his touch disappeared just as quickly. Before I had time to mourn the loss, his hand landed on my stomach, skating down until it dipped beneath my underwear. He wasted no time in dragging his finger through my wetness.

"Damn, Iris." He squeezed my neck again, nothing about it causing me pain, and I pushed my hips further into his hand. Nick eagerly obliged, making small circles on my clit as he held my throat. When we locked eyes, I read the surprise in his. Truthfully, I was shocked too. I'd never had a boyfriend hold me this way before. But Nick wasn't choking me, he was putting just the right amount of pressure, and it made me wonder if he'd ever done this before.

"You're so wet," he murmured as he slid a finger inside me. My breath hitched and one of my hands reached out to grip the server while the other held on to his shoulder. His mouth met mine, a sweet and tender kiss that made the hand around my neck and the finger inside me feel even more sensual.

Our tongues danced together as he slowly pulled his finger out only to thrust two back in. I whimpered in the back of my throat and tried to pull my mouth away, but I had nowhere to go—his hand was still holding me steady.

When Nick finally ripped his mouth away we were both panting. His lips stayed close to mine, resting on my cheek and pointed toward my ear. Nick's fingers picked up the pace and he squeezed my neck once more, a delicious reminder of his power.

"That's it," he whispered, his breath ghosting over my skin. "Ride my hand. Fuck my fingers and show me how much you love my hand around your throat."

I whimpered, doing what he said, my fingernails digging into his upper back as I used him for more leverage.

"Nick…" My breath caught when his thumb found my clit and he made small, tight circles. "Yes… Nick… oh… please…" He curled his fingers until I was seeing stars. "Right there… gahhhh…"

I was too lost in chasing my orgasm to worry about how unsexy my sound effects probably were. Nick cut them off, his lips slanting over mine. Nothing about this kiss was innocent or sweet. This kiss was primal, messy, and still absolutely perfect. Our teeth banged together, our tongues didn't always connect, but his affection more than made up for it. He kissed me like I was the air keeping him alive, like I was the passion that gave his life purpose. He kissed me like he never wanted to stop.

My thoughts from our first date came back to me as I rode out the last waves of my orgasm.

I wasn't into clothes being ripped off or up-against-the-wall sex. I didn't need rough and fast to feel how much Nick wanted me…

Had I really thought that? Maybe I didn't *need* rough and fast, but now there was no way to deny how much I enjoyed it. Because somehow he still made it feel tender. It was the way his fingertips lightly brushed my skin or the way his eyes were soft on mine as he watched me climax.

My lips slacked and he pulled away, just enough to give us air, but every single move still made our lips touch.

"That was perfect," he growled. "I love watching you lose control. I love feeling you give yourself over to me. I've never… I've never done this," he said, punctuating the words with a gentle squeeze of my neck. "Never wanted to, but my God, Iris…"

"Nick, I'm…" I couldn't finish; surely my shaking body

spoke for me. The shudders moved through me as the last of the pleasant tingles faded. I clenched around his fingers, causing him to groan.

"Iris." He sounded pained as he dropped his head to my shoulder. "Stop sounding so fuckable or we're never gonna make it to dinner."

"You started it."

Nick lifted his head and finally pulled his hand from my underwear. "Has hanging out with children all day crippled your ability to come up with a better comeback?"

I stuck my tongue out at him, and we both dissolved into laughter.

♥♥

We'd been driving for about fifteen minutes when Nick started getting weird. Maybe he was more nervous about meeting my family than he let on.

"Hey, are you okay?" I asked, my eyes nervously shifting between the road and Nick's darkened expression. We decided it'd be better if I drove since I knew where we were going.

"Yeah." He cleared his throat and released the death grip he had on his knees. "It's just… this road…"

"The accident?" I guessed. Nick gave a quick jerk of his chin, and as ridiculous as it was, I quickly morphed into the perfect driver. Hands at ten and two, back straight and my eyes forward. I didn't even look over at Nick when I heard a reluctant chuckle.

"Thank you," he said as he pulled one of my hands away and placed a gentle kiss on my knuckles.

I smiled, a bit embarrassed. "I'm sorry. This is the only way to and from their house. The other entrance is blocked by some construction that's been going on since April."

"It's okay. Where does your sister live?" he asked, clearly trying to distract himself.

I itched to pull my hand away and put it back on the wheel. "Calla and Kent live a couple neighborhoods over. They're probably already at the house."

"She's pretty close to your parents?" Nodding, I took a breath once we made a turn and left the road behind. "But you didn't want a house near them?"

"You'll see why when we get there." I chuckled. "These aren't exactly homes you live in by yourself. I'd love to move closer to them someday, but right now I'm content where I'm at."

We were silent for the rest of the drive, but as Nick started leaning down to get a better look at the houses we passed, I could only imagine what his reaction would be. He knew we were well off, but it was completely different to be able to see it.

"Wow," he whispered when I pulled up to the house and parked the car. "You weren't kidding when you said your family had money."

I gave him a small, slightly nervous smile before I watched Nick exit the car and walk around to the driver's side. I didn't even attempt to get out on my own anymore. After the first five or six times he placed his hand on my arm to stop me, I figured out that he was always going to want to help me. It wasn't a one-time thing.

He grabbed my hand and softly shut the door. We walked around to the trunk I'd just popped open. Nick let go of my hand, immediately grabbing the wine and the homemade potato salad he'd insisted on making.

"Look," he began as I shut the trunk. "I know I was weird about your money in the beginning. But I promise I won't be rude." Apparently I wasn't hiding my nerves as well as I thought.

"I know." I grabbed his upper arm and squeezed. "I'm not worried about that. I'm just nervous in general. You all are so important to me, I just… I really want you all to like each other," I said, my gaze darting to the front door.

"Hey," he murmured. I looked back to see him frowning down at his hands, like he wanted to wrap me in a hug but was angry because the stuff he was holding was stopping him. "It'll be fine. If they're even a quarter as wonderful as you, how could I not like them? And me…" He trailed off with a smirk. "Well, I'll do my best to make the greatest first impression I've ever made."

With a smile, I let out a breath of relief. After double-checking the lock, I wound my arm through his and let him lead me to the front door. Nick eyed the perfectly placed flowers lining the walk and the beds framing the house. I gripped his arm a little tighter when I saw him smile as he looked at the row of irises.

We stopped in front of the door, adorned with a wreath made of rich fall-colored leaves, but before I could knock or ring the bell, Nick stopped me. He turned his body toward mine and, with only the power of his lips, pulled me into the world's sweetest kiss. A few swipes of his lips later, he backed away.

"Thanks for inviting me. I don't know if I told you how much it meant to me."

Thank you. It was so simple, just two words, and yet it had such a big impact.

"You're welcome."

"Okay," he said with a lift of his shoulders. "Let's do this."

I laughed at the over-the-top game face he put on, feeling the tension drain from my body. I reached forward and rang the bell.

My mom opened the door a minute later with a bright smile and rushed us in. "Iris." She pulled me into a quick hug before turning toward Nick.

"Nick." She looked down at the offerings with an even bigger grin. "This was so sweet of you. You shouldn't have," she said as she plucked both from his hands and put them on the table by the door. Before he could even respond, she wrapped him up in a hug. I was surprised when he eagerly went. When she pulled back, her hands rested on his shoulders. "It's so good to finally meet you. We've heard nothing but wonderful things."

"Iris, you shouldn't lie to your mother," he joked, looking slightly nervous at how my mom would react. He needn't have worried. She was practically beaming as she looked between us.

"I didn't. I just left a bunch of stuff out," I said. Nick's expression relaxed as he grabbed my hand and looked back at my mom.

"Thanks for having me, ma'am."

"Ma'am?" My mother scoffed. She turned my way. "Did he *ma'am* me?"

Before I could respond, Calla came in, bouncing a giggling Mirielle in her arms. "It's what I've been telling you, Mom—you're getting old."

Our mother turned toward my sister, but she couldn't hold her fake anger, not that she would have been able to much longer. "I guess I've earned the title. I am a grandma after all," she finished wistfully, pushing the tiny wisps of my niece's hair from her forehead.

My eyes connected with my sister's, the good humor fading from her face as she gave me a tense smile. I saw my mom face Nick out of the corner of my eye, but I kept my sights on

Calla, even when she broke our connection and looked down at her daughter.

"Please, call me Sarah. I won't have it any other way."

"Of course, Sarah."

I finally turned back and saw her smile widen. My mom turned toward me to whisper, "He's a keeper."

My gaze lingered on Calla as they both walked toward the kitchen, my mom grabbing the wine and potato salad on the way.

"Hey, you okay?" Nick asked, lightly touching my elbow. I shook off the weirdness and turned toward him.

"Yeah." I gave him a small smile, but he wasn't buying it. Right when he went to speak, my mom called us in from the kitchen.

"Later?" he asked. I nodded and he wrapped an arm around my shoulders.

I didn't really know what I was going to say, though. There had never been this kind of wedge between Calla and me before. I was hoping that by the end of dinner there would be nothing to talk about at all. That the strain would be gone, and that the tightening in my belly was just hunger disguised as fear.

Nick

Dinner was weird.

And even though Iris had been nervous, I didn't think she was actually worried about something like this. Her parents were great, asking lots of questions about my ma and me, about my childhood and my career as a chef. They were all smiles, and every time Sarah looked over at Iris, her eyes soft and approving, my heart soared.

But Kent and Calla's presence was more than a little draining. The main course was just finishing up and they'd barely said anything. And when they had, it was mumbles. Iris and her parents seemed equally confused, so I assumed it wasn't about me and was maybe just other marital issues.

Until Kent started talking about the accident.

"We were sorry to hear about your accident," he began, shocking the hell out of everyone.

"Oh, uh, thank you." Iris told me they knew everything, and it wasn't that surprising. Iris didn't seem like the type to keep things from the people she cared about.

"Did they catch him yet?" he asked, sounding oddly detached, almost bored.

"No, not yet."

Nodding, he picked up his napkin and wiped his mouth before setting it next to his plate. "I wouldn't get your hopes up. No-contact car accidents are hard to close, plus given the amount of time that's past…" Kent trailed off when he noticed all eyes on him.

My jaw clenched. "I know. But I'm still optimistic."

Oh, the irony. Mr. Pessimist is suddenly the optimist.

Kent's eyes narrowed. "Is it about the money? Because I'm sure—"

"Kent," Iris hissed as her hand landed on my thigh. I looked over to see her eyes shooting fire at him.

"Perhaps that's enough for tonight," her dad said, looking between Kent and Calla—who'd remained quiet with her gaze on her daughter.

"Yes. It is." Iris stood, gripping my arm and pulling me up with her. Sarah quickly followed suit and walked us to the door.

"Thanks for having me," I said, my tone stiff and robotic.

Sarah shot her daughter a worried look.

"Of course." Her voice was just as strained. "Come back anytime."

I tried to soften my scowl. Sarah and her husband had been nothing but nice, but it was proving difficult. I gave her a quick nod before reaching for the door.

"Oh, and let me go get your dish—"

"Don't worry about it," I cut her off. I couldn't even revel in the fact that they ate my entire potato salad. My eyes landed on Kent, who was standing in the archway between the kitchen and the main hallway, staring at me. "It may not be up to your standards, but I can certainly afford another one." With another bitter smile, and not a second glance at Iris or her mother, I turned around and walked out.

♥♥

The silence was unbearable. It wasn't anything like our usual rides. My hand wasn't on her thigh, her fingers weren't wrapped around my neck, playing with my hair. And her soft laughter wasn't floating through the air.

I hated it.

But I didn't know how to fix it, not with this burning anger inside me.

"I don't think they liked me," I tried to joke. It didn't work; my voice sounded rough, and I tried not to let the pit in my stomach deepen.

"My parents loved you," she said softly.

Shaking my head, my hands fisting the steering wheel, I said, "Maybe they think I'm just some poor asshole, too. Someone looking to make a quick buck." I'd asked Iris if I could drive us back to her place. I wondered if she was regretting it now.

"They don't think that." I could practically feel her frown fill the car.

"No? How can you be so sure? That's how most people in America think, especially the wealthy. I, like all poor Americans, don't have pride and I'll do whatever I can for some money. Kent obviously thinks that, and Calla didn't look far behind. It's not a leap that your parents would, too."

Out of the corner of my eye, I saw her rub her forehead. "That's not it at all, Nick. I don't know why Kent acted that way, but Calla isn't—"

"You're so goddamn blind." I angrily shook my head. "You're not doing anyone a favor by turning a blind eye to everything that's wrong in the world. You want to skip around in a field of daises, convincing everyone to hold hands and play nice? You want to pretend the world is perfect and the people in it are fair? Fine, go ahead. But you're not doing the world any favors, Iris. You aren't helping anyone."

Somehow it felt quieter than the silence that reined minutes earlier. I gave myself another sixty seconds, trying to calm down, before looking over. Her head was facing the window, and what I saw in the reflection caused my heart to splinter. Her lip was quivering as she bit it, and her eyes shimmered with tears.

Dammit.

We were only a couple minutes away from her house. "Iris—"

"Don't," she whispered.

I stayed silent until we pulled into her driveway, but only because I wanted all my focus to be on her when I apologized. If she could see the regret in my eyes, feel the reverence in my touch, it would hopefully strengthen the thing I was horrible at: apologizing.

I had just put the car in park when I heard her seat belt clang against the door before she shoved it open.

"Wait—" My hand flew out to grab her elbow, like I did whenever she tried to leave the car.

She froze, one leg hanging out and the other planted on the floor bed ready to push off. Turning toward me, she shifted until we weren't touching. But she stayed. Without an ounce of embarrassment, she sat there as tears started streaming down her face, letting me see the damage I'd caused. She didn't hide it to save face or make me feel better; she gave me everything.

And it hurt like hell.

When I was younger I always got angry when Colleen would hide her feelings from me, when she would turn away and wipe her tears before I could see them. Even though I knew it would hurt—seeing the tears I caused—I wanted it because it meant she trusted me.

Now, I was wishing Iris would pretend. I was hoping she'd throw out some lame excuse about allergies and run away before I could see her fall apart. Because this didn't come close to how much I imagined it would hurt. I expected an ache in my chest, not a grenade that completely blew me apart.

Iris was quickly becoming the greatest joy I'd ever known, but that also meant she became the deepest sorrow when she was hurting, especially when me and my big, stupid fucking mouth were the cause.

A sorrow that was made worse by her next words.

"I choose to see the good in people because too many people see the bad. I decide each morning to count my blessings rather than lament my troubles. It's not always easy, and there are days when I need a break. But this is who I am and I'm not ashamed of it. I've seen the power of positivity, whether you believe me or not, whether there's an explanation for it or not." She looked down and picked some invisible lint off her clothes.

"You're right. I know there are people who probably look at you and your circumstance and think like that, but those people are not my family. And I'm not being blinded by devotion or loyalty. I don't know what was wrong with Kent and Calla tonight. But I do know them, and they are good, fair people. And isn't expecting them to be a certain way because they have money the exact same thing as people judging you for not having it?" She shook her head and adjusted her purse, like she was preparing to deliver one last verbal blow before leaving. Iris made sure she looked me in the eye when she spoke again.

"I know you don't understand how I can be so optimistic. Not many people do. They think I'm strange or they feel intimidated or whatever—I've heard it all. I've gotten used to my relatively solitary life. I guess I just thought"—she sniffled before taking a deep breath and finishing—"I thought I'd finally found someone who understood enough to want to be with me the way I am. I'm a good person and I do help people. If you can't see or appreciate it, that's your loss."

And with that, she stepped out of the car, taking all my happiness with her. She waited by the hood for me to exit. I moved slowly, my mind racing for a way to fix this. But when I got close enough, she snatched the keys out of my hand, locked her car doors, and swiftly moved toward her house.

She didn't look back once, and I stood frozen in her driveway.

I'd never seen Iris cry like that before. Truthfully I hadn't known it was possible. She always seemed so strong, too happy to be brought down by anything. But I guess that was the problem with strength. Sometimes it became synonymous with indestructible.

We saw strong people as invincible.

We imagined them unbreakable.

But that was a big mistake. Invincibility didn't exist. It was an illusion that made humans seem like something more. And we became careless.

I became careless.

I saw Iris as strong.

Invincible.

Unbreakable.

And without meaning to, I crushed her.

Sixteen

Iris

I IMMEDIATELY SLUMPED AGAINST THE DOOR, THE TEARS cool on my face. I hated crying. I wasn't this person.

Think of something positive.

Something good has to come out of this.

But I had nothing. Just a whole lot of hurt.

I easily forgave his assumptions when we first met. He hadn't known me, and he certainly didn't owe me the benefit of the doubt. His distrust came from his past and the people who'd wronged him. That had nothing to do with me, so it was a grievance I was easily able to let go of.

But now? Now he knew me. I thought he *trusted* me. The fact that he didn't broke my heart a little bit, and it made me feel like a fool. How much of what I thought he was feeling was the truth?

Slowly picking myself up, I walked toward the kitchen. Just a few hours ago, he'd made me feel like the most important person on the planet. But maybe that was my mistake. Maybe I was confusing sex with something more. Maybe Nick—

I'd just put my clutch down and was bending over to take off my new shoes, when a knock sounded at the door. And if possible, the knock sounded frantic. Or maybe that was my imagination, because I knew there was only one person it could be.

I hesitated for only a couple seconds before his fist pounded again and I reluctantly walked to the door. Hand on the knob, I took a deep breath before pulling it open.

It felt odd to be in the exact same position we were in five hours ago. Only this time there were no butterflies. My heart was content to stay in my chest, protected by the cage that kept it. And it felt like it would take a lot of work to get my lips to lift again.

Nick cleared his throat. "Can I come in?"

I slowly backed up and let him through. After shutting and locking the door, I followed him toward the family room. He was standing by the fireplace, looking at pictures. I followed his stare to the family portrait. My brunette hair was like a beacon against my blonde family. Out of the corner of my eye, I saw him turn toward me.

"I'm sorry," he whispered. "Money is a sore spot for me, but I shouldn't have taken it out on you. All those things I said…" I looked over to see him shaking his head. "They were lies."

"You're not wrong about the world. Or how I see it." I shrugged and wrapped my arms around my waist, trying to stop any more tears from falling. "I guess I thought that was one of the things you liked about me."

"I do." Nick quickly stepped forward and held out his hands, but I backed up. He frowned and stuffed his hands in his pockets.

Looking down, I studied my shoes and thought about how excited I'd been to wear them and for Nick to meet my family. I certainly hadn't counted on everything going down like this. His words hurt because they hit a nerve. I'd tried not to think about it, but it was always nagging in the back of my mind.

I finally looked up and asked, "Why did you want to take me on a date?"

"What?" His expression twisted in shock.

"I know I haven't said anything, but you aren't the only one who's been insecure in this relationship. I thought about how annoyed you got in the beginning and I don't understand what you see in me." Nick opened his mouth, but I waved my hand to stop him. "I'm proud and very happy with who I am. I'm not asking this because I need reassurances about myself, I'm asking because, just like you, I've wondered if we're too opposite." I took a deep breath, ready to release my biggest fear. "And sometimes I wonder, even though you didn't act grateful in the beginning and you were insistent on not giving me anything, if you feel like you owe me. Maybe you would have wanted to be with any girl who gave you a kidney and tried to befriend you."

Nick started shaking his head.

"You're wrong. I'm with you because I fucking want to be. The only reason I was annoyed was because I was scared you were too good to be true. I don't feel indebted to you either." This time when he stepped forward he didn't give me a chance to back away. Nick grabbed my hands and leveled me with his gaze.

"Iris, you said, maybe I would have ended up with anyone who gave me a kidney. But don't you see? *No one* else would have done that. You're one-of-a-kind. You amaze me. Even if your optimism annoys me on occasion, it's not something I want to change. I need you, just as you are."

I let out a breath of relief and when he pulled me into a hug, I didn't fight him. "I'm sorry," he whispered into my hair once more.

"Me too."

Nick abruptly pulled backed and held me by the shoulders. "You have nothing to apologize for," he said forcefully.

Shaking my head, I said, "Not for me. For Kent… for Calla." I frowned. "I don't know what got into him, and Calla just hasn't been herself lately. But I promise they aren't like that. Maybe they're stressed or sleep deprived. I know Mirielle was colicky earlier on, maybe some of that is still happening? Or—"

He cut me off with a quick kiss, and I felt those butterflies come back and my heart started to pound again. "It doesn't matter. I shouldn't have reacted the way I did."

I nodded. "I don't want to talk about this anymore."

"Me neither," Nick readily agreed.

"What do you wanna do?" I whispered.

His eyes heated as they dropped to my bare legs and moved down. "I remember you saying something about wanting to break these heels in…" Nick's hands skimmed down the front of my thighs, stopping at my knees and curling around.

At dinner I told my mom the shoes were new and I couldn't wait for the pinchy feeling to go away once I broke them in, but I had a feeling Nick meant a different kind of "break in."

I let out a squeak as he knelt and tugged me forward, his fingers brushing down my calves before landing on my ankles where the straps of my heels met skin.

Nick kissed each knee as his fingers continued to dance over my legs, eliciting tiny shivers with each pass. "I want to wrap these gorgeous legs around me. I want to feel the spikes digging into my shoulders as I eat you out. I want there to be marks on my back because you came so hard."

"Nick..." My breaths were coming out quick as I watched him stand and wrap his hands around my waist.

"Then I'm going to make love to you slowly, with so much tenderness you won't have any doubts about how sorry I am."

I didn't tell him that he'd already assuaged my doubts; instead I let him lead me down the hallway and deliver on *both* of his promises.

"Tell me something no one else knows," Nick said as he leaned against the headboard and I sat on his lap. His hands were resting on my hips and my arms were loosely wrapped around his neck. It was hours later and both of us were exhausted, but we weren't even attempting to go to sleep. He'd thrown on a pair of boxers and I was wearing his shirt—something that seemed to make him extremely happy.

My cheeks burned as I thought about something no one else knew. "Oh, it's good, I can tell." Nick laughed as he squeezed my sides and drew me closer. "Tell me."

"I took a couple of pole and lap dancing classes."

His hands fell away as his jaw dropped. Nick's eyes began roaming down my body as if he'd never seen me before. "You... damn, that is something I'd like to see."

I slugged him in the arm. "Yeah, well, we did it for fun. No offense to all the strippers out there, but I'll never take my clothes off for money and gyrate on a stage or a stranger's lap."

I took pity on him when he started pouting. "We don't have access to any poles, but I think lap dances might be a boyfriend perk that can be awarded at some time."

Licking his lips, he murmured, "I think you're right.

C'mere." I shuffled closer, doing my best to look as desirable as I felt. Nick's hands landed on my thighs, skimming from my knees and disappearing under the shirt I had on.

"You pretend to look proper and nice… you never swear or go over the speed limit. You never wear a skirt above the knees, never show too much cleavage." He looked like he was in pain as his eyes lingered on the top of his shirt I was wearing, with no trace of cleavage.

"All of which I'm proud of," I responded. The last word came out a little breathy as he leaned forward and began laying kisses along my exposed throat.

"But underneath all that, underneath this…" His hands trailed up my side and stopped at the neckline, gently pulling it down until he saw the tops of my breasts. His shirt was so large on me it didn't feel uncomfortable. The soft touches he left had me shivering. "You're not a very *good* girl, are you?"

Nick's fingers moved to the bottom hem of the shirt, toying with it without bringing it up. My mind was stunned into silence.

Are we really having this conversation?

"I bet you like to get spanked." My nose crinkled and some of the lust receded. I'd like to think I was open to new things, but having my butt—or any part of me—smacked didn't hold much appeal.

And it wasn't us. The spanking. The punishment. To each their own, but that wasn't something either of us got off on. When Nick held my neck it was never about pain. He never hurt me—never even came close.

It was about trust. Comfort. Which seemed contradictory, but it wasn't if you really thought about it. The only thing that made it dangerous or painful was intent. And Nick never intended to hurt me. Knowing he had the power to, but had no intention, made me feel safer than anyone ever had. Than anyone ever could.

I moved back when I felt Nick's chuckle vibrate against my chest.

"I cringed the second it was out of my mouth." He shook his head and we both started laughing uncontrollably.

"That's not us, is it?" he managed to get out when we'd calmed down.

"Nope. Not us at all."

Our laughter faded to content smiles, which eventually turned thoughtful.

Us.

We were frozen as the word settled in our laps.

We were an *us*. It wasn't *him* and *me*, it was *we*. The two of us, for some extended period of time, were one.

"Us," Nick whispered, like he was thinking the same thing.

I didn't respond with words; instead I leaned forward and swept my mouth across his, sealing the unspoken promise.

Nick

We were finally winding down for sleep, Iris tightly wrapped around me, when she whispered.

"Nick?"

"Yeah?"

"My birth dad used to pick me up and twirl me around in the kitchen while my mom made dinner. And sometimes he'd tickle my stomach until I thought I'd throw up. The hands of someone who held a gun on a cashier and cut lines of cocaine were also the hands that made me feel loved beyond measure.

"I remember watching my birth parents. They'd dance in

the kitchen, make out like teenagers on the couch—keeping it PG, of course—and hold hands pretty much everywhere we went. Their love was so pure, so unguarded and beautiful. They had their wedding rings tattooed on. People would look at them like they were crazy. Told them they'd never make it. They made it almost eight years, and when it was over, it wasn't by choice." I stayed silent, just running the tips of my fingers down her arm.

"When the Chamberlains adopted me, I didn't understand. They didn't act the way my birth parents had. When I asked Mom why she didn't love Dad, she frowned and asked me why I thought that. I told her it was because I never saw them kiss or dance in the kitchen. She smiled like she understood. She tapped me on the nose and told me to watch a little bit closer."

"What'd you see?"

She tipped her face toward me and smiled. "Their kind of love. I watched while they made dinner, as they tucked us in at night, or when they had a fight. In the kitchen, they moved around each other in perfect harmony, like a dance they'd been performing their whole lives, only they never touched. He knew what she needed without her saying a word, and when he handed it to her, she gave him a look that only a person in love could. When they would stop by our bedrooms to check on us one last time, Dad would always smooth out the blanket at the end of the bed before he let Mom sit there. Apparently she had sat down on one of Aster's train toys when he was younger. The little weirdo liked to sleep with them." Iris smiled.

"And when they fought?" I whispered, reminding her.

"When Dad screwed up, because it was always his fault," she teased.

"But of course." I grinned down at her.

"Mom would banish him to the couch. And every time when he walked to the hall closet to get the blanket and pillow he used, he would come back and a book would be on the coffee table, whatever book he was reading at the moment. He'd smile, pick it up, and place a soft kiss on it before he started reading. Mom knew how much he enjoyed reading before bed.

"They showed me that love could also be subtle and private. Where my birth parents' love was loud, passionate, and heartbreakingly real, my adoptive parents' was soft, compassionate, and just as real. Both couples loved the only way they knew how. They made me see that there are all different kinds of love in this world."

Iris's face dipped back down, her fingers softly swirling over my chest. "Sometimes I think my birth parents had to love that way. Like maybe, somehow, they knew their forever would be shorter than others, and they wanted to fit as much love in as they could."

We were both quiet for a minute, letting her words digest. When I looked down I saw her drawing hearts now. Iris chuckled, stopping her fingers and laying her palm over my heart.

"I'm sorry, I'll just get to the point. We're both exhausted and I'm rambling—"

"Hey, I'll listen to your rambles any time you want." I felt her smile as she kissed my chest.

"Thank you. But I think I'm about to pass out from my rambles."

Squeezing her hip, I waited for her to continue. "So my point… my father did a horrible thing. He did it for the right reason, but it was still horrible. And he had one of the purest hearts I know. Colleen…" Iris hesitated when I froze. "She did a horrible thing for a selfish reason. I can't say much because I didn't know her. But maybe she did love you, just not in the way you needed."

My breathing regulated as she started ghosting her fingers along my skin again. "There are so many different ways to have a pure heart, Nick, just like there are vastly different ways to love a person. Maybe they don't always line up with what we need, but I'd like to think that, deep down, most people are good.

"And maybe if we stop searching for all the ways we're different from other people, and start seeking out all the ways we're the same, we'll finally be able to see that."

Seventeen

Iris

MY HEAD ROLLED ON THE LEATHER SEAT, A LAZY grin on my face as I slowly woke up and looked toward Nick. He briefly glanced over at me, flashing me a smile—complete with dimples—before his gaze moved back to the road. My lips tipped up even more when he grabbed my hand and brought it to his mouth, placing a gentle kiss on my knuckles.

The weekend of Kevin and Lindsay's wedding was finally here. Nick told me it was going to be small, only their family and closest friends. Right now it was early Friday morning, and he was driving us up to the White Mountains of New Hampshire, where the wedding was taking place.

I checked the time. We'd already been on the road for almost two of the three-hour drive from Boston.

"Sorry," I mumbled around a yawn. "I didn't mean to leave you hanging with no one to talk to."

"No worries," he responded easily, still holding my hand on his thigh. "Besides, you should be resting now. You'll get absolutely none this weekend." I laughed when his hand tightened around mine and he winked.

Now fully awake, I leaned over the console and placed a kiss on his bearded cheek before whispering in his ear, "I'm looking forward to it."

I swore I heard him growl as I pulled away. And when he released my hand and gripped the steering wheel with both of his, I knew I'd succeeded in riling him up.

"*That* was not cool."

Chuckling, I grabbed a blanket from the backseat before wrapping it around me. I shifted my body his way. "Why'd they pick a winter wedding?" I asked.

Nick let out a breath. "Lindsay loves the snow. She grew up in the Southwest. Never had a white Christmas until she moved to Boston at the start of high school." He shrugged. "But as a kid, since it was so foreign to her, she kind of associated snow with magic. When she got engaged it was kind of a no-brainer for her."

"Kevin didn't mind?"

Nick smirked, his eyes flicking to mine. "Lindsay could tell him to dress up as an elf, and he'd do it. That guy is stupid in love with her."

I smiled, thinking about my parents. "But that's what it's about, isn't it?"

"What?"

"Love," I said simply. "It isn't the anniversaries or the flowers. It's not about sex or kissing. It's all the little things. It's bringing him lunch when you know he's too busy to go out and get something. Or holding her hand when she's nervous about meeting his family. Love isn't in big fancy weddings or huge romantic gestures. It's in the simple things, like knowing how your boyfriend takes his coffee or what your girlfriend's favorite movie is. It's all the stuff no one else really thinks about."

I saw Nick swallow as my palms grew damp. I hadn't meant to take the conversation in such a serious direction.

"Have you ever felt that way?" he whispered.

I'm feeling it now.

"Not completely," I hedged. I didn't want to lie, but I also didn't want to start this weekend by freaking him out. Aster never invited women to weddings because he said it gave them all sorts of fantastical ideas.

Does Nick think that's what I'm doing?

"Iris?" he asked, breaking me out of my paranoid thoughts.

"Yeah?"

"Three months ago I wouldn't have had a clue what you're talking about. But now… it makes a lot of sense."

Our eyes met for the briefest of seconds as he looked away from the road. It was quick, but I saw everything I needed to. We both knew how the other felt; we didn't need to say it. There were no freak-outs. Just contentment.

I relaxed against my seat and brought my hand back to his thigh, gently massaging it as we continued in silence.

An hour later we arrived, and my breath caught as we pulled up to a giant lodge covered in snow. It looked like it could've been splashed across a postcard—I sincerely hoped it was somewhere.

"Wow." My feet were firmly planted on the bed of the car as I leaned forward and looked up to the top of the building, basking in the fairy lights lining the roof.

Nick parked the car and I heard him unbuckle his seat belt before his hand gently wrapped around my upper arm. I'd just fully turned my head when his mouth met mine and his other hand cupped the side of my face, holding me to him. His lips made gentle sweeps across mine before he traced the seam of my lips with his tongue. I immediately opened for him, and what started out sweet quickly turned hungry as he pulled me closer. My stomach was digging into the center console as his hands began wandering.

One of mine sneaked toward him, settling on his lap. He groaned when I palmed him through his jeans. A moan of my own echoed through the car as I felt him grow hard.

"BOO!"

I jumped back, hitting my head on the roof as I looked out the windshield. Kevin was cackling with a few men I didn't recognize. Nick rolled the window down.

"What's wrong with you, asshole?"

Kevin smirked as he leaned in. "I'm pretty sure I paid for a fancy room for this kind of thing." His wiggling eyebrows dropped when he saw me rubbing my head.

"Shit. Are you okay, Iris?" he asked with a wince.

I waved him away and leaned back over the console. "I'll live. So how does it feel? Last night of freedom?"

"Terrible. Lindsay's mom and sisters are adamant I can't see her. I thought the point of this shit was so I could see her all the time." Nick rolled his eyes as Kevin's other friends called for him at the front of the lodge.

"I'd ask if you're coming out with us tonight, but…" Kevin trailed off, snickering at the expression on my boyfriend's face. Kevin and Lindsay already had combined bachelor and bachelorette parties in Boston last weekend.

"Right. Well I'll see you for all the fun and games tomorrow, Nick." He dipped his head in my direction. "Iris. Sorry about the head. I'm sure Nick here will kiss… something and make it all better."

He was sprinting away—cackling—before Nick could react. But Nick was chuckling himself as he rolled up the window and turned my way. Then he frowned as he reached forward and gently rubbed the back of my head.

I sighed as he guided me forward and rested our foreheads against one another. "Sorry," he whispered, still massaging my head. "It'd been nearly four hours since I was allowed to kiss you. And that's way too long to be in your presence and not kiss you like you deserve."

I grinned, not bothering to point out that he kissed me at the gas station two hours ago, and gave me a quick peck at a stoplight thirty minutes before we arrived.

"Kevin was right though."

"About what?" he murmured, eyes closed.

"I think I am gonna need a kiss… somewhere."

I was smirking when Nick's eyes flew open.

"I'll go check us in," he said, scrambling for the handle. I laughed, clutching my stomach when he almost slipped on a patch of ice in his hurry to get to the lodge.

This weekend felt like a huge deal, and not just for Kevin and Lindsay.

♥♥

I gasped, my hands burrowing further into Nick's hair, pulling at the strands until I was convinced I was going to yank them straight out of his head.

He didn't seem to mind. If anything, it encouraged him. He growled against my clit, sending delicious tingles radiating through me.

"N-Nick…" My head turned to the side, and though the

curtains were shut, I could see the lights dangling outside and the gentle snowfall.

His hands came up and palmed my boobs, roughly squeezing while his tongue continued to work me over until I exploded, seeing stars. When the pressure become too much, I tried to push him away. He held me close and continued eating me out like he was never going to stop. I felt it building again, but…

"N-Nick… I c-can't… I… oh… God…"

He mumbled something against my core, but I was too busy writhing in pleasure to make it out. I couldn't believe I was coming for a fourth time. And I couldn't even berate his smug smile because he earned it. I was wiped out.

After he gave me one orgasm with his fingers against the hotel room door, he took me on the bed two more times—once missionary and then with me riding him—before he moved down my body and coaxed one final orgasm out of me.

"I'd return the favor," I managed to get out, still gasping for air. "But I think you've killed me. Is death by orgasm a thing?"

I heard his chuckle and felt his warm breath ghost over my stomach as he kissed his way up my body.

"If so, we'd better stop. I'm actually pretty fond of you."

"Oh yeah?" I teased, my eyes shut as my brain tried to regain function. When he didn't say anything, I opened my eyes to find him staring down at me with a serious expression on his face.

"Yeah," he whispered right before he brought his lips to mine, offering me a sweet kiss that stole my breath all over again. Nick pulled back and brushed the hair from my face, like he couldn't stand for any part of me to be hidden from him.

"C'mon. Let's get you cleaned up."

I groaned. "Nick, I can't stand, walk, lift my arms above

my head—AHH!" I finished with a shriek as he picked me up, forcing my tired arms to wrap around his shoulders.

"What are you doing? I just told you—"

"I'll take care of you."

He slowly moved us into the bathroom. The porcelain was cool on my skin as he gently set me on the countertop and turned toward the bath. Nick's hand hovered under the stream as he adjusted the temperature until he was satisfied. Once he was he quickly jogged back to the bedroom.

Apparently my sex-coma was no match for his butt, because my eyes tracked him all the way to his suitcase. When he returned he dumped some liquid in that immediately foamed up in the water and released a lemony scent. After testing the temperature again, he turned off the faucet before picking me up and carefully lowering us both into the steamy and bubbly bathwater.

I moaned. It felt like heaven on my sore muscles.

"Does it feel nice?" he murmured as his hands lightly stroked my arms. I nodded against his shoulder. Ever since we left the bedroom, his looks held affection and his touches were no longer demanding. Nick became tender and attentive, solely concerned with my well-being.

I knew he meant the bath, but my thoughts were somewhere else. I wished I had the courage to tell him that nothing in this universe was a match for how *he* made me feel, for how I was starting to feel about him.

When he started massaging shampoo into my scalp I was an absolute goner.

"I'm seriously going to fall asleep in here."

He kissed the shell of my ear before running his fingers through my hair until he reached the tips. Gently tilting my head back, he grabbed a cup, turned on the faucet to fill it, and rinsed the shampoo from my hair. He did this three or four times until my hair was free of suds. Then he picked up the conditioner and slowly worked it into my ends, doing it exactly how I did.

My words from earlier floated back to me...

Love isn't in big fancy weddings or huge romantic gestures. It's in the simple things... in all the stuff no one else really thinks about.

Like how I washed my hair.

As my eyes fluttered closed, tired and overwhelmed with the surety that I was in love with Nick, I leaned my head to the side. Nick read me so well, I was hardly waiting a second before his lips sealed over mine.

And he may not have known it, but for me, the kiss sealed something far more precious.

Nick

We'd gotten in around two o'clock, and after the quick sex coma, bath, and nap, it was a little after seven o'clock.

Iris stretched on the bed next to me. I grabbed her hips and quickly lifted her onto my lap. She let out a squeak as her hands found my chest.

"I wanna explore."

Grinning, I pushed some of her fallen hair back from her face. "What happened to your death by orgasm?"

"I've resurrected." She kissed my chest. "Pretty please?"

"Of course. Just give me a minute." I gave her a pat on the ass and watched her flop onto the bed next to me. Unable to stop myself, I gave her one last kiss before getting out of bed and padding toward the bathroom.

After using the toilet and brushing my teeth, I walked out to find Iris leaning against the wall next to the window. Her hand was holding the curtain back as she stared at the falling snow, a soft smile on her lips. She had changed into jeans, a long-sleeved burgundy shirt, and thermal socks. Her jacket, scarf, and boots were waiting on the chair behind her.

As if she felt my gaze, she turned her head and our stares collided.

"Are you almost ready?" she asked quietly. Without a word, I nodded and walked toward my clothes in the corner. We were both living out of our suitcases for the couple days we were here.

I quickly pulled on my clothes from earlier—they smelled clean enough—before walking over to where Iris was about to put on her coat. Molding my front to her back, my hands landed on her hips and squeezed.

"Let me," I whispered against the back of her neck before placing a gentle kiss there. She nodded, letting go of the coat when I wound my arm around her and took it. I shook it out before tapping her left shoulder.

Iris looked to her side, catching me in her periphery, as she slid one arm in and then the other. When I finished, I gently massaged her shoulders for a few seconds before smoothing out the material. Then I turned her around, cupped her face, and gently kissed her.

When I broke away, we were both winded. I focused on her lips, all my thoughts and feelings whirling around me, almost too great for me to comprehend.

Always kiss like it's the first time and the last time.

I remembered hearing that advice before, but I'd never really understood it. But I was finally starting to get it. It wasn't even a choice I had to make. I kissed her and I felt everything.

I felt nervous and unsure, like I still couldn't believe it was happening. And whenever we were about to stop, I panicked a little. Each time I kissed her a little stronger, to make sure she knew how much it meant to me that she let me kiss her, hoping I left as big an impact as she was leaving on me.

Both of us had been looking down, at the other's lips, but like magnets, our heads came up at the same time, our eyes connecting once again.

"C'mon." I reached down and laced my fingers through hers. "Let's go explore."

She beamed up at me as I grinned down at her.

It was perfect. Or was there a word greater than perfect? Because if there was, that was what this was. I didn't know it could be like this; even before I became jaded, I just didn't know. And I knew I'd never be able to go back.

The hotel was surprisingly quiet. We nodded at a few other couples before heading toward the back doors. The temperature was hovering in the high thirties, but the back deck had a few heaters so it wasn't completely unbearable. Besides, it gave me the perfect excuse to wrap my arms around Iris and pull her into my chest.

We were right in front of the fence, overlooking the back section of the hotel where the reception would take place. Both of us sucked in a breath at the sight before us.

"It's gorgeous," Iris whispered. I couldn't speak; I just nodded dumbly even though she couldn't see my agreement.

It was dark out, but the trees were lined with lights that casted a subtle glow over everything. It would undoubtedly look like the fairy tale Lindsay wanted tomorrow at twilight.

I'd been to a couple weddings over the years, all for distant relatives of Colleen's. There were always so many people, and apart from Colleen's parents, we knew no one there. But this had a completely different vibe. Instead of large round tables that held nearly a dozen people, the tables were small, seating only four people. To the left there was a decent-sized pool with several waterfalls providing a soothing background in the far corners.

Iris looked back at me. "I know a lot of people get lost in planning their wedding. It's nice to see something so reminiscent of the actual couple."

"Yeah," I murmured. She grinned as I shoved my hands into the pockets of her coat. Her eyes fluttered shut as her head rested against my shoulder.

We stayed like that for several minutes until I heard the back door open.

"Nicky?" an excited voice asked. Both of us turned toward my ma.

"Catherine." Iris's enthusiasm matched hers as she stepped out of my arms and quickly walked toward her. I frowned down at my empty arms before lifting my gaze to see the two of them hugging. Looking past them, I saw Trevor—I wasn't allowed to call him Dr. Moore anymore—checking the two of them in. His gaze was trained on my mother—the concierge had to tap on his arm to get his attention. It was such a strange sight, to see my ma with someone, but the second I looked over and saw her wide smile, my lips lifted.

I couldn't remember a time when she'd looked so happy. My stomach sank at the thought that I might have been the reason she never dated. I knew my dad leaving didn't break her, but that didn't mean she was whole.

This seemed glaringly clear now that I'd met Iris. Neither my ma nor I had been irreparably damaged by the people we'd been with, but that didn't make us complete. Because I was starting to think we all came to this planet incomplete, and even if we were happy, we'd never feel truly whole until we found the person we were meant to spend our life with.

I didn't know if Trevor was that person for my ma, but I was seriously starting to believe Iris was that person for me.

"Dear?"

I blinked, looking down at my mother and trying to clear my thoughts. My lips dipped down as I looked around and found Iris gone.

"She went to the bathroom," my mother explained. Nodding, my eyes moved to Trevor, who was finishing up.

"The drive was okay?" I asked, my gaze coming back to her. I'd been worried about them getting such a late start considering the snowy conditions.

"Yes. Trevor was extremely cautious."

"Good. Good," I said absentmindedly. My ma's hand came to my cheek, bringing my gaze back to her. She was wearing a worried frown.

"Are you okay?"

"Of course." I smiled, but it was smaller than she would have liked.

"What have I said about lying to your mother?"

My smile grew, nothing forced about it. "That a puppy is kicked every time I do."

"Exactly."

"I figured that lie out quite a few years ago."

We both chuckled. I didn't even point out the irony that she lied when lecturing me about lying. Any lie my mother told was white. I believed and trusted in her one hundred percent.

I suddenly leaned forward, catching her off guard, as I wrapped my arms around her. She laughed, slightly confused, but still hugged me back. I could be on fire and she'd hug me, burning right along with me. That was just how she was.

"Thank you," I whispered.

She pulled back, still holding on. "What for?"

"Everything. I don't know if I've ever really said it. You've given up so much for me and I need you to know how much I appreciate it." My eyes unconsciously moved to Trevor once more. He was standing just inside the door, watching the two of us with his lips tipped up.

Ma caught the move, and when my gaze met hers again, she was giving me a soft smile. "You say it every time you randomly show up with flowers or with my favorite cupcake. You say it every time you listen—extensively—about my day before saying a peep about your own." Shaking her head, she continued, "You say it every single time you look at me, Nick."

She took a deep breath and removed her arms from my waist to grab my hands. "There were a lot of things about my life with your father that weren't perfect. Most of them, probably. My options were limited, and Tyson's proposal felt natural and foolproof. If I'm being honest, I'm not sure I ever loved him. We'd gotten pregnant young, before we knew what we wanted out of life. But the second I found out about you, Nick, I knew I wanted you. There was not a single moment of hesitation. Being your mother is the greatest joy of my life." I tried to ignore the tears in my eyes, but it was no use.

"I could have dated throughout the years," she said, picking up on my thoughts from earlier. "I didn't stop because of you. You more than filled my heart; I didn't need anyone else. I never felt the need. Even now, I could be happy with just you—"

"But you deserve so much more, Ma."

Her grin widened. "So do you. And I think God has finally graced us with them."

Both of us looked inside to where Iris was now standing with Trevor. The two of them were so lost in their conversation they didn't notice us staring.

"Yeah," I whispered. "I think He has."

Eighteen

Nick

I was straightening my tie, my thoughts on Iris and how we spent last night after we left my mother and Trevor, when she stepped out of the bathroom.

My jaw dropped along with my hands. She looked fucking stunning.

Her makeup was simple: no color on her lids, just black liner and mascara, some light pink blush on her cheeks, and a slight sheen to her lips. Her brown hair was curled and brushed to one side, looking so damn soft I immediately wanted to run my fingers through it. I roughly swallowed at the thought of messing it up. Somehow I restrained myself as I took in her dress. I'd seen it already, but somehow it seemed brand new now that Iris was in it.

It was a deep forest green color to match the trees surrounding the lodge. The material clung to her chest, the top of it resembling a heart as it offered a modest amount of cleavage, and the sleeves rested halfway down her shoulder, like the dress was moments away from slipping off.

God, I wish.

But while the top half hugged her body, everything directly below her chest easily flowed. She was running her hands along the fabric when she met my gaze.

"What do you think?" Iris held out her arms, genuinely unsure of how she looked in it. Not because she was insecure, but I was pretty sure she was still having a hard time stepping into someone else's dress, someone else's role. I already knew from Lindsay that Iris had tried it on more times than Lindsay's cousin ever had. And honestly the dress looked made for Iris.

I brought a hand up to my mouth, rubbing my jaw before shaking my head. "Iris, you look… my God… you…"

"Really?" she asked with a pleased grin. "That's the look every girl aims for."

"What? To make men stunned, stupid, and speechless?"

Her laughter floated across the room, wrapping around me and making me feel at home. Iris walked forward, picking up my tie and finishing what I'd started. "Yes. The three S's. And not for *men*, but for *her man*."

I stared down at her, my eyes trained on her lips, on how her smile lingered. Her joy was beautiful, infectious. And I needed to taste it.

She'd just finished, preparing to step back when I carefully grabbed her neck, hauled her to me, and crashed my lips down on hers. It wasn't gentle or poetic, and it was probably messing up the stuff on her lips. I braced for a slap to the arm or worse—a knee to the groin—because Colleen hated when I kissed her after she'd done her makeup. But that wasn't what happened.

Iris groaned, moving closer as her hands made their

way into my hair, holding on as the kiss deepened. All other thoughts disappeared when our tongues tangled and my hand fell to her waist, bringing her closer. I could still taste the toothpaste on her breath and the faint scent of lemons drifted over me as my kisses moved across her cheek, my nose nudging her hair.

"Nick..." she whimpered.

"Hmm?" Her head was tilted back, and I moved my mouth across her jaw toward her bare neck on the other side. Iris squeezed my biceps, and I felt her legs clench below me. My hand skimmed lower—

Bang. Bang. Bang.

With a squeak, Iris jumped back. I looked at her mussed hair and raw lips, but I felt no guilt. And thankfully she didn't look affronted by having to fix them either.

"Nick?" my ma called through the door. I shook my head and dropped my hand to adjust myself before walking toward her voice. After taking a breath, I grabbed the handle and pulled it toward me.

Trevor had his arm around my mother's shoulders, grinning at me, while my ma squinted suspiciously. I held the door open wide, glancing back to find an empty room. Iris must have gone back to the bathroom to freshen up.

"You look beautiful, Ma," I said sincerely as I took in her dark purple dress. It was as long as Iris's, but the neckline was up to her collarbone and she had sleeves that ended just above her elbows.

She started fidgeting, so unaccustomed to wearing a dress. "Thank you, dear."

"I told her that she shouldn't be showing up the bride like this, but she insisted on wearing it," Trevor said with a large smile, putting his hand on the small of her back. My mother blushed as she leaned back into him.

Oh, he's good.

"Iris…" my mother breathed, eyes wide. I turned around to see my girlfriend exiting the bathroom again, and just like the first time, she nearly knocked me on my ass. She and my ma gushed over their outfits and makeup for a few minutes before Trevor asked if we were all ready to go.

I watched with a smile as he held his arm out to my mother and she eagerly took it. The door clicked shut behind the four of us, and Iris's fingers tangled with mine.

We walked down the hallway toward the bank of elevators.

Side by side.

Hand in hand.

Moving toward something so much bigger than us.

My ma and Trevor sat in the front row beside Kevin's parents. I was standing behind Kevin's brother—his best man—while Iris stood opposite me next to Lindsay's sister—her maid of honor.

I tried to keep my eyes on Kevin and Lindsay, but they invariably strayed to Iris. And every single time, like I was calling her, she looked over at me too.

"You may now exchange your vows," the officiant said, looking at Kevin first.

He cleared his throat before beginning. "I always pretend to hate my middle name, but it's actually one of my favorite things about myself," he started, staring directly at Lindsay. "Do you remember the first time we spoke?"

She chuckled and the sight seemed to make Kevin fall even more in love. "Yeah, I do."

He turned to the small audience. "I was pretty nervous. I wasn't as suave as I am now. It took me seven pep talks to get the courage to walk up to her." We all laughed. "I'm serious. She was intimidating as hell."

Kevin faced her again and took a tiny step closer. "She was the most beautiful girl I'd ever seen. Still is. And when I first heard her laugh, I fell, without even knowing if there was a safe place to land. Truthfully I didn't care." I saw Iris's eyes well and when I looked at Lindsay, hers were too.

"So I walked up to her, repeating what I was going to say in my head, when all of a sudden, her friend started screaming. But she was a teenage girl, so naturally she thought she was whispering. She kept saying, 'Oh my God, he's coming this way. Oh my God. Oh my God.' Over and over until Lindsay looked like a tomato." He turned toward the audience and "whispered."

"She had a huge crush on me." Everyone chuckled as Lindsay rolled her eyes. Then she pulled him back toward her. When he spoke next, he spoke directly to her.

"I was thrilled to hear you felt the same way, but you looked ready to bolt. So what could I do?"

She smiled, remembering. "You said, 'You think that's embarrassing, try having the middle name Macy,'" Lindsay finished in a deep voice meant to mock Kevin. The crowd laughed, and my gaze moved to Iris, catching her beautiful smile.

"Not my best line. But we were young so I blamed it on youth. Truthfully it didn't matter. It could have been the worst line in the world, but it became my favorite that day. Because it got you to relax. When you laughed, I felt like I was falling all over again. First I was nervous, because as a teenager everything is the end of world. And surely you knowing my embarrassing middle name was, like, the worst thing to ever happen," he exaggerated. "But it saved the conversation. You loosened up and we ended up hanging out after school and talking for hours." Kevin turned completely serious, his eyes now shimmering with tears.

"It was one of the best days of my life, Linds. And it was just the beginning. All my best days include you, and I know they will for years to come. All the birthdays, anniversaries. All the childbirths and family vacations. All the fights and the dreams. I want everything you can give me."

Lindsay was nodding, and there were tears in both their eyes. The officiant then indicated for Lindsay to give her vows.

"Kevin Macy," she began, and everyone laughed. "The first time I truly realized how much you loved me was senior year in high school. We'd been dating for almost four years and saying the words for three, but…" She shook her head, like the memory was causing her pain. I could imagine Kevin's pinched brow and worried frown.

"I wanted to find my birth father." The room froze with her confession. Kevin had told me the story, but he'd made me promise to never say anything to Lindsay. I looked at Lindsay's mom, pain and tears swimming in her eyes, as her husband drew her closer.

"You said you'd help me. You ended up finding him. And he… he didn't want to see me. Didn't want anything to do with me." I expected to see sadness in her gaze, but there was only her love for Kevin.

"You lied to me and said you couldn't find him. You cussed him out and told him you felt sorry for him, that he was missing out on the greatest girl in the world, and that he needed to stay away from me. He didn't. I guess he felt a little bit of guilt because he found me and told me all this. He said he was sorry and that it wasn't me, it was him." Lindsay shook her head and looked down. When her eyes came back up, there were tears in them. But her expression made it clear they were tears of joy.

"That should've destroyed me, but I didn't care. Kevin, you healed my heart before he even had a chance to break it. And that's when I realized how deep your love for me ran. Deeper than I think I will ever know. Because that's what love is. I think it's what you do for the person that they'll never be aware of. But I still feel it. I feel how much you love me, and I can't even imagine all the things you've done that I haven't been able to properly thank you for."

She shuffled forward and finished, "You are, without a doubt, the best thing that's ever happened to me, and I can't wait to spend the rest of my life with you, where I belong. Where I've always belonged."

My eyes moved to Iris as they continued with the ceremony. The promises of love and devotion. Being there in sickness and health. She had already given me all that. Where would we be in ten years? Would we still be together?

God, I hope so.

It didn't scare me that I was having these thoughts either.

I'd never had a serious girlfriend before Colleen, so I'd often found myself wondering if she was "the one." It seemed to make sense seeing as she was the only woman I opened myself up to. But my mind strayed, curious as to how everyone else was so certain of "the one." There were so many other people in the world; how could you promise to feel the same way forever?

And when things ended with Colleen, the person I decided was as close to "the one" as I would get, I wondered how I'd be able to trust myself again. How could I possibly assure myself of another woman when my first instincts were so off?

But as I stood here and listened to Lindsay and Kevin say "I do," and heard the catcalls as Kevin dipped his new wife down and kissed her, I realized the flaw in my thoughts.

All those times I wondered if she was right for me, I was giving myself an option. It required deliberation, and there were three different answers: yes, no, or maybe.

And that was how I knew this was different.

There were no options.

No deliberations.

And only one possible answer.

Yes.

Iris

We were back in our hotel room. My leg bounced as I sat on the side of the bathtub, waiting for Nick. I came into the bathroom to change and he told me to wait while he set up something in the room. My eyes drifted to the bathroom door that had started to open, Nick's grinning face peeking through.

"All set?" I asked, dying to know what he was doing. Instead of answering, he simply walked forward and grabbed my hand, lifting me from the tub. Nick cupped my cheek and brought me forward into a kiss. Our tongues tangled as he slowly walked backward into the bedroom. I registered the soft hum of music and the faint scent of lemon.

With a grin, I pulled away and slowly opened my eyes. My gaze stayed on Nick, but I saw the flicker of candlelight throughout the room as well as the open window drapes revealing the snowfall outside. I felt all the air leave me as I glanced at the bed, where dozens of yellow rose petals lay.

Nick followed my stare. "Yeah, it's all pretty cheesy. But…" He shrugged and turned back toward me. "I don't really care."

"Me neither," I whispered. The moment felt too intimate for anything else. I felt my grin widen as I stepped closer to him and wrapped my arms around his neck. But unlike the last time we danced, Nick seemed eager to wind his arms around my waist and slowly sway.

"Do you remember the first time we danced?" I asked.

Nick laughed. "Of course. You were practically twerking."

"I was not. Take that back."

"I certainly didn't mind." He shifted his hand until he was grabbing my butt, his hungry gaze roaming over my body, like he'd just noticed the tiny black satin robe I was wearing. "W-what's under there?" he croaked out.

Stepping back, I wrapped my hand around one end of the belt holding it closed. I made no other move to open the robe, and Nick growled in response.

"Take that off… before I do it for you."

My lips curled into a saucy grin, even as my thighs clenched together. "That's supposed to be a threat?" Without waiting for a response, I slowly pulled it open anyway, revealing the black and cream lingerie underneath.

Nick's mouth dropped open, and his hands briefly turned into fists at his side. He stepped forward, his hands immediately going to the material up by my shoulders. I stayed frozen as he slowly pushed the robe off until it fell down my arms and pooled at my feet. Grabbing me by the waist, he turned me so my back was to the window, and carefully pushed me toward it.

I let out a yelp when my skin met the cool pane. The ledge stopped just before my butt, so the only thing any passerby would see was my bare back and the strap of my bra.

Nick grinned as he slowly knelt in front of me, his hands resting on the back of my thighs. When his fingers wandered higher, he let out a tortured groan.

I'd always been modest when it came to clothing. My skirts rarely went above the knee, my tops never showed more than a tiny bit of cleavage and my underwear often resembled that of a ten-year-old girl. I liked cute designs or little bows, and sometimes I went with more luxurious material, but I never ventured into thongs. My butt was always covered. So the fact that I was wearing cheekies felt like a big deal.

I would probably never venture into thongs, but I had severely underestimated the power of alternative underwear. Because knowing these were under my dress all day had made me feel sexy. And if the hungry look Nick was giving me was any indication, he thought so too.

"Fuck..." he murmured as his hands molded around my cheeks, squeezing and bringing me closer to his face. I braced my hands against the frame of the window as he stared up at me. His hands skimmed up to my lower back before dipping into my underwear and dragging it down my legs.

"We're definitely keeping those," he said, tossing them to the side. Before I could reply, before I could even *think* of replying, his mouth was on me. I startled when he lifted one of my legs over his shoulder. But the shock quickly left as arousal took its place. My head tipped back and I moaned as he began lightly kissing my clit.

One hand rested on my backside while the other moved toward my aching center, running through my folds. He slid two fingers inside and slowly pumped them in and out. The movement pushed me up the window and I could feel the top of my butt against the glass.

I wondered if anyone was outside. I wondered if they were watching. It was obvious what we were doing, but I didn't know how clear of a view they would have. Regardless, I couldn't stop the excitement running through me.

"It's turning you on, isn't it?" he whispered.

"W-w-what?" I said, even as I felt a blush race across my

chest. His eyes darkened.

"The idea that there's even the smallest possibility someone could see us."

Again, he didn't give me time to answer. Nick's fingers sped up as his mouth put more pressure on my clit.

"N-Nick…"

My hands moved from the window and I grabbed his head, holding him to me as my orgasm ripped through me, quick and unexpected.

Everything felt like a contradiction.

The heat spreading through me against the cool of the window.

The roughness of Nick's fingers against the tenderness of his gaze.

The scream begging to be ripped from me against the whimpers that softly fell from my lips.

Nothing with Nick was how it seemed.

As I came down from my high, I started brushing the hair back from his face. He stood up and drew me away from the window before closing the blinds. My hand in his, he led us to the bed and we stared down at the rose petals.

"I might not have thought this through." He turned to look down at my near-naked body. "I mean, isn't it possible for one to get caught up your…?"

I chuckled. "I love it, Nick."

"Yeah?"

"Of course. And we can crawl under the comforter. No harm. No rose petals in inappropriate places," I said with a grin.

He smiled. That heart-stopping, dimpled smile that never failed to make me weak in the knees. But there was also something different about. It was softer somehow, and his eyes… he almost looked like a man in love.

Before I became the stereotypical girl who got wild ideas of love just because we were at a wedding, I leaned in and pressed my lips to his.

It was the kind of kiss that brought tears to your eyes and contentment to your heart. Nick's lips slowly moved over mine, tender and sure, like I was the last person he'd ever kiss this way.

Then we slipped under the covers and made love the exact same way.

Nick woke abruptly. I was still reading in bed when he shot straight up and his wild, panicked eyes met mine.

"What's wrong?" I reached for his hand, and found it warm and clammy. He held it firmly as he struggled to catch his breath.

"I remembered something… about the accident."

"That's great." I knelt next to him, holding one of his hands to my chest, while I started rubbing his back with the other. "What do you remember?"

"Lily…"

I felt the air in my lungs still as my grip became punishing. "What?"

"The guy… he called back to someone in the car, he called her Lily, and she was… she was screaming." His eyes became haunted. "She sounded scared. She kept saying 'we're gonna lose her.' And I remember thinking how strange that was. Dammit." He bent forward, disconnecting us, and gripped his head.

Lily.

Lose her.
That road.
Could it be…?

Lily was Calla's middle name, a nickname Kent called her on occasion.

No.

They wouldn't leave him…

But they might, if it saved their child.

He would turn himself in later…

But he wouldn't, not if it took him away from his daughter. And not after what happened to his brother.

All the questions were floating around in my mind, and yet in my heart I knew. Somehow, without any explanation, I knew what had happened that night.

Kent was the driver who ran Nick off the road.

Nineteen

Iris

NICK DROPPED ME OFF AT MY HOUSE AND BEFORE HE even left the neighborhood, I threw my luggage in the trunk and got in my car.

My mind was whirling. Even though I had no proof. Even though all I had was "Lily" and "we're gonna lose her," I knew the driver had been Kent. I *felt* it. Just like I felt the pit in my stomach telling me this would not end well for me.

God, what had he been thinking? How could he leave Nick there?

Guilt immediately plagued me. I might not have a niece—or even a sister—if he had stayed. How screwed up was that?

For the first time in my life, my heart felt like it was being pulled in two completely different directions. I always tried to do the right thing. The paths were always clear, like a child's fairy tale. One was bright and lined with flowers, while the other was darkened, decayed weeds leading you in to what was sure to be a miserable existence.

But now both paths looked the same. They were plain, with no distinguishing characteristics to tell me which was the right one to take. And did I even have a choice? Kent and Calla had sent me on their path without me even knowing it.

They must have known who Nick was; the dinner a few weeks back suddenly made perfect sense. Kent wasn't looking down on Nick. He was panicking.

My breathing stalled as I pulled up to their house. It was the picture-perfect home. Red door. Blue shutters. Wraparound porch and a white picket fence.

Legs shaking, I pulled myself from the car and walked up their front steps. I knocked quickly, still not able to process that this was the first thing I was doing after my incredible weekend. I'd been expecting to lounge around in bed and reminiscence about it all. Now it all felt tainted.

"Where's Kent?" I asked my sister as soon as she opened the door, practically storming by her on my way in.

Her worried eyes searched mine as she held Mirielle on her hip. "In his office," she answered slowly. "Why?"

"Good. Follow me."

The echo of my shoes followed me down the hallway, Calla's bare feet barely making a sound behind me. We reached the door and, without even knocking, I pushed it open.

"What's the—?" Kent had started to stand, but froze when he saw me with his wife.

I waved Calla inside and watched as the two exchanged a terrified look, like their world was seconds from imploding. I imagined this kind of fear had been a very present aspect of their relationship lately. How could it not be when they were carrying around a loaded weapon?

My sister took a deep breath. "Iris—"

"When?" I asked.

"What?" Kent finally snapped out of his trance and walked around his desk, taking my sister's hand.

"When did you know it was Nick you ran off the road?"

Even though they might have been expecting the words—actually hearing them—seemed to knock them backward. Kent's hand moved to Calla's lower back to support her, while she held Mirielle a little tighter.

Kent cleared his throat. "Since the beginning, when your mom told us you were donating your kidney to someone who'd been in a car accident."

"*Six* months? You've known for six months and haven't said anything? To me? To the police? What were you thinking?" Of course I knew what they'd been thinking. I was still having the same thoughts.

Kent hung his head and grabbed the back of his neck. "You make it sound so simple."

I knew it wasn't simple, but still… "You left a man to die—"

"Grow up!" Kent shouted.

I blinked and stumbled back. Even my sister looked shocked. Kent never raised his voice. He rarely even got upset. That was why his behavior toward Nick had been so bizarre.

"Just grow the fuck up, Iris. Not everything is black and white. Or have you forgotten your sister was in labor? Dealing with a pregnancy that was already unlikely. Calla could have had a stroke or bled out. Mirielle almost…" His eyes watered as he slumped against his desk and ran a hand over his face. When he looked back up, his eyes were terrified. My sister was softly crying as Mirielle started squirming, probably because Calla was holding her too tight.

"I didn't know what to do," he said softly. "Calla was screaming and crying and I… I panicked. I saw another car coming up the road, so I hopped back in and drove her to the hospital, hoping the other car would see him. I had every intention of reporting myself, I did. But then…" He trailed off and looked down at his daughter. "Then Mirielle was born and I didn't want to be taken from her. You know what happened with Keith…"

Everything froze. He hardly ever talked about his brother. I didn't even know the particulars; it had happened right after high school, before Kent was in our lives. What I did know was that Keith spent two years in prison for a crime he didn't commit. And even though he was eventually cleared of all charges, it forever altered his life—and his family's. So I could most definitely understand Kent's reluctance to trust the justice system.

My brother-in-law cleared his throat. "I'm not saying it's a good excuse. But… that's all I've got."

I felt drained—I'd already argued this point with myself countless times since Nick's nightmare last night. And not once could I envision a different scenario in which all the people I loved came out okay. I couldn't imagine the kind of craziness that ensued that night. I didn't know what I would have done.

But he'd gambled with Nick's life…

"How am I… how am I supposed to keep this from him? Oh God… what if he thinks I knew all along?" My hand was shaking as I brought it up to my mouth.

"He won't, Iris. Anyone who really knows you could never think that," Calla tried to reassure me.

"You don't know. You don't understand. He doesn't trust easily. And he trusts me." I looked over at my sister with tears in my eyes. "He finally trusts *me*."

I believed in a world of gray. Nick didn't. He would never understand. But more than that, I would never be able to keep this kind of secret.

"Calla, I can't live with something like this."

"Iris, I know what we're asking is a lot, but I need Kent. You know how long we've been trying. It was an accident, and look"—she waved her hand around the room with a forced smile—"everything is okay."

"We're lucky everything is okay, Calla," I said softly. "Nick could have *died*."

Her eyes shimmered with tears. "I could have too. Or Mirielle. Or both of us."

I stopped. Stopped breathing. Stopped blinking. Stopped hearing Calla's pleas to understand. Stopped seeing Mirielle's crying face right in front of me. And mostly, stopped pretending I didn't understand.

I did.

She was right.

Her pregnancy had been high risk. They were lucky to have gotten pregnant at all, and the doctor said if they'd arrived any later they would've most likely lost the baby. It would have ripped all our lives apart. But if Nick had died, it would have ripped Catherine's whole life apart.

How could the right thing also feel wrong?

How could I justify something that *happened* to turn out well? Kent had no way of knowing Nick would've survived. So what mattered more? His choice or the outcome?

Everything was muddled. There was no right answer. I couldn't justify one either way. I felt like I was drowning in a sea of gray.

"I… I have to go." I started to move on autopilot toward the door.

"Wait!" My sister grabbed my arm and swung me around. When our eyes met, I saw undisguised panic in hers. Before she could ask, I reassured her—well as much as I could, anyway.

"I'm not going to say anything. At least not right now. The truth is I have no idea what I'm feeling or what I'm going to do. But I promise I'll talk to you and Kent before I make the decision, okay?"

Her hand fell away, and even though I knew she was worried, I also knew she understood. "Yeah, okay," she responded softly.

"Iris?" Kent called out. I froze, but kept my back to him. "He doesn't need to know. The damage is done and if he's already moving forward, maybe this would just hurt him more…" His soft voice trailed off.

I continued out of their house without another word. Honestly, I was afraid of what words I'd say, and sometimes one word was all it took to destroy something. Like the word Nick recalled from his nightmare, the word that sent me down this path.

Lily.

A perfect weekend shattered by one word. In the right context, a single word had the power to derail my entire life.

I could feel it. It felt like a large weight on my chest, one that was with me all the time, and day after day it got heavier and heavier. I struggled to breathe.

I'd been avoiding Nick for the past couple days. I didn't want to, I didn't even *plan* to, but somehow something was always coming up. And it always seemed like the most important thing in the world.

But when Catherine called me and asked me to come over for dinner on Friday night, I had no excuse, and I didn't want one. I missed Nick.

When Friday night finally arrived, my nerves were at an all-time high. I knocked on Catherine's door, rocking back on my heels. It immediately flung open to reveal Nick's bright smile. The dimples that normally set my heart aflutter now felt like a taunt. I kept thinking, *How many more times will I get to see them? How many more times will they be aimed at me?*

"Hey." He leaned forward and wrapped an arm around my waist, pulling me into him. Nick's lips met mine, hungry, and it took everything in me to match him. Because I didn't want hurried kisses, I wanted slow and sweet. I wanted to remember…

Nick pulled away and brushed some of the hair back from my face. "You okay?"

"Yeah. I'm just a bit tired." I smiled—hoping it didn't look as forced as it felt. His hand moved to the back of my head, gently massaging.

"Hopefully not too tired." His mouth dipped to my neck and he lightly kissed my pulse. "I've missed you," he breathed.

"Me too," I whispered.

"Quit hogging her," Catherine yelled as she came up beside us. I chuckled and backed away. She immediately pulled me into a hug.

"Hi, Iris." Trevor waved, and I took one hand off Catherine's back to do the same.

She stepped back and held me at arm's length. "Now I know you've been spoiled by Nicky's cooking, but just remember, you loved mine at one point."

Everyone chuckled, but mine tapered off a little early. She noticed and brought the back of her hand to my forehead.

"Are you all right, dear?"

"Yeah. Yeah." I tried to wave off her concern, but she frowned, unconvinced.

Nick began rubbing my back, looking down at me with a little more worry, before addressing his mom. "We might bug out early, just so I can make sure she gets some rest." And I could tell he actually meant rest this time.

"Of course."

"That's really not necessary—"

"You've had a pretty busy week," he said to me. Guilt sat heavy in my stomach, spreading. "We'll just relax this weekend. I'll take care of you."

Catherine looked incredibly pleased as she bounced toward the kitchen. Nick smiled and led me to the already set table. He held my hand and began asking me about my week. I felt like I was on autopilot as I answered them.

"Sorry." I rubbed my head. I'd just answered with "good" for the fourth time.

"Don't worry about it."

"Are you sure—?"

"Dinner's ready," Catherine chirped as she came over and set a large platter on the table. After Nick helped his mother and Trevor bring out a few more dishes—he insisted I stay seated—we all joined hands while Nick prayed.

"Dear Heavenly Father. Thank you for this food you've blessed us with today. Thank you for my loving mother. And thank you for Iris, one of the most caring and genuine women I've ever known…" He squeezed my hand and it might as well have been my lungs, because I stopped breathing. "Thank you for this wonderful family. Amen."

"Amen" echoed around the table, and when I opened my eyes Nick was staring at me. His hand was still in mine and he gave it one final squeeze before he let go. I looked down at my plate, one word circling in my head.

Family.

He thought of me as family. I had started to see him that way too. Where were my loyalties supposed to lie?

I loved my family. It had never mattered that they weren't blood; I loved them like they were. And when Calla met Kent freshmen year in college, he easily became a part of our family as well.

A family's job was to protect one another. To protect those you loved at any cost. But… I loved Nick and Catherine, too.

Where was the justice in any of this?

The only way I could help one was to destroy the other.

He doesn't need to know.

Kent's traitorous words kept flashing through my head, and with each passing day they dug down a little further, cemented themselves a little more, until the idea didn't seem as ridiculous as it had when he first suggested it.

But I knew—ridiculous or not—I wouldn't be able to continue my relationship with Nick, not with this lie between us.

Nick

Our hearts were pounding fast. Unlike that dance in her kitchen months earlier, they were the same speed. Both living to the fullest. Both living with so much pleasure our hearts wanted to burst free.

I tried to get Iris to relax when we got here, but as soon as I walked through the door she pulled me into a thought-shattering kiss, and an hour later here we were. Sweaty and spent, and tangled in her sheets.

She was lying on her stomach, her head tilted my way with her eyes closed and a small, exhausted smile on her face. Her bedding was bunched around her waist, covering her legs and leaving her back exposed. My fingers itched to trace her spine, to feel her shivers as they dipped beneath the sheet and found her center, circling her clit until she was writhing and panting for more. Then I'd lift her to her knees and slam into her from behind…

Despite my fatigue, my cock suddenly thought that was a brilliant idea, sinking into the woman I loved…

Because I did. I loved her. More than anyone. More than I thought humanly possible. And I couldn't hold it in any longer.

"I love you," I whispered. She stilled and her eyes slowly opened as I held my breath. I hadn't said those words to a woman in four years. I hadn't planned to do it tonight. But sometimes the right moment couldn't be planned. It could only be seized.

"What?" she choked out, shocked.

Scooting closer, I rested my hand against the center of her back. "I love you."

Iris sat up, my hand dropping in the process, and wrapped the bedding around herself completely.

I tried not to let my disappointment show when she didn't immediately respond—especially since she looked troubled by the prospect. But the feeling was coursing through me as naturally as the blood in my veins.

Iris's mouth opened and shut as she teared up. Regardless of my dejection, I didn't want her to feel bad for something she might not be ready for. She deserved as much time to figure out her feelings as I did.

"It's okay. Wait until you're ready." I smiled and ran my hand through her hair.

"Nick, I'm sor—"

"Don't apologize. It's okay, really." Leaning forward, I gave her a kiss. She still seemed unsettled, and part of me almost regretted saying it. Maybe it had been too soon. We'd only been officially seeing each other for three months.

I pulled her into my arms, hoping to calm her turmoil. Unfortunately it did nothing for the mounting anxiety inside me.

Iris

I could see the naked vulnerability as he told me he loved me, anxiously waiting for me to return the words. But I couldn't do it.

He told me he loved me.

And I was just sitting here.

Oh God.

But how could I say it back when I was lying to him? Keeping something so monumental from him? How was this ever supposed to work out in my favor?

My thoughts were spiraling, and I felt tears of frustration build in my eyes.

"Hey, hey," Nick whispered, scooting closer. "Really, you don't need to say it back. That's not why I told you. I don't expect you to return it. I took my time, you take yours."

He interpreted my freak-out wrong.

I wanted to shout, OF COURSE I LOVE YOU! But I couldn't.

"Seriously, I don't need you to say it back." And with a smile he leaned forward and placed a gentle kiss on my lips. My hand curled into a fist around his T-shirt, my heart swelling and breaking all at once.

Everyone wanted to hear it back. I didn't care if you were the nicest, most patient person on the planet, when you told someone you loved them, you wanted to hear it back. Even if you weren't hurt, you were a little disappointed—you had to be.

So I tried to say it in other ways.

My hands said it as I caressed his chest.

My lips whispered it as I kissed him.

"Lie down," I murmured. He obeyed, scrambling backward. I crawled after him, my hands brushing his legs every time I moved. I was midway when I paused. My left hand was on the mattress by his hip, while my right skimmed the inside of his thigh. My touch was light and teasing, and I loved watching his eyes heat as he looked at me.

"Iris…" he whispered, his hands forming fists to keep himself from touching me.

Flattening my palm on his leg, I moved up slowly until I was cupping his balls, gently rolling them in my hand. I felt my underwear become damp at Nick's low moan. He sounded completely tortured.

I decided to put him out of his misery, leaning down and wrapping my lips around the tip of his dick.

"Shit." His hand snaked out and gripped my hair, pulling me closer. I eagerly opened my mouth, taking as much of him as I could. "Fuck yes."

My other hand fisted around the base of him as I slowly worked him over. I groaned as he grabbed my hair tighter and started slowly pumping, taking control. Nick's pants echoed throughout the room and just when I thought he was close, he pulled me up and smashed his lips against mine.

"I wanna come inside you," he whispered against my mouth before kissing me again. I had no complaints.

Then he pushed into me—the first stroke since saying *I love you*, and I closed my eyes at how perfect it all felt. But also because I wasn't sure I wouldn't cry. This kind of perfection just highlighted all I had to lose.

That night, I fell asleep with his kiss on my lips, and I knew I would wake up tomorrow with his love wrapped around me.

But for how much longer?

Twenty

Iris

LIES WERE LIKE A VIRUS, TOUCHING EVERYTHING, infecting everything... even the truth. I couldn't find solace in a single thing I said to Nick. Everything was tainted because of a single lie.

I didn't understand how people could do this so frequently; it felt like I was suffocating under the weight of it.

"Iris, are you okay?" Catherine asked as she placed a hand on my arm. Snapping out of my trance, I turned to face her.

"Oh, yeah. Sorry. I guess I spaced out." I smiled and moved to step around her when she stopped me.

"Are you sure?" Her voice was low and concerned. "Maybe you're coming down with something." She put the back of her hand to my forehead. I felt like the small child she was treating me as.

I gently grabbed her wrist and pulled it away. Trying to

give her a more reassuring smile, I said, "Yes. I'm fine. Just stressed with the end of school, I suppose."

It was the middle of December, classes were wrapping up and it was a plausible enough excuse. But truthfully I was overwhelmed. I rarely felt this way, but surrounded by everyone I loved (minus Aster, who wasn't flying in until the twenty-second), and with a black cloud hanging over us, I felt completely alone and incapable of handling what was to come.

My parents decided to have a Christmas party. They wanted Kent and Calla to have a do-over with Nick, and they also figured it was a perfect time to meet Nick's mom. But they invited over other friends so it didn't resemble the ambush from a month earlier.

Catherine brought Trevor, and that was who Nick was currently talking to. Kent and Calla had done an excellent job steering clear of him, and every time my mother noticed she frowned and looked at me in question. I shrugged and downed whatever drink was nearby.

So now I was lying to my mom.

And every time Nick looked over at me, he seemed worried. Not for himself, but because, like Catherine, he thought I was getting sick. They had all this concern—all this love—for me and I was lying to them.

I spotted Calla across the room, bouncing Mirielle and staring at her husband with a faraway look, like she'd already lost him.

My hand laid flat against my stomach. I was truly going to be sick.

"Really, dear. Maybe you should go lie down…"

My eyes met my sister's. She nodded—resigned—and inclined her head toward the bedrooms before disappearing down the hall. I looked back at Catherine. "That sounds like a good idea. Will you let Nick know if he asks?"

She smiled. "You mean when."

"Huh?" I asked, already distracted by the conversation Calla and I were about to have.

"You mean *when* Nick asks about you." Catherine pushed a stray strand of hair behind my ear. "Because he will. I've never seen him like this with someone. Like he always wants to know where you are. Not in a creepy way," she rushed to add, providing me with my first real laugh tonight.

"You're just…" I held my breath as she thought of the word. "The sun. *His* sun. He orbits around you, like he has no choice. Like you're necessary to his survival."

My heart stopped. It was quite possibly the sweetest thing she could have said.

You're lying to her. You're lying to him.

That thought kick-started my heart, cracking it right down the middle.

"Listen to me." Catherine blushed and waved away the words. "I start dating and become a sappy romantic."

Leaning forward, I hugged her. "Thank you," I whispered. I didn't know what for, possibly for everything. For coming into my life. For bringing Nick into my life. Or just for being who she was.

We pulled away and with one last watery smile, I turned and left before I could blurt everything out. My steps were quick as I walked down the hall toward the room my parents had set up for Mirielle.

I stopped short in the doorway when I heard my sister's soft cries. She had put her daughter in the crib and was standing above it, staring down at her. With one last glance down the hall, I stepped through and shut the door.

"I never wanted to put you in this position," she whispered.

"I know, and I…" I stepped away from the door and went to her side. "I don't know what I'm supposed to do. I love you and Kent. But I love Nick, too."

Calla sniffled. "I know you do." She looked up at me with a small smile. "It's in your eyes."

I reached down and rubbed my niece's cheek.

"He told me he loved me, but I couldn't say it back. Not when…" I pulled my hand away when I felt it clench in frustration.

What did my love mean if he didn't know? Like a tree falling in the forest when no one was around, was my love of any use if I couldn't tell Nick?

"I've tried, Calla. I have, but I can't do this anymore. It's only been a week but I feel like I'm being ripped apart. I can't lie to him. Every day he looks at me with so much love and trust, and every time I continue to say nothing, I'm betraying that. I love him. And I haven't been able to say it because I don't want to do it with a tainted heart. *Please…*" I started crying.

My big sister pulled me into her arms, holding me secure with one hand around my back and comforting me with the other as she ran her hand down my hair.

"Shhh… I already talked to Kent last night. We both understand. We're… we're so sorry, Iris. This wasn't how any of it was supposed to go."

Mirielle slept peacefully, her soft snores filling the room, while Calla and I held on to each other and fell apart.

Nick

Iris was acting weird. I tried not to read into it. I tried not to assume it had anything to do with me saying "I love you." But nearly a week had passed and she was still fidgety.

I was standing with Trevor, talking about how I was looking into taking a couple business classes so I could start making owning my own restaurant a reality, when my eyes landed on my ma. She was standing by herself, staring down the hallway I knew led to the bedrooms.

"She's worried about Iris." I looked back to see his eyes on my ma as well, a frown pulling at his features.

"Me too. She…" I blew out a breath and grabbed the back of my neck. "I told her I loved her. I think it might have freaked her out." But even as I said it, it didn't feel right. I just couldn't imagine what else was going on.

"Your mom told me what happened last time you guys were here," Trevor said with a shrug. "Maybe she's worried about a repeat."

Nodding, I looked around for Iris. It was a possibility, but again, it didn't feel like the truth. I frowned when I couldn't find her—also noting that Calla was missing—before excusing myself to go talk to my ma. Trevor said he'd hit the bathroom and join us, but really I think he was just giving us privacy.

"Hey," I said as I walked up. She turned toward me, throwing on a bright smile.

"Hi, dear."

My lips lifted, trying to match her smile. "Do you know where Iris is?"

"Oh. She still wasn't feeling well. I told her to go lie

down." My smile dropped as I moved away from my ma, but she stopped me. "Maybe give her a few minutes?"

I tried to relax as I nodded, but it was really just to appease my mother. When Iris and Calla stepped out of a bedroom door ten minutes later, I felt my muscles loosen. They were whispering, their shoulders hunched over like a painful weight rested on both of them.

Iris's eyes met mine when they split up at the mouth of the hallway. My mother and Trevor had been talking amongst themselves for the past five minutes, so I didn't bother saying anything before I made my way to Iris.

"Hi." She smiled—nowhere near as bright as normal—in response, but didn't say anything. "You feeling better?"

"A little." I pulled her into a hug and rubbed my hands up and down her back. Her arms wrapped around my waist and settled on my lower back. And I felt her sigh in relief as she snuggled closer to me, assuaging some of my unease.

Iris stayed close to me for the rest of the night. I didn't mind, but it felt like such a one-eighty from her pulling away that I felt a building dread in my stomach. One that told me I was about to be crushed.

The only good thing about my mind being this preoccupied with Iris was that I barely had any time to think about Kent. We exchanged a few tense nods, but other than that, it was like he didn't exist.

Until the end.

Everyone else had cleared out. The only people left were Iris and her family, my ma, Trevor, and me. Kent and Calla were in the nursery, checking on Mirielle, while the rest of us said goodbye in the foyer.

"Nicky, why don't you and Iris go say goodnight to Mirielle? Trevor and I will wait here," my ma said with a wide grin. I knew what she was doing. She was trying to get me to have at least one conversation with Kent tonight. Iris seemed a bit taken aback, and she looked like she was about to let me off the hook. But I knew how much this would mean to my mother.

"Sure, Ma," I said as I grabbed Iris's hand. "We'll be right back."

It felt like I was dragging her down the hallway. We both stopped when we heard low voices and sniffles coming from the room.

"It'll be okay. Please believe me," Kent said. I frowned as Iris froze next to me.

"I'm scared," Calla cried.

"Don't be. We're going to make it through this as a family. I promise."

"I love you."

"I love you, too, Lily."

Now it was my turn to freeze.

Lily?

"Lily, I don't…" He sounded torn.

Iris's hand jerked in mine and I let go.

It couldn't be…

This is the only way to and from their house…

Fertility treatments…

Lose her…

As the pieces fell into place, I felt myself being torn apart. But I tried to hold out hope. I turned my head toward Iris, ready to find her confused.

When my eyes met hers, my knees nearly buckled.

She wasn't confused.

She knew exactly what had happened.

And like an idiot, I'd let myself fall… again…

I knew it. I fucking knew it.

That was the first conscious thought I had once I got over the shock.

"Nick," Iris began, reaching for me. I stepped back and glared, swiftly shaking my head before I stormed past her and into the room.

"It was you?" I asked Kent as the door slammed against the wall. They both looked down into the crib as I felt Iris come up behind me.

"Can we talk somewhere else? She's sleeping…" Calla whispered.

"Sure. Let's go in the backyard and have some hot cocoa and sit around the fire pit while we discuss this," I bit back.

"Nick—" Kent began.

"No." I was tired of lies. "Did you run me off the road?"

He swallowed, running his gaze over his wife before looking back at his daughter. With his head still facing the crib, he said, "Yes."

"We're sorry. It was an accident—" Iris's sister started before I cut her off.

"Stop. I don't want to hear any of it. I just… I can't believe I was actually this stupid."

"Nick, you weren't—" Iris spoke up again.

"Don't. Just don't." I shook my head. "I have to get out of here." I about-faced and walked toward the front door. There had been no shouts, so when I heard their laughter abruptly cut off upon seeing my face, I wasn't surprised.

"What's wrong?" my ma asked as she stepped forward.

"Is Mirielle okay?" Iris's mother immediately asked, looking ready to race down the hall.

"She's fine. I'm leaving."

"Nick, wait," Iris said as she joined us, Kent and Calla closely behind her. "I'm sorry."

"What's going on?"

Iris turned toward my mother, ready to explain, but I beat her to it.

"Remember how I wondered why a perfect stranger would give someone their kidney?" Iris paled as my ma's wide eyes shifted between us. "Kent here is responsible for putting me in the hospital. That's why Iris sought you out, why she gave me her kidney."

I turned to face Iris, really looking at her for the first time. "Was it out of guilt? Or were you hoping to keep me quiet in case I remembered something?"

"What?" she gasped—and I had to give her credit, she looked genuinely horrified. Her face paled further and her lips went slack. But I wasn't falling for it. Not again. I still couldn't quite wrap my head around the fact that I was in this place again, betrayed by someone who I thought loved me…

But she never said it back, did she?

"Please, Nick… that wasn't it at all. I love you. I didn't—"

"Oh, *now* you love me?" I asked, my hands clenching into fists. "Well if that's not a Hail fucking Mary, I don't know what is. I said it a week ago, and what did I get? Nothing. Not a damn word. Just a smile and a kiss. Like that would keep me from noticing the three words I *didn't* get back? But now that you're in hot water, all of a sudden you love me?"

I could feel my lips curl into a snarl. "Let me guess? I'm not to go to the cops with this? That's why I'm suddenly worthy of your love, right?"

"N-no, of c-course not. I—I…" She trailed off as a loud sob racked her body. "I didn't want to lie, but I felt like I didn't have a choice."

I firmly planted my feet and crossed my arms. I would *not* walk over to her. I would *not* comfort her.

"Everyone has a choice. The choices may suck. They may be hard as hell to make. But everyone has a choice. *You* had a choice, and it wasn't me."

I watched her flinch and stumble back, like I actually hit her, and I'd never hated myself more. Her sister was softly crying in the corner as Kent stepped forward.

"Nick—"

"Don't," I growled, my head swinging toward him. "Don't you say a fucking word! You left me for dead on the side of the road without a care in the fucking world."

"That's not true."

I shook my head and turned to leave when Iris reached out and grabbed my wrist. "Please—"

I ripped my arm away and watched in horror as she lost her balance and fell to the floor. She looked up at me like she didn't know me.

At that moment, I didn't either.

Iris waved away any offers for help and stood up on her own. Then she wrapped her arms around herself, like she was holding herself together. Something that was supposed to be my job.

"I know you don't believe me, but I didn't know—"

"You're right, I don't," I interrupted.

"Nicholas," my mother hissed. I turned to find her disapproving eyes on me. How could she still not see?

"I'm leaving." Shaking my head, I headed toward the door.

"Nick," Calla called out frantically. "I know we have no

right to ask anything of you, but… could you wait until after Christmas before you call the police? I… we'd like to see our daughter's first Christmas."

I shut my eyes against the pain. Not just mine. Calla's. Kent's. Iris's. Hell, everyone's. We were all hurting for different reasons.

I didn't answer as I continued out the door, ignoring the cries and shouts for me to stop, to understand, to let them explain… I ignored it all.

Their explanations would fall on angry, deaf ears. In that moment, I truly didn't care. I didn't want excuses or to be comforted. I wanted to be alone.

Anger was the easiest mask to slip on, the most readily available. It was bulletproof—nearly indestructible. Little could penetrate it. Not grief, reason, or love.

Twenty-One

Iris

YOU HAD ZERO CONTROL OVER HOW YOU FELL IN LOVE. You didn't get to choose the speed or what was waiting for you at the bottom. You didn't get to decide if there were obstacles in your path, or what kind they were. You didn't even get a say in whether you had a parachute and would float to the ground safely, or if you'd crash and burn.

I had thought I was safe on the ground, only to discover I had been caught on something in the sky. Now all that was left was for me to fall. There were no more obstacles because Nick was done with me.

There was just the fall.

No parachute.

No soft landing.

Just a hard, unforgiving slab of concrete.

And the higher up you were, the faster you fell, and the more the impact hurt.

It freaking *hurt*.

I touched an ornament on my Christmas tree, the one Nick said was his favorite, and tried not to cry.

It had been two weeks since I'd seen him. Two weeks of nothing but tears and heartache. I tried calling but he never answered. I sent texts that all went unreturned. I stopped by his apartment but he was never home or he ignored me. And every single time one of those things happened, I felt another piece of my heart fracture.

A heart doesn't break once. It breaks dozens of times, and sometimes there weren't even pieces left to be put back together. Sometimes a heart broke so much that there was just dust, remnants of what once was. I feared that was how this would end.

Stepping back, I sat on the couch and stared at the tree. It looked perfect, just like I thought it would when Nick and I had picked it out.

A loud knock startled me and had me jumping from the couch before I could think twice about it. I had enough sense to look through the peephole first.

My heart deflated slightly; it wasn't Nick.

But it was another Blake. I smoothed my palms along my yoga pants before opening the door. I didn't know what to expect. Catherine had always been kind to me, but then again I'd never deceived and broken her son's heart before. I hadn't seen her since that awful night either.

"Oh, dear." She stepped forward and immediately wrapped me up in a hug. My tense muscles relaxed and I crumpled against her, overwhelmed by the fact that she didn't hate me.

"I'm sorry," I whispered through my tears. "I didn't…"

"Shhh… it's okay," she said over my sobs, her hand brushing back my hair just like Nick used to. After I calmed down, she shut the door and brought me back to the couch.

"Let me get you some tea."

I started to stand. "No, no. You're the guest—"

"Iris," she began sternly. "You haven't seen this side of me yet, but I do not take no for an answer when it comes to consoling."

Catherine didn't give me another chance to say no, she simply walked out of the room and started rummaging through the kitchen. I'd almost forgotten she had never been here. We'd exchanged phone numbers and addresses when we first met, but she hadn't had a reason to come over.

"You have a beautiful house," she said when she came back a few minutes later and set the cup in front of me. I thanked her before taking a sip. I was smiling as I put it back on the coffee table.

Lemongrass.

My favorite.

"How have you been?"

"Oh. You know… super. I'm spending Christmas Eve alone, wallowing in my house. That's normal, right?" I had been trying to make a joke of it, but my breath hitched at the end, revealing my near sob.

"Okay," she said. "No small talk it is. I'm just going to dive right in."

I didn't know if that was better or worse.

"Nick never chased Colleen," she began. "First and foremost, remember *that*."

He wasn't chasing me either…

I kept that thought to myself.

"Let me start at the beginning." She cleared her throat and leaned forward. "Nick was angry when his father left. He became instantly distrustful of the world and I don't think he ever got over that. He was always waiting for someone to be proved distrustful, so when he learned what Colleen had done, he wasn't all that surprised or heartbroken. She apologized and she wanted to work it out. I believe she did love him, just not as much as her career. And she knew how both Nicky and I, being Catholic, would feel about the abortion. She did what was best for her, and I think that gave him the reassurance he needed, that people couldn't be trusted. But, he never thought about going back to Colleen. He's always been firm: once a liar, always a liar, circumstances don't matter."

I wondered if she knew she was breaking my heart, if she knew she was slowly chipping away at the little bit of hope I'd let build in my chest. Looking down toward my cup of tea, I felt tears welling once more. This was crueler than any insults she could have thrown at me. I knew she didn't mean it that way— Catherine was the sweetest woman I'd ever met. But hearing this, hearing he'd never forgive me and that I'd have to live the rest of my life with this all-encompassing love, knowing it'd never be returned again… well, it killed me.

Nick walked away. Just like he did with Colleen. Just like he said he'd do if he thought the fight wasn't worth it.

I wasn't worth it.

And when I thought I couldn't hurt any more, she reached out and gently squeezed my hand. "Iris," she said softly. I forced my gaze up and found her frowning with tears in her eyes as well. Moving her hand, she cupped my cheek like she would a small child's.

"I'm not saying this to hurt you."

I nodded. "I know, you're just… you're being honest. And I-I'm grateful. I'd probably have gone my whole life holding on to the hope that he could someday look at me like he once did, love me like he did. So… t-thank you." I pulled her hand from my face and gave it a squeeze. I needed to get her out of the house before I started full-on bawling.

"I-I appreciate it, and I'm not trying to be rude, but I'm not feeling well. I think I need to go lie down now." I tried to smile but somehow those signals never made it from my brain to my mouth, because I felt my lips stay in a flat line. I moved to stand when Catherine gripped my hand and pulled me back down.

"I wasn't done, dear." I closed my eyes as my butt hit the cushion, because really... she was killing me. "When their relationship ended he was just more surly, more angry. I think he hated to be proven right, but he was settled because he felt confident in his assumption that people only looked out for themselves."

She stopped, forcing me to open my eyes. I found a bright smile on her face, like whatever she was thinking about gave her more joy than she'd ever known. So I was floored when she said, "And then you came along, and completely blew his expectations away. I remember the first time he saw you, the first time you started speaking... Lord, he looked so scared." She laughed as she let go of my hand, finally convinced I wasn't leaving.

"That's a good thing?" I sniffled.

"Oh, yes. A man in love is a man afraid. Or at least a man who has the potential to fall in love." Her laughter tapered off as she scooted closer and wrapped her arm around me. It struck me that this was very similar to the day we met, how she held me in the hospital chapel when we prayed.

"He wants to forgive you, Iris," she said softly. "He's sad. I don't think I've ever seen my Nicky sad. He gets angry, sure. But sad? Never." I frowned. I never wanted to make him sad. "That's another good thing." She elbowed me in the side, getting a small grin out of me.

Catherine brushed my hair back from my face. "He's not a perfect man, Iris. But he's a good man."

"The best," I whispered. "You don't need to convince me."

"I had a feeling not, but I needed to make sure. And you're one of the good ones too."

"Are you on your way to Nick's?" I asked, eyes forward.

"Yeah," she said softly.

I stood and walked over to the tree before bending down to pick up Nick's present. Catherine appeared beside me as I stared down at it, a single teardrop landing on the laughing Santa wrapping paper. Quickly wiping it away, I pivoted and held it out to her.

"Will you give this to him?" I gazed down at the card neatly tucked under the bow in one corner. Her eyes stayed on my face as I gently pulled it out and set it on the mantel. "Maybe you shouldn't tell him it's from me. Just… I want him to still have it," I finished on a whisper.

"Of course." She looked toward the coffee table. "Well I know you're tired, so I'll get out of your hair. Do you happen to have a to-go mug for my tea? I hate to impose, but—"

"Oh no. Don't worry about it. Gimme a second." I quickly filled up a cup for her and met her at the door where she was standing, tightly clutching her purse.

"Thanks, dear," she said as she took it. Catherine managed to balance the gift and the mug as she gave me a one-handed hug. "Don't lose faith. He'll come around."

I gave her a small smile and held the door open for her. "I'll try."

She quickly walked to her car as I closed and fell back against the door.

It wasn't until Catherine was long gone that I realized Nick's card was too.

Nick

It was Christmas Eve, and I was spending it sitting on my couch with a bottle of beer in one hand and the TV remote in the other.

I wasn't any closer to making a decision. I'd picked up the phone countless times to call the detective from my case, but I could never dial the number. Despite my initial shock and anger, the only feelings left were confusion and sadness.

I thought back to Iris's words from all those weeks ago when I showed up with flowers after being an asshole… *I don't believe in holding grudges. I believe in forgiveness. But that doesn't mean I hand it out for free.*

The problem was I didn't know how to hand it out at all. I didn't know if I could forgive her. I wasn't as pure as Iris. I didn't forgive the driver who cut me off in traffic; I honked and gave him my middle finger. I didn't forgive Robby Stewart who broke my favorite Tonka truck in the fifth grade; I never spoke to him again.

I wasn't a man who forgave. I was a man who held grudges. And even though that made me a jackass, that was who I was, and I didn't know how to change it.

But as I sat there thinking about it, I realized my grudges never really mattered to the parties who'd wronged me. The driver kept going, none the wiser. Robby made new friends. And if I couldn't forgive Iris, she'd find someone else.

Sucker punched. That's what that thought felt like.

Hearts were weird. And the concept of breaking them even stranger.

Apparently a broken heart could love just as much as a whole one, because even though she'd lied, I still loved her.

I froze when a knock echoed throughout my apartment. "Nicky, it's me." Blowing out a breath, I tried to convince myself it was relief and not disappointment I felt when I heard my mother's voice.

On autopilot, I got up and unlocked the door before slinking back to the couch and resuming my position. I heard her lock the door and set something down on the table before she moved across the room to where I was.

"You're an idiot." I looked at my mother then back at the TV.

"Is that a general statement or are you referencing something specific?" I could only imagine the unimpressed look on her face. But when she stormed in front of me and shut off the TV, I didn't have to imagine anymore. Because I was looking right at her. Her face was set in a deep frown that managed to look sad, pissed, and worried all at once.

"Nicky," she said sadly.

"Ma—"

"No. I'm talking now. I understand, okay? I do. But Iris is not Colleen. I know it. You know it. Iris is a wonderful person who was caught in a terrible situation. You talked about the right choice like it was something universal. It wasn't. There was no *right* choice that night. What if I had been in that car, bleeding to death, and you had to decide, knowing there was another car coming up, what would you have done?"

I sighed and pulled my feet from the coffee table. The truth was I *did* understand. The more I thought about it, the more I realized the entire situation was a clusterfuck and there was no right answer. But understanding didn't take away how much it hurt.

"I can tell she loves you, dear. But I can also tell you this: she is not a girl who will wait around. She's down right now because she's hurting and she knows she hurt you. But she recognizes her worth. She knows she deserves someone who can forgive and move on." My ma kicked my foot until I looked up. "And I know that's one of the things you love about her."

She came to sit next to me. "You've always had trouble trusting people. Even before Colleen. Despite your belief that your problems began with her, that's not the truth. You only noticed it then. They began long ago, before you even realized it. It began with your father."

I opened my mouth to refute her, but she stopped me. "Let me finish. You may not think that's the case, and maybe it wasn't the 'big' shift, but it was the seed. No one's born a certain way, believing certain things. It all comes to us as we grow. And just like a flower, it all starts with a tiny seed. Your father planted that seed of doubt, distrust, and fear." She grabbed my hands. "Colleen was just the water and sun that let it grow until eventually it was so big you couldn't ignore it. You were forced to see the truth of some people. But you're so busy looking at that one flower, that you can't see all the beautiful ones surrounding it.

"Fear can be overwhelming, it can block out everything else. But if you move just a little bit, Nicky, you'll see all the greatness this world has to offer. There is great love to be had in this world. Don't confuse that message with the people trying to deliver it. People make mistakes." She wrapped her arm around my shoulders.

"You're hurting. I'm not saying you shouldn't be. But she's hurting, too. And even though technically we can find people to blame, sometimes situations just suck. Don't wait too long to figure it out."

I nodded, letting that sink in right before she threw something else at me.

"I went by Iris's place tonight."

My heart stopped. It took everything not to ask about her.

How is she?

Did she look good?

Is the tree up?

Is my ornament still on it?

I looked over and saw my mom giving me a knowing smile. Rolling my eyes, I turned to face her completely, her arm falling away, and cleared my throat. "How was she?"

"She's looked better."

I looked toward the TV, that knowledge hurting me more than anything else. Iris never deserved to feel down, and the only reason she was was because of me.

My gaze was still on the TV when my ma bent down and kissed me on the cheek. Only when she pulled away did I notice she'd gotten up and grabbed a box. She gently set it down on the coffee table before walking to the front door.

Pausing with her hand on the knob, she said, "If you can't trust what I'm telling you. Trust *that*. I don't know what the card says or what Iris got you. But I have no doubt that it's perfect for you. Because the woman I know, the woman you *love*, is incapable of anything less."

She left, and I got up to lock the door behind her, my head hitting the wood as tears filled my eyes.

When I was younger I let my father fill my head with fantasies of him returning. But he said all that out of guilt. He hadn't been thinking of me at all. He just wanted to make himself feel better, and when he changed his mind he made sure he wasn't there to see the consequences: my pain and devastation.

When Colleen lied to me, at least she didn't give me any fake excuses. She owned what she did. That didn't mean I could forgive her, but she faced it.

But right now, with Iris, I had no clue how to handle it. How do you forgive someone for a betrayal they weren't even aware of?

My knee-jerk reaction had been that she was lying and I was being manipulated again. But with some thought I realized that that reaction was based on nothing more than my past experiences, because I hadn't been thinking about Iris. I thought of my father and Colleen.

Expectation comes from experience.

The more thought I gave it, the more I realized Iris couldn't have faked it all. Three months of touches, kisses, love… there was no way to fake all that.

I turned around and my stare immediately landed on Iris's gift. Without another thought, I strode forward and grabbed the box, running my fingers over the card.

My heart felt like it was about to beat out of my chest as I sat down and opened it. I knew whatever the gift was would pale in comparison to the words she wrote. The card was simple; the front depicted a lone Christmas tree and the inside was blank except for her handwriting.

Nick,

Merry Christmas!!

I've never been more excited to spend Christmas with someone. Every single day we spend together is my new favorite day. You mean more to me than I'll ever be able to express. I've never felt so safe in someone's hold. I've never felt such peace in someone's touch. I've never felt so much love in someone's kiss.

I can't wait for what comes next.

xoxo,
Iris

Below that was a new note, in a different color, like it was added on later.

I love you.

I needed to say it (or write it, I guess) at least once and imagine you believe me. Maybe it's easier knowing you'll never read this.

But I do, I love you more than I know how to say. The only reason I never told you earlier was because I didn't want it to be said on a breath of lies and misplaced trust.

I look back to this card I wrote before everything went to hell and I think, I can't believe I was so naïve. My hand is shaking as I write this. Is that weird? Is it weird that my heart constantly feels like it's breaking? It's not just once, I've discovered. Every time I think of you, it shatters, which is pretty much every single second of the day.

I'm sorry. I'm sorry for lying. I'm sorry for what Kent did. I'm sorry that part of me is still conflicted over what the right choice was that night. I'm just sorry. But mostly I'm sorry I was another example, another lesson in your belief that you shouldn't trust people. I hope you don't lose the lightness you've found. You deserve to be happy.

I know I screwed up. But I can't help but feel like I was set up for it. You can't live your life waiting for people to fail you. If you do, they will, one hundred percent of the time. Especially if you won't accept an explanation. I guess I thought it was different between us, but maybe not. Either way, I own up to my mistake.

And I'm not saying you need to apologize to me. I just hope you don't spend your life waiting for the other shoe to drop. I hope you enjoy what you have, and if a time comes where your next partner does disappoint you, I hope you'll give her the benefit of the doubt.

I hope you'll find the woman you love enough to fight for. I'm just sorry it wasn't me.

My eyes watered as I placed the card aside and unwrapped the gift. Once I saw what it was, there was zero chance of stopping the tears from falling over and running down my cheeks. It was a set of expensive knives, complete with an engraving on the outside of the wooden box holding them. It read: *Nicholas Blake, Executive Chef & Owner.*

There was a post-it, explaining that the blank space below was left so I could add my restaurant's name once I had one.

My chest ached. She was right. Just like I had with Colleen—inadvertently or not—I had been waiting for Iris to hurt me. If we were a sinking ship, she would have been the water that was accidentally pulling us under, but I was the one who fucking drilled holes in the bottom.

It took two to dissolve a relationship. But sometimes there only needed to be one to fight for it. I didn't know where her head was at. It had only been a couple weeks, but my mother was right—Iris wouldn't wait forever.

Either way, she was about to find out that she was the only woman I could love enough to fight for.

Twenty-Two

Iris

It was awkward. No one knew what to say to me, Kent, or Calla. I watched as Kent held Mirielle close to his chest, like she was about to be ripped away from him at any moment. Calla looked on with the same kind of horror and despair on her face.

We'd never had dinners like this—especially Christmas dinner—it was my mom's favorite holiday, and I hated that we were ruining it for her.

My loneliness was bearing down on me as I gazed at the three couples. Even wrapped in sadness, fear, or awkwardness, I was jealous of what they had.

My parents. Kent and Calla with Mirielle. And Aster, who brought his new girlfriend, Becky. They all had someone, and while I was happy for them—I truly was—it was hard to watch.

I missed Nick. He should be sitting here beside me. But I was slowly coming to think that nothing I did would have mattered. Our fate was decided the moment Kent ran him off the road. We would always be linked by that night. I could have told him my suspicions the second he woke up from his nightmare. I could have driven to his house and revealed everything after I confronted Kent and Calla. At any point in the last two weeks of our relationship, I could have said something, and I still would have ended up here alone.

Because even if Nick forgave me, even if he never had to worry about forgiving me in the first place, he wouldn't forgive Kent.

And could anything ever blossom between us when he couldn't be around my family? They were important to me, just like Catherine was to him.

I loved him. But I could also recognize his flaws. One of which was that he was someone prone to choosing grudges over forgiveness, pessimism over optimism, sadness over happiness, and hate over love.

It hurt to think the love I imagined… the love I thought we'd had… wasn't enough. We needed to meet halfway. I was willing to talk through it. Even after two weeks of silence, I still held out hope. But after Catherine left last night and I realized she took the card with her, my original panic flared with the most hope I'd felt since that horrible night.

I hardly got any sleep last night, waiting for Nick to call or show up. I left an hour later than I should've this morning because I didn't want to miss him in case he dropped by.

He never did.

So either he had no interest in even reading the card, or he read it and didn't believe my words. Both options felt like a kick to the stomach.

When it came to what hurt more, words or a hit, I honestly couldn't tell the difference. They didn't feel separate to me. At least not when they came from the people I loved. Words could feel like a deep punch to the gut, just like a slap could feel like a sting on the soul.

Either way, neither hits nor words were the most painful thing. Silence was.

And this morning, on Christmas, I decided that maybe it was time I accepted a truth I was too naïve to accept before: Nick wasn't coming back.

I looked up and found my mother staring at me, sympathy swimming in her blue eyes. My gaze dropped to her hand still holding my father's. I cleared my throat and started to stand.

"I think I'm going to head out," I said with a nod toward the entrance of the house.

"But we haven't even had dessert. Your mom made lemon bars," my father said with a frown. "They're your favorite."

I tried to give a small smile, but I didn't think it worked. "My stomach doesn't feel too well. I think I'm going to go home and sleep."

"Why don't you stay here?" my mother chimed in, now standing up with me. I wanted to say yes, for no other reason than to remove the heartbreak from her eyes, but I couldn't.

The hope that Nick would show up was gone, but I wanted to be alone. Nothing had ever hurt this much. It was the kind of hurt that didn't want company.

The kind of hurt no one should have to deal with on Christmas.

"I'd rather be in my own bed tonight. I'm sorry, Mom."

"Okay. Well at least let me wrap up some lemon bars to go." She scurried away too quickly for me to refute.

"Hey." I looked over my shoulder to find that Aster had stood up. "Can we talk for a minute?" he asked.

"Sure." I let him lead me away from the dining room and

toward the library Mom had in the front of the house. Talking was the last thing I wanted to do, but I hardly ever saw Aster anymore.

I walked toward the window, watching the snow fall and the lights in the front yard. It painted a happy picture that didn't exist in this house right now.

"How are you?" he asked softly as he came up beside me.

"I've been better." I smiled sadly. "What about you? New York must be treating you well; Becky seems really sweet."

Aster shrugged and looked down at the floor. "Yeah. She's pretty cool."

My smile was more genuine this time, because *She's pretty cool* equaled *I'm in love with her* when coming out of Aster's mouth.

"I was sorry I didn't get to meet Nick." He looked at me from the corner of his eye. I knew my parents had told him everything, and I was really hoping that would have been enough.

"Me too. I think you guys would have gotten along. He thought I was crazy half the time, too."

He frowned and rubbed a hand across his jaw. "He doesn't think you're crazy, Iris. He'll come back."

My eyes filled with tears. Shaking my head, I walked over to the large chair in the corner and took a seat. His steps echoed across the wood as he joined me. The chair was big enough for three or four people so we had no trouble fitting.

I looked down at my hands as my tears started to fall. Aster scooted closer and wrapped his arm around my shoulders. "Mom said he didn't really yell. That he seemed… well, a little calm. That's good, right? Somewhere deep down he knows that—"

"No," I whispered. "That's not good at all."

I thought about his relationship with Colleen, how he

walked away without a backward glance.

"Nick doesn't... he's told me about his past relationships. He doesn't look back, let alone come back."

My brother tapped me on the nose. "That was before he met you. You've changed him."

"How do you know?" I whispered.

Aster was quiet for a minute as he collected his thoughts. "Because of how I see you." I swallowed nervously, waiting for him to continue. "I don't think you're crazy, either. I may say it but... the truth is you scare me."

I straightened, my lips pulling down into a frown. "Scare you? How?"

"I worry about you. I worry you'll hurt yourself trying to help others. That you'll wander into the darkness and not see that sometimes people aren't sitting there and holding roses, just waiting for someone to notice they're decent people. Sometimes, they're holding axes. Some people belong in the dark." He shook his head. "It's easier now that you're older. I know you're smart and that you have a good head on your shoulders. But when you were younger I was terrified every time you left the house.

"There are people in this world who would look at someone like you as prey. They'd take advantage of you or hurt you. As your big brother, I couldn't stand that. I didn't mean to make you feel crazy or like a freak. Or any of the other stupid shit I said when I was a kid. I thought I was helping you. I didn't want you to be in a dangerous position. Sometimes I think you're too good for this world."

I shook my head. "Aster—"

"Most people don't know how to handle that," he kept going. "But once someone knows what it's like to be around you, they can't live without you. You make everyone's life better just by being in it. So that's how I know he doesn't think you're crazy and that he'll come back. He's in awe of you."

Now I was crying for a completely different reason. "Aster…"

"I'm only speaking the truth." He leaned down and kissed the top of my head before pulling me into a hug.

A few weeks ago I would have dismissed his words, but tonight I held on to them like the life raft they were.

Nick

I was parked across the street, creepily in the shadows, when Iris came home. My eyes flew to the clock. It was only seven o'clock. I'd only been here an hour but I was expecting to wait much longer.

After I had an early dinner with my ma and Trevor, I figured I'd give them some alone time. I didn't tell them where I was going, but somehow Ma knew. She kissed me on the cheek and wished me luck before I left. I hugged her extra tight.

I'd ducked down the second she got out of the car, but she didn't spare me a glance. She didn't spare *anything* a glance.

Her neighbor directly next to her was out, grabbing something from a car, and she didn't acknowledge him at all. I frowned and looked over at him. He looked equally confused. Iris always said hello. But it was like she was on autopilot, almost robotic, as she grabbed a bag from the backseat of her car before trudging up the steps and into her house, not even bothering to plug her lights in.

Once she locked herself inside, I grabbed her present off the passenger seat and exited the car. I slid the small, wrapped jewelry box into the pocket of my jeans and crossed the street.

My foot had just hit the sidewalk when I heard a car pull up behind me. Turning my head, I saw Calla get out of her car. She did a double take and slowly walked toward me, like a zookeeper would approach a caged lion.

"Hey," she whispered as her eyes nervously darted toward the houses behind me.

"Hi."

"What are you doing here?" she asked.

"I'm here to see my girlfriend."

Calla's eyes grew hard. "Oh? I wasn't aware she still had a boyfriend."

I clenched my fists. Not because I wanted to hit her, but because I was genuinely considering punching myself in the face. It probably wouldn't hurt as much as her words.

"Iris left early because she said she wasn't feeling well. She didn't even have any lemon bars." She lifted a container filled with them as proof. "They're her favorite."

"I know that."

She raised her eyebrows. "Do you?"

"Yes," I said a little too loudly.

"I may have been distracted these last few weeks, but that doesn't mean I haven't seen how much pain Iris is in. And it kills me to know that I'm responsible. That I'm the reason my baby sister is hurting. But you're responsible too."

"I—"

"No. I'm talking now."

What is it with every woman telling me to shut up lately?

"Iris isn't perfect. If you thought so, that was your mistake. You can't pretend everyone is perfect and be dismayed when you find out they're not. *That* is on you. If you loved her like you claimed to, you'd love Iris for her flaws, too. Love can't exist in a perfect world. And if that's where your head has been, thinking you were in love with her because she was perfect, then perhaps you were right, and it was all a lie. Because if you were in love with her, you'd love *all* of her. And if you can't, she'll find someone who can."

She looked down at the ground. "I'm sorry we asked her to lie," she whispered. "We shouldn't have. We were just trying to keep our family together. But I never considered I'd be breaking up hers. She doesn't deserve this. So I'm asking…" Her gaze rose to meet mine. "I'm *begging* you, if you're not here to forgive her, please don't go up there. If you need to yell or hate someone, use me. Not her."

"I'm not here to yell at her." I pulled the wrapped gift out of my pocket. "Would I bring a present if I was?"

Calla blinked and looked at it, a tiny smile stretching across her lips. "To be honest, I didn't even see that. I've been a little out of it lately."

I sighed and put the gift back in my pocket, feeling the pain in my chest building. "I'm not going to say anything," I admitted.

Her eyes snapped to mine and her mouth fell open. "What?" she whispered, her hand flying to her chest.

"There's a difference between being a bad man and a man who did a bad thing. I think I've been confusing the two for quite a while. I don't know, I guess it was easier to only see things from my perspective, but I remembered hearing the panic in his voice that night. I remembered the indecision and fear. It wasn't a choice he made lightly."

"It wasn't, I promise. And I… he told me he was going to the police after I delivered. But I was hysterical, begging him not to. He wanted to do the right thing—"

I stepped forward and placed my hand on hers. "It's okay." And it was. It wouldn't be better overnight. But my mother's words really sank in.

Calla shivered. And for the first time I realized she wasn't as bundled up as I was. "You should head on home." I nodded toward Iris's house. "I'll take care of her," I promised. We shared easy smiles for the first time, and she squeezed my hand before handing me the lemon bars and walking toward her car.

"I do love all of her," I called after Calla. "I may not have trusted her in the beginning, but everything she's about… how she goes out of her way to help people, I think it's amazing. I think she's completely unprecedented and unlike anyone I've ever met. Even the things that drive me crazy, I don't want her changing them. She wouldn't be her without them.

"I love how she snorts whenever she watches an animal video on YouTube. I love her inability to bypass a musician on the street without pausing to dance and throw some money in their tip jar. I love her weird obsession with lemon bars. And I love that she wanted to give some random guy her kidney, even though I was a complete asshole." I paused, tears filling my eyes. "It would be impossible for her to be anyone else's because *she's mine*. She has been since I pulled my head out of my ass long enough to recognize and accept it. She's mine," I repeated, saying it like a fact. Because that was exactly what it was.

The sky was blue.

The Earth was round.

And Iris Chamberlain was mine.

Twenty-Three

Iris

I'D JUST RETURNED TO THE SOFA WITH A GLASS OF WINE when someone knocked on the front door. I put the glass down and walked toward it, expecting it to be a neighbor asking for sugar or something random like that. And even though I wasn't in the mood for *anybody*, I tried to paste on a smile.

With a sigh I opened the door, smiling and preparing the lie that I was fine in case they asked about my slightly ruined makeup, when I stopped short. It wasn't a neighbor on the other side.

It was Nick.

Honestly, the last person I'd expected. My heart felt like it was about to beat right out of my chest. I couldn't remember a time I felt more nervous.

"Hey." He gave me an unsure smile, no dimples, as he rocked back on his feet.

"H-hi," I stuttered. My fingers were aching from the grip they had on my doorframe. "You're... you're here."

He nodded before his eyes moved to the room behind me. "Can I come in?"

"Yes, of course, sorry." I stepped back so quickly I tripped over the rug, and suddenly I was falling backward. I made an unintelligible shriek and closed my eyes, bracing myself for the inevitable impact with the wood floor.

It never came. Instead, strong, warm, and familiar arms circled around my waist and stopped my momentum.

My heart was still pounding fast and I hesitantly opened one eye at a time before peeking to the left of me, confirming what I already knew. I had to take a deep breath before I met his eyes.

I was incredibly grateful for it the second our gazes met. He was looking at me with such warm affection I could feel it wrapping around me like a blanket on a cold winter night. I didn't think I'd ever get that look again.

He slowly righted us until I had my balance, but he didn't let me go; if anything he held me tighter. One palm pressed against my lower back, while the other lingered. It was then I remembered briefly seeing a Tupperware container in his hand.

"Breathe." He chuckled softly as I let out the air I'd been keeping hostage.

"Sorry. I'm n-nervous," I blurted out.

Nick frowned before lifting a hand and pushing back a piece of hair that had fallen. "I never want you to be nervous around me."

I nodded, but remained quiet. I couldn't help it—I *was* nervous. I mean, how could I not be? The love of my life was standing in front of me and I had no idea what he came for.

His arms loosened and I stepped out of his hold.

"What's in there?" I asked, nodding to the container.

"Oh." He gave me a sheepish grin before removing the lid. I couldn't stop the tears that came to my eyes when I saw my mom's lemon bars inside. Once she gave them to me at the house, I handed them off to Aster as he walked me to my car. I didn't want to waste them when I knew I wasn't going to eat them.

Shaking my head, I lifted my gaze to his. "How did you…?"

"I ran into Calla outside. She was bringing these over." I hadn't spoken to her before I left, and we'd said very little the whole day. It wasn't a conscious decision. She was focusing on Mirielle and I was just trying to make it through the day. I was almost amazed I'd made it home, I was so out of it. It was one of those drives that I could hardly remember by the time I arrived home.

"Calla said you left without having any." He lifted the container and smiled. "I didn't think it was physically possible for you to walk away from these."

I shrugged and wrapped my arms around my waist.

"My stomach hurt." His grin dropped with my confession.

"What about now?" He held it out to me. I took the container, but still didn't feel like eating any.

"Thank you. Maybe later." I gave him a small smile and put the Tupperware on the coffee table.

We stood in awkward silence, our eyes fixed on one another while we said nothing. After a few moments, he crossed his arms and cleared his throat. "I got your gift. Thank you. It's beautiful."

I nodded, my throat suddenly tight. "You're welcome."

"And I read your card..."

My gaze dropped and I looked toward the tree. Noticing an ornament was crooked, I moved to fix it. Despite my earlier hope that he would read it, now that I knew he had I felt incredibly vulnerable. Everything I wrote was the truth and I didn't regret it. But that didn't mean I wasn't scared.

"Your mom took that," I said, still focusing on my task.

"I figured. But I'm glad she did."

I lifted my eyes to his. He had a point. "I guess if she hadn't you wouldn't have reached out. So even though I'm a bit embarrassed—"

"I would have," he interrupted. "It might have taken me a little longer, and that would have sucked because we've already wasted so much time, but I would have reached out."

Turning toward him, I decided to bite the bullet. "When I confronted them and found out what they'd done..." I shook my head. "I couldn't believe it. I was shocked. Horrified. Guilt-ridden. And about a hundred other things. But then I really began to think about it, and..." I trailed off, not knowing if this would make him hate me more.

"I don't know if Kent made the wrong choice. I don't know if there was a right choice. Obviously I hate that you were left there. Obviously I wouldn't have wanted anything to happen to you. But if they'd stayed? If he'd tried to get you out? My sister and her baby could have died... how can I say I wish he made a different call when the one he made kept all the people I love alive?" I shrugged again, and looked at Nick for an explanation. I genuinely wanted to know how you made a black-and-white situation out of all this gray I was swimming in. He was usually able to.

Nick took a deep breath and looked toward my fireplace. "I don't... I don't know if there was one either," he whispered.

I froze, completely in shock. His gaze met mine.

"I know it was an accident. He tried to trust that someone would help me. I think Kent did the best he could with what he was given. It doesn't mean I fully forgive him—I think that will take time. But you're right. Maybe his intentions and the inevitable outcome have to count for more."

I thought for sure I was about to fall over.

"You told me that you didn't believe in grudges, that you believed in forgiveness," he continued. I nodded. "I want to be that way. It'll take time, but I already feel like I've gotten better since meeting you."

Nodding once more, I curled my hands into fists. The need to touch him was stronger than ever before, but I was still unsure where we stood.

I crossed my arms across my chest and started talking. "I didn't give you that kidney with any expectations. I just wanted to help, but I shouldn't have lied to you. Even if I understood where they were coming from. I shouldn't have kept it from you. Not even for a second—"

"It's okay."

I kept talking over him. "But I panicked when I realized what Kent had done. I didn't know what to do. I was protecting them, but I was also protecting myself." Nick's eyes looked haunted, and I knew it was because I was becoming hysterical as I continued to explain, but now that I'd started I didn't think I'd be able to stop. "I knew I'd—"

He crossed the room and cut me off with a quick, sure kiss. His lips didn't move, they merely rested against mine. It wasn't a kiss of passion or desperation. It was just a reminder that he was there.

He pulled back and cupped my cheeks. "Iris, breathe." Nick looked sad as he pulled me in for a hug. "I'm not leaving." I melted into him as I wrapped my arms around his waist and buried my face into his chest.

"I'm sorry for freaking out like that. I'm not used to being the asshole."

Nick let out a surprised laugh as he pulled back. His eyebrows were high on his forehead as he grinned down at me. He looked at me with so much affection it made me dizzy with want. Shaking his head, he said, "I've never heard you swear before. You'll never stop surprising me, will you?"

I froze at the use of future tense.

"Iris…"

"Yeah?" I was surprised I could get the word out since I was holding my breath.

"Lucky for us, I'm an expert on being an asshole. You're not one."

I started laughing.

Nick smiled.

And everything fell back into place.

Nick

We were both quiet as she led me to her bedroom. Iris let go of my hand and sat on the edge of her bed before slowly unbuttoning her shirt, each pull revealing smooth skin or white cotton. I swallowed before reaching behind my neck and quickly removing my own. Her hands worked on my belt as I bent down and unclasped her bra. She shivered as the air kissed her skin, and my eyes instantly zoned in on her nipples.

With a smile, she shuffled backward and propped herself up on her elbows. I slowly climbed onto the bed until I was hovering above her. She tilted her head up, her face bare and beautiful, her brown hair falling sensuously over her shoulders and down her back. I straddled her, balancing on my knees as my hands softly cupped the back of her head and brought her closer. Her hair was soft and smelled like lavender. I pulled her toward me until our lips met. Our eyes were closed as we opened our mouths and our tongues tangled. It was soft and intimate, and quite possibly the most perfect kiss we'd ever shared.

"Nick," she whispered as my mouth traveled away from hers. My lips moved across her cheek until I reached the spot behind her ear.

"Yes, dear?" I heard her breathy chuckle.

"Saying *dear* reminds me of your mother."

I pulled back with a scowl. "I feel like this should be self-explanatory, but talking about my ma in bed is a complete turnoff."

"My bad," she murmured as she tilted her head to give me more access to her neck. I pulled away and her eyes fluttered open. Moving my hands to her shoulders, I gently pushed her flat against the bed. My hands moved down her chest, and we both let out a content sigh as they found her breasts. One of the things Iris told me she loved was that I didn't immediately go for the kill. I took my time, admiring and kneading. It wasn't exactly a hardship to keep that up.

Her hands went to my shoulders and she dug her nails into my bare skin.

"Oh how I've missed you," I whispered, my eyes dead set on her left nipple, which I was pinching between my fingers. Iris whimpered when I drew it into my mouth, softly sucking, while my other hand kneaded.

"I don't know how you survived," she joked.

"Hmmm?"

She chuckled, breathy. "It had to be torture to go two weeks without a pair."

I frowned and pulled away.

"I had been without 'a pair'"—I felt my scowl deepen—"for a year. It's not about that. It's because they're yours. I've missed *yours*." My hands squeezed again. She opened her mouth to respond but I cut her off. "Now hush, we're trying to get reacquainted."

"Not much has changed." Her smile was soft as she gazed down at me, her fingers brushing the hair off my forehead.

"I'll be the judge of that. Besides, they look lonely." I grinned.

Iris's laugh was so full of joy, she appeared weightless. "They missed you too."

"I'll bet. Fucking gorgeous." I dropped soft kisses until I was at her right nipple.

"Don't think I forgot about you." I drew a reverent circle around it before sucking it into my mouth, a little harder than the other. She laughed when I continued to whisper sweet nothings to them. Her giggles quickly cut off as my bare chest brushed against hers, our nipples grazing. I hissed right before my mouth met hers in a gentle kiss.

I pulled away, my eyes closed and my forehead resting against hers. Soft pants filled the space between us. "I missed you so much."

"Me too," she whispered.

I sealed our lips together again, groaning when her tongue slipped out and connected with mine. My hands wandered down and carefully removed her pants before I broke away to sit back and take off my own. She reached into her nightstand and grabbed a condom.

My eyes were on her; she was panting and squirming as

she waited for me to roll it on. Both of us moaned when I settled over her and slid inside.

It had only been two weeks but it felt like so much longer. That was what missing someone did. Time slowed to a crawl, especially if you didn't know when you'd be seeing them again.

Iris wrapped her legs around me as I began a steady rhythm. I lifted myself up on one elbow, bringing my other hand to her neck, gently holding her in place. She bit her lip and her eyes fluttered closed as her head tipped back.

"Iris," I whispered until her gaze was back on me. "Keep them open."

Nodding, she fisted the sheets as I sped up. One hand came up and wrapped around my back, her nails digging into my skin. She whimpered when I pulled back to my knees and grabbed her hips, angling her so I could go deeper.

"N-Nick. Oh God…"

I brought one hand to her clit and began making fast, tight circles, while I continued thrusting into her. My groans competed with her moans as we got closer.

And when we finally came minutes later, we did it together. Our bodies were wrapped around one another so tightly hardly any air passed between us. But between our labored pants, we had plenty.

I'd collapsed against her, still giving her room to breathe, with my sweaty forehead resting against her shoulder.

"Fuck," I muttered before pulling back and kissing her once I caught my breath.

"Yeah…" she agreed. "My hand just wasn't the same."

My eyes widened as she grinned, playful and sexy all at once. Shaking my head, I kissed her again.

"You really will keep surprising me, won't you?" I asked

against her lips. I didn't give her a chance to respond before I took them again. It didn't matter. I knew.

Iris was predictable in the fact that you never quite knew what she would do. All you really knew was that it was going to be amazing. She wasn't merely one thing. She was like a kaleidoscope. There were so many different sides to her, and they were all beautiful.

My body was exhausted, but my mind felt wide awake. Almost like I didn't want to miss out on a single second of Iris's company. I lay on my back, my legs kicked out in front of me, while Iris was draped across me, her arm slung over my stomach. My arm ran along her back and my hand was on her hip, holding her to me.

There was one thing that was still bothering me, though.

"Hey, Iris?" I whispered into the darkness.

"Hmm?"

"You're the woman worth fighting for." She froze for a second before slowly peeling herself away. Thankfully she kept herself connected, just giving herself enough room to look down at me.

"In the card you said—"

"I know."

"Can I ask why you thought you weren't? I hate that you thought that, and that you were surprised when I showed up here. I hate that you didn't know how much I love you… or how big of an idiot I am, with a tendency to shove my foot in my mouth."

She laughed at my attempt to lighten the mood. "That last

one I knew." Her smile faded a bit as she began drawing on my chest with her finger.

"It just seemed a lot like Colleen."

I frowned. "What do you mean?"

"You said that when you broke up with Colleen, you didn't yell. You asked her for the truth and left. Just like you did with me."

Grabbing her hand, I weaved our fingers together. "It was different. I walked away from Colleen because I had nothing to say. When I walked away from you… I was hurt beyond belief, Iris. But I didn't want to cause you any pain, and I thought if I stayed, I would have said something I'd regret. I didn't walk away because I *don't* care, I walked away because I did." Iris still looked glum.

"What is it?" I asked, giving her hand a shake.

"I love you." She said it simply and gave me one of her wide grins. "I realized I hadn't said it yet. Not with the air cleared and you believing me. It feels good."

"It sounds good," I agreed with a smile.

"I love you. I lo—"

I lightly tugged on her hand and leaned forward, immediately capturing her lips. It was my favorite kind of kiss, where I could taste her smile and feel the vibrations of her laughter. It was one hundred percent Iris.

When she pulled away, I swayed forward. Her kisses tasted like sunshine, and her hugs felt like home. And both always made me want to go back for more.

"Hey, I almost forgot something." I gently nudged her until she moved back.

"What?" she asked as I climbed out of bed and looked for my pants. Once I found them, I easily dug the small jewelry box out of my front pocket before crawling back into bed.

"Your Christmas present." I held it out to her. She was holding the sheet to her chest with one hand and reached out with the other to take the gift.

I was silent as Iris carefully unwrapped and slowly opened the lid. Her wide eyes flew between me and the box. "Nick, it's beautiful." She ran her fingers over the necklace.

I'd heard her talking to my ma at the wedding about how she'd always wanted a teardrop necklace. Once I went home and googled what the hell that meant, I immediately started looking for one.

The necklace was simple, just a small Rose Quartz bead in the shape of a drop on a silver chain. But when I saw it, I didn't even think twice before buying it. It seemed perfect for Iris.

"It's perfect," she echoed.

"That's not even the best part. Look at the company."

Iris looked at the tiny card inside and squinted. "I've never heard of them."

"Exactly! Get this," I said excitedly as I placed a hand on her knee. "All the proceeds from this shop are invested into different charities. So every time you wear this, you'll know some foundation is benefiting—"

She quickly shuffled closer, the sheet falling away, and pressed her lips to mine. "Thank you." Iris shook her head. "You've given me so many gifts tonight. The necklace. The place where you got it from. And the fact that you know me better than anyone else. I couldn't have asked for a more perfect Christmas." She wrapped her arms around me and held on tight.

"I want to give you the world," I whispered.

"I only need you." Iris kissed my cheek before we resumed our earlier positions, her curled around me.

She may not have needed anything else, but that didn't mean I didn't want to give her *everything*. Iris was the girl you gave your all to.

And that was exactly what I planned to do.

Twenty-Four

Nick

KENT AND I STOOD IN THE NURSERY. HIS EYES ON Mirielle, my eyes on him. It was New Year's Eve and Iris's parents were having a party, with all the same people who were at their Christmas party. Things were especially tense when Kent, Calla, Iris, and I met in the foyer. The last time we'd all been in that place, lives felt destroyed and confidences betrayed. But as the night wore on, the strain ebbed.

Still, I knew we needed to clear the air.

"May I?" I asked, gesturing to Mirielle, who'd just woken up. Kent slowly nodded and stepped back. I walked forward and gently picked her up, cradling her to my chest, making sure her head and neck were supported. Looking into her wide blue eyes, I tried to dig through my emotions and find an objective truth in our situation.

But the longer I stood there, the more I realized there

wasn't one. The truth was a funny thing. It was supposed to be objective, when in reality it was relative. And not just to different people, but to time and place as well. It would be nice if certain things were true all the time. It would be comforting because then people would't have to think.

But the truth was never *this* or *that*, it wasn't black or white like I'd originally thought. It was gray. It was messy. It was complicated. And pretending it was anything else had been a mistake.

Kent had his beliefs, and I had mine. Neither was correct. There was a semblance of truth to both, but until we could admit that, we'd never get anywhere. Until we could look at the other side and say, *yes, I see some truth there*, we'd forever be stuck.

"There isn't anything I wouldn't do for her," he whispered. "If that makes me a monster, or just a parent, I'm not sure, but it's the only truth I know for certain right now."

Nodding, I looked up at him. "I know your choice wasn't an easy one. Truthfully, I don't know what I would have done, had I been in your shoes."

"You don't have to condone something to understand it. I won't ask for your forgiveness—I don't want to put that kind of pressure on you. Just don't treat Iris any different because of it. She did the best she could in the situation Calla and I put her in. I know you're here and she says everything is sorted out, but I need your word that you've completely forgiven her, that there's no lingering resentment."

I started bouncing Mirielle when she began to fuss. "There was never anything to forgive."

"Good." He walked closer and rested a hand on his daughter's head. "Iris has never looked at anyone the way she looks at you—it's like you're as vital to her survival as oxygen. Even from the beginning, we all knew you were different. It was never anything she said, but the way she said your name..." Kent trailed off, shaking his head.

"I feel the same way. She's changed me in ways I could've never imagined. Sometimes I just stop and stare at her, because I still can't believe she's real, or that she's mine."

Kent wore an affectionate smile as he looked down at his daughter. "Yeah. Iris is one of the good ones, isn't she?"

I chuckled and shook my head. "She's not one of the good ones. She's the best one."

There was no gray in that thought—it was the truest statement there was.

Iris

I loved the start of a new year. The possibilities. The excitement. Even if most resolutions fell to the wayside, it was nice to see how much everyone wanted to change.

Things felt especially wonderful this year.

Nick wouldn't become best friends with Kent and Calla overnight, but he and Kent began mending that bridge, and that was all I could really ask for.

It was a few days after my parents' New Year's Eve party and I was waking up in Nick's bed, one of my favorite places. Kevin, Lindsay, Nick, and I were going ice skating at Frog Pond in downtown Boston later today, so I was soaking up my last few minutes of sleep. I knew I'd need my energy—ice skating was not my forte, and we were up late last night. I'd already heard Nick get up and start getting ready in the bathroom.

My hands met the headboard and my toes curled as I stretched. I heard footsteps getting closer, and as I relaxed back into bed, I felt Nick press butterfly-soft kisses along my shoulder blades. I moaned, low and breathy, as I wiggled around. One of his hands found my waist while the other palmed my butt over the bedsheets.

"Morning," he whispered against the shell of my ear.

"Mmm…"

"I gotta run an errand."

My hair shifted against the pillow as I nodded. I internally fist-bumped because that meant more sleep for me. "M'kay. When will you be home?" I mumbled, already being pulled back under.

We both froze.

Home.

I liked the way that sounded… *a lot.*

With a blinding smile on his face, he answered, "In an hour or two."

"Okay. Kiss?" I turned my head toward him, eyes closed, mouth waiting.

He pressed his lips softly to mine. "Do you need anything?" he asked when he pulled away. I shook my head, eyes still shut.

"Just you, so hurry back."

"Don't forget about our double date with Kevin and Lindsay." He laughed because when Lindsay suggested it, apparently I looked terrified.

I mumbled my agreement and listened to him walk away and leave the apartment.

It felt like I'd just fallen back asleep when I heard the door shut again. Looking at the clock on the nightstand, I saw that an hour and a half had passed. I sat up and leaned against the headboard, holding the sheet to my chest in the process.

Nick walked in a few minutes later, dropping a bag from

my favorite bagel place in my lap and a kiss on my cheek. "I have something I want to show you."

"Okay." I greedily took the bagel out and bit into it. He chuckled when he came back in.

"You don't waste any time, do you?"

"Nope." I nodded to the wooden box in his hands. "Is that...?"

"The best present I've ever gotten? Yup." I sat a little straighter. "I had the restaurant name engraved."

My eyes bulged. "Already?"

"Yeah. I've had a name in mind for a while."

I brushed my hands off on the napkin that was in the bag and reached for it. "Let me see," I said excitedly. We hadn't talked about his restaurant much. For as excited as he was, I was pretty sure a big part of him was nervous.

He handed it over and I turned it toward me. I read the inscription out loud.

Nicholas Blake, Executive Chef & Owner
Bacio del Sole

"Nick..." I whispered. He shuffled closer until our knees bumped.

"It'll be an Italian restaurant, and the name is 'Kiss of Sunshine' in Italian... obviously." His nervous chuckle brought my eyes up, and I heard one of our past conversations in my mind.

"Sunshine..." he whispered.

"Hmm?" I asked.

"Kissing you, it's what I imagine kissing sunshine would be like. Warm, bright, soul-filling. A balm to a depressed mood," he answered.

"Are you serious?" I asked now. He always talked about me not being real, without even realizing I felt the exact same way about him.

"Yeah."

He looked down, suddenly shy. And even though my heart was already bursting, I still felt it grow in size. It felt impossibly full, brimming with something more than love. He'd become my best friend. I was lucky enough to be in love with my best friend.

I leaned forward, grabbing his chin and pulling his lips to mine. It was a slow and sweet kiss. And if I hadn't already been in love with him, this would have made me fall.

Two months later, on March 10, my twenty-seventh birthday, we were all together again. My parents, Kent, Calla, Mirielle, Aster and Becky who were back for a short trip, Catherine, Trevor, Lindsay, and Kevin. We were at my parents' house, celebrating my birthday with a simple dinner—which was always my preference. Right now my parents were putting the leftovers away while everyone else dispersed. I was sitting at the dining room table with Lindsay, Catherine, and Calla.

"I can't believe you convinced her to go," my sister said.

"I don't know why she was so worried. She only fell four times, and that's not bad," Lindsay said as I took a sip of my iced tea. She was right, but she didn't know it was the fewest number of times I'd ever fallen whilst ice skating.

"Her numbers are usually in the double digits." The four of us laughed.

"I just feel bad that I kept taking Nick with me," I said.

Lindsay grinned. "He could have easily let go. Nick *chose* to go down with you."

Catherine smiled. "That's exactly what a man in love should do."

My lips tipped up as my gaze traveled to him. He was holding Mirielle as he talked to Trevor and Kent. The couple times we'd seen my sister and brother-in-law since the disastrous Christmas party, Nick had always insisted on holding my niece for part of the night. Sometimes I wondered if he was trying to remind himself of what else had been at stake that night.

"He's doing better." I turned back to the table at Catherine's soft voice. Calla and Lindsay had started a separate discussion.

"I think they'll be okay."

"Me too." She smiled.

"Are you?" I suddenly asked.

"Am I what, dear?"

I hesitated, my eyes quickly going back to her son. "You never said how you felt about Kent. I just wondered what your thoughts were."

Catherine was quiet for a minute as she considered it. "You know, as a parent, I understand Kent's decision. And as *Nick's* parent, I also felt anger at the thought of my son being left on the side of the road." I cringed and stared down at the table. Her hand found mine and she squeezed. When I looked back up, she was smiling.

"But above all else, I consider myself a child of God, and I believe everything happens as it's meant to. Who am I to question Him? I'm grateful things turned out the way they did. I forgave Kent before I even knew it was him. Not necessarily for his sake—I had no way of knowing his intent at the beginning—but because all that anger would only eat at *me*, the way it did Nick. And trusting our Lord only works if you have faith in everything He does."

When she finished, I noticed the other side of the table had gone quiet. I looked over at my sister, who was looking at Nick's mother with so much respect it stole my breath. Catherine noticed and took Calla's hand. "And once I met Kent and Calla," she began again, talking to me but looking at my sister, "I saw the true purpose of it all. Not only to bring a baby safely into the world, but to save Nick as well."

She turned to face me now. "My son was saved in more ways than one thanks to you, Iris. And well… if that accident was the only way for it to happen, so be it. This has only strengthened my faith in our Lord."

"I agree." I jumped at the sound of Nick's voice behind me. When I turned around he was smiling down at his mom. He held out his palm and helped her up before turning my way. "I think it's time for presents," he whispered as he offered me his hand. With a wide smile, I accepted and let him lead me toward the couch. Everyone quickly found their spots.

"I'd like to go first if that's all right."

"Of course, Nick," my mom said with an easy smile. He walked forward and held out a rectangular box decorated with yellow wrapping paper and a pink bow. Everyone laughed when I tore into it and lifted the lid. Whatever it was was wrapped in white gauzy paper.

I gently pulled back the paper and found a framed chalkboard inside. I completely lost my breath at the sight of it. "Nick…" I whispered, my fingers gently tracing the edges. It read:

> **Nick & Iris**
> He saw her...
> May 17, 2016
> He stopped being an idiot...
> August 29, 2016
> He kissed her...
> October 6, 2016
> He loved her...
> December 3, 2016
> He asked her to be his...
> March 10, 2017
> He promised to be hers forever...

Tears splashed the glass that was protecting the writing as my emotions got the best of me. There was a blank space for a future date. I looked up and found a blurry Nick down on one knee in front of me. I heard several people sniffling in the background, but I couldn't tear my gaze away. He took the gift away from me before grabbing my hands, and out of the corner of my eye I saw a ring box balancing on his knee.

"You told me that your birth parents married quickly because they knew their forever would be shorter than everyone else's," he began. "But I don't know if that's necessarily true. Coming from a man who knows what it's like to be completely and overwhelmingly in love, I can safely say that, no matter the length, they wanted their forever to last as long as it could. Because no amount of time is enough when you're with the right person. And when it's right, you know. Even if everyone else thinks you're crazy. Even if the whole world thinks you should wait."

My gaze instinctively flickered to Aster. He chuckled and raised his hands. "Why do you automatically look at me?" The rest of the room laughed as he wrapped an arm around Becky. I looked back toward Nick.

"No one said any of that," he assured me. "I just know what public perception is. But I don't care. I want our forever to last as long as it can.

"You're a part of me." He looked down toward his stomach. "*Literally*. I hated my scars—the emotional and physical ones. I thought they showed the weakest parts of me. But you made me see how wrong I was. They don't show my weakness, but my strength. They're proof I lived. They tell my story. There's no more pain, only strength. Just skin hardened through determination to fix itself.

"Iris, you taught me a new way of looking at everything. And even though you never intended to get anything out of it, you still got something."

My smile wobbled as more tears fell. "What?"

"My heart." His own eyes misted and he opened the box. It was a simple ring, a small diamond set in a rose gold band. It was absolutely perfect.

Nick grabbed my left hand and held the ring up. "Iris, will you marry me?"

"Yes," I said softly. "Of course."

He tenderly slid the ring on my finger before leaning forward. Nick grabbed the back of my neck and pulled me into a kiss as everyone cheered in the background. It only lasted a few seconds before our laughter and tears forced our lips to part. Nick removed the box from my lap and dragged me down with him before hugging me. One hand cupped the back of my head and the other wrapped around my waist. I held on to his neck tightly.

"Thank you," he whispered, almost like he couldn't believe I'd said yes. When he pulled back, some of the nerves I'd noted these last few months seeped in.

"If this was seriously too fast, we can have a long engagement." I chuckled and went to speak when his eyes moved to the framed picture and he said, "We can also take out the idiot part, that's probably not very romantic." He looked adorably worried as he rubbed the back of his neck.

I laughed, grabbing his cheeks and forcing his eyes back on me. "I love it. It's *you,* and it's me. It doesn't get more romantic than that."

"I love you," he breathed.

"I love you too." I put my hand over his heart and felt the beat he had been so sure was destined for no one. Dragging my hand down, I rested it against his stomach, feeling the puckered skin of his scar underneath his T-shirt. I smiled as I remembered his words.

You're a part of me. Literally.

Grabbing Nick's hand, I rested it against my stomach. "I hope that, someday, I'll have a part of you in me too."

I realized after the fact how those words could be twisted into something dirty. But he didn't make a joke of it. He looked as excited by the idea as I was.

"Me too," he murmured. I sighed as my fiancé kissed my nose and hugged me again.

Fiancé…

I grinned into his shoulder. Life had never felt so good.

Twenty-Five

Nick

Three years later...

I LOOKED DOWN AT MY NEWBORN DAUGHTER, SAFE AND secure in my arms, and I understood Kent in a way I never had before. I didn't want to leave my daughter to go take a piss, let alone to leave the hospital and turn myself in to the police, not knowing when—or even if—I'd return.

I forgave him years ago. I said all the right things, and I accepted his apology, but I never truly *understood*. I now knew I never could have, not until I first heard the cries of my beautiful baby girl.

Iris and I married a year after I proposed. We ended up waiting another year to start our family once I realized how difficult it would be to get a new restaurant off the ground. *Bacio del Sole* opened a year ago, and we began trying shortly after.

Gazing over at my wife, her face red and splotchy, her

brown hair stuck to her face with sweat, and her body limp with exhaustion, I fell in love all over again.

I remember as a kid my ma told me, *One day you'll fall in love, dear, and it'll change you forever.*

She was wrong. I didn't just fall in love once, I fell in love hundreds of times. All with Iris. And every single time, it changed me for the better.

But this? Holding my daughter was all of that times a million.

Iris hadn't been asleep long, and she made me promise to wake her up if she did drift off, saying she didn't want to miss a moment. She'd kill me for letting her sleep, but I couldn't bring myself to wake her. Not after she'd spent fourteen hours in labor.

I walked toward the window. It was a beautiful spring morning, but nature had nothing on my girl. I smiled down at her. She would be a daddy's girl, just like I had been a mama's boy.

"Hey, mister, you were supposed to wake me up."

Grinning, I turned around and walked toward my wife. "My apologies." I bent to kiss her forehead.

"Yeah, right." Iris shimmied up the bed and scooted over, giving me room to sit. I angled our daughter her way. "Oh my God, she's perfect," she whispered, her eyes welling with tears, just like they had every time she looked at her in the last few hours.

"I know. Thank God she looks like you," I said.

"She's not even a day old. She looks like—"

"Don't say it," I interrupted. I would have silenced her with a hand over her mouth too, but I was afraid of only holding my daughter with one arm.

"A potato," she finished with a wide grin.

"How can you say our daughter looks like a potato?" I shook my head, even though my lips tipped up.

"A cute potato," she amended.

I laughed and pulled the blanket tighter around her.

"We still need a name," Iris said softly.

"Actually… I've been thinking." I gave her a sheepish grin.

"What?" She smiled, exhaustion pulling at her features, but she'd never looked more radiant. Unable to stop myself, I leaned forward and softly kissed her. When I pulled away she was still smiling and her eyes were closed. They slowly fluttered open.

"So what's the name?"

I looked down at her, my little girl, my *daughter*, and felt overwhelmed all over again. "Florence," I whispered, and just as I did, her little eyes opened and bright blue irises collided with mine. It felt like a sign.

Iris was quiet and I looked up to see her staring between the two of us.

"It's okay if you don't like it," I rushed to assure her. "I was messing around on the computer and saw it. It seemed perfect for how your mom loves gardening and you love Italy—" She quickly leaned forward and placed a finger on my lips.

"It is perfect. I love it." We both smiled down at the squirming baby in my arms. "Florence Grace Blake. Grace was the name I was playing with."

I grinned. "Wow, I hope they're all that easy." I handed Florence to her mother. Iris carefully took her and held her as close as she could.

"It's crazy," I whispered.

"What is?"

"How I ever thought Kent made the wrong choice. It seems so simple now. I'd leave myself dying in a ditch if it meant our daughter was okay."

Iris looked up. "I know what you mean. The world seems completely different now, doesn't it? A little brighter."

"A little scarier," I countered.

She rolled her eyes. "Some things never change."

"Thankfully the important stuff did."

"Oh, yeah? Like what?"

"Like my faith in people." I definitely wasn't at Iris's or my ma's level, but I had gotten better at giving people the benefit of the doubt. "I'm still a little rusty though." I was careful as I leaned over and kissed her forehead. When I pulled away, I said, "I hope she always sees the world like you do."

"She will. We'll make sure of it, Daddy." She grinned and looked down at Florence. My eyes followed hers.

Yes. We will…

Iris

It was four months later, in the heart of June, and we were finally settling into a routine.

I put Florence down in her crib for her afternoon nap and walked to the kitchen. Stopping in the doorway, I studied the scene before me. Nick and Mirielle were "baking." He stood at the counter and rolled a piece of dough. My niece, who'd just turned four, was standing on a step stool that Nick bought her for her birthday last month. It was painted with "Nick's Favorite Assistant." When Kent explained to her what that meant, I thought he was going to cry. Calla almost did too. I most definitely did.

The two of them were very close. Nick's lap was the one she always climbed on when we were sitting on the couch. She hugged him the longest, and trailed after him when he left the room.

Mirielle loved her mother and father dearly, but every child needed that extra adult to make them feel special. Nick beat me by a long shot. I didn't mind; their relationship was one of the most beautiful things I'd ever seen.

Mirielle was obsessed with the kitchen, and everything in it. Whether that was innate and the reason she loved Nick, or Nick inspired her love for cooking, I wasn't sure. But I loved watching them together.

Right now, my niece didn't look too happy. Her lips were downturned as she pounded on the dough.

"Miri," my husband said, using her special nickname. "What's wrong?"

"Nothing." She pouted and hit the counter again. With a small grin, Nick put his hands under her armpits and lifted her up before setting her on the counter. Mirielle immediately crossed her arms and started swinging her legs. He brought his hands to her knees, squeezing gently until she stopped kicking.

"What's gonna happen to me?" she muttered.

He frowned. "What do you mean?"

"When Fourence becomes your favorite assissant, what about me?" I barely suppressed a giggle at her butchering of our daughter's name.

"Why do you think that would happen?"

"She's your baby, you're gonna love her more."

Nick scoffed. "Impossible. I love you both the same."

Mirielle stayed silent, clearly disagreeing.

"You know when we have tea parties?" Yes, Nick had tea parties with her. I just about died every single time, too.

"Yeah?" She perked up a little at the memories.

"What if I told you you could only bring Bubu or Fuzzy

Butt?" he asked, using her names for her stuffed hippo and panda.

She groaned, long and loud. "That's stupid. I can't pick."

"Exactly." Nick grinned. "You can love more than one person, or stuffed animal."

Her face bunched up in adorable confusion. "You can?"

"Of course. I love you, and I love Florence. Maybe she'll be your assistant."

Mirielle sat up straighter, her smile wide. "Really? Daddy says only impotant people have assissants."

Nick smiled, but didn't correct any of her words. "That must mean you're important."

My niece started kicking her legs again, this time with excitement. Her arms extended toward him and he easily wrapped her in a hug. "I love you, Uncle Nicky," I barely heard her whisper.

"I love you, too."

His eyes met mine as I stepped into the kitchen. "Hey, guys."

Mirielle spun toward me and shouted, "Aunt Iri!" She was smiling as I helped her down and onto her step stool again.

"What are you guys making?"

"Cookies!" she yelled again.

"Shhh… Florence is asleep, and she needs all her rest if she's going to be your assistant."

Her smile got even bigger. "Okay," she whispered. "Where's Grandma Cat?"

She was talking about Nick's mom. She and Trevor, her husband of a year and a half, were over here frequently. Our families became close, and now instead of a two-person Sunday dinner, Nick was making Sunday dinners for nine, now ten with Florence. And sometimes thirteen when Lindsay, Kevin, and their two-year-old son, Samuel, came over.

"She's on her way," Nick said. He stopped me before I could walk by him. With a grin, he crooked his finger in a *come here* motion. My smile melted as I moved forward and our lips met.

"Just like sunshine," he whispered when we broke away. With a soft grin, I leaned my head against his shoulder and watched Mirielle run around the kitchen until she stopped by the tea table we had set up in the corner. She always had a short attention span. More often than not, all she and Nick did were a few prep steps before Nick finished up the rest.

"C'mon," she whisper-yelled. With his arm wrapped around my shoulders, we walked over and sat down on her tiny chairs. I always chuckled as I watched Nick squeeze into them.

This time I didn't. I just stared, picturing this table filled with all our children.

It was the greatest future I could ever imagine.

Epilogue

Catherine

I STOOD IN THE DOORWAY OF THE CLOSET AND TOOK IN THE state of it. It was bursting with bright-colored clothes and stuffed animals. My smile widened as a pair of arms wound around my stomach.

"Hey," my husband whispered in my ear.

"Hi." I turned around in his arms and placed my palms on his chest. Trevor looked down at me, smiling from ear to ear.

"About done, love?"

"Never. It's a grandma's job to spoil her grandchildren."

Gazing behind me, his smile somehow widened. "I think Florence is set, and it's only her first birthday after all. You need to leave room for all the others."

My lips playfully dipped down for a second before rising into a full grin.

"Ma?" Nick called.

"C'mon." Trevor weaved our fingers together and walked

us downstairs. We passed by the master bedroom and I saw Iris putting on her earrings.

"Yes, dear?" I asked when we walked into the kitchen where my son was feeding Florence.

"How crazy did you go?" Nick questioned. Trevor brought a hand up to cover his smile as he squeezed my hand. "That bad, huh?"

"Not bad," I insisted. It was Florence's first birthday party, but Iris suggested I only wrap one gift and leave the rest in my granddaughter's bedroom.

"I heard you make four trips upstairs."

Shrugging, I reached forward and pushed a wisp of my granddaughter's hair behind her ear. "Do you think it's too much, sweetheart?" I asked. She giggled and started babbling. With a smile, I leaned back. "That's an affirmative if I've ever heard one."

I caught the end of Nick's eye roll. "I'd give up if I were you," Iris said as she walked into the room, pausing to kiss me on the cheek before moving toward her husband and daughter.

"She's not dressed yet?" she asked Nick as he wiped Florence's dirty hands clean. "People will be arriving soon."

"In case you've never noticed, our daughter prefers to wear her food. I thought it wise to wait."

"Which is why I told you to start feeding her forty-five minutes ago."

Stepping forward, I lifted Florence from her seat, careful of the food splattering her shirt. "I'll dress her."

"Thanks, Catherine." Iris smiled warmly before turning back toward Nick. I left the chattering behind as I climbed the stairs and brought her to her room.

There were a few times over the years when I considered the idea of bringing another child into our family. Not naturally, of course—I was almost fifty. But the idea of adoption floated around in late-night conversations between Trevor and me. Ultimately we decided against it. Between Mirielle and Florence, plus Lindsay and Kevin's now two sons, plus knowing that Calla and Kent were in the process of adopting another child and that Nick and Iris would have more someday, it just made sense. It was a wise decision—we always seemed to have one of the children at least one day during the weekend.

Looking down into my granddaughter's laughing face, it was hard to remember that I'd once been lonely. It was hard to imagine a time when Nick's world seemed completely destroyed.

"Gahaha!" Florence giggled, like an exclamation point on my thoughts about the transformation of her father's life. I finished dressing her and lifted her to my hip with a wide grin on my face. She played with the buttons on my blouse as I walked downstairs with her.

I paused at the bottom when I found my grown son running around the kitchen island, chasing his wife. They were both laughing wildly. Trevor lightly grazed my arm as he came to stand next to me.

I smiled up at my husband and he gave me a soft kiss on the corner of my mouth. My lips inched higher as I thought about my life—the good and the bad. When Nick's father left all those years ago, I didn't see it for the blessing it was. Even though it hurt him at the time, it would have caused Nick far more pain had Tyson stayed.

Not everyone was meant to be in our lives. Some by choice, like Nick's father. Some against our will, like Iris's birth parents. But standing here right now, I truly believed we all ended up where we needed to be, standing next to the person we were meant to be with.

We always think we want life to go a certain way. That we'd be happier if *this* or *that* hadn't happened. But we knew so little about what was in store for us.

I was glad I didn't have the power over my life that others scrambled for. Because this life was greater than anything I could have imagined.

"What's going on?" I finally asked.

"I have no idea." Trevor wrapped his arm around my shoulders. "One minute they were arguing and the next…" My husband shrugged just as Nick caught Iris. Nick wrapped his arms around his wife's waist and pulled her against his chest. Her laugh echoed around the kitchen when he began whispering in her ear.

Florence started clapping and kicking her chubby little legs. Nick and Iris spun around and looked at their daughter with huge smiles. We all cringed as her giggles reached a shrieking level. Though, it was hard to be annoyed when she was so happy.

"Thanks for getting her dressed," Iris said as they walked over. Nick's arm was wrapped around her waist and he was smiling, like he didn't have a care in the world.

"It's no problem," I assured them.

"Dada." We all froze and slowly looked down. "Dada," she repeated. Florence had talked before, she'd even said "dada," but we all knew she hadn't connected the word to Nick yet. She had just been babbling.

Until now.

This was different. This was done with intent. Her arms were outstretched toward Nick, and her legs were kicking with even more excitement.

Nick was still frozen, seemingly unsure this was really happening. And while some mothers might begrudge the fact that "dada" was her baby's first word, Iris was grinning wide.

"Did she...?" my son asked.

"DADA!" Florence wailed, frustrated tears welling in her eyes as she tried to wiggle out of my arms. Nick snapped out of his haze, rushing forward almost comically to lift his daughter into his arms. And when he did, her expression broke into one of pure joy.

"Dada!" she happily screamed while slapping his face. It didn't faze him, he was too choked up.

"I... I love you, sweet girl," he whispered, like they were in their own world. Because they were. Nick may not have had a father growing up, but he knew exactly what he was doing. Florence would never wonder where her father was, or if he loved her. Nick would give her the childhood that every kid should have.

One with joy.

One with trust.

And one with so much love, she would have no choice but to see the world with bright eyes and a trusting heart.

Extended Epilogue

Iris

TEN YEARS.

It was almost surreal. Nick and I had been married for ten years, and yet every single day felt like the beginning of our story.

Today Nick and I were renewing our vows at *Bacio del Sole*. It was just a small party, like our wedding had been, consisting of only our families and close friends.

"Mama." Looking down, I saw my daughter, Caterina, staring up at me with wide, terrified eyes. I was currently in Nick's office getting ready, where I had changed into a simple, white summer dress that stopped right above the knees.

"What's wrong, honey?"

"I'm scared," she whispered.

"Why don't you practice?" I suggested. She nodded, eyes on the ground, and grabbed her basket of flowers.

"Wooohoooo…" Now my eyes were drawn to my other

daughter, Liliana, who was sitting upside down on the couch, her dress bunched up around her waist and the tips of her hair touching the ground.

They were complete opposites, which was ironic since they were identical twins. Nick and I had the girls a few years after Florence, and we named our almost four-year-olds after Nick's mother and my sister.

Today they were our two flower girls, while Florence was my maid of honor.

I'd just put my second earring on when Caterina tripped and fell to her knees, smashing her basket.

Rushing over, I placed a hand on her back and asked, "Are you okay, sweetie?" She didn't respond. "You don't have to walk out there if you don't want to." My youngest daughter—by nine minutes—was terrified of people, and I didn't want her to do this if it made her uncomfortable.

Caterina's head snapped up. Her father's warm brown eyes stared back at me. "I-I still w-wanna be in the f-family, Mama."

Liliana was quick to help. She flung herself off the couch and skipped over to her sister. I stepped back and watched Liliana wrap her arm around a sniffling Caterina.

"Cat, you can walk with me and share my basket."

Caterina rubbed her eyes and gave a small smile. "Thanks, Lil." Then she turned toward me. "Can I find Nana?"

"Sure. I'll take you both out there." The three of us walked down the hallway, and when we reached the end, Liliana immediately ran off, while Caterina easily found her target and shuffled over. I looked out at the rest of my family and friends.

There were four tables, two on each side, to make the shortest aisle in history. Aster was sitting at one of the farthest-away tables. His arm was wrapped around his wife of eight years, Briana, the girl he met after Becky left him. Their six-year-old son, Ricky, named after our dad, sat on the other side of him. When they found out Briana was pregnant, Aster moved his family back here to be closer to us.

Calla and Kent were at the table next to them, sitting with their eight-year-old son, Jackson, whom they adopted four years ago, and our parents.

Catherine and Trevor were sitting at the table across from them, the one closest to us, and Caterina sat in her lap. Even before she learned of her namesake, Caterina always had a special bond with Nick's mom. It was never a surprise when my daughter sought comfort from her.

At the last table sat Lindsay and Kevin with their four sons and Florence. That table was the most chaotic. My eldest daughter was slowly becoming a tomboy, constantly trying to outdo whatever the boys were doing.

I'd always wanted a boy, but I'd heard enough horror stories from Lindsay to know I'd never want four of them.

Smiling, I placed my hand on my stomach.

"You ready to be my best woman?"

Turning toward the bar, I saw Nick talking to our niece a few feet away. Mirielle was nodding vigorously. When found out Nick got to pick someone to stand up with him, she was adamant it should be her. At twelve years old, she was most definitely a ballbuster. She refused to accept societal norms, and while her parents loved her unique, take-no-bull personality, they were probably at high risk for ulcers.

When we were debating how far we wanted to go in renewing our vows, we decided to include the children as much as we could considering only Mirielle was here last time, and she was too young to remember.

With a grin, I turned around and walked back toward Nick's office. I picked up my flowers and lovingly rubbed my slightly swollen belly. Nick and I had found out I was pregnant a couple months ago—today I was nearly five months along. We decided to do the gender reveal today—only I knew so far, and it had determined the color of my bouquet. Nick and I combined the two events because we knew how hard it was for everyone to gather like this.

I gazed down at the flowers, all white except for three perfectly placed ones that revealed the baby's gender. Nick would see them first since we were walking down the aisle together this time. When he told me that was what he wanted, I asked him why. I still got butterflies thinking about his answer.

He'd grabbed my hands and said, "Ten years ago you walked down that aisle toward me, alone, and I promised myself that would be the last time you did anything without me."

I'd sassed him back of course, saying, "Well, technically, I wasn't alone. I had my dad—"

Nick had grinned, expecting the response, I guessed, and placed a finger over my lips. "Hush. I'm trying to be romantic and sentimental and you're ruining it."

I stifled a chuckle now. Who would have thought the surly man I met nearly twelve years ago would turn into a giant softy who let his daughters paint his toenails and treated his wife like a queen?

"Hey." I whipped around at the sound of his voice, keeping the flowers hidden behind my back. He was grinning as he shut the door.

"Wow," he breathed. "You're gorgeous."

I smiled, loving how he phrased it that way. It was never "you look," always "you are." It didn't matter what I was wearing or if my hair was in an elegant updo (like today) or a messy bun with Fruit Loops buried in it (like yesterday morning).

Nick walked forward, stopping a foot away from me, and

anxiously looked down at the empty space where my hands should be.

"Are you gonna keep me waiting?" He was practically bouncing on his feet. I slowly unwound my hands from behind my back until they were resting in front of me, gripping the flowers tightly when he teared up.

"Stop that," I chided. "You know I can't watch you cry without crying myself. And my makeup is perfect."

He ignored my words as he dropped to his knees in front me and rested each palm against the sides of my distended stomach.

"We're having a boy?" he asked reverently.

Placing one of my hands over his, I nodded. His eyes lifted to mine as he smiled, so wide and bright he could challenge the sun. Nick stood up and gently cradled my head before wrapping me in a hug. My hands landed on his back, taking care not to jostle the bouquet too much.

We never explicitly said so, but I think we might have kept going because we wanted a boy. Nick loved his girls with all his heart, but I honestly wasn't sure if he'd be able to handle another one. He was already fretting over them wearing makeup and dating. He wanted a son. He never said so, for fear of hurting the girls, but I knew.

"Do you have any idea how happy you make me?"

I chuckled and pulled away. "I'm pretty sure you were a part of it too. Or do you not remember?" I quirked an eyebrow.

"Oh, I remember," Nick said on a laugh. It quickly faded as he became serious. "I remember everything."

My breath caught. He was looking at me like he did ten years ago. Like I was the best thing to ever happen to him.

"I remember how you saved me, how you welcomed me into your life when I gave you no reason to. I still don't know why you chose me, but I thank God every day that you did."

I placed my hand over his heart and drummed my fingers. "I picked you because of this. Because of *your* pure heart. You've always had one, Nick." I could tell he struggled to believe it, so I added, "It was dark in there for a little bit. But it was always pure."

"The darkness didn't scare you off?"

"No. Darkness is only the absence of light. It can never win against it."

Nick grinned, dimples and all. "So you're saying I never stood a chance?"

"Nope." We both chuckled.

"Good." He held out his arm. "Are you ready, Mrs. Blake?"

I placed my hand in the crook of his elbow and let him lead me out the door.

Toward our future.

Shining brighter than ever.

Playlist

"Prove You Wrong"—He Is We

"Give Your Heart a Break"—Demi Lovato

"The Only Exception"—Paramore

"Shake It"—Metro Station

"Gold"—Owl City

"You and Me"—Lifehouse

"Somewhere Only We Know"—Keane

"Chasing Cars"—Snow Patrol

"Say You Won't Let Go"—James Arthur

"Come to Me"—Goo Goo Dolls

Acknowledgments

This was the fastest turnaround time I've had for a book. It was nerve-racking and I definitely wouldn't have been able to do it without the support of my friends and family. I've been a hermit these past few months, even more than usual, so thank you guys so much for putting up with it! I know it's not easy, but you have been awesome and are part of the reason this book exists <3

To my beta readers: Briana Pacheco, Jenny Baker Reimer, Kristen Humphry Johnson, and Kingston Westmoreland, the feedback was amazing! Thank you for being so detailed and not getting annoyed by all my follow-up questions and emails :)

Thank you, Taylor Henderson for answering all my medical questions and ensuring I was accurate in my portrayal.

Thank you to my editor, Stephanie Parent! I'm still amazed by how quick you are ;)

To Hang Le, thank you for this gorgeous cover and the amazing teasers!

Thank you to my formatter, Stacey Blake at Champagne Formats, for putting up with my latest <3

As always, thank you, the readers. This wouldn't exist without you.

xoxo

About the Author

Jeannine Allison is an author of contemporary and New Adult romance. After waffling between many degrees in college, she finally graduated with a BA in English Literature from Arizona State University. She loves writing and reading—obviously :)—but when she's not, she enjoys playing with her two dogs, watching her favorite YouTube beauty bloggers, drinking coffee, googling new tattoos, and pretty much anything else that allows her to wear yoga pants and a sweatshirt.

Stalk Her!

Facebook: www.facebook.com/jeannineallisonauthor

Instagram: www.instagram.com/jeannina517

Goodreads: www.goodreads.com/author/show/14847745.Jeannine_Allison

Website: www.jeannineallison.com

Pinterest: www.pinterest.com/jmall13

Other Books

The Unveiling Series

Unveiling the Sky

Unveiling Chaos

Unveiling Ghosts

Unveiling Fate (Coming Fall 2017)

unveiling the sky

prologue

Alara

Glass rained down around me, blood dripping from my hand to the tile below. I tried to take a deep breath, but the air wasn't there. My breaths grew louder, and with another cry, I slammed my bloody hand into the mirror. After that fourth hit the pain barely registered anymore, and I collapsed against the opposite wall. I watched myself disappear from the mirror as I slid down the wall until my butt hit the floor.

The knocks on my front door were getting louder, and my phone continued its insistent ringing. The only time it stopped was during the three-second intervals between calls when Naomi hung up and dialed again. I watched it vibrate across the counter until it teetered at the edge, precariously balancing, one shake away from crashing to the floor. Exhausted, I finally reached forward to answer it.

"Alara?" Naomi's frantic voice shouted. "Open the door."

"I-I'm tired," I choked out on a sob.

"I know, honey. I know. Just… I need you to open the door." The normal cheer was gone from her voice, replaced by undisguised panic and sorrow. I closed my eyes and leaned my head back as more tears ran down my face.

Ending the call without responding, I slowly got up, checking to make sure the towel was secured around me. I glanced down to see my long blonde hair was still dripping wet, the water trickling to mix with the blood. As I made my way to the front door, I glanced at the contents of my closet scattered about on my bedroom floor and wondered if this was my life now. Despair. Destruction. Pain. Exhaustion. The thunderous knocks from Naomi's tiny hands ended as soon as I unlocked the door and stepped back. Not even a second later, she burst in, and her wide brown eyes took in my appearance.

"Oh God. What happened?"

"I'm just so, *so* tired, Naomi." My shoulders sagged and my head dropped as I started crying harder. She was at my side in an instant, rubbing small circles on my back and telling me it was going to be okay.

"Alara…" she began softly. "I need you to tell me where the blood is coming from." I looked down, taking note of the red streaks on my feet and legs. I wordlessly held up my left hand, which she quickly turned over and began examining. She was shifting her focus back and forth between my eyes and hand. "Shit. I think this needs stitches."

I withdrew my hand and shook my head. "N-no. I don't want to g-go anywhere," I hiccuped as I cradled my hand to my chest.

"I know. It's okay. You don't have to. Sher's already on her way over. She should be here any—"

"Fuck. What the hell happened? Is she okay?" Sherry's

voice sounded as she raced through the front door and slammed it behind her. Her burgundy hair was wild and curly around her flushed face, and her chest heaved under her Arizona Cardinals T-shirt, giving the impression she ran here.

Their voices became muddled as they moved me to the couch. I closed my eyes, trying to control my breathing and stop my tears. I thought back to my childhood when I got in trouble for talking too much and laughing too loud, and I couldn't help but wonder how it all changed. How could the happy child I was turn into *this*? I tried to think of the exact moment when I felt the change, the exact moment when simply waking up seemed like a chore, but I couldn't. I opened my eyes to the white plaster above, only vaguely aware of Sherry and Naomi sitting on either side of me. As I continued to stare at the ceiling, I started counting and realized this had been going on for three years. I'd felt this despair, destruction, pain, and exhaustion for three freaking years, yet I'd done nothing about it. I constantly wrote it off, telling myself I'd be okay. I had time. It hadn't broken me… until tonight.

"Alara." Naomi's voice became clearer, and I realized my tears had slowed and my breathing was more manageable. She came around and knelt directly in front of me before giving me a slight shake. "Alara," she repeated.

I brought my head up and looked at her. She let out a relieved breath and sat next to me again before grabbing my uninjured hand and giving it a squeeze.

"Sher knows how to stitch you up. She left for the drugstore. She should be back in ten minutes."

I nodded while my sorrow continued to subside and I slowly slipped into numbness. I turned my head into the back of the couch, feeling the rough texture against my forehead as the last of my cries disappeared. Naomi hugged me from the side and rested her head on my shoulder, all the while whispering, chanting, that everything would be okay. But for the first time in three years, I didn't believe it, because when I closed my eyes, all I saw were more days just like this.

one

Alara

Eight months later...

THE MOANS AND GRUNTS WERE GETTING LOUDER. I pulled my pillow over my head and burrowed between it and the mattress, but it proved useless. Naomi and Caleb had been having sex all night and my roommate was an unabashed screamer. It was on her fourth or fifth plea to God that I finally threw the covers off, quickly slipping a bra on under my shirt and changing into running shorts. I had just reached the door and shoved my feet in my shoes when I heard the distinct sound of an ass slap.

Grimacing, I slammed the door as hard as I could before taking off toward our apartment complex's tiny gym. Thankfully no one was there, and when I glanced at the clock I realized why. 5:30 a.m. On a Sunday. On the second to last weekend before school started. I was going to kill Naomi.

Caleb had been gone all summer, and I thought about

how disgruntled she'd been up until ten hours ago when he showed up at our door. I was comparing the pros and cons of a sex-deprived Naomi and a sex-crazed Naomi as I climbed on the treadmill closest to the window. Both sucked, one figuratively, and sadly, I knew the other was quite literally. Caleb was an atheist, but whenever Naomi's mouth was on him, he conveniently forgot that fact. Loudly. At least he had the decency to blush in the morning.

I only had enough energy to work out for forty-five minutes. *That's what only four hours of sleep gets you.* Climbing off the elliptical, I stretched my sore legs and wiped the sweat from my brow before making my way back toward our (hopefully silent) apartment. I sent up a quick prayer as my hand closed around the doorknob, and I pushed it open. Smiling, I took in the silence and made my way into the kitchen to fill up my water bottle.

"God, I missed sex."

I jumped and whirled around at the sound of her voice. Naomi stood in her neon-green sports bra and black boxers as a grin spread across her face.

"Yeah, I figured that out."

"Were we loud?" She wore an expression of mock innocence and barely contained her laughter as she reached forward to swipe my now filled bottle.

"No, *you* were loud."

She shrugged and jumped on the counter, swinging her legs. "So what are you up to today? Caleb and I were thinking of catching a movie."

I raised a skeptical eyebrow. "You know you can't have sex there, right?"

She frowned and took a sip before tossing my bottle back to me. "Hmm… well, we can at least do some hand stuff." I chuckled and shook my head at her serious tone before walking by her and toward my room. "So that's a no?" she hollered as I crossed the threshold.

"That's a hell no," I yelled back before closing the door on her laughter. I smiled as I walked into my adjoining bathroom and started the shower. After quickly throwing off my sweat-soaked clothes, I stepped under the cool stream and let out a content sigh.

My arms were tender as I lifted them above my head and washed my hair, slowly moving the suds in circles. I made quick work of conditioning my ends before grabbing my favorite coconut lime body scrub and rubbing it down my legs and arms. When I reached my left wrist, I paused before reverently tracing the slightly raised scar that ran from the center of my palm to the heel of my hand. The night I'd gotten that was the worst of my life, but it could have been so much worse if it weren't for Naomi.

Even though we'd been friends since the second grade, we'd never thought about living together in college. We had heard the horror stories about rooming with friends, and we didn't want to do anything to rock the boat. Unfortunately, the boat was rocked anyway.

My depression had never been worse than it was at the end of last year. I was living by myself, and the numbness crept in so slowly I didn't even notice it until Naomi barged in one afternoon, yelling at me for blowing her off again. She told me she felt like I didn't care about our friendship anymore. She cried. I hadn't seen her cry in years. But there she was, crying in my living room while I lay on the couch I'd barely moved from in three days.

I think that was the first time I realized my depression affected more than just me. But it was just so easy to lose myself in it. I felt so worthless and unloved that I honestly believed she'd be relieved all those times I canceled on her. But she wasn't. She was hurt and confused, and that was on me. So yeah, the boat was rocked. That bitch was practically waterlogged.

We moved in together shortly after, and in those first few months, I slowly realized our fears of living together were completely unfounded. Because even though most friendships were surely tested by it, I forgot Naomi wasn't like most friends. She wasn't perfect. She left her clothes in the dryer for days, never took out the garbage, and her crap was constantly cluttering the common area. And let's not forget the loud sex. But that didn't matter because she was still my best friend and the best person I knew. So if she wanted to have loud, crazy sex and leave her stuff everywhere, she could go right ahead. I'd take the bad, because in the end, it paled in comparison to the good.

But as I continued tracing the scar and the water ran cold, I couldn't help but think one day she would wake up and realize my good could never outweigh my bad.

Naomi and Caleb had successfully removed themselves from bed an hour ago to go to the movies. I'd just slipped into jeans and a T-shirt when I remembered my niece's party was supposed to be at the park this year. If I didn't know how hard it was to say no to Megan, I'd hate my sister for agreeing to this. Living in Arizona meant I typically limited my outside excursions to the months of October through April; anything else was a sure death sentence. Like right now, in the middle of freaking August.

Quickly removing my clothes, I settled on a knee-length

mint-green dress instead, even though it would only make a minimal difference in the triple-digit heat, but anything would be better than jeans. I grabbed her present off my desk before rushing out the door and to my car. The party didn't start for an hour, but my sister had put me in charge of watching Megan while she set up everything. I pulled in just as Jackie was slumping down on the bench.

"AUNTIE ARA!" Megan screamed as she came running toward me. I bent down, taking care to keep my dress tucked under my knees, and waited for her to launch herself into my arms. She barely slowed down as she plowed into me, and I rocked back with the force of it.

"Hey, sweetheart. What's going on here today?" I made a big deal of looking around at all the decorations my sister had piled on the table, getting ready to set up.

"It's my birthday party, Ara. Duhhh... remember when I gived you the pretty pink invitation with all the glitter?"

"Gave," Jackie corrected from behind her. "You *gave* her the invitation, sweetie."

Megan nodded, trying to look stern like her mother. "I gave you the invitation, remember?"

Jackie chuckled a little while I tried to keep a straight face. I hit myself on the head as if I just remembered. "Of course. What was I thinking? Wait... did I forget your present?" Again, I made a show of looking at the bags around me and frowning.

"You got me a present?" she asked excitedly as she hopped around in front of me, her big brown curls bouncing with her.

"I sure did. Now tell me. What was the one thing you wanted more than anything else?"

"Daddy, I wanted Daddy to come home. That's the wish

I made this morning on my breakfast pancake." I saw Jackie's face drain of color as she stood behind Megan and a look of complete torture came over her face.

"WAIT!" Megan yelled and grabbed my hand, bringing my eyes back to her now pale face. Her lips trembled and her eyes were wide with tears. "It doesn't come true if I tell you. Mommy says it's not gonna come true if I tell you."

My sister sprang into action, coming around and kneeling with us. She squeezed her daughter's hand as she reassured her. "That's only on birthday cakes, sweetie, not pancakes. There are never any rules on pancakes."

"Really?" We both nodded earnestly until the tears that had sprung up began receding. "Pinky promise." She pouted, daring us to tell her we were lying, before sticking her pinky in Jackie's face. After we both locked fingers with her, Megan gave us a wide grin and let out a sigh of relief.

"Why don't you go play on the swings for a little bit?"

"Okay, Mommy." Megan turned to run away before pausing and spinning around to face us again. She quickly ran and hugged me once more before whispering in my ear, "I missed you, Auntie Ara." And with that, she was skipping toward the swing set.

"Hey, Jax," I said, using her nickname from when we were kids. She smiled and pulled me in for a hug once we were standing. We stayed that way for several seconds before she reluctantly let go. I'd never been much of a hugger, but lately, every time Jackie hugged me, I held on a little tighter. It was beginning to feel like that was the only thing holding her together. "Have you heard from him?"

She shook her head. "Not yet."

"He'll call. He'll find a way. He loves that little girl more than anything." I pointed toward Megan as she swung higher and turned to talk to an imaginary friend on the empty swing next to her.

"You're right." She paused. "I know you're right. I just never pictured her fifth birthday being this way. I never imagined I'd be doing all this alone."

"Mom and Dad—"

"Are busy." She cut me off. "I can handle this. This is just one of those bad days, Al. You know?" She gave me a pointed look because, yeah, I did know.

Jackie walked away and began setting up the games while I went over and pushed Megan a little higher, feeling guiltier than I had in a long time. I couldn't even begin to understand the type of stress and pain my sister was going through. And even though she never said it, I knew there was a part of her that wondered how I could be the depressed one when she was the one with so much crap on her plate.

Some people couldn't understand depression without a source; my sister was definitely one of those people, and some days I could feel it—the resentment and disbelief. She never meant to make me feel that way. She was my sister and she loved me fiercely. But at the end of the day, some people just expected more… but sometimes there was no more. Sometimes there was no trauma. No death. No PTSD. Nothing.

Megan's giggles broke me from my thoughts as she became almost parallel with the ground. I looked over at the set-up on the picnic tables and grimaced as my thoughts collided with reality.

Sometimes there was no more. Sometimes there were just giggles, balloons, and a happy little girl talking about blowing bubbles, but you were still depressed and you still couldn't figure out why.

Gabe

One year. Today marked a full year I'd been without my mother. Three hundred and sixty-five days since I last heard her voice, saw her smile, or felt her touch.

When I left for Europe and told my sister I'd be gone for *a little while,* I honestly hadn't meant for it to turn into six months. She never said anything negative about me being gone; she even stopped asking when I was coming home around the three-month mark. But I knew it had to be killing her.

It had been two weeks since I last spoke to her, and even though I'd already bought my plane ticket, I hadn't told her I was coming home. I told myself it was because she was preparing for her senior year of high school and I didn't want her to be concerned with anything but that. But really, I was afraid she was giving our father updates, and I was in no way ready to deal with him. Especially today.

I sat in my car outside my childhood home and looked into my mother's kitchen, bristling at what I saw. A blonde model, at least fifteen years my father's junior, was hanging around his neck as he gave her a few absentminded pecks on her lips. It was a horrible thought, but I couldn't help but wish he were the parent who was six feet under.

I swallowed the breakfast that threatened to resurface and moved my eyes toward the driveway. Sam's car wasn't there, so I assumed my father and his mistress of the month were the only ones home. Despite my need to see mom's favorite place, her garden in the backyard, I couldn't make myself go inside right now. Not with the scene currently taking place, and not with all my thoughts about what happened the last time I was in that kitchen.

Samantha was softly crying as my father and I continued to scream at each other across the kitchen. She was fingering the jewelry around her neck, a simple silver pendant with the phrase "I still believe in 398.2" etched into it. Our mother had given it to her on her thirteenth birthday.

"It's time you took your life seriously. We all loved your mother"—I scoffed at his lie while he continued like nothing happened—"but her death is no excuse to throw your life away. It's been six months—"

"And while that might be an appropriate amount of time to grieve for a coldhearted bastard like yourself, some of us need a little bit more," I bit out.

Again, he continued as if I hadn't made a sound. "It's been six months, and you've made too many drastic changes. You broke up with Miranda, dropped out of your master's program, quit your job, and those are just the things you've made me aware of. You need to grow up and accept death is a part of life. The world isn't going to wait for you to get back on your feet, and I certainly wouldn't be doing you any favors by tolerating this childish fantasy."

I crossed my arms over my chest and leaned back against the counter. "I know you think you own the world, but this isn't your decision. This is my life and that means I decide what the hell I do with it."

His mouth flattened into a line and his eyes narrowed as they raked over me thoughtfully. "You're not ready." He spoke quietly, as if he were talking more to himself than to me. After a disgruntled sigh, he closed his eyes and pinched the bridge of his nose before refocusing his attention on me. "You have until the New Year. It's only the second week of March, so that should be plenty of time to sort out whatever it is that's going on up there." He waved his hand toward my head. "Then you will come back and do what's right by this family. You will get your master's, come work for me at the company, and refocus your attention back on Miranda. Do you understand?" He eyed me expectantly and let out an annoyed sigh when I didn't answer. "Gabriel, this is the only arrangement I will allow. Take it or leave it."

Sam's cries had softened, and when I looked over at her, I saw her staring down at her hands resting in her lap. "Samantha, will you be all right if I leave for a little while?"

"She'll be fine," my father answered for her. "She's sixteen years old. Besides, she has Brody."

I was still looking at her and saw her stiffen at the mention of her boyfriend. She looked up at me and gave me a smile before speaking for the first time since we started arguing. "Of course, Gabe. You need some time away from this place," she said as she pointedly looked at our father.

My plan to travel around Europe for a few months was impulsive, and even though I didn't have a lot of money (not by dear old Dad's standards anyway), I did have enough to get by until I figured out a more long-term plan.

I had followed the rules my whole life, and what did I have to show for it? Not a damn thing. For as long as I could remember, I'd been groomed to follow in my father's footsteps, and to the outside world, it seemed like a lifestyle I wanted. But in reality, it was just a ten-year-old boy's pathetic attempt at getting his father's respect and love. And somewhere in the middle of seeking my father's approval, I started believing it was what I'd wanted, too. But it wasn't. It only took my mother dying of cancer for me to realize it.

But I had let it go on for so long that I didn't know who I was anymore or what I wanted. I couldn't go back, but I didn't know how to move forward either. So instead, I existed in a kind of limbo, and the plan became simple—do whatever I wanted and not worry about the consequences. I was no longer Mr. Punctual, Mr. Do-the-responsible-thing, or Mr. Proactive. Because those things didn't matter much in the face of everything that was important. Those things couldn't save my mother any more than they could help pull my sister from her despair. So what was the point of any of it?

I shook my head, and as I stared at his impatient expression, I realized I didn't have to give him the truth. What would be the point in having this completely useless argument with my father now when I could deal with it later? When I could deal with it without Sam in the room or three shots of vodka in my system? I nodded in what he no doubt thought was submission. "Fine. Deal."

He gave a curt nod in return before leaving my sister and me alone in the kitchen.

I'd barely heard his office door close before Sam ran over and hugged me. "Are you sure you're okay if I leave for a little while?" I asked. But I didn't know if I'd be able to stay even if she begged me.

"Yeah," she mumbled into my shirt.

I knew she was lying, but I took the life raft she was offering and held on for dear life. Swallowing my shame and guilt, I quickly kissed the side of her head before turning around and taking the stairs two at a time until I reached the top.

When I reached my old bedroom, I opened the door to the mostly bare room and moved toward the closet. Most of my stuff would stay in my—well, I guess now it was just Miranda's—apartment until I returned. But here was where I kept all I had left of my mother. I carefully removed the back from one of the frames until I had the worn picture in my hand. After staring at it for several seconds, I folded it until it fit in the plastic frame of my wallet. The air began to feel heavy as I closed the box and shoved it back with all the others before I jumped up and headed toward the door.

My father's car was gone when I got to the garage only twenty minutes later. I slowly pulled out of the driveway and gave my mother's house one last look. Movement in an upstairs window caught my eye, but when I looked up to what I knew was Sam's window, all I saw were the fluttering curtains where her face must have been. A face I could barely look at because of how much it reminded me of our mother.

I drove away as I felt tears roll down my face and a painful thought took residence. If I had trouble looking at my sister, how the hell did she look in the mirror?

Maybe she was simply stronger than me. Maybe she wouldn't be haunted by our mother's death like I was. But as much as I tried to convince myself of those maybes, I couldn't. All the maybes in the world couldn't erase what I saw in her eyes that day— that she was suffering just as much as me, and I was too selfish and weak to do anything about it.

But how could you save someone who was sinking, if you were drowning right there with them?

I left the house before he could see me. Confronting him without any kind of plan would be a suicide mission. I hadn't spoken to my father in over three months, and our last conversation wasn't one I was eager to repeat. It ended with my fist in the wall of a cheap motel room.

What would your mother think? You think she'd be proud of the man you've become?

His words had been on repeat in my mind ever since I hung up on him. Not just because they were vicious, but also because they were most likely true. My mother would not be proud of who I'd become. But not for the reasons he thought.

He wasn't proud because all he saw was a college dropout (even though I still had a bachelor's degree) with no job and little to no aspirations or plans beyond the next ten minutes. He'd expected me to be married to Miranda with the first of our two point five kids on the way by now. And for a while, I wanted that, too. I wanted the wife, the kids, and the white picket fence. I was ready to settle into that average life.

But what I realized when my mother died was I would have hated it all. I would have graduated with my expected business degree and entered into an accounting job at my father's firm, all with a genuine smile. But I would have woken up in forty years dissatisfied, resentful, and filled with regret. Because I'd never done what my mother was always pushing me to do, and that was to find my passion. For so long, I stuck with the status quo and what I was good at, despite whether or not I really loved it.

It was the same thing with Miranda. I didn't love her, at least not in the way you're supposed to love a wife. I guess growing up in my household, I never got to see that, but in the six months since I'd been gone, I saw a lot. I saw passion and love and spirit in ways I never would have dreamed possible. All the things my mother had always pushed us toward. So while my father was sure I was a disappointment because I quit my job and broke up with my girlfriend, I knew my mother wouldn't have felt the same way.

What would gut my mother the most was what I did to Samantha. How I abandoned her. I'm sure she would have understood the first month, maybe even the next two. But leaving for six months? Not even my saint of a mother could justify that.

I guess the only defense I had left was I didn't feel like myself anymore. As my mother withered away, so did the pieces of my life. Things that seemed important before suddenly didn't matter at all. Once those things were gone, it felt like I had no idea how to do anything anymore, and I convinced myself even if I had stayed, I would have been worthless. Everyone else seemed to still know how to live, and all those things I lost still mattered to other people. And while I hated my father, I couldn't deny he was very right about one thing: the world doesn't wait for you to grieve.

My head was throbbing by the time I pulled into the parking lot of the cheap motel I was going to stay at tonight, and I couldn't wait to lock myself inside my room and not have to deal with anything or anyone for the rest of the day.

I had been lounging on the bed for three hours, and it was just past 7:00 p.m. when my phone rang. Glancing at it, I saw the incoming name: *Samantha*. I stared at it until it went silent, and I blew out a breath of relief. Unfortunately, my relief only lasted a minute before the ringing started again. *Samantha*. When was the last time Sam called me twice in a row? My stomach felt heavy and my vision grew blurry at the thought of the last time that had happened. Exactly a year ago. Snatching my phone up, I breathlessly answered, "Hello? Sam? What's wrong?"

"Hey, hey. Calm down. Nothing's wrong," she said in a hurry.

"Oh."

"Something's got to be wrong for me to want to talk to my big brother?" she asked with a slight edge to her tone.

"Of course not. I just…"

"You just wouldn't have answered if you thought it was just to talk to me?" Sam didn't sound mad. She just sounded…

resigned, and her disappointment was evident in the heavy exhale that followed.

I opened my mouth to correct her, but what would be the point? We both knew the truth. And the truth was I probably wouldn't have answered.

"I just wanted to see how you were doing," she said, graciously overlooking how much of an asshole I was. "You know with today..."

"I'm doing fine, Sam. How about you and Dad?"

She was silent for a moment, and I smiled because I knew she was sitting there nodding into the phone, a habit both her and Mom had. It usually only took them a couple seconds to remember the caller couldn't see them. "I'm all right. It's hard but... school's starting in a week and senior year is supposed to be the best, right? So I'm excited for that. I haven't seen Dad much though. He's been traveling on and off for the past few months."

That son of a bitch would leave his only daughter to fend for herself without a care in the world. A voice in my head asked me if I was any better.

She cleared her throat before asking, "So what city has the honor of your presence today?"

I hesitated before clearing my throat and answering, "Carillo."

"Carillo." She drew out the word slowly. "As in..."

"Yeah. I got back this morning."

"You're home? And you didn't tell me?" Sam finally let her armor crack, and I heard a soft sniffle come through the line.

"Sam. I just didn't—"

"Hey, it's all right. I u-understand. I do. But I have t-to go. I'll talk to you later, okay?" she rushed out. But instead of just hanging up like any other woman would when she desperately wanted to get off the phone so she could cry in solitude, Sam waited for me to say goodbye, too.

"Yeah, Sam. I'll talk to you soon," I said in a low voice. She mumbled another strained goodbye before hanging up. I clutched my phone for several seconds before dropping it to the floor and putting my head in my hands, hoping like hell what I'd just said wasn't a lie.

Printed in Great Britain
by Amazon